I0761097

ROBERT LUDLUM'S

THE BOURNE REVENGE

THE BOURNE SERIES

ROBERT LUDLUM'S THE BOURNE ESCAPE (by Brian Freeman)

ROBERT LUDLUM'S THE BOURNE VENDETTA (by Brian Freeman)

ROBERT LUDLUM'S THE BOURNE SHADOW (by Brian Freeman)

ROBERT LUDLUM'S THE BOURNE DEFIANCE (by Brian Freeman)

ROBERT LUDLUM'S THE BOURNE SACRIFICE (by Brian Freeman)

ROBERT LUDLUM'S THE BOURNE TREACHERY (by Brian Freeman)

ROBERT LUDLUM'S THE BOURNE EVOLUTION (by Brian Freeman)

ROBERT LUDLUM'S THE BOURNE INITIATIVE (by Eric Van Lustbader)

ROBERT LUDLUM'S THE BOURNE ENIGMA (by Eric Van Lustbader)

ROBERT LUDLUM'S THE BOURNE ASCENDANCY (by Eric Van Lustbader)

ROBERT LUDLUM'S THE BOURNE RETRIBUTION (by Eric Van Lustbader)

ROBERT LUDLUM'S THE BOURNE IMPERATIVE (by Eric Van Lustbader)

ROBERT LUDLUM'S THE BOURNE DOMINION (by Eric Van Lustbader)

ROBERT LUDLUM'S THE BOURNE OBJECTIVE (by Eric Van Lustbader)

ROBERT LUDLUM'S THE BOURNE DECEPTION (by Eric Van Lustbader)

ROBERT LUDLUM'S THE BOURNE SANCTION (by Eric Van Lustbader)

ROBERT LUDLUM'S THE BOURNE BETRAYAL (by Eric Van Lustbader)

ROBERT LUDLUM'S THE BOURNE LEGACY (by Eric Van Lustbader)

THE BOURNE ULTIMATUM

THE BOURNE SUPREMACY

THE BOURNE IDENTITY

THE TREADSTONE SERIES

ROBERT LUDLUM'S THE TREADSTONE RENDITION (by Joshua Hood)

ROBERT LUDLUM'S THE TREADSTONE TRANSGRESSION (by Joshua Hood)

ROBERT LUDLUM'S THE TREADSTONE EXILE (by Joshua Hood)

ROBERT LUDLUM'S THE TREADSTONE RESURRECTION (by Joshua Hood)

THE BLACKBRIAR SERIES

ROBERT LUDLUM'S THE BLACKBRIAR GENESIS (by Simon Gervais)

THE COVERT-ONE SERIES

ROBERT LUDLUM'S THE PATRIOT ATTACK (*by Kyle Mills*)
ROBERT LUDLUM'S THE GENEVA STRATEGY (*by Jamie Freveletti*)
ROBERT LUDLUM'S THE UTOPIA EXPERIMENT (*by Kyle Mills*)
ROBERT LUDLUM'S THE JANUS REPRISAL (*by Jamie Freveletti*)
ROBERT LUDLUM'S THE ARES DECISION (*by Kyle Mills*)
ROBERT LUDLUM'S THE ARCTIC EVENT (*by James H. Cobb*)
ROBERT LUDLUM'S THE MOSCOW VECTOR (*with Patrick Larkin*)
ROBERT LUDLUM'S THE LAZARUS VENDETTA (*with Patrick Larkin*)
ROBERT LUDLUM'S THE ALTMAN CODE (*with Gayle Lynds*)
ROBERT LUDLUM'S THE PARIS OPTION (*with Gayle Lynds*)
ROBERT LUDLUM'S THE CASSANDRA COMPACT (*with Philip Shelby*)
ROBERT LUDLUM'S THE HADES FACTOR (*with Gayle Lynds*)

THE JANSON SERIES

ROBERT LUDLUM'S THE JANSON EQUATION (*by Douglas Corleone*)
ROBERT LUDLUM'S THE JANSON OPTION (*by Paul Garrison*)
ROBERT LUDLUM'S THE JANSON COMMAND (*by Paul Garrison*)
THE JANSON DIRECTIVE

ALSO BY ROBERT LUDLUM

THE BANCROFT STRATEGY
THE AMBLER WARNING
THE TRISTAN BETRAYAL
THE SIGMA PROTOCOL
THE PROMETHEUS DECEPTION
THE MATARESE COUNTDOWN
THE APOCALYPSE WATCH
THE SCORPIO ILLUSION
THE ROAD TO OMAHA
THE ICARUS AGENDA
THE AQUITAINE PROGRESSION
THE PARSIFAL MOSAIC
THE MATARESE CIRCLE
THE HOLCROFT COVENANT
THE CHANCELLOR MANUSCRIPT
THE GEMINI CONTENDERS
THE ROAD TO GANDOLFO
THE RHINEMANN EXCHANGE
THE CRY OF THE HALIDON
TREVAYNE
THE MATLOCK PAPER
THE OSTERMAN WEEKEND
THE SCARLATTI INHERITANCE

ROBERT LUDLUM'S

THE BOURNE REVENGE

BRIAN FREEMAN

G. P. PUTNAM'S SONS
NEW YORK

PUTNAM
— EST. 1838 —
G. P. Putnam's Sons
Publishers Since 1838
An imprint of Penguin Random House LLC
1745 Broadway, New York, NY 10019
penguinrandomhouse.com

Library of Congress Cataloging-in-Publication Data
has been applied for.

ISBN 9798217046218

Printed in the United States of America
1st Printing

The authorized representative in the EU for product safety and compliance is Penguin Random House Ireland, Morrison Chambers, 32 Nassau Street, Dublin D02 YH68, Ireland, https://eu-contact.penguin.ie.

ROBERT LUDLUM'S

THE BOURNE REVENGE

Eight Years Ago

DAVID WEBB SAVORED HIS FIRST DAY IN PARADISE.

He held a frozen hurricane drink in one hand and a dog-eared paperback of a Nelson DeMille novel in the other. His body sank into the deep orange cushions of a lounge chair, his back slightly inclined. A baseball cap dipped low on his forehead and Nike Bandit sunglasses covered his eyes. In front of him, the water of the Mandarin Oriental's circular swimming pool shimmered in turquoise. The condominium towers of Miami rose like a stacked line of dominoes on the other side of the channel from Brickell Key.

It was October, but Florida summer hadn't yet given way to Florida fall. The blistering afternoon sun scorched David's bare chest and his muscular legs below his swimsuit. He didn't mind. The raw heat from a cloudless blue sky felt good after a subfreezing month spent on the coast of Greenland, battered by frigid winds. The Russians had landed a six-person scientific team in the fifty-person village of Iliminaq, ostensibly to conduct research on ice fields offshore. Treadstone suspected they had other intentions, so David had been sent to observe and intervene if necessary. He concluded quickly that the Russians were less interested in puffin populations and more interested in tapping into the undersea communications cables that passed out of Canada near the Greenland coast.

"That cut looks bad," a voice above him said as a shadow fell across the pages of his paperback.

From behind his sunglasses, David looked up to see a Hispanic woman with jet-black hair smiling down at him. A thong bikini barely covered her mocha skin and skinny five-foot frame. Her eyebrows arched sharply over dark eyes, and she had a petite, rounded nose. She was probably on the south side of thirty years old. With her index finger, she pointed at an eight-inch gash that stretched below David's knee.

"How'd you get it?" she asked.

"Oh, that? Knitting needle accident."

The woman cocked her head with amusement. "Yeah, those can be rough."

"Always knit with a partner for safety."

"I'll remember that."

David grimaced as he moved his leg, still feeling the sting of the wound three days later. The Greenland mission had ended with a fight on a Zodiac in open water. One of the Russian spies had wound up dead with a bullet in the middle of his throat, but not before delivering a slashing wound down David's leg.

"Mind if I join you?" the woman asked.

"Go ahead."

She stretched out on the recliner adjacent to him, her body all legs and breasts, her dark hair snug in a ponytail. She closed her eyes to the bright sun, although he could see that she'd left them open a slit so she could see whether he was admiring her. Which he was. "I'm Martine, by the way."

"Charlie," David replied. "Charlie Briggs."

"Vacation?"

"Yeah. You?"

"Sort of. A little business, a little pleasure. What do you do when you're not knitting, Charlie Briggs?"

"Investment banking. San Francisco. What about you?"

"I'm in the import business," she said.

"What do you import?"

"Alcohol mostly," Martine said, her mouth breaking into a grin. "Imported into me, that is."

"Then maybe I should buy you a drink."

"Maybe you should."

David signaled a poolside waiter. Martine ordered herself a caipiroska with Grey Goose. As she waited for her drink, she rubbed Neutrogena sunblock onto her exposed skin, fingertips edging under the cups of her bikini top. When she was done, she asked him to do her back, which he did. Her skin was supple and warm. Caressing a woman's body again felt good, but as he smoothed the cream over her neck below the rope of black hair, he found his fingers tightening. An image of his hands locked around the Russian's neck during their fight flashed through his mind.

"That's a little rough, Charlie," Martine said.

He shook himself. "Sorry."

"No worries. Rough can be good."

He returned the bottle of sunblock to her, and Martine gave him another flirty smile. Her drink arrived, and she took a sip, licking her pale pink lips. David eased back into his chair and realized he was sweating, but not from the Miami heat. Another flashback jolted him, this time a memory of the kill shot, drilled through the man's throat. He saw the Russian falling backward into the ocean; he saw the man's eyes as he realized he was about to die.

Stop it!

But his brain kept replaying the scene on a loop, over and over.

The Russian was his first kill since his inaugural mission for Treadstone a couple of summers earlier, when he'd eliminated four members of an alt-right extremist group in a mountaintop Swiss chalet. Despite the violence, despite the adrenaline, his emotions felt switched off. That was exactly what Treadstone wanted, exactly how he'd been trained. On the other hand, David also realized that he could remember every detail of the Russian's face, just as he could with the terrorists in Switzerland. Targets stayed in his head with a special vividness, as if the images of their death masks were burned into his brain.

He'd told Mo Panov, the Treadstone psychiatrist, about his memories. Whenever you killed someone, they made you see a shrink, to make sure you weren't cracking up. *I see dead people*, he said to Mo, trying to turn it into a joke.

Mo didn't laugh.

Instead, he'd insisted David take a vacation and forget about Greenland. Go somewhere hot. Drink a lot. Have sex. So here he was, ready to soak up the Florida sun and take advantage of opportunities that came his way. Like the woman next to him. She was making the opportunity very clear.

But forget Greenland? He couldn't do that. He couldn't forget how it had felt to kill again.

If there was one thing David Webb had, it was perfect recall.

"Oh, fuck," Martine murmured.

She had her drink at her mouth, the glass wet with condensation, but her brown eyes were focused on the other side of the Mandarin Oriental pool.

"Not enough vodka?" David asked.

"No, no, it's fine. But I really am in the import business. One of my most demanding clients just showed up early. If he's here, that means he needs me to do something. Sorry. I have to go. This guy doesn't like waiting."

"That's all right."

"Maybe we could have dinner tonight," she suggested.

"Maybe we could."

"Or we could go straight to dessert."

"I like that idea, too."

Martine stood up and donned a yellow linen cover-up that hung to the middle of her thighs. She pushed her feet into sandals and blew him a kiss and waved goodbye. He watched her as she headed for the far side of the pool, leaving a very nice view from the back.

That was when his attention shifted to the man waiting near the pool railing.

"*Fuck*," David hissed, echoing Martine's reaction.

He recognized that man.

His first name—that was all Treadstone knew—was Fang. He'd been on the agency watch list for more than a year, ever since he slipped across the southern border near Nogales. An alert ICE official had detained him and sent in his details and photograph, but Fang snapped the man's neck before they reached the detention center. Then he melted away into the Arizona desert hills. He hadn't been spotted since then.

Fang was a Chinese spy. And an assassin.

David pretended to read his paperback as he studied the man from behind the protection of his sunglasses. Fang was small, no more than five foot six. He wore a dark blue sport coat with an open-collared shirt and weathered blue jeans. He was about David's age, around thirty, with slightly jutting ears and a tight, thick crown of dark hair. His nose was slim with wide nostrils, his mouth expressionless, his eyes piercing and intelligent. The bulge of the coat flap near his heart suggested a shoulder holster.

As Martine joined him, Fang spat a couple of angry sentences at her. A moment later, his gaze shifted pointedly across the pool at David. The book still in his hands, David gave no reaction, other than taking another sip of his hurricane. He didn't look away; looking away exposed you faster than staring. Fang showed no recognition of David or his profession. David was relatively new to Treadstone, and his hat and sunglasses sheltered his face.

But if they met again, Fang would remember him. Good agents always did.

Martine and Fang shared a brief, uncomfortable exchange by the pool. Then the attractive young Hispanic woman hurried toward the hotel. Fang took a last look at David before turning around, hands on the white railing, and staring off toward the Miami skyline. Not even ten minutes later, Martine returned, now dressed in a red blouse and white slacks, with high heels. She joined Fang, and the two of them left the pool area together, taking steps down to a paved trail that led along the water.

David grabbed his white polo shirt from the table where his drink was. The shirt hid his Smith & Wesson CSX 9mm, which was compact enough to fit into the baggy pocket of his swimsuit. He slipped the loose polo shirt over his chest, then shoved his bare feet into rubber-soled sneakers and took off after them.

The sidewalk on the water's edge led underneath a string of palm trees, with the hotel tower looming overhead and blocking the sun. Even in the shadows, the heat didn't yield. The water of the channel was blue and calm. Ahead of him, a short bridge led from Brickell Key back to the mainland. Martine and Fang walked together. She was on her phone, far enough away that David couldn't hear what she was saying. Fang used short, fast steps, and the woman had to hurry to keep up. He looked back once, but David saw the man's shoulders moving in time for him to duck sideways, where he couldn't be seen.

They reached the front of the hotel near the east end of the island bridge. David watched from the sidewalk, staying hidden. Five minutes passed, enough to make Fang impatient, and Martine had to calm him down. She made another phone call. Not long after that, a long black town car crossed the bridge and glided silently to a stop in front of them. Fang used his own phone to alert someone about the limousine's arrival. Almost immediately, three Chinese gentlemen in black suits walked slowly toward them down the hotel driveway, their steps fragile. They were older, all in their sixties or seventies, all with an official look about them.

CCP, David thought.

A young Chinese woman accompanied them. He recognized her, too, from a Treadstone security alert. Her name was Rose, but she was no fragile flower. According to the alert, she was every bit as lethal as Fang.

Two assassins. Three Chinese party members.

What the hell was going on?

With his phone, David snapped pictures of all of them.

The crowd of six climbed into the back of the limousine. Fang was last, holding the door for Martine, whose pretty face looked scared and unhappy, as if she didn't want to get inside the car. Then the limo headed into the turnaround. It reversed direction and rolled onto the bridge back to the city.

David moved fast. He spotted a blue Mercedes turning his way off the bridge, and he jogged into the middle of the ramp that led to the hotel entrance. With a casual smile, he waved his hands to stop the car, then walked around to the driver's door. The man behind the wheel, fiftysomething and dressed like a golfer, rolled down the window. David noticed a carry-on bag with a Delta tag in the back seat.

"You checking in, sir?"

The man in the Mercedes gave him a confused look. "Yeah, that's right."

"Name?"

"Bill Morrison."

"This your car, Bill, or is it a rental?"

"A rental. Why do you—"

David thrust the barrel of his CSX through the open window and pressed it into the green satin fabric of the man's golf shirt.

"Sorry, Bill, you're a little early for check-in. Move over. We need to take a detour."

The annoyance on the man's face immediately switched to sweaty terror. Quickly, he undid his seat belt and awkwardly scrambled over the gearshift into the adjoining seat. He reached for the passenger door handle to escape out the other side, but David took his wrist and twisted hard, keeping him where he was. "I'll let you go soon, Bill. You won't be harmed. But for now, sit where you are and stay quiet."

"*Shit*," the man whispered. "Shit, shit, shit, who are you? What do you want?"

David pointed the gun across the seat. "*Quiet*."

He navigated the Mercedes into a U-turn and sped onto the bridge toward Miami. A sidewalk and a low railing adjoined the westbound lane. He noticed the man's phone on a wireless charging pad and rolled down the passenger window. He slowed the Mercedes and said, "Toss your phone into the water."

"Are you fucking kidding me?"

"I'm not kidding, Bill. Do it."

A jab of the gun convinced the man, and the iPhone flew out the window and into the Miami channel.

David kept driving, focused on the traffic ahead of him. He spotted the town car at the far end of the bridge and accelerated, closing the gap, but keeping a couple of cars between him and the limousine. The car turned off Tamiami and headed north toward downtown, then crossed the river and wound around to Second Street, where it turned west. David could see signs for I-95, but before the limo reached the freeway turn at the Metromover tracks, he saw it pull to the curb near the entrance to a parking garage.

David stopped, too, idling the engine outside a CVS a block behind them. Fang got out of the back seat, dragging Martine with him. She clearly knew the score. Wherever they were going, it was a party of five, not six. Fang dragged her squirming into the darkness of the garage, and her scream carried down the block. David reached for the door handle to intervene, but Fang returned almost immediately, alone, sliding his gun back in its holster. He tugged calmly on the sleeves of his sport coat and climbed into the rear of the town car. David slammed the dashboard in frustration.

Sitting next to him, Bill Morrison reacted with horror. "Oh, Jesus! What did he just do? Did he fucking kill her?"

"Time to get out, Bill."

"He killed her! Jesus!"

"Yeah. He did. My advice is, don't tell anyone what you just saw. Right now, no one in that car knows you're a witness. If that changes, believe me, they'll find you and eliminate you."

"*Shit!*"

David waved the CSX at the passenger door, and Bill didn't need to be told twice. The middle-aged golfer spilled out of the Mercedes and took off through the Miami streets at a stumbling sprint.

Meanwhile, the limo headed for the freeway. David stayed a quarter mile back, not worrying about losing the town car in the stalled traffic on I-95. The vehicle inched along, speeding up then slowing down, making slow progress. Half an hour later, it exited on a westbound ramp near Biscayne Gardens. The limo wound through the streets along the railroad tracks, but soon enough, its destination became clear. They were heading for the Opa Locka Executive Airport, where the private jets of the rich came and went. Rather than turn at the airport's main entrance, the limo detoured down a side road past a hangar building, all the way to a barbed-wire fence and a locked vehicle gate.

A black Gulfstream II waited on the other side of the gate.

As soon as the town car arrived, a Chinese man in a pilot's uniform came down the jet's steps and waved at a security officer to open the gate. The limousine drove through. From the other end of the street, David snapped more pictures as Fang and Rose escorted the three older Chinese men onto the plane. When the passengers were all on board, the steps immediately retracted, and the jet taxied away from the hangar building toward the airport runways.

David stayed where he was, watching the Gulfstream take off like a bullet into the sky.

Then he dialed a number on his phone. On the third ring, a woman answered with the name of a Miami bar.

"I'm looking for a man named Kodak," David told her. "If he's not there now, he will be soon. I need to talk to him before he starts drinking. Tell him to call me. Tell him Charlie Briggs needs his help—"

SUDDENLY, DAVID'S EYES SNAPPED OPEN. HE AWOKE WITH A START.

He lay on his back in a king-size bed on top of the sheets. The room was dark, the curtains closed. The cool air from the vents smelled stale. Nothing looked familiar to him in the shadows, no clues as to where he was. His mind spun with confusion, empty and disoriented, as if he'd been jolted out of a violent dream.

He threw his legs sideways off the bed, but as he got up, pain drove like a spike through the middle of his skull.

Jesus!

His face convulsed; his eyes squeezed shut. For a moment, he thought he would vomit. He staggered to the window and threw the curtain back, then winced as sunlight flooded the room. Below him, he saw a circular swimming pool, sunbathers dotting the lounge chairs. A bridge crossed a narrow channel. Condo towers lined the Miami waterfront. David blinked at the view.

He knew this place. The Mandarin Oriental.

But how did he get here?

He tried to remember, and his first thought was of Mo Panov. The therapist's voice echoed in his head. *God, David, you're a mess. Get out of here. Go somewhere. That's not a suggestion, my friend, that's an order.*

Yes. He'd gone to Florida.

And then what?

He looked down at his body; he was naked. A gash on his leg was beginning to scab over, no longer stinging when he moved. Where had it come from? *Greenland.* With a rush, he remembered the fight in Greenland, the gunshot, the dead Russian. He remembered returning to Washington to give his report and flying from there to Miami for a vacation. And then, with barely a stop at the hotel room, he'd gone straight to the pool.

Shrink's orders. Swim. Drink. Read. Forget about everything.

That was—*today.* Friday afternoon.

But he didn't remember coming back to his room.

What was happening to him?

David went into the bathroom and grabbed the sink to steady himself. His square, handsome face in the mirror stared back at him, laser-like blue-gray eyes and swept-back hair so dark brown it was almost black. He hadn't shaved in days, his chin rough with stubble. On the side of his neck, below his jawline, he saw an ugly, purplish bruise. When he grazed it with his fingertips, he winced from a stab of sharp pain. This was definitely fresh. Not from Greenland. Then he felt a stinging in his hand, and when he held it up, he saw a straight cut lacing across his palm, still red and tender.

It looked like the kind of wound a metal wire would make.

Where had it come from?

Nothing made sense!

He ran the faucet and splashed cold water on his face, trying to jolt himself awake, trying to unscramble his mind. *Think! Remember!* He saw and heard fragments of a dream. Faces. Screams. Blood. Rain. But the images blew away like torn-up paper as he tried to assemble them, and nothing was left.

David staggered back into the middle of the hotel room. He glanced at the nightstand next to the bed and saw a paperback of DeMille's *The Charm School*, plus his CSX pistol and his phone. Everything was where it should be. He went and snatched up the phone and opened the photos app, but he found no recent pictures. The last images he'd taken were from the Greenland coast, nothing from Miami.

Then he noticed the day and date on the phone.

Oh, God! Oh, *shit!*

It wasn't Friday. It was *Tuesday.*

The phone spilled from David's hand to the carpet. He pressed both fists against his forehead and tried to remember, but all he felt was more pain, hot and blinding. He grabbed the hotel phone and stabbed at the button for the front desk. The calm male voice of the clerk answered on the first ring.

"Yes, Mr. Briggs, how can I help you?"

"What day did I check in?"

"I'm sorry, sir?"

"My check-in at the hotel. What *day?*"

"That was last Friday, Mr. Briggs. You have three more days with us on your reservation."

"Are there any charges to my account? Anything other than the room rate?"

"Let me see. Yes, there are two charges from the pool bar on Friday afternoon. That's all. Nothing since then."

David hung up the phone. He didn't understand. It was *impossible!* His mind was totally *blank!*

He didn't remember anything at all from the last four days.

PART ONE

NOW

1

JASON BOURNE KNEW THE DAY MIGHT COME WHEN HE WOULD HAVE TO kill Shadow.

Ever since he'd met her in Switzerland more than a decade ago, she'd lied to him, betrayed him, manipulated him, and put his life in jeopardy for her own ends. Now she was the head of Treadstone, and that meant she owned him. He was her personal agent for off-the-books missions, which gave her a power over him that she relished using.

They'd also become lovers the previous summer—something that no one else at Treadstone knew.

None of that changed the risks of their relationship in and out of bed. Shadow was who she was, and she would never change. Someday she would step over a line from which there was no going back, and he'd have to put a bullet in her head. They both knew it. They'd admitted it out loud to each other. That reality hovered in the background whenever they were together.

Bourne kept an eye on her security detail as they walked along the river trail in Anacostia Park in Washington. Wherever the head of Treadstone went, half a dozen agents always kept watch. A man walked a dog fifty yards behind them; two men in suits kept pace ahead of them; an SUV rolled slowly down the nearest lane of Anacostia Drive. Bourne could also feel by instinct the threat of a long gun pointed at him from a construction crew located on the bridge over the river.

Shadow took his hand, her nails scraping along his palm. Part of that was cover. A couple on a romantic stroll attracted less attention for anyone who might be surveilling them. Part of it was also Shadow's acknowledgment that things were different between them since they'd slept together in Greece. But with her, he never knew how much emotion was real and how much was staged to keep him under her thumb.

"I appreciate you flying over from Paris," she said. "You haven't been back to the U.S. in a while. It's been a long time since we were together."

That was true. It was a cold February in Washington, and he hadn't seen Shadow since a meeting in the Tuileries before Christmas. She had a way of disappearing until she wanted him, either on a mission or between her legs.

"Your message sounded urgent," Bourne said. "What's going on?"

She didn't reply quickly, as if she were reluctant to explain the next step. Finally, she said, "I need you to talk to Mo Panov."

Bourne showed no reaction, but he was surprised. He hadn't expected that. He knew Mo well, and their therapist relationship went back a long time, but he hadn't talked to him in almost two years. "Why is that?"

"I'd like him to regress you. I want to see if he can unlock any more of your memories."

Bourne said nothing as they kept walking. Remnants of overnight snow clung to the winter-brown grass, and the cool wind off the river blew through his leather jacket. Next to him, Shadow wore a long wool coat that draped to her ankles, but no hat. Her lush blond hair hung loose, and her pale skin was flushed in the cold, pink against her burgundy lips. She let go of his hand with a shiver and shoved her hands in her pockets. Ahead of them, across the water, he could see the Navy Yard and the white arches of the Capitol Street bridge.

"Regression hasn't been too successful in the past," Bourne pointed out.

"I'm aware of that, but Mo's willing to try again. Are you?"

He thought about the many hours he'd spent in Mo's office.

Treadstone had sent him there after his first memory loss, when he'd been shot on a mission in the Mediterranean and had his entire past wiped out. Mo had tried hypnosis and drugs, but they'd done little to help Jason remember any details. His memories were still there—that was what Mo believed—but they were locked away in a place his brain couldn't find. Whenever he tried to force his mind to go back, all he got was a sharp pain drilling behind his eyes. He couldn't push himself to remember. It didn't work that way. Instead, memories returned to him when he least expected it, in bits and pieces, fragments of a puzzle that would never be completed.

Last year, it had happened again. He'd almost died in an explosion, and once more he'd found himself stripped of identity, his memories gone. But this time, the recent past had come back faster, leaving only the years before he'd been shot as a blank slate. He'd dealt with it himself, rather than turning to Mo for help. His instinct was to avoid the raw vulnerability of being on the couch.

"I'm willing to try, but what's going on?" Bourne asked.

Shadow stopped on the trail and faced him. "Have you kept abreast of our briefings on Chinese espionage activity in the U.S.?"

"I've seen the reports, sure. Volt Typhoon."

"Yes, that's the umbrella code for their operations. The level of infiltration is massive. We believe they're ramping up more and more each year. Spy balloons, drones, public and private data hacks, tech viruses inside critical infrastructure, property acquisitions near sensitive installations, police stations inside U.S. cities to target dissenters. Political blackmail, too. As you well know."

"Adam Hill," Bourne said.

"Exactly."

Bourne saw the man's face in his mind, and it still prompted a wave of fury that tightened his chest. Adam Hill had been the U.S. vice president until his resignation the previous year. He'd also been a Chinese spy, a literal Manchurian candidate steps from the Oval Office. Bourne had managed to take him down, but the mission had come at a devastating personal cost.

A woman he loved, a woman named Johanna, had been killed.

"Hill's gone," Bourne pointed out. "He shot himself the day after Christmas."

Shadow frowned, doubt creasing her beautiful features. "Did he, Jason? Or did you help him along? I didn't ask you before now because I wasn't sure I wanted to know. But I wouldn't have blamed you."

"It wasn't me. Not that I didn't think about it."

"Then it was probably the Chinese themselves. They must have figured Hill knew too much about their domestic operations to leave him alive. Regardless, it doesn't matter. Taking Hill down was a victory, but he was just one big fish. The school of other fish swimming around is even more dangerous. We have to assume there are dozens of moles inside every layer of government, plus utilities, corporations, media, all of our critical industries. That doesn't include the Chinese spies that have poured across the border in the last decade. Hackers. AI experts. Saboteurs. Assassins."

Assassins.

A strange sensation traveled through Bourne's mind, like a sense of déjà vu. He felt himself close to remembering . . . *something.*

But then it was gone.

"What's their goal?" he asked. "What's the endgame here?"

Shadow started walking along the trail, and Bourne stayed beside her. "I think they're testing us. They're looking for pressure points, weaknesses. The L.A. fires, the New Jersey drones, the Nevada blackouts, a dozen other regional crises. I'm convinced the Chinese played a role in all of them. They want to see how we react when things go wrong, see what it takes to get us off balance. But everything that's happened up to now, that's just laying the groundwork for the real attacks. Imagine things like that happening all at once, on a hundred different fronts with a hundred times the severity, just as the CCP moves on Taiwan. Americans are used to war happening somewhere else, but the Chinese aim to destabilize the homeland whenever the conflict starts. And they don't need tanks, bombs, and infantry to do it."

"I get the risks," Bourne said, "but I'm not sure what this has to do with my memory."

"I'm getting there, Jason. You see, overall control for Volt Typhoon is obviously run out of Beijing, but the actual plans involve boots on the ground right here in the U.S. You can hack remotely, you can gather data from anywhere in the world, but the sophisticated work involves human intelligence. Old-fashioned spy work. You need to conduct long-term surveillance of physical infrastructure. You need to observe behavior, gather data on security procedures and processes. Moles need to be researched, influenced, recruited, run, handled. You need face-to-face meetings and dead drops."

"In other words, they need an American network."

"Exactly. This all has to be organized and managed. That means leadership, someone running the operation, setting priorities, assigning resources, coordinating all the moving parts. At the center of the giant web is a giant spider. A person in charge. Not overseas. Not in China. Someone here in the U.S."

"Do you know who?" Bourne asked.

"I only know a name," Shadow told him. "Bai Ze. Have you heard that before?"

"I haven't."

"Bai Ze is a beast in Chinese mythology," she continued. "A white tiger with horns and the face of a man. Plus eyes on its back so it can see everything. It's supposed to know all the secrets of the ghosts and the gods."

"And you think Bai Ze is the code name for the leader of China's American espionage operations?"

"I do. We flushed a Chinese mole at a nuclear plant in Pennsylvania. Mid-level IT engineer. That's the kind of threat we're talking about, ordinary American hiding in plain sight. This guy's a nobody, family man, married for fourteen years, two kids. Security clearance, no red flags in his background. But he was in a position where he could plant a virus that would corrupt the plant's operating software and take it out of service for weeks. So the Chinese targeted him. They found a weakness. In his case, it was a sister who needed expensive cancer drugs. The family was running out of money. A recruiter used that information to turn the engineer and get him to install the virus. We were lucky. One of his colleagues spotted an anomaly in the code and reported it. We got to the man's devices before he erased them, so we were able to locate the Chinese agent who reached out to him. The recruiter's texts made references to someone named Bai Ze calling the shots on the operation. It was clear Bai Ze was high up, had direct communication with top officials in the CCP. I think only the network leader is likely to have that kind of access."

"The agent you captured, did he know anything more about Bai Ze? Like who he is? Or where he is?"

Shadow shook her head. "No, he was killed before we could interrogate him. So was every other agent in that chain. These guys don't mess around. But we did learn one interesting thing. I'm pretty sure Bai Ze *isn't* Chinese."

"You think he's American?" Bourne asked.

"That's my guess. For one thing, the myth of Bai Ze involves a *white* tiger. I don't think that's an accident in terms of code names. Sounds to me like an inside joke by the CCP. But there's more. An agent who was part of the operation in Pennsylvania complained in a text message about taking orders from a *guizi*. That's racist slang for a foreigner."

Bourne frowned. "But you don't know who Bai Ze might be."

"No."

"Well, whoever he is, he needs acccss, right? He has to have high-level connections."

"You're right," Shadow agreed. "That's why I've been extra cautious lately—including last year, when you and I went after David Abbott. I don't know who to trust, inside or outside the intelligence community. Other than you."

Bourne didn't bother telling Shadow that trust was a one-way street. She might trust him—although he was sure she was lying about that—but he would never trust her. He never trusted anyone. That was what kept him alive. Even his mentor, David Abbott—the man who had originally brought him into Treadstone—had his own motives. Shadow and Abbott would both sacrifice Bourne in a heartbeat if it led them to their goals.

"Holly Schultz at the CIA was working with Adam Hill," Bourne reminded her. "She claimed it had nothing to do with his Chinese connections, but if she's a double agent, she'd be in a perfect position to develop strategies to cripple U.S. interests."

"Agreed. She's on my suspect list. And not just because Holly and I are adversaries."

"Bai Ze could even be you," Bourne pointed out.

"That's true," she replied. Her cool face had no expression. "I could deny it, but that wouldn't mean anything, would it? Maybe I'm testing you, Jason. Maybe I'm sending you after Bai Ze because I want to see if my cover is deep enough to hold."

He heard an echo of his voice from the previous year. *One of these days, I may have to kill you.*

And he thought about Shadow's reply. *Oh, I know. I fully expect it.*

"So you want me to find Bai Ze," Bourne said. "Then what?"

"We squeeze him. We get him to give us a road map of Chinese infiltration, and we begin dismantling Volt Typhoon piece by piece."

"Okay, but if you have no clues about who he is, where do I start? It seems like I'm searching for a needle in a haystack." Then Bourne's eyes narrowed as he understood the motive behind this meeting. "Except you do have a clue, don't you? Somehow this all involves me."

"That's right."

"Based on what? Where did you get your information?"

"The Files," Shadow replied.

Of course.

The Files. Shadow's secret weapon. The Files were an AI software engine developed by the Chinese, which worked in conjunction with massive data hacks obtained from public and private sources. The Files collated trillions of data points, seeing clues and trends in the minutiae that the human mind would never catch. More than a year ago, Bourne had stolen the Files. He thought he'd destroyed the laptop with the master software so that no one could use it again. Instead, Shadow had deceived him in order to grab the Files for herself. Since then, she'd used the AI engine ruthlessly to amass power for Treadstone.

"So what did the Files tell you about Bai Ze?" Bourne asked.

"That's the trouble. I don't understand it."

"What do you mean?"

Shadow examined the Washington park around them, as if she were suddenly worried about surveillance. She leaned in closer, her face inches away. In her heels, they were eye to eye. "Are you familiar with a small town in Wisconsin called Fish Creek? It's in Door County, northeast of Green Bay."

"I've never heard of it."

"You've never been there?"

"Never."

Her deep-red lips pushed into a thin frown. "That's what our records show, too. As far as Treadstone goes, you've never had a mission anywhere near there. Not as David Webb. Not as Jason Bourne. I also talked to Abbott. He wasn't aware of any personal or family connections you had in Wisconsin. You had no reason to go there."

Bourne was puzzled. "So? What's the problem?"

"The problem is that the Files say otherwise," Shadow told him. "According to the Files, you were in Fish Creek, Wisconsin, eight years ago in the middle of a Chinese espionage operation. And you *saw* Bai Ze."

2

"DAVID!" MO PANOV EXCLAIMED HAPPILY.

The therapist had a song by Foreigner playing on his stereo, and he used a remote control to switch off the music. "My God, it's good to see you again, old friend. Sorry—I know you go by Jason these days. I need to stick to the appropriate covers. But to me, you'll always be David Webb."

"With you, David is fine," Jason told him. He studied the psychiatrist's plush new office, which was located on the twelfth floor of a Tysons Corner high-rise. The floor-to-ceiling windows gave a view toward the Potomac and the monuments of DC. "You're coming up in the world, Mo. These are nice digs."

"Well, if I had to pay for it myself, I'd still be working out of my basement. But CIA headquarters is only five miles away. The agency wanted me somewhere closer, and they like the corporate cover. Did you see the sign on the door? MP Logistics. Apparently, I run a global shipping business. I'm pretty sure you can send a container of Nvidia graphics cards anywhere in the world by going to my website."

Bourne chuckled. "I'm impressed you've heard of Nvidia."

"Only because of my 401(k). Just don't ask me to tell you what a graphics card does."

Mo waved at a microfiber glider positioned near one of the windows. Jason sat down. The chair, at least, was familiar to him. He'd spent hours in that chair when it was located in the lower level of Mo's home in Rockville. Mo was the go-to shrink for intel agents who experienced mission trauma but who couldn't share details of their assignments with anyone who lacked a top secret clearance. Their relationship went back longer than Jason remembered—all the way to the aftermath of his first mission in Switzerland—but there had been bumps in the road between them along the way. When Jason lost his memory after being shot in the Mediterranean, Treadstone had gone to Mo to figure out the source of his erratic behavior. Mo resisted making any kind of diagnosis without talking to David directly, but he finally admitted it was *possible* that David Webb had turned traitor. That was enough to get Treadstone to send a hit team after him.

Later, when Mo learned about David's memory loss, he'd raised holy hell at Treadstone and insisted on treating David personally. For Jason, the therapy had helped with the emotional ramifications of what he'd been through, but it had done little to bring any of his memories back. He was still a man with no past.

"Shadow filled me in about this mission," Mo said with a little chiding in his voice, "but to be honest, I expected you here long before now." He crossed from his desk to an overstuffed sofa near the glider. His right leg dragged slightly as he walked and his left arm was stiff—both products of a shooting a few years earlier. But he was still energetic for a man in his late fifties. He took a seat on the sofa and put a white mug of coffee on the table next to him. "What has it been, two years?"

"About that."

"I've kept tabs on you, David, even if you weren't coming in for appointments. In fact, when Shadow took over Treadstone, the first thing I did was ask for a meeting to talk about you. A lot has happened in your life. I heard about your new bout with memory loss last year. That was something we should have worked on together. You've also struggled with relationships, right? Abbey Laurent. The death of Nova. And now Johanna. I'm sorry about that. It's obvious she was very important to you."

"I was in love with her," Jason admitted.

"I hear you went off the grid for several months after that."

"I did."

"But now you're back."

"It was time," Bourne replied with a shrug.

"Time for what?"

Jason said the first word that came into his mind. "Revenge."

"Ah."

Mo didn't say anything more. He studied Jason with his penetrating brown eyes and let that confession sit there in the open. His long legs jutted off the sofa, and he smoothed his bald head as if he still had a full crown of dark hair. Bourne tried to outwait him, but Mo had more patience than Jason did.

"Not that I'm out there looking for revenge," Bourne went on eventually. "I'm not."

"No?"

"No. I lost Johanna. I grieved. I'm over it."

"Really?"

"That's right. I mean, am I still angry? Sure. Definitely. But I can manage that."

Mo tapped a finger softly on his lips. Again he let the silence drag on, but then he finally continued. "Believe me, David, I know something about loss. I know what it does to a man, how it changes him, how it forces him to reevaluate everything in his life. You were in love with Johanna. As I understand it, Holly Schultz ordered her to be killed at the request of Vice President Adam Hill, who turned out to be a Chinese spy. In the process of trying to rescue Johanna, you were forced to kill another Treadstone agent, Vandal. Is that what happened? Do I have that right?"

Bourne frowned. "Yes."

"But that's all in the past, is that what you're telling me? You're *over it.*"

Mo had him in a corner, and Jason knew it.

"All right, no, I'm not over it at all," Bourne admitted. "It eats me up. It crushes me. I can't sleep, and when I do, I have nightmares. But I'm learning to live with it. I put all of that in a box when I came back to Treadstone."

"And yet the first thing you talk about is revenge. Which leads me to ask, revenge against whom, David? Adam Hill killed himself."

"I didn't have anything to do with his death."

"I didn't say you did. But Hill's gone. Who's left for your revenge? Holly Schultz?"

"Holly was just a pawn. I'm sick of killing pawns. My anger is at the ones in charge, the ones who really made it happen. The

Chinese, the CCP, they controlled Hill. He was their mole. Ultimately, they're responsible."

"Okay, so here you are with a mission that allows you to strike back at the Chinese," Mo concluded. "Your job is to find this mystery agent, this Bai Ze. Then what happens? Shadow told you to bring him in so she can interrogate him. Do you intend to kill him instead? Is that payback? Is that your *revenge?* Will it give you some kind of satisfaction for what they did to Johanna?"

Bourne's hands tightened into fists. "You're a son of a bitch, Mo, you know that?"

"Yes, I am. Sometimes I have to be." Mo leaned forward, and his voice dropped to barely more than a whisper. "Here's what I *should* do, David. As a therapist, I should call Shadow and tell her that you are the wrong person for this mission. That you can't separate your grief over Johanna from what she's asking you to do. That in my professional opinion, you are at risk for an emotional overreaction, that your behavior on this assignment is likely to be unpredictable even to you. Is that what you want me to tell her?"

"*No.*"

"All right, then we'll keep this between us. God knows you've earned a reprieve from me ten times over, given our past. But I want you to know that *I* understand exactly what's going on in your head. Maybe you can fool Shadow. You can't fool me. And I'm not kidding when I say you may find yourself at the end of your rope emotionally, that you're at risk for spinning out of control on this one. If that happens, you need to *call me.* Got it? Don't try to deal with this alone. Don't fake your way through it like you've been doing for two years."

"Is this your idea of tough love, Mo?" Bourne asked.

"Goddamn right."

Jason exhaled slowly. "Well, I appreciate it."

"You'll keep me in the loop?"

"Agreed."

Mo smiled with satisfaction. "Good. So let's get down to the business at hand. Shadow told me what she wants, but I want to hear it from you. Then we'll decide what strategy makes sense."

"Well, Shadow says she has evidence that I was in a small town in Wisconsin eight years ago. Apparently a major Chinese espionage operation was under way. She thinks I saw Bai Ze during that operation, whether I realized it or not at the time. But of course, I don't remember any of it. It's lost in my past. The trouble is, the Treadstone records don't put me in Wisconsin at all. I was in Miami that week on vacation."

"And yet Shadow has faith in her information?" Mo asked. "She believes it's accurate?"

"She does."

"Sometimes fragments of memory come to you. Do you remember anything from back then? Either in Wisconsin or in Florida?"

"Not a thing," Bourne said.

"Do you remember *why* you went to Florida? Why I wanted you to take a vacation?"

"You?"

Mo nodded. "Yes, me. It was my idea. You'd been on an assignment in Greenland. It ended violently. You killed a Russian spy. That was the first time you'd been involved in a fatality in several years, and you were shaken. You were still young back then, David, still green as far as emotional maturity for the work you do. I told you—really, I pretty much ordered you—to get away from work for a few days. Do you remember any of that?"

"Sorry, no. Not Greenland, not Florida, not Wisconsin, nothing."

"Understandable. The bullet in the Med did its work very thoroughly. Well, I can tell you, that *is* what happened, David. Of course, you picked Miami for a holiday without consulting me. I would have told you *not* to go there."

"Why not?"

"Because you'd been there on a mission once before. You'd already stayed at that same hotel, the Mandarin Oriental. You checked in under a legend you'd used in the past. The whole point of taking a vacation was to remove yourself entirely from your work life. Instead, you picked a place where you had Treadstone history. Psychologically, that was a mistake, but I can't say I'm surprised. You didn't *want* to go on vacation at all. You never do. That's who you are."

"But now I wonder if I went there at all," Bourne said. "Miami may simply have been a cover. Maybe, for some reason, I went to Wisconsin instead."

Mo pursed his lips. "Well, let's see if we can find out, shall we? You know the drill."

Jason did.

He had never believed that he could be hypnotized. He assumed his mind was too stubborn for that. But at their earliest session years ago—a session he no longer remembered—Mo had told him that he was, in fact, highly susceptible. Since then, Mo had proven it time and time again, by leading him into a hypnotic state in a matter of seconds. That was one of the reasons he'd avoided seeing Mo for such a long time, despite everything he'd been through. Hypnosis made him feel vulnerable, as if his mind and memory could be manipulated. He didn't like it.

But once again, Mo did his magic, and Bourne was gone.

He didn't hear Mo's voice guiding him into the past. He had no awareness that the things happening around him weren't real or of how much time was passing. For a long time, he seemed to float in a kind of nothingness. Then the world grew strangely vivid, and all of his senses felt exaggerated. He experienced intense heat on his body, the smell of chlorine and sunblock, the blue of the water, the rough pages of a paperback book sticking to his fingers—damp because he'd been swimming. Beautiful people walked by him; voices and laughter rose above the whistle of the ocean wind. He walked along the Miami channel. He tasted wine on his lips and ate crispy pork belly.

And yet there was something else. Something *missing.*

Images and sensations pushed at his brain, but the details seemed lost in a fog. He felt his hands caressing a woman's bare back, saw her silky black hair and the honey-colored curve of her jaw. Her teasing voice was in his head. *No worries. Rough can be good.* If he saw her face, he would remember her, but as she turned toward him, she melted away, and the lounge chair beside him was empty.

He saw a man on the far side of the hotel pool, wearing a sport coat over jeans. The man stared at him, but his face was blurred, out of focus compared to the vivid detail of everyone else around him. *I know that man.*

But he didn't remember him.

And then—nothing.

Bourne's eyes blinked open. He was still in Mo's office, and Mo was watching him intently, waiting to hear what he had to say. When Bourne checked his watch, he saw that nearly two hours had passed.

"What did you see?" Mo asked.

"I *was* in Miami that week," Jason murmured, still trying to bring himself out of the fog and separate reality from hypnosis. "I remember that part of it. In fact, the whole week is oddly vivid compared to the rest of my past. But something happened there, too. Whatever it was, it's gone now. I wasn't able to pry the memory out of my head, just a couple bits and pieces."

"This was in Florida?" Mo asked.

"Yes, I was definitely in Florida. But the Files say I was in Wisconsin. That's what makes no sense. How could I be in two places at the same time?"

3

THE FLASHBACKS BEGAN AS SOON AS BOURNE ARRIVED AT THE MANDA-rin Oriental. Echoes. Faces. His memories fought through the cloud.

The Uber dropped him off at the east end of the Brickell Key bridge. The lineup of Miami towers loomed on the city side of the channel, and the Powell Bridge arched over the water to the south. It was a perfect day, warm and breezy, just like it had been eight years ago. That first day of vacation. He could feel the peace of Florida trying to grab his mind away from the violence of Greenland.

Bourne closed his eyes, letting images of the past come back to him.

A town car.

Yes, a black town car had arrived *right here*, where the bridge ended, near the driveway that led up to the hotel doors. He'd seen it. He watched it. Men got inside. No, men *and* women, including one woman who didn't want to go, who sensed danger in that journey. He'd felt frustration tighten his chest because he couldn't help her.

Who were they? What did they look like?

But he pushed his mind too hard, too fast. His brain rebelled. The images vanished, and sharp pain stabbed his eyes.

Bourne walked up the ramp to the hotel entrance and into the lobby, which was a showpiece of glass and gold stone. Metal sculptures of sea creatures dangled over his head. He went to the desk and checked in under the name Charlie Briggs, which was the cover he'd used eight years earlier. Treadstone still had the receipt that showed him checking in and checking out a week later.

He went to his room. Showered. Changed. Put on a swimsuit. He sensed that he'd done all of this before. He went downstairs to the pool area, and he dove into the warm water and did laps across the diameter of the circular pool for half an hour before drying off and settling into one of the lounge chairs.

His phone said it was three o'clock in the afternoon.

The Treadstone contact arrived on time.

A man in his midtwenties, dressed in a black tank top and cargo shorts, climbed the steps from the channel walkway to the pool area. He was medium height and muscular, and tattoos covered most of his right arm. His hair was shaved down to his scalp on the sides, with an ocean wave of dark curly hair on top. His blue eyes were oddly light against his tanned skin and dark beard line. He scanned everyone in the pool area without seeming to do so, and he noticed Bourne without letting his gaze linger on him. He strolled to the pool bar, ordered a Corona with a lime in the neck, and brought it to the lounge chair next to Jason.

"Cain," the man said. "I'm Levi. Welcome to Miami."

"Thanks. Any local activity I should know about?"

"There's nothing serious right now, but hell, by nightfall that could change. You know what they say. Drugs, girls, guns, cigars, anything you want comes across the water and checks in here. In Miami, everybody's in the import business."

Bourne closed his eyes. A fragment of a lost conversation echoed through his mind. Sarcastic. A joke.

I'm in the import business.

What do you import?

Alcohol mostly. Imported into me, that is.

"Cain?" Levi asked, interrupting his thoughts. "Is something wrong?"

"No, I'm fine. How long have you been stationed here?"

"A year. This is actually my first post. I spent two years in training after getting my national security degree at Arizona State. But don't worry. When I go somewhere, I get the lay of the land pretty fast."

Levi shoved the lime wedge into the beer bottle and took a swig, but he actually drank nothing at all. His pale blue eyes did another survey of the pool area. Bourne could tell: He was young, but he was smart.

"Did you get the intel request I sent?" Jason asked.

"I did."

"I'm interested in the second week in October eight years ago."

"Yeah, I checked it out. There's nothing in the Treadstone records from back then. Other than you. The log says you were here that whole week. But you didn't report anything, at least not through official channels. Anyway, I assume you already knew that, so my guess was, you were looking for intel outside Treadstone. That's where I focused my efforts."

"You're right."

"Well, I reached out to a few sources who have been around the area for years," Levi told him. "I thought somebody might remember if anything big went down during that stretch eight years ago."

"And?"

Levi waited as an attractive woman passed in front of them, a frozen strawberry drink in her hand, her sandals clopping on the pavement. When she was safely out of earshot, he went on. "Well, one report sounded interesting, but it was unconfirmed. I talked to a longtime drug dealer who feeds dirt to the FBI now and then to keep them off his back. He said he passed along a tip to them back then. He remembered it because he was pissed. The feebs checked it out and found nothing, so they thought he'd made it up. They didn't pay him his usual finder's fee for intel. But he swears it was legit."

"What was the tip?" Bourne asked.

"He claims he spotted someone on the FBI watch list down in the port area. The guy was meeting an incoming boat, smuggling something into the country. People, cargo, who knows. But he was sure about the face. It was a Chinese assassin, someone we really wanted. Went by the alias Fang."

Fang!

Bourne knew that name.

For a moment, the fog lifted. He stared across the glimmering hotel pool, and he saw Fang standing near the railing. The memory startled him with its clarity, jumping into his head. He remembered the man's sharp, smart eyes picking him up with a kind of radar. That was the face he'd tried to grasp when Mo helped him search his memory.

A Chinese assassin.

Here at the Mandarin Oriental.

If David Webb had seen him, he would have followed him.

"What happened to Fang?" Bourne asked. "Did we ever find him?"

"No, he disappeared. As I say, the FBI never caught a whiff of him around here. Either the dealer got it wrong, or Fang didn't stay in the area for long. Anyway, he never turned up again. Maybe he was killed under whatever alias he was using, or maybe he went back to China."

Bourne knew he was close. The wall that kept him from the truth had begun to crumble, letting him see peeks of what was behind it.

"Did you find anything else?" he asked. "Anything strange going down back then?"

"It's Miami, Cain. Everything's strange."

"What about murders? If an assassin was in town, were there any hits?"

"I thought about that, too. Yeah, there were a couple of gang and drug hits, but nothing you'd hire an overseas pro to handle. The only unsolved murder was a woman in a parking garage. Tap to the head. Police figured it was probably a mugging gone bad. The woman was some kind of event planner, travel arrangements for the rich and famous, that kind of thing. Lot of demand for that down here. Her name was—"

"*Martine*," Bourne murmured.

Levi cocked his head in surprise. "That's right. Martine Díaz. You knew her?"

Images tumbled over one another in Bourne's head. He saw a woman in a bikini, white smile, ebony hair tied in a ponytail. She flirted with him from her lounge chair, their connection ripe with possibilities. Then he saw that same woman struggling to get free as she was dragged from the back seat of a town car into a parking garage.

Dragged by Fang.

The pieces began to fall into place, one after another. The town car started from the Mandarin Oriental, and David Webb followed it to—

"The airport," Bourne said suddenly, seeing a vision of a black Gulfstream rocketing into the cloudless sky. He focused on Levi again. "Where do most of the private jets take off around here? What airport do they typically use?"

"Opa Locka," Levi said.

Bourne nodded. *Yes.* That was right. Fang had taken three Chinese men to Opa Locka. He *saw* them.

Then what?

I'm David Webb, I just saw a Chinese spy leaving Miami on a Gulfstream. What do I do?

I follow them.

"If I needed a pilot down here," Bourne asked, "someone who didn't ask a lot of questions, someone who didn't keep records, who would I talk to?"

"I can think of one guy," Levi replied. He tapped a finger against the neck of his Corona bottle. "But you'll want to grab him before he has too many of these. He lost his license for drinking, but that doesn't keep him out of the sky. He's been doing under-the-radar flights around here for twenty years, everything from Cessnas to Gulfstreams. Name's Konrad Dachowski. Goes by Kodak."

BOURNE PARKED HIS RENTED CAMRY ON A DIRT SHOULDER NEXT TO THE railroad tracks, under an overpass for the Palmetto Expressway. He was a stone's throw from Miami International. Every few minutes, the thunder of a jumbo jet landing on Runway 9 rattled the ground. This was an industrial area, mostly populated by warehouses, with an almost constant parade of semitrucks kicking up dust. But there was also a salsa bar that attracted cargo workers at lunch and club dancers at night. It shared a strip mall with a row of anonymous tenants whose windows were covered over with butcher paper.

Using binoculars, Bourne kept an eye on the bar's parking lot. According to Levi, this place was Kodak's favorite hangout.

Kodak.

Bourne knew his face, knew he'd used him in the past. But he remembered nothing else. His instincts told him that he would have reached out to Kodak for help after watching a jet take off from Opa Locka. But the details of whatever happened next didn't exist for him anymore. It was as if the next few days of his past had simply been painted over.

Bourne sat behind the wheel of the Camry and waited. Four o'clock passed. Then five. Then five thirty. The after-work drinkers began to arrive.

At six o'clock, he spotted a white F-150 pickup pulling into the lot near the rear of the building. The man who climbed down from the truck was short and stocky, with an almost completely round face. His hair had thinned to a black crown at the back of his head, and he kept a bushy salt-and-pepper mustache. His large wire-rimmed glasses would have been in style back in the 1970s. Despite the Miami heat, he wore a weathered leather bomber jacket over worn blue jeans. He was smoking a cigarette, which he crushed on the pavement before disappearing into the bar.

Bourne checked the area for other surveillance and saw none. He left the shadows of the overpass and crossed the street. Inside the bar, most of the tables were already full, and a stage was being set up for evening music. He spotted Kodak sitting by himself at the counter, pawing at a bowl of mixed nuts and chatting up the attractive bartender, who treated him like a regular. He had a low-ball glass of what looked like vodka on the rocks in front of him.

The chair next to Kodak was empty, and Bourne sat down. The Polish pilot gave him a sideways glance and then did a double take, recognizing him. His mustache wriggled as he let out a loud sigh. When he spoke, his voice still had a thick Eastern European accent. "Ah, shit. You. I figured you were dead."

"Nice to see you, too, Kodak."

"What do you want, Cain? I work with you two times, you almost get me killed both times. Do you remember? First time, a flight into the Everglades. Gunfire forced the plane down into the swamp, and I had to run for my life from fucking gators. I hate gators."

"You live in Florida," Bourne said.

"Yeah, well, I fucking hate orange juice, too. So what?"

"I need your help."

"What, you want to fly somewhere? Call JetBlue."

The young bartender, who sported a curly pile of flaming-red hair, wandered down the bar and leaned her elbows on the counter in front of Bourne. Her green eyes twinkled at him. "You want something, hon?"

"How about a Coke? Lots of ice."

"You got it." She smiled at Kodak. "What about you, sweets? Top you up?"

"Yeah, sure, why not."

Bourne put a hand over Kodak's glass. "Actually, he's done for the night. Pour this one out, and give me the bill."

"Ah, shit," Kodak said again.

Jason waited until the bartender brought him his Coke and then left them alone. He checked the other tables with a casual glance around the bar and spotted a young Asian woman, dressed for salsa dancing, concentrating on her phone. She had a half-empty cosmopolitan in a martini glass in front of her. He stared hard at her, waiting for her to feel his gaze, but if she was aware of him, she didn't look up.

That was a tell. They'd already found him.

Bourne turned back to Kodak. "What about the second mission we ran together? Tell me about it."

"Why tell you what you already know?" the man asked, his tone crabby.

"Humor me. When was it?"

"Do I look like a fucking calendar? Long time, seven, eight, nine years, who knows."

"What happened?"

"You know what happened. You call me. Right here, you leave a message, and I call you back. You say, Kodak, I need you. I tell you, get fucked. You say, no gators this time, no guns."

"What did I want?" Bourne asked.

"You gave me a tail number on a Gulfstream. Wanted to know if I could get its flight plan from Opa Locka."

"And could you?"

Kodak snorted. "Who you talking to? Of course I could. Jet was on its way to Green Bay, Wisconsin. Must be a load of Packer fans, huh? Why the fuck else would anyone go to Wisconsin?"

"I hear it's pretty up there," Bourne said. "October. Leaves changing."

"Do I look like I fucking care about leaves?"

Bourne chuckled. "I asked you to fly me up there. Right?"

"Right. All I could find was a twin-engine Beechcraft that I borrowed off a lawyer who likes me to fly packages for him from Port-au-Prince now and then. Took hours to get there. Had to refuel in fucking Kentucky. We didn't land until midnight."

"What about the Gulfstream?"

"It was still there. But no one around. Is this some kind of test, Cain? You were there. You know what happened next."

"Just tell me," Bourne said.

Kodak sighed heavily. "All right, all right. You went off and found ground crew, paid them to find out where the passengers went."

"Where did they go?"

"You think you fucking tell me? No way. And I don't care."

"Then what?"

"Then we find a motel outside the airport. I try to sleep, you don't. You sit in a chair, watching the door, like you expect something to happen. And guess what? Something fucking happens. Guy picks the lock, comes in all quiet, gun, silencer. I wake up, and the two of you are tearing up the place. Gun goes off, practically blows my fucking head open. You break the guy's neck, drag him into the woods behind the motel. Me, I'm not happy about any of this, you know?"

"I'm sure."

Kodak shook his head. "Five in the morning, I go fly the Beechcraft back, you go wherever the fuck you go. Never figured I'd see you again, and I didn't, not until tonight."

"You didn't fly me back to Florida?"

"No."

Bourne frowned. Kodak didn't take him back to Florida—and yet he *did* go back to Miami. He checked out of the Mandarin Oriental on time the following Friday. He had room service charges on the fifth and sixth days.

But nothing on days two, three, and four. *Why?*

The answer was obvious now. Because he was in Wisconsin. But why was there nothing in the Treadstone reports? If he'd stumbled onto a Chinese spy operation, he would have written it up, and yet he let Treadstone believe he'd been in Florida the entire time. This was long before he was shot in the Med.

Long before he lost his memory.

Wasn't it?

Bourne took another look around the bar. The Asian salsa dancer had finished her cosmopolitan and was gone. The clock was ticking.

"Come on, Kodak, we need to get out of here."

"Why the fuck do I need to go anywhere with you?"

"One, because I need you to fly me to Green Bay again. Now. Tonight. Two, because I figure we have less than five minutes before a heavy assault team arrives outside. If you're still here, they'll grab you to find out what we talked about, and then they'll put a bullet in your head."

Kodak made a noise like a cat hacking up a fur ball. "Ah, shit."

4

AT TWO IN THE MORNING, BOURNE FOUND HIMSELF FOURTEEN HUNDRED miles from Florida in the middle of a deserted airport. Kodak, who had no desire to spend any more time than necessary with Bourne, didn't linger after landing in Green Bay. He dropped Bourne near the terminal, then turned his lawyer's Beechcraft around and took off immediately on a return flight to the sunshine of Miami.

Bourne was alone and in need of transportation. There were no rental car agencies open, but five hundred dollars in cash to a bored airport janitor bought him access to a hangar where a recently deceased Cessna pilot kept a 2010 Ford Taurus. He found the car keys in the glove compartment, and after he coaxed the cold engine to life, he made his way out of the city on Highway 57, heading northeast toward Door County. He kept his eyes on the mirrors, but for now, no one followed him.

A light snow fell, making the road slippery. His high-beam headlights showed nothing but empty wilderness around him, the road framed by dense stands of oaks, birches, and evergreens. Highway signs warned of deer, and he spotted several snow-covered carcasses on the shoulder to back up the signs.

The gas tank of the Taurus registered as half full, and the gas stations he passed were all closed for the night, but fortunately, he didn't have far to go. Less than an hour later, the map on his phone showed that he was approaching Door County, which was a peninsula shaped like a witch's scrawny thumb jutting out of the mainland and separating the turbulent waters of Lake Michigan from the Green Bay inlet. Based on the billboards he passed, it was a tourist region of small towns, B and Bs, cherries, and lighthouses—not exactly ground zero for Chinese spy activity. And yet, according to the Files, David Webb had encountered Bai Ze eight years ago at a resort hotel called the White Gull Inn in a small town known as Fish Creek.

The signs told him he was thirty miles away.

However, things went wrong before he got there. Ten miles later, near a town called Carlsville, he spotted headlights behind him, a car turning out of a dirt driveway as soon as Bourne passed. When he slowed his speed, the car slowed; when he accelerated, the car kept pace. The driver had to know that Bourne had spotted him, but he didn't seem to care about being discovered.

Two miles later, Bourne knew why.

A second vehicle turned onto the highway a quarter mile ahead of him. The car adopted a slow speed of fifty miles an hour, but when Bourne went to pass him, the driver accelerated to keep him where he was. He also noticed the vehicle behind him creeping closer, the two cars readying a pincer where they could come at him from two directions and run him off the deserted road.

Bourne checked his map. He saw one turn ahead of him at a

place called Monument Point Road. He kept his speed steady, not slowing down, waiting until the car ahead of him cleared the intersection. Then he hit the brakes sharply and turned the wheel hard, feeling the rear of the Taurus lurch wide on the slippery pavement. The car kept turning, spinning through a full three-sixty, until the nose of the car aimed west. Bourne shoved down the accelerator, and the wheels spat and spun and finally gained traction. He shot down a country road barely wider than the car, with the winter branches of trees on both sides waving their arms at him. Slushy snow sprayed across the windshield.

In his mirror, he saw headlights. The car behind him turned sharply, went out of control, and then corrected. The leading vehicle did a U-turn and brought up the rear. Bourne drove fast, despite the snow, despite the darkness, trying to stay ahead of the two vehicles chasing the Taurus into the empty woods. When he glanced at the map, he saw an intersection coming up, the road splitting in three directions. He barreled ahead, keeping straight toward the waters of Green Bay. Then another sharp turn forced him to slam on the brakes, and again the rear of the Taurus spun wide as the wheels lost traction. He swerved onto the shoulder, kicking up snowdrifts, then veered back. Beyond the curve, the road bent right, but he was going too fast to make the turn, and the car shot across the opposite lane onto an even narrower road, where the snow hadn't been cleared. As he punched into the heavy, wet, six-inch pile, the Taurus's wheels groaned in protest and skidded to a stop.

Bourne climbed out of the car into deep snow. His Glock was in his hand. Behind him, the engines of the other two vehicles growled as they got closer. He figured he had only a few seconds before they reached him. He plunged into the woods, fighting through drifts up to his knees, and leaving an easy trail for the men to follow. When he stopped and looked back, he saw twin beams of flashlights crisscrossing the trees. Two men.

He kept going, blind in the darkness, the jagged branches of trees scraping his face. His breathing grew labored as he struggled forward, trying to carve a trail through heavy wet snow. Then, with no warning, the woods ended, and he spilled onto a ribbon of rocky beach. The waters of Green Bay stretched out in front of him under the starlight. A fierce, frigid wind slammed his face, mixed with balls of ice. On the beach, the falling snow melted as it landed in the surging waves, and he jogged north, splashing in and out of the freezing water, no longer leaving a path to follow.

But the men were close behind him. When he looked over his shoulder, he saw their flashlight beams cutting through the night. He dove from the beach back into the cover of the woods, where he was invisible. He crouched down, silently threaded a suppressor onto his Glock, and waited.

The two men emerged from the trees not even a hundred feet away. They stood in the water, dark silhouettes looking both ways, unsure which way Bourne had gone. They split up. One man went north; the other went south. Both had serious weapons, AR-15s braced against their sides. Around here, no one would care about the crack of rifles, even if they were awake to hear it.

Bourne realized he was frozen in place, with nowhere to go. If he fired his Glock and missed, he'd invite a rain of gunfire on his location. If he ran again, they'd hear him crashing through the woods.

The first of the men inched closer, approaching his hiding

place step by step. He was good; he was smart. He stayed in the ice-cold water, ten feet offshore, far enough away that a pistol would have to be perfectly aimed to take him down. In the darkness, with the wind swirling and changing directions, Bourne doubted he could make the shot. But he might have no choice but to try.

The man was near enough now that he could make out some of his features. He was white, with blond hair and pale skin. Steam clouded from his mouth in the cold. His eyes were two black beetles at night, studying the woods. The man knew Bourne was close; he was a pro, and he could *feel* him even if he couldn't see him. They'd been only steps behind in their pursuit through the woods, which meant Bourne couldn't have gone far.

Silently, Bourne stared at him, and the man behind the rifle stared back into the blackness. The AR-15 barrel was pointed at the trees. The man's finger was on the trigger. Still in the water, he stopped almost exactly opposite Bourne, as if his instincts told him he was in the right place. Bourne examined the rocky beach, but could see no footprints that would give him away. Even so, the man had decided he knew where Bourne was hiding. And the trouble was, he was right.

In the next few seconds, the man would fire. He'd unleash rounds into the woods, his aim shifting a few inches with each pull of the trigger. If he got a hit, he'd hear the grunt of pain. If he got close, he'd hear Bourne diving for cover. One way or another, Bourne had to make a stand right here.

He stretched out his right arm and braced his wrist, aiming the barrel of the Glock through the brush. The wind swooped and howled, and he could barely keep the gun steady. If he fired, he'd only get off one shot before the rifle ripped apart his hiding place.

He needed at least three or four shots to zero in on the man's torso, and even with the suppressor, he'd give himself away.

The man in the water took one step closer. Not more than that. Just one. Not close enough. Urgently, silently, Bourne unfurled a leg and eased himself down, conscious of the branches that would snap if he touched them and the slushy snow that would make him lose his balance in a rush of noise. He lowered himself inch by inch until he was flat on the ground, buried in snow, keeping his Glock aimed toward the water. From there, he used the wet earth to balance his arm against the wind.

It was still a risky shot.

He reached up with his left hand and found a dangling branch a couple of feet over his head. With his fingers, he broke it, causing a low crack over the gales.

The man in the water didn't hesitate. He fired. The rifle snapped with each pull of the trigger, but his bullets all went high. Bourne ignored the onslaught and used the cover of the noise to squeeze the trigger of the Glock, which made a low hiss as the first bullet fired. The hiss was mostly soundless against the crack of the AR-15.

He missed, fired again, and missed again.

The third bullet landed home, tunneling into the middle of the man's face. The rifle dropped; the body dropped, thudding into the bay with a splash. One down. But the exchange of gunfire drew the second man along the beach at a sprint, already firing, already blowing apart the woods. Bourne had no choice; he had to move. He crashed on his hands and knees through snow and trees, then threw himself forward when he knew the second man was close enough to hear him. He held his breath, trying to stay hidden. His awkward angle on the ground trapped his gun arm beneath him.

Twenty feet apart, they confronted each other.

The wind howled.

The man held his fire now, listening, keeping a safe distance. Waves rose and fell around him in the starlight, throwing up clouds of spray. Snow whipped sideways, creating a kind of white fog between them. Bourne felt the wet cold invading his bones. His face half covered, he watched the man, who was barely more than a ghost. The standoff lingered, both of them wondering what the other would do.

Then flame spat through the snow, another wave of rifle fire. It started high and wide, then got closer, kicking up slush and mud. Bourne steeled himself, motionless as the barrage came within inches and cut his face with shrapnel from the trees. He tasted blood dripping down his cheek and across his mouth. Just as the bullets ripped open the ground six inches in front of him, the fire stopped. Smoke blew through the wind, sharp and pungent. The man kept the rifle leveled and inched closer through the surf. He didn't know whether Bourne was alive or dead, whether the assault had left his body riddled with bullets. Making a mistake would be fatal, but he couldn't walk away not knowing. So Bourne waited for him, prone among the trees. The man came from the water; his boots crunched on rock. One eye open, the other under the snow, Bourne watched him come.

Fifteen feet. Then ten.

Two or three more steps, and the man would see Bourne's body, dark against white drifts. He'd fire, a last inferno with perfect aim, making certain Bourne was dead. Slowly, quietly, Bourne freed his right arm and swung it around, the Glock no more than a couple of inches off the ground, barrel turned sideways toward the water.

The man took another step, cautious and suspicious. Bourne sighted down the barrel, tried to keep the gun steady, tried to see the meat of the man's torso through the night. It was a tough shot, a long shot, but he couldn't wait. The man stiffened now with a sudden recognition, his eyes separating the shadows and picking out his target lying on the ground. Dead or alive didn't matter. He was about to fire.

Bourne fired first. He pulled the trigger four times, each shot finding the man's chest in a tight circle of bullets. Then he slithered forward, expecting return fire, which he got. Wounded but not dead, the man jerked on the AR-15, his aim erratic as the recoil made him stagger, the barrel tilting high in the trees. Bourne twisted onto his back, took aim, and fired twice more, this time through the man's stomach.

The drilling of multiple bullets finally caught up with the killer on the beach. The man's grip loosened and the rifle fell to the rocks. His hands clutched at his chest, then his stomach, and then dropped limply to his sides. He took a few crazy steps before crashing sideways into the waves.

Bourne pushed himself to his feet. The snow wiped the blood from his face. He walked unsteadily onto the rocky beach, shifting his Glock back and forth between the two assassins. But they were dead. He listened, hearing no sirens over the wind, no disturbances. He doubted that anyone had even heard the firefight. Keeping his gun ready, he checked the body of the first man, which was being pushed toward the beach by the waves. The man was face up, eyes open and dead, and Bourne took a photograph. When he checked the man's pockets, he found no identification.

Then he checked the second man, who was facedown in the

water. Bourne flipped him over by his shoulder and lit up the man's face with his phone. He had black hair, wet and matted against his skin, and a trimmed beard. A dragon tattoo snaked from under his shirt to the bottom of his beard line.

But what Bourne noticed most of all was the horizontal scar on his cheekbone. He'd been there when the man got that scar. They'd worked together on an operation in Thailand almost a decade earlier.

He *knew* him!

The dead man was CIA.

"HE'S ONE OF HOLLY SCHULTZ'S MEN," BOURNE TOLD SHADOW. "AFTER I lost my memory, I saw my mission files. This man was in them. His code name was Chess, but I don't know his underlying identity."

"I got the picture you sent. I'll run him through the database."

It was five in the morning in Washington, but Shadow sounded wide-awake. Bourne found himself wondering whether she'd been alone in her bed when he called. He hated that he even cared about that.

"Bai Ze was waiting for you," Shadow went on. "I don't like that."

"Yeah. He had people in Florida, too. Somewhere we've got a leak. I think we have to assume that whoever Bai Ze is, he knows I'm on his trail."

"What's your next move?"

Bourne looked through the windshield of the Taurus, but snow had already covered up the glass. When he lowered the window, he felt cold wind through the car. But he was alone. No one else had followed him. He'd dug out the tires to free the Taurus from the drifts and then driven miles from the scene of the firefight. Now he was off the road in the driveway of what looked like a deserted summer home. He saw no signs of an alarm system guarding the house. It would be easy to break in.

"I need to clean up. Then get some sleep. In the afternoon, I'll head to the White Gull Inn in Fish Creek and see if I can figure out what operation I stumbled onto eight years ago. But it's strange. I have no idea what Bai Ze would be doing in a place like this. This is a tourist area. There aren't any government or corporate operations worth infiltrating."

"At least we know that you really were there," Shadow said. "And you were on the trail of the Chinese when you left Florida. So far, the Files have been proven right."

"Yeah." His voice betrayed his doubts.

"Is something wrong?"

Bourne frowned, listening to the hiss of snow. "How would the Files know about that? Where would they get the information to conclude that I was in the middle of a Chinese operation?"

"I don't know," Shadow admitted. "Even when I ask the software to reveal its sources, it seems reluctant to do so. Sometimes I think it out-and-out lies, like it has its own agenda to protect. There's a lot about the Files, a lot about its capabilities, that I haven't begun to discover yet. But one thing I've learned is that the software is *ravenous* for information. It hacks everything it gets near. Wi-Fi. Phones. Smart devices. As an experiment once, I took the laptop to a coffee shop and booted it up. In about ninety seconds, the software had hacked every phone in the place, plus the retailer's local Wi-Fi. From there it traveled up the chain and hacked into the computers for the corporate headquarters. Then it sent me an encrypted email with all the access codes it found."

"Scary."

"But useful," Shadow said. "My point is, the software for the Files was developed by the Chinese, but perhaps on some level its capabilities worked against them without their being aware of it. When the software was being developed, it may have hacked some of their own systems and retained information about their operations. Including reports from whatever happened eight years ago."

"Okay, but that doesn't explain *me.* If I saw this assassin Fang back then, if I followed him to Wisconsin, why didn't I report it?"

He heard a smile in her voice.

"You're a lone wolf, Jason. You always have been, even when you were David Webb. Do you think I don't know that? If you were on his trail, you wouldn't stop to let anyone else know what was going on."

"But why wouldn't I file a report afterward? Nobody at Treadstone knew I was here, and I didn't report the sighting of a Chinese assassin on the watch list. The only footprints I left were small enough that it took the Files to uncover them."

"I don't know what to tell you. Whatever you do or don't do, you usually have a reason."

"Maybe. Or maybe it was something else." Bourne felt his eyes blinking shut. Aching stiffness made it hard to move. "I should go."

"Hang on. I'm getting a report back about Chess."

Bourne waited. When Shadow's silence dragged on, he finally said, "So what's the deal? Do you have anything more about him? Is he still active with the CIA?"

"He's dead," Shadow told him.

"I know that."

"No, Jason, he was killed on a mission years ago. Or at least, that's what the CIA records show. Someone faked his death so he could be resurrected in the shadows. New life, new identity."

"What was the mission?" Bourne asked.

"The details are blacked out. Even I don't have clearance to unmask the report, which is very odd." She hesitated. "But when he went missing, he was in China."

5

A STEEP HILL LED BOURNE DOWN TO THE LAKESHORE IN THE TOWN OF Fish Creek. He parked the Taurus on a backstreet where it wouldn't be seen and explored the area on foot. The overnight snow had stopped, but it was still cold and windy, and clouds made the day steel gray. Offseason, on a Friday morning, he had the town mostly to himself. It reminded him of New England, with a harbor for fishing boats—now empty and fringed with ice—and houses built with gables, front porches, and white siding. A few of the shops were open, but many were closed for the winter. The same was true of the inns and B and Bs. It looked like a town in hibernation, waiting for the spring sunshine to wake it up.

Eight years ago. October.

What had drawn the Chinese *here?*

In the early afternoon, Bourne walked to the White Gull Inn, which was tucked away near the water's edge at the west end of Main Street. It was open year-round and dated back to the late nineteenth century. The inn didn't appear to be large, not even twenty suites, some in the main two-story building, some in free-standing cottages tucked away in the woods. A pristine layer of snow covered the grass and coated the branches of the trees. Bourne let his gaze travel around the grounds, waiting for some kind of echo or instinct that he had been here before. Normally, he remembered places, even if he didn't recall people or events. But this time there was nothing. The hotel, the town, the area, didn't resonate in his mind at all.

His memories seemed to have been wiped clean.

He walked up the neatly shoveled walkway and into the lobby of the inn. Chambered windows faced the street, and a huge fire crackled in a rough-stone fireplace. The hardwood floor glistened. Bourne generally melted into new settings with ease, but he was also a man of urban alleys and cramped apartments, and he felt out of place here, as if he'd crossed into a Norman Rockwell painting from decades earlier. Automatically, he reached into the pocket of his leather jacket and curled his fingers around the butt of his Glock.

Nothing is what it seems to be.

Treadstone.

A fortysomething man, wearing a yellow turtleneck and pressed gray slacks, greeted him with a pleasant smile. He was tall and lean, with slightly unruly brown hair and a prominent chin. His smile wavered just a little when Bourne told him his name was Charlie Briggs, but that he didn't have a reservation.

"We *highly* recommend reservations," the man told Bourne. "Most nights we're fully booked, even during the winter. And especially weekends. We get lots of honeymooners and family reunions, even in the offseason. But you're lucky. We had a couple of cancellations because of the snow. You'll be fine with one of our cottages?"

"Sure."

"All right then. It's Friday, by the way, so you're in luck. We're doing our winter fish boil tonight. If you haven't experienced that before, you really should. It's a Door County tradition."

"What's a fish boil?" Bourne asked.

"Oh, we boil whitefish and potatoes outside in a large pot over an open fire. At the end, our master boiler tosses kerosene on the fire, which triggers a boilover that gets rid of the fish oils. It's quite a sight to see. Plus there's cherry pie for dessert. We only have a couple of seats left for tonight if you want a reservation."

"Why not."

"Excellent, I'll put you down. I hope you enjoy your stay, Mr. Briggs. You'll find brochures in the cottage about winter activities around the area. There's actually a lot to do throughout the year. Once you've stayed here, I guarantee you'll want to come back during the warmer months, too."

"Actually, I was here once before," Bourne told the clerk.

Was he? Why wasn't any of this familiar?

"Oh, yes? When was that?"

"Eight years ago," Bourne said. "It was October. In fact, I was wondering if you could look up my stay back then and tell me what room I was in. Just for curiosity. I was down with the flu most of the time, so I don't remember much about that weekend."

"When in October?" the man asked.

"The second week. So it would have been October twelfth or thirteenth."

"Well, let me look. Our records should go back that far." He tapped on the keys of his computer, but then his forehead crinkled and his mouth pursed into a frown. "Were you with a group back then, Mr. Briggs?"

"No. I was on my own."

"Then I'm afraid you must have the wrong dates. The entire inn was reserved for a special event that week. There were no outside reservations."

"I'm pretty sure about the dates," Bourne told him. "Now that I think about it, I recall some kind of big group here that weekend. Maybe there was a cancellation like today and I got lucky. What was the event?"

The man's frown persisted. "I'm not sure. Honestly, this is rather strange. There's no details on the event or on the people occupying the individual rooms. I don't even see any information about billing."

"That's unusual?" Bourne asked.

"Very unusual. I mean, we get corporate and private events that take up the whole inn quite often, but it's uncommon to have no record of it in the computer. It's almost as if the details were manually erased sometime after the event took place. I've never seen anything like this."

"Were you around back then?"

"No, I've only worked here for two years."

"Is there someone else who might remember?"

A flicker of suspicion crossed the man's face. "Why do you want to know?"

Bourne smiled and made up a lie. "To be honest, that first evening, before I got sick, I had a very nice conversation with a woman in the room next to mine. We really hit it off, but we never connected again. It's foolish, I know, but as long as I was back here, I thought I might get her name out of you. Of course, eight years is a long time, but we really did seem to have chemistry."

"I'm afraid I wouldn't be able to give you any names of our guests regardless," the man informed him. "That's against our privacy policy. But it's a moot point, as I said. There's nothing in the system."

"Well, I appreciate you looking."

"Certainly, Mr. Briggs. We'll see you at the fish boil tonight."

Bourne turned away, but behind him, he heard the man tapping on the computer keys and muttering half to himself.

"Someone certainly had a lot of clout," the man said. "Or a lot of cash."

A PRIVATE EVENT EIGHT YEARS AGO. NO RECORDS. NO DETAILS.

Bourne was sure that whatever the event was, it was at the heart of the espionage operation the Chinese had been conducting. He needed more information, but when he searched online, he found no evidence to suggest what had been happening in the midst of autumn leaf-changing season in Fish Creek. He also stopped by the local library to check headlines in the county newspaper, but it was already closed for the day. So for now, he had to focus on the present, not the past.

At six thirty, after dark, he made his way to the terrace behind the inn's restaurant for the traditional fish boil. It was crowded, as the clerk suggested, with tourists from around the county making their way to the White Gull for whitefish and cherry pie. A few flurries blew in with the wind, and most of the people were bundled up in heavy coats, their faces dancing in the shadows of the flames cast from the large stone firepit. The smell of kerosene and smoke mixed with the lake breeze.

Bourne stayed on the edge of the crowd, largely invisible in the darkness. His gaze went from face to face, examining the people. Bai Ze's men had been waiting for him when he arrived in Wisconsin, and he assumed they'd be looking for him here, too. The threat hadn't gone away.

At first he saw no one who raised his suspicions.

Then he spotted the woman standing off by herself.

She stood at the fringe of the trees, seemingly not part of the group gathered for the fish boil. She was in her late thirties, like Bourne, with shoulder-length chestnut hair, but she was too far away for him to make out many details of her face. She was small and fit, wearing a black sleeveless down vest over a long-sleeve white nylon top. Her phone was in her hand, and she was taking pictures of the crowd.

He wasn't sure if she could see him clearly—any more than he could see her—but her stare kept shifting his way in the darkness. Then the chef squirted kerosene on the fire, triggering a cloud of flames around the boiling pot. He felt a wave of heat, and he knew the sudden brightness of the fire had lit up his face. At the same moment, the woman raised her phone again, the camera aimed directly at him.

He was sure she'd just taken a series of pictures of him.

Ignoring the crowd in the courtyard, Bourne took off toward the trees. Seeing him, the woman immediately turned and vanished. He continued to the woods and then to the street that led to the lakefront, but he saw no sign of her.

But she'd been watching him. He had no doubt of that.

Bourne returned to the hotel, where the food from the fish boil was being served in the dining room, and ate a quick dinner. When he was done, he went outside again, checking the trees where the woman had been, then continuing to the dead end of Main Street, which was covered with a dusting of snow. A handful of parked cars lined both sides of the road. He kept his hands in his jacket pockets, his hand secure on the Glock. The woods showed him nothing in the darkness, and the nearby homes had no lights. He made his way to the very end of the street, where a postage stamp of grass overlooked a rocky beach and the expanse of Green Bay glistening under the starlight. He took a seat on a bench near a low stone wall that fronted the bayshore.

Moments later, he heard footsteps behind him in the snow.

In one smooth motion, he swung around, the Glock at the end of his outstretched arm. The same woman was there. Seeing the gun, she screamed and threw her hands in the air.

"Jesus! Hey, sorry, sorry, I didn't mean to startle you. I come in peace. Really."

"Then why were you spying on me at the hotel?" Bourne asked, not lowering the gun.

"I wasn't—that wasn't what I was doing. Not really. I mean, I wasn't there to see you. I like to check out the fish boils from time to time. It always makes for great pics when they do the boilover. Especially the winter ones at night."

"You were staring at me," Bourne said, "and taking pictures. And here you are following me to the beach."

"Yeah. You're right. Busted." The woman shrugged, breaking into a sheepish smile. She wore a blue wool cap, and her stringy brown curls swished across her face as the wind blew. "I saw you there, and yeah, I was looking at you, but only because I'm sure I know you from somewhere. I'm not a stalker or anything."

With a glance, Bourne checked out her body from top to bottom. He saw no indication that she was armed. He bent his elbow and let the Glock go loose, and then he returned it to his pocket. "Who are you?"

"My name's Laney Reese."

"You live around here?"

She nodded. "Yeah. Well, on the other side of the peninsula in Baileys Harbor. I'm a Door County lifer. Not many of us left around here. The rich FIBs have bought up most of the houses so they can spend their summers at the lake."

"FIBs?" Bourne asked.

Laney smirked. "Fucking Illinois Bastards."

"Ah. Right."

"Look, do you mind if I sit down? You won't shoot me or something?"

"Go ahead," Bourne said.

She took a seat next to him, staring out at the darkness of the lake. He noticed that she kept her hands on the knees of her blue jeans, rather than put them in the pockets of her vest, which he might take as a threat. Despite the night, she was close enough to him that he could see her features clearly. She had a thin face and neck, with dark, twinkling eyes and a mouth that turned naturally upward into a smile. Her compact nose was rounded at the end, her cheekbones soft and flushed. A few lines around her mouth and eyes attested to her age, but she had a quiet prettiness about her, as well as an easy confidence in who she was.

"That wasn't just a line, by the way," Laney said. "You really do look familiar to me. Have we met before?"

"Not that I know of."

He stared back at her, searching his mind for clues, but as with everything else about Door County, he felt no glimmers of familiarity. If he'd met Laney Reese, he didn't remember it at all. But she seemed to know *him*.

"What do you do, Laney?" he asked.

"Oh, a lot of things. I'm a Jill of all trades. In a seasonal place like this, it's hard to have one job that pays the bills. I waitress at a fish place in Baileys Harbor during the summers. I sell pottery at farmers markets. I also write for the local newspaper. It's mostly an online blog, stories about new restaurants and shops. Not exactly the *Milwaukee Journal Sentinel*, you know? But it makes me feel like my journalism degree wasn't entirely wasted."

She cocked her head, still studying his face with curiosity.

"Anyway, that's me. Not to pry, but you are . . . ?"

"Briggs," Bourne replied. "Charlie Briggs."

The name elicited no reaction. "Hmm. Can't say I know a Charlie Briggs, but wow, you still look *so* familiar. Are you on vacation here?"

"Sort of."

"What do you do that makes you carry a gun? If you don't mind my asking."

"I'm in investment banking. I'm cautious when it comes to security."

"I guess so. You from Chicago? If so, sorry about the FIB thing."

"New York," Bourne said.

"No kidding? You're a long way from home."

"I've got relatives in Madison." The lie came to him without any thought. That was one of the things Bourne disliked about himself. He lied too quickly and too well. But a man without an identity had to put on other identities as easily as changing clothes.

"Oh. Okay. Madison's a cool town, pretty funky. Or as funky as it gets in Wisconsin. So, Charlie Briggs, are you married? Sorry to be so forward, but when you're thirty-eight and single, you learn not to beat around the bush when you meet someone new. Particularly a good-looking investment banker who's not wearing a ring."

Bourne smiled. "I'm not married."

"Me neither. Or did I already mention that?"

"You already mentioned that."

"Just making sure you caught it." Laney winked.

"How long have you worked for the newspaper?" Bourne asked.

"More than a decade now. They pay shit, but every little bit helps. Like I said, it makes me feel like I'm not a complete professional failure. I don't have a choice, though. Dad's dead, and Mom's got Parkinson's. She's in assisted living, so it's not like I could go off and see the world, right?" Laney shook her head. "I also have a way of oversharing with strangers. That may explain why I'm thirty-eight and single."

"Don't worry about it," Bourne said.

"Well, good. I really don't want to scare you off. In fact, not to put you on the spot or anything, but do you want to join me for a beer? Bayside Tavern is a couple blocks away, and they're still open. Then maybe I can figure out why I know you. Or maybe you just have that familiar look." Laney stopped talking as her phone started ringing. She reached for her pants pocket, but then hesitated. "I'm just going to answer my phone. Really. No guns or anything."

"Go ahead."

Laney pulled out her phone and listened, and her upturned smile turned downward. Bourne listened to one side of the conversation.

"Seriously? Where? You heard it on the scanner? Yeah, yeah, thanks, I'll check it out right now. I appreciate the tip."

Laney ended the call.

"Let me guess, you need a rain check," Bourne said.

"I do. So sorry about that. Could we meet in the morning? You around for breakfast tomorrow?"

"Sure."

"I'll meet you at your hotel. The stuffed French toast is great."

"It's a date. But you've got me curious now. What's so urgent? It seems like they roll up the sidewalks at night around here."

"Normally, yeah, but I've got a source in Sturgeon Bay who likes to listen to the police scanners. It's pretty quiet most of the time, but he just heard the radio going wild. Somebody reported two bodies on the beach a few miles south of here. Both of them shot multiple times from the look of it. Around here, that's big news, let me tell you."

"I guess so."

"So I need to write it up and get an article on the website," she went on. "Typically, nobody gets killed in Door County unless they decide to pull the trigger themselves. And two people? That's crazy. Last time we had a double murder anywhere around here must have been eight years ago."

"Really," Bourne said. "Eight years."

6

THE SPY KNOWN AS BAI ZE PUNCHED IN THE TEN DIGITS OF THE COMBI-nation code that unlocked the warehouse door in the industrial area near the Baltimore port. He watched the light turn from red to green, activating the hydraulics that slid the oversize door open. When he climbed back behind the wheel of his Ford Expedition, he drove inside the warehouse, then closed the door and resecured the lock.

Bright halogen lights came on inside, illuminating the huge space. Underneath the high ceiling, he was surrounded by a maze of crates and shipping containers stacked forty feet tall, bearing labels and RFID tags that identified shipments of soy sauce, mirin, and green tea, among other Chinese imports. He shut off the truck and crossed the wide, oil-stained floor of the warehouse to the rear wall. There, he used an app on his phone to slide two sets of containers smoothly sideways on rails like barn doors. Behind the false containers was a door and another combination lock, which he opened with a separate ten-digit code.

The door led to his command center, from which he directed all of the ongoing Chinese espionage activities across the U.S. Once he was inside, he closed the door and felt the vibration as the heavy crates slid back into place on the opposite side. This new room was large, forty feet square, but lushly appointed, with plush carpet and brickwork on three sides. Chinese art adorned the walls, and dozens of lanterns hung from the ceiling. The fourth wall was made entirely of black glass, masking an oversize screen.

Bai Ze illuminated the hanging lanterns, plus a handful of LED sconce lights—he preferred semidarkness—and then took a comfortable seat behind a massive cherrywood desk with legs hand-carved into dragons. He booted up an Apple Mac Pro M2 Ultra and watched one of his curved fifty-seven-inch Samsung screens come to life. For the next hour, as he kept an eye on his watch, he reviewed reports from operatives around the country. IT engineers in Palo Alto. Drone operators in Cocoa Beach. Restaurant owners in Manhattan's Chinatown. Prostitutes in DC, working out of the Capitol Hill lounges. Wheat farmers in North Dakota, living on land adjacent to the Grand Forks Air Force Base.

In particular, he reviewed the reports that had just arrived from Miami Beach and from Green Bay, Wisconsin.

When he noted the time again, it was almost midnight. He shut down his computer, slipped headphones over his ears, and switched on the screen that occupied the full-size wall across from his desk. The video call began precisely on time. His superiors were prompt. As the screen changed, Bai Ze saw what he always did—a mostly dark room with a long wooden table and draped burgundy wall in a building located somewhere in the Zhongnanhai government compound in Beijing. Nine men in dark suits sat in a row behind the table. All wore elaborate Chinese opera masks that obscured their faces and protected their identities. Individual spotlights from above lit up each of the masks, making the artificial faces seem wild and alive in their many colors.

He didn't know the names of these men. He had no idea whether the same men were on every call, or whether some of the bodies at the table changed from month to month. It didn't matter. The effect was designed to be intimidating, and it was.

"As always, it is an honor to be with you, gentlemen," Bai Ze said in his American English. He knew that, seven thousand miles away, his words were being smoothly translated into Chinese.

The man in the middle of the table, whose black-and-white Li Gang mask was painted to be particularly fierce, made his clipped reply without small talk or introductions. "Your report."

Bai Ze didn't know if this man was formally the leader of the group, but he always guided the meetings and was the first to speak. Whoever the man was, he used only Chinese, but Bai Ze heard it through his headphones in the monotone of a female translator, whose English was heavily accented. Sometimes he struggled to understand her.

He began to talk about the status of key plans he was mounting around the country, starting with a honey trap put in place over the past six months that had ensnared a Texas rocket engineer and given them access to his laptop. The project had already produced a trove of schematics related to the latest generation of rotating detonation engines, which Chinese scientists were hungry to analyze. But he'd talked for less than a minute when the man in Beijing interrupted him impatiently.

"The other projects can wait. First talk to us about Jason Bourne."

Bai Ze stopped. He knew better than to argue. "Yes, of course. Well, as you know—"

"Bourne has proven to be an exasperating threat!" the man continued, interrupting him. Bai Ze could hear anger in the man's raised voice, but the translation came through in the Chinese woman's same bloodless tone. "He is responsible for the loss of Adam Hill. Hill was our most valuable mole, years in the making. He would have been president come the next election. Can you imagine the utility to us of having our man in such a position? Instead, we were forced to eliminate him to make sure he did not expose *our* operations throughout the country. A disaster!"

Bai Ze waited until he was sure the man was done with his diatribe. "Yes, the loss of Hill was a setback, to be sure. I regret the situation. Controlling Hill gave us years of priceless intelligence, and no doubt we could have expected much more. But he was still only one cog in our larger machine. He had limited awareness of the breadth of our operations, so there is very little sensitive information he could have given the FBI before we were able to eliminate him. As you know, I keep different segments and projects compartmentalized so that exposure of one presents minimal risk to the overall strategy. The left hand never knows what the right hand is doing—apart from myself and all of you, of course."

"You are avoiding the question," the man snapped. "Tell us about the situation with Bourne."

"Cain is back in service," Bai Ze admitted.

"For Treadstone?" another man at the table asked, his red devil's mask showing fangs and horns. "Is he once again with Treadstone?"

"Yes, we believe so. Following the incident in Salzburg where his lover was killed, Bourne was offline for several months. Our efforts to find and target him during that period were unsuccessful. The duration of his absence led many of us to wonder if he'd permanently severed himself from intelligence work. But no. He is back, working directly under Shadow again as her personal operative. The two of them are a formidable combination, both intelligent and resourceful. However, as you all know, Bourne's background also makes him an unusual agent. The loss of his memory has resulted in a man who is more volatile and more prone to emotional attachments."

"Are you saying Bourne and Shadow are involved?" the man in the devil's mask asked.

"They've attempted to hide it, but yes, the information that has come across my desk suggests a sexual relationship between them began last year during the David Abbott affair. That could prove to be useful. Shadow's history of betrayal makes it unlikely that Bourne will ever truly trust her. The right incentive might make it possible for us to drive a wedge between them."

"We want Bourne eliminated!" the first man insisted, slamming the table. "We do not want to get inside his head. We do not want to use him or turn him. We want him taken off the playing field so that he does not interfere with us again."

Bai Ze hesitated. He was always reluctant to tiptoe into an argument about strategy with these men. "With the greatest respect, gentlemen, I disagree. Yes, of course, the endgame must be to remove Bourne entirely. But between now and then, I believe we can find a way to make him our ally."

A long silence followed.

"How?" the leader in the Li Gang mask asked finally. Before Bai Ze could say anything more, he charged ahead. "Where is Bourne right now? Do you know? Have you been able to track his movements?"

"Yes, we have. He started in Miami, but now he is in Wisconsin. It appears that he has made a connection with the operation we conducted there eight years ago. He knows that he was involved."

The leader erupted again. "Impossible! You insisted to us that he would have no memory of those events."

"He doesn't," Bai Ze replied. "The connection was discovered by Shadow, not Cain. She used the Files."

The immediate hissing from all nine men made them sound like a den of snakes.

Bai Ze continued before any of them could speak again. "Yes, gentlemen, your frustration about the Files is noted. And yes, initially, I was as concerned as you when I learned that Bourne had begun to dig into our exercise from eight years ago. But perhaps it was inevitable. My instinct was to take him out before he could get any answers. However, our attempts to do so failed in both locations. Since we're struggling to remove him, I think we should play a different game."

Silence lingered at the table.

"In what way?" one of the men finally asked. He wore a Jiang Ziya mask, and his face, like his voice, looked old.

"I believe we have an opportunity to turn this situation to our advantage," Bai Ze told them. "Bourne is highly skilled, but the last few years have demonstrated that he can be manipulated. Lay down the proper breadcrumbs and we can lead him where we want him to go. He can get us what we want, what we *need* for the ultimate success of our plans. Then, and only then, we can pluck that thorn from our paw. But the whole thing must be subtle. He must be certain that *he* is the one in charge. If he sees our hand pulling the strings, then we lose."

The man in the middle leaned forward. "You are playing a dangerous game, Bai Ze."

"I'm aware."

"Eight years ago, Bourne stumbled into the middle of our plans. We lost two of our best agents as a result. You convinced us back then that eliminating Bourne was too risky, that a high-profile loss would alert the CIA and Treadstone about our activities far before we were ready. But now I wonder if your advice was wrong. If Bourne's memory returns, he will realize who you are. Everything we've worked for will be lost."

"I understand," Bai Ze said. "I know the risks of this operation. Trust me, Bourne's memory will never return."

7

LANEY WAS RIGHT. THE CHERRY-STUFFED FRENCH TOAST WAS excellent.

Bourne sat with her in a corner of the White Gull Inn dining room, at a table that looked out on the shadows of the snow-covered woods. It was early morning, barely past dawn, and he could see that she was tired. Her eyes were bloodshot, her curly brown hair messy, her pretty face devoid of any makeup. She kept yawning and apologizing to him. The story of the murders, she said, had taken her until almost two in the morning to research, write, and post on the Door County website.

"So what happened?" Bourne asked. "Tell me about it."

"The local police aren't really sure. They don't have any clue who the victims are, or any suspects for who did it. But the crazy thing is, they're not the ones in charge anymore."

"How so?"

She shook her head. "Around midnight, the feds showed up. FBI. They took over the investigation and kicked the locals out.

Not that we've got the bandwidth around here for dealing with this kind of thing. But the cops were pissed. Anyway, once the feds came in, the pipeline of information shut down. Nobody was saying a word or answering any questions. They even tried to play tough guy with me. They told me I shouldn't post stories about this. National security risks, blah blah blah. Like anyone believes that bullshit from the FBI anymore."

Bourne pasted a sympathetic look on his face. He knew the agents who'd arrived weren't FBI, no matter what their identification said. They were Treadstone cleaners, trying to put the genie back in the bottle. "You said they don't know who the victims are?"

"Two white guys, but probably not locals. Nobody recognized them, and around here, somebody would know them if they lived on the peninsula. They had no wallets, no ID, nothing to suggest who they really were. One of the cops said that meant they were probably pros, whatever that means. Anyway, it was lucky anybody found them at all. The bodies had been pulled off the beach into the woods, where nobody could see them. But some guy was taking a late-night walk with his dog, and Fido went running off when he smelled the blood."

"Blood?"

"Yeah. Whatever went down, it was messy. Both of the vics were shot multiple times. The cops figure it probably had something to do with drugs. Even around here, we have plenty of problems with that shit. We're on the lake and connected to the seaway. Smugglers may be trying a new way of bringing stuff into the country. Less snooping in a remote area than you'd get in Milwaukee or Chicago."

"Could be," Bourne said.

Laney picked at her breakfast. She didn't look hungry. She'd ordered a Bloody Mary, but it sat on the table untouched. She eased back in her chair, rubbed her eyes, and then worked her fingers through her curls. "Anyway, enough about me. What's your story, Charlie Briggs? Last night I said you looked familiar, like we'd met before. You probably figured that was just my way of coming on to you."

"I didn't think that," Bourne said.

Her brown eyes zeroed in on him. "No? Then damn, I must have been way too subtle, because I *was* coming on to you. Not that I stand much of a chance looking the way I do. I slept through my alarm and didn't have time to put on my face."

"Your face looks good to me."

"Oh, sure, very smooth," Laney said, her lips crinkling into a smile. "Well, so does yours, believe me. But I really do feel like I know you from somewhere. Like we've met before. Call it an instinct. That's how I remember things. You said you had relatives in Madison, right?"

"Cousins. But I don't get out here very often. Do you go down to Madison a lot?"

"Hardly ever," Laney replied. "I live in paradise, so why leave? But if your family's down there, why come up to Door County on your own? Just needed a getaway from the investment banking biz?"

"Something like that."

"Are you staying long?"

"I haven't decided."

"Wow, you just can't shut up about yourself, can you? Talk talk talk."

Bourne laughed. "Sorry."

"No, I'm sorry, prying is an occupational hazard. But once I start, I can't stop. Have you been to Door County before? Or are you a virgin in Cherryland?"

"I was here once eight years ago," Bourne said. He watched her reaction closely, but he didn't see her make any connections.

Eight years.

"That's a long time. But if you were here, who knows, maybe our paths did cross."

"Maybe so."

He saw her phone light up on the table with an incoming text. Laney snatched it up and then let out a hiss of anger as she read the message. "*Fuck!* Fuck, you've got to be kidding me. I can't believe this!"

"What's wrong?"

She didn't answer immediately. Instead, she tapped out a short reply on her phone—he saw that she'd written *GODDAMN IT!*—and then she switched to the Safari app and plugged in the address of a website. When the site loaded, she scrolled with her thumb in quick, impatient swipes until she reached the bottom. She cursed again, loud enough to attract stares from the people around them, and shoved the phone into a pocket of her jeans. Her cheeks were flushed, and she looked close to tears. "They killed my story. They fucking killed my story. It's not out there anymore."

"About the murders?"

"Yes! The first real journalism I've been able to do in like forever, and it's gone! That was the sales manager for the website. The fucking feds leaned on the site owner and got him to take it down. They made all sorts of threats. I mean, do we still have a fucking First Amendment in this country, or what?"

"In my experience, the government usually gets what it wants," Bourne said.

"No shit." Laney pushed away her plate. She glanced across the table, where Bourne was three-quarters of the way through his breakfast. "Listen, I'm sorry to rush you, and I know I'm making a shitty first impression, but do you mind if we get out of here? I'm not going to be able to sit still."

Bourne pushed away his plate, too. "No problem."

"Thank you."

She got up without waiting for him and headed across the restaurant, her feet landing heavily, her fists opening and closing as she walked. Bourne asked the waitress to add the meals to his room charge, and then he followed her to the lobby and out into the cold morning air. She continued to the street, where she stood in her boots in a few inches of snow, her arms wrapped tightly around her chest.

"Do you think I'm overreacting?" she asked.

"No, I don't."

"Yeah, I'm totally normal, for sure." Laney rolled her eyes. "Like I said, you're very smooth. Seriously, this isn't how I wanted our date to go. Did I tell you this was a date? Because for me, it's a date. Look, how about we take a drive? I can show you the Cana Island lighthouse. It's really pretty in the winter. About half an hour away."

"Okay."

"And yeah, I know, I talk a lot."

"Don't worry about it."

"Right, Mr. Smooth. Do you have a car?"

Bourne pointed at the old Taurus parked under the trees across the street. "That's me."

Her eyebrows cocked with surprise. "No offense, but shouldn't you be in a Jaguar or something? Or one of those butt-ugly Tesla Cybertrucks?"

"It's my cousin's," Bourne said. Another lie spilled easily out of him.

"In Madison?"

"Yeah."

"Well, okay, whatever. You drive the clunker, I'll play navigator."

They got into the Taurus. Bourne did a U-turn, heading up the street into town. He navigated past the shops and restaurants of Fish Creek and then climbed a shallow hill, where Laney instructed him to take a right turn onto County Road F. Not long after, they left the small town behind and ended up in remote land in the middle of the peninsula. More light snow fell, dusting the two-lane highway, which had been plowed overnight, leaving drifts on the shoulder. Power lines dangled overhead, and winter trees crowded the road.

Laney seemed to be off in her own world, still stewing with resentment about the loss of her story. He liked her, and he felt bad about manipulating her. She was interested in a date with a handsome stranger; he was interested in finding out what she knew about events eight years earlier, which were still a blank slate in his mind.

He was also sure that Shadow had been the one to spike her article.

But as they drove east, Bourne realized he had bigger problems.

They'd found him again.

A pickup truck appeared in his mirror, no more than a red dot against the gray horizon. He accelerated, watching the other vehicle close the distance quickly. His adversaries didn't seem to be playing games today, not hiding in his wake. As fast as he went, the truck went faster, trying to overtake him.

"Easy on the speed," Laney commented. "The snow can be slick."

Bourne said nothing. Behind him, the truck had the horsepower to outmuscle the old Taurus, and all it would take was one sharp crack on their bumper at high speed to send them toppling end over end. His mind worked quickly, developing a plan as he pushed the speed of the Taurus harder. The chassis began to shimmy on the highway, kicking up white clouds on both sides.

Laney finally noticed that his eyes kept shifting to the mirror. She glanced over her shoulder. "What's going on? That truck back there, is he *following* us?"

"No, he means to run us off the road," Bourne told her.

"*What?*"

"We've got less than a minute or so before he catches us."

"Are you kidding? Who is he?"

"I don't know."

"Well, how do you know he's coming after us?"

"I can tell from how he's driving. He'll slam us from behind, and either the impact will knock us into a tree or we'll launch skyward and roll. Either way it's not good."

"Can't you just stop?"

"I could, but I'd rather not get into another firefight with you in the car."

"Another . . . *Jesus!* You mean like with guns? Fuck, fuck, was it *you?* Were you involved in what happened yesterday?"

Bourne ignored the question. "Are there any intersections ahead of us?"

"What?" Laney said again.

"Intersections. Are we close to any other roads?"

She pushed her hair out of her eyes. Her voice stuttered. "Um, yeah, yeah, we're going to cross County A soon. What are you going to do?"

"Play chicken with him, but just me, not you," Bourne said. "I'm going to hit the brakes and turn around. Hold on tight and close your eyes if you need to. You'll have a couple of seconds where the car is stopped. As soon as I tell you, dive out, okay? Then go hide in the woods. Do *not* come out until you see me come back."

"Charlie, what the fuck is going on?"

"I'll explain once we're on the other side of this, but right now, just get ready to jump when I say. Okay?"

Ahead of him, through the trees, he saw the road widening as they neared County Road A. He tapped the brakes and felt the car skid, so he took his foot off the pedal and let the Taurus drift, still going sixty miles an hour. The car plunged through a stop sign into the middle of the intersection, and he nudged the wheel enough to send the car twisting like a game of spin the bottle. Next to him, Laney screamed. The Taurus made half a dozen wild rotations before it finally ground to a halt, and as it stopped, Bourne called to her.

"*Now.* Get out now. I'll come back for you."

Laney fumbled with her seat belt. She pushed open the Taurus door and half climbed, half fell out of the car onto the snowy pavement. He didn't bother trying to close the door. He made sure she stumbled to her feet and began running away, and then he jammed down the accelerator. The Taurus squealed in place, its tires spinning, churning up snow. He eased off the gas, letting the car grind through the ruts, then increased speed as he felt himself lurch forward. Bourne aimed at the tree-lined road from where they'd come. He ignored the lanes and drove down the middle of the highway, pushing harder until the pedal was on the floor.

The red pickup was directly ahead, coming straight at him.

They tested each other's nerve, neither one moving, neither one shifting out of the way. The distance closed, swallowed up by speed, the open door of the Taurus flapping back and forth like a broken bird's wing. Bourne could see the man's face taking shape through the windshield ahead of him. White. Dark hair. Beard. They were that close to each other. Bourne tensed, waiting for the collision, bracing for the impact and the airbag exploding into his face. But in the final split second, the other driver panicked. The man jerked the truck out of the way, skidding onto the shoulder, and ramming down a highway sign. The pickup's right wheels crashed into two-foot drifts, and the vehicle flipped sideways. It landed upside down, its roof pancaking as its momentum carried it into the trees.

Bourne let the Taurus ease to a stop in the middle of the road. Carefully, he reversed course. As he passed the crash site, he saw the truck, its front end wrapped around the trunk of an oak tree. Smoke and steam hissed from under the hood. He paused, not seeing any movement, not hearing any doors open. If the driver was alive, he wouldn't be coming after them any time soon.

He continued back to the intersection at County A, where the snow showed crazy markings like crop circles made by the Taurus as it spun. He stopped, letting the motor run, and got out into the cold. Around him, the trees whistled with the wind. Frigid air and flurries blew into his face. Everything around him was empty.

He saw no sign of Laney, and he wondered if she'd done the smart thing and run as far away from Charlie Briggs as she could.

But no. On the southwest corner of the intersection, he saw a boarded-up building with a red roof that looked as if it had once been a fancy supper club. From behind one of the walls, Laney appeared, peering cautiously at the street. When she saw him, she walked with quick steps toward the car, casting her gaze up the road, where the smoke of the accident had begun to rise above the treetops. She got inside the Taurus and fastened her seat belt, and for a few seconds, she said nothing at all. She just breathed through her nose, loud and fast, and stared straight ahead through the windshield.

Then her head turned, and she faced him. Her voice barely rose above a whisper.

"Who *are* you?"

THEY STOOD TOGETHER ON THE BEACH, WITH THE COLD WAVES OF LAKE Michigan swishing over fragile ice sheets near their feet. The white tower of the Cana Island lighthouse rose immediately behind them, an old beacon of the rocky coast through storms and fog. No one else was around. Laney shivered, more from fear than the temperature, and Bourne put an arm around her shoulders. She leaned into him.

"You can ask me whatever you want," he told her. "I'll answer what I can. But that's not much."

"Let me guess. This is off the record."

"Far off the record," Bourne said.

"Well, what's your name? Because I assume it's not Charlie Briggs."

"Call me Jason."

"Jason what?"

"Just Jason, for now."

"Who do you work for? Are you a cop? Or are you one of the bad guys? Like a terrorist or something?"

"If I were a terrorist, Laney, you'd be dead."

"Those men they found on the beach, did you kill them?"

"I can't talk about that."

"Who were they?"

"I can't talk about that, either."

"The feds who showed up, are you one of them?"

"I—"

"Can't talk about that. Yeah. But you'll tell me everything you can." Laney sighed. "Did you spike my story?"

"No, but I suspect that someone I work for did. I'm sorry."

"Why are you here? And why are these people trying to kill you? This is a tourist area, for God's sake. Things like this don't happen here."

"Well, something happened in Door County eight years ago," Bourne said. "That's why I'm here. Whoever these men are, they don't want me getting answers about it. They want to keep me in the dark."

"What was it? What happened?"

"I don't know. I could use your help in finding out."

Laney stared at him. "Me? How can I help?"

"You were here."

"That may not matter," she said, a strange look on her face. "But I'll do my best. What do you want to know?"

"Do you remember anything unusual going on at the White Gull Inn in October eight years ago? I checked at the desk. The inn was completely booked for some private event, but the records from back then have been erased. No guest names, no record of who paid, no history of what the event was. Do you know what it could have been?"

"I have no idea, but there's nothing unusual about them being booked. They get large parties all the time. Plus, October is peak leaf season. The whole peninsula is crazy with tourists. Every hotel and B and B around here is always sold out."

"You mentioned a double murder eight years ago," Bourne pointed out.

"Yeah. That was unusual."

"Was it in October?"

"It was. You're right."

"Tell me about it," Bourne said.

"I'll tell you what I can," Laney replied, again with an odd undercurrent in her voice and an inscrutable look on her face. She bent down and dipped her hand in the cold lake water. "I've been over my notes from back then a hundred times, believe me. But I don't have any answers."

"Anything at all will help me. Who got killed?"

"The victims were a young Chinese couple. Man and woman, both of them no more than thirty. They were staying at a guest cottage in Ephraim north of Fish Creek. Their bodies were found in the woods near there."

"How did they die?" Bourne asked.

She looked up at him, her face dark. "They were shot in the throat."

He kept his reaction off his face. In his mind, he had a vision of the assassin who went by the name Fang standing on the other side of the pool at the Mandarin Oriental in Miami. And a woman. Bourne had seen him with a woman, too. *Rose.* He'd followed both of them from Florida to Wisconsin. He'd followed them *here.*

And he'd killed them.

He was sure of that. A suppressed Glock. Two shots in the throat.

"Did the police know who they were? What were their names?"

"They had Chinese passports. That's pretty unusual around here. In fact, it's weird enough that I heard about these two *before* they were killed. The woman who owns the cottage in Ephraim called me about them. Just gossip, sort of racist, but it is what it is. When the couple checked in, the woman told the clerk they were on their honeymoon, but my source at the inn said they didn't act like it. Two beds in their room, not one. No lovey-dovey stuff, no romantic dinners. Never smiling. Around here, weird stuff gets noticed. People talk."

"What did you do?" Bourne asked.

"I spied on them. Just to see if anything funky was going on.

I'm not necessarily proud of that, but it's what reporters do. I got the license plate of their rental car and traced it back to the Green Bay airport. I have a source there, too. He clues me in if celebs come to town. We do get a few, every now and then. Turns out this 'honeymoon' couple arrived on a private jet with a handful of old Chinese gentlemen in suits. Official types. That's also weird. But if they came to Door County with the lovebirds, they kept a low profile. Nobody saw them around here, nobody talked about them. So I don't know who they were or what the hell they were doing in this area."

"Then what?"

"Then I don't know."

"What do you mean?"

"Everything I'm telling you is from my notes. The rest is secondhand. I didn't write the story about the murders. Somebody else did. According to him, the Chinese embassy used their clout to torpedo the investigation. Just like your people did with the murders overnight. The bodies of the victims got transferred to their authority. They even got the police to destroy their paperwork. It was like it had never happened."

"So you don't have any idea what was really going on?" Bourne asked.

"None."

He stared at her, seeing that same enigmatic look on her face. "Why didn't you write the story?"

"I was in the hospital."

"Why? What happened?"

"The night of the murders, I was in a car crash. Somebody

T-boned me. I spent two weeks in the hospital. By the time I got out, it was all history, the murders swept under the rug. Not that it mattered to me. I didn't remember any of it."

"You didn't remember the crash?"

Laney took his hands. She was quiet for a while, her face close to his, flurries landing like shiny crystals on her skin. "I didn't remember *anything*. The crash took away my whole life. I woke up and my past was gone. I didn't know who I was."

8

I DIDN'T KNOW WHO I WAS.

For Bourne, it was like discovering a twin flame, or reading an ancestry report to find a sibling he didn't know existed. He'd never met anyone who'd gone through what he had. Losing their past, their memories. Losing their entire identity. Having to start over and build a new life out of nothing.

Everything Laney said had deep echoes for him because he'd experienced it himself. The parallels took his breath away.

"My past is two-dimensional," Laney said. "It's flat. Not real. Just facts in my head. I know who I am, but only because I read all about it after the accident. Letters and emails. Social media. Photographs. School yearbooks. Things my mom and my friends told me. I've put the pieces together like a puzzle, but many of the pieces are missing. It's like my life began eight years ago, because that's the only part of it that I actually remember. The rest may as well belong to a stranger."

Bourne thought: *That's it exactly.*

But he struggled with what he could say to her, how much of his own secrets he could share.

They wandered back through the snow-covered park past the looming tower of the lighthouse. The narrow dirt causeway to the mainland lay ahead of them, the Taurus parked on the other side. He kept one hand in his pocket, caressing the Glock, but he saw no evidence of anyone nearby. For now, he'd dodged his pursuers.

"I'm sorry if I sound like a busted toy," Laney said. "I'm not looking for sympathy for what I went through. I'm long past that. To be honest, I don't tell a lot of people what happened to me. They don't know what to say or how to react, so it's easier not to tell them about it."

"Do you remember anything at all from before the crash?"

"Bits and pieces. Certain things will trigger flashbacks for me. Sometimes I see faces, sometimes places. It's disconnected from anything else, but I know it's real. Other times it's mostly instinct. I remember something without actually remembering it. It just comes to me, and I don't know how or why. Like a password or a friend's birthday. I know what it is, I know I'm right, but it's just there in my head, not like a real memory." She laughed quietly to herself. "I realize that doesn't make any sense."

"No, I understand what you mean," Bourne said.

"For a long time, I tried to force my brain to do better. I would push myself to remember things. I figured it all had to be in there, right? So if I dug deep enough in my head, I'd be able to grab it and get it back. But that never worked. In fact, it made things worse. Instead of remembering, I'd get frustrated, and then I'd get—"

"A headache," Bourne interrupted.

Laney stared at him in surprise. "Yes."

"But worse than any normal headache. Even worse than any migraine. It's like a spike being driven through your brain and trying to come out through your eyes. So intense you want to throw up."

She shook her head. "That's right. That's just how it is. How do you know that?"

Bourne hesitated, and the silence sounded loud. He watched the sluggish lake water, which had frozen into jagged patches of ice near the dirt trail between the lighthouse island and the mainland. "My past is gone, too."

"What? Are you serious?"

"Yes. I have no memory of who I was."

"My God! Really? Like me?"

"Just like you. It's like staring into a fog where the rest of your life should be."

"Yes! Exactly! How did it happen to you? When?"

"I was shot," Bourne told her. "A few years ago, I was on a boat in the Mediterranean, and I took a bullet to the head. A drunk doctor saved my life, but I lost my memory in the process. I don't know whether it was the bullet, or the surgery, or both, but I woke up with no identity."

"I've never met anyone else who's been through it," Laney said.

"Neither have I."

"It's strange. I've spent the last eight years feeling like I was the only survivor on a desert island. Now I find out somebody else is living there with me. I don't know how I feel about that. I'm not sure whether to be happy or sad."

"I get it."

Suddenly, Laney pushed herself up on the toes of her boots.

Her fingertips came around the back of his neck, and she pushed against him, their bodies pressing together, their mouths meeting in a gentle kiss. He felt the cold and the heat of her at the same time. Her curly hair brushed his face, its aromas of rosemary and mint filling his senses. The kiss lingered, soft and curious. Then she let go of him, looking embarrassed. She took a step back, slipping on the ice, and he had to grab her arm to steady her.

"Sorry," she said.

"Don't be."

"I usually don't make the first move with a guy, but there's this closeness about us. About what we share."

"Yes, there is."

"But I'm being stupid."

She turned away, but he didn't let go of her arm. He pulled her to him and lifted her off the ground, and he kissed her back. There was nothing soft this time. It was hard and hot, like a flame melting the winter ice. When he put her down, she laid her head on his chest and laughed breathlessly.

"Okay. I liked that."

"Me too."

They walked again. It felt different between them, like they'd crossed a bridge together. When they got back to the Taurus, Bourne opened the passenger door for her, but she didn't get in right away.

"I couldn't explain it before," Laney said, "but now that you know the truth about me, I should tell you what's really in my head. It's not a vague 'you look familiar' kind of thing. I know we've met before. It's one of those instincts I talked about. I don't remember you, but I *know* you."

"That probably means we met eight years ago," Bourne said.

"I guess so. Except I don't know how or why."

"Neither do I."

"Well, am *I* familiar to you?" Laney asked. "Do you remember me at all? Even if it's just instinct."

He frowned. "I don't. But that's not you. Everything about Door County, about what happened eight years ago, is blank to me. That's strange. Normally it doesn't work like that. Normally I do get instincts, sensations of familiarity, even if the details are gone. But not this time. When I tried regression to that time of my life, I remembered being *somewhere else.* It was vivid in a way my recovered memories rarely are."

"What does that mean?"

"I don't know, but I don't think it's a coincidence that both of our memories are gone from the exact same stretch of time eight years ago. If we met, if we were together, then I think we were part of something. Somebody doesn't want us to know what it was."

Laney's eyes widened. "Are you saying it wasn't an accident? The car crash? What happened to me?"

"I'm saying I don't believe you *lost* your memory. I think it was *taken* from you."

BOURNE STARED AT THE FACE OF MO PANOV ON HIS PHONE. BEHIND THE therapist, he could see the Washington, DC, skyline through the windows of his office. Mo had been silent for a couple of minutes, chewing on the end of a pen, after Bourne described what he suspected about Laney Reese. And about himself.

"I guess what I want know is whether it's possible," Bourne said. "Can someone's memory be proactively erased?"

Mo rubbed his chin with a frown. "My best clinical answer, Jason, is *maybe.* I know that doesn't help you. Obviously, scientists understand that memory is a fragile thing. Your experience in the Med showed that it's possible to lose everything. Physical and psychological traumas can produce varying degrees of memory loss, sometimes temporary, sometimes permanent. But could it be done with *intent?* I don't know. It would certainly be very risky."

"I don't think risk would deter the Chinese," Bourne said.

"No, I imagine you're right."

Bourne sat on the floor of his cottage at the White Gull Inn, his back against the wall. A fire crackled in the log fireplace, warming him. He'd dropped Laney off at her house outside Baileys Harbor, and then he'd come back here to dig into the mysteries from eight years earlier.

But first he searched his room. He found multiple audio and video listening devices that had been planted since he was gone.

They knew where he was. They were listening. Watching.

Was it agents for the Chinese who'd been following him since he arrived in Wisconsin?

Or was it Shadow, who always wanted to keep a close eye on her prize?

Either way, he'd destroyed the devices. For the moment, he felt secure talking to Mo.

"Is anyone in the intel community working on memory manipulation?" Bourne asked. "Are *we?*"

"Of course. Memory is a hell of a weapon. If you can erase it, replace it, change it, manipulate it, recover it, you can wield a tremendous power over someone's psyche. Believe me, we've put millions into memory research, and if we're doing it, then you can bet the Chinese are, too. But nobody wants to admit how far it's gone. It's all super-classified."

"But it's possible," Bourne said.

"Like I told you, maybe."

"You mentioned memory *recovery*. Not just erasing it, but getting it back. Is that part of the research, too?"

"Of course. You of all people can appreciate the possibilities. Imagine being able to trigger a memory in someone's brain from any time, any place, and throw it up on a screen in 4K detail. The implications for everything from police work to espionage are staggering. But if you can trigger a memory at will, the question is, can you also *modify* it to show whatever you want? Once the technology is out there, how do we know what's true? Could we ever rely on the accuracy of what we remember? AI making up shit is bad enough, but imagine it happening inside your own head. It's scary at every level, from governments down to individuals. A wife finds out her husband is having an affair and threatens to leave him. The next day, she doesn't remember it at all, and the affair goes merrily on. See what I mean?"

Bourne closed his eyes. He stared into the fog of his past. Automatically, he pushed himself to remember something, anything. A moment from his childhood. His teen years. His parents. But instead, the spike came back, a bolt of pain behind his eyes that made his whole body convulse.

What if he could remember? What if he could bring his past back?

"The thing is, Mo, I'm beginning to wonder if the Chinese have already done it," Bourne said.

"How so?"

"Well, think about it. We know—we *know* for sure now—that I was in Miami, and then I followed a group of Chinese agents, officials, assassins, whoever they were, up here to Door County. The pilot, Kodak, confirms he flew me to Green Bay. But I never reported it. I never gave any information to Treadstone about the mission or what I found. Instead, I acted as if I'd been in Miami at the Mandarin Oriental the whole time."

"It's suspicious, I agree," Mo said.

"It's more than suspicious, particularly when you add Laney into the equation. The night of this double murder—the killing of two Chinese agents here, probably *by me*—Laney was involved in a car crash and lost her entire identity. She's convinced we were together at some point, and I think she's right. The question is, what was going on? What did we see? How did both of us *lose* so much time?"

Mo stood up from his chair in Washington and took his phone to the window. "I get it. The implications aren't good. So how can I help?"

"I'm supposed to see Laney tonight. Can you talk to her? Can you regress her like you've done with me? I want to see if there's anything left in her memories. See if you can get around whatever's blocking her."

The therapist hesitated. "Has she agreed to this?"

"I said I had a friend who might be able to help her. I didn't give her any details about who you were."

"I don't know, Jason. I don't like doing this with someone who isn't a patient and who isn't in government. It's also not the kind of session I like to do remotely. It's hard enough in person. Even if I can get her into a receptive state, I'm not sure we'd retrieve any memories. With you, the results have been minimal at best."

"Laney and I are different people," Jason said. "I was shot. She wasn't. I can't prove it, but I'm willing to bet the car crash was staged to cover up what they did to her. So it's worth a try if there's even a chance of finding out what was going on eight years ago. Because if I saw Bai Ze, maybe Laney did, too."

Mo sighed, giving in. "Yes, all right, but I want to hear from her that she's really okay with this. I want to make sure she goes into this with eyes wide-open."

"Fair enough. Thanks, Mo."

"Thank me if it works," the therapist replied.

Bourne nodded, but he didn't end the call. The face-to-face session lingered between them, and Mo noticed.

"Is there something else, Jason?"

"No. Forget about it. It's nothing."

"And yet you're obviously troubled. What is it?"

Bourne exhaled slowly. He felt the heat of the fire on his skin. "I was thinking about being shot in the Med. About Geoffrey Washburn trying to put me back together on the operating table in Port Noir. That was when I lost my memory, my identity, but—"

"But?" Mo said.

"But what if it goes back further than that? What if someone was already messing around in my head years earlier?"

9

BOURNE CHECKED THE LOCAL LIBRARY, NOW THAT IT WAS OPEN, LOOKing for any kind of information about goings-on in the area eight years earlier. But news of the twin murders had been deliberately played down—people being shot was bad for tourism—and he found nothing to give him any clue about a private event at the White Gull Inn.

If the hotel had been fully booked, a minimum of a few dozen people had to be involved. Probably more. Who were they? Where had they come from?

What was the event that brought them together?

And who paid?

Then it occurred to him that just because the White Gull had been fully booked didn't mean that the attendees had *only* stayed there. If it was a large gathering, then maybe other hotels in the area had been included, and maybe one of them had a manager who would remember what was going on.

Over the next two hours, he visited half a dozen of the larger inns in Fish Creek and the adjacent towns of Egg Harbor and Ephraim. He used an IRS identification badge under the name Edward Sands. No one challenged him. The mere mention of the IRS usually loosened tongues—particularly when he told the hotel staff that his audit involved a different organization, not them.

He soon found out that he was right.

Of the six hotels he visited, three had been fully booked eight years ago during the second week in October for a special event. Like the White Gull Inn, all of the underlying records, including billing and payments, had been erased.

Whatever had been going on, a great deal of care had been taken to make sure none of the participants could be identified.

In Ephraim, however, he found a man who'd owned one of the fully booked hotels for nearly twenty years. His name was Bruce Walthers, a big balding fellow who was drinking coffee in a gazebo on his property as he took a break from mowing the hotel's wide front lawn. Behind him, the hotel's white paint and two-story railings looked fresh and neat. Walthers took care of his place. He welcomed Edward Sands with a wary smile behind his mustache, even after he saw Sands's IRS badge. But Walthers's smile vanished, and the man lost all interest in strolling down memory lane when Bourne expressed interest in the bookings at his hotel from October eight years earlier.

"Yeah, sorry, no can do, buddy," Walthers told him. "My records from that week don't exist anymore."

"Why is that?"

"Because I erased them."

"Really? It's interesting that you remember one specific week from so long ago."

"I've got a good memory."

"And you're sure there are no backups?"

"I'm sure. It's my place. One computer, that's all. I replaced the hard drive. Destroyed the old one."

"Why did you go to so much trouble?" Bourne asked.

"Get me a warrant or a subpoena and maybe I'll tell you."

"Sounds like this was a very unusual booking," Bourne said.

"No comment."

Bourne stroked his chin and studied the big man, who didn't look intimidated. "That kind of nonresponse makes the IRS prick up its ears, Mr. Walthers. Makes me wonder if you're hiding something in your records."

"You want to audit me? Audit me."

Bourne noted the dense woods looming immediately behind the hotel building, and he made a guess. "We may do more than conduct an audit."

"Meaning what?"

"Meaning there were two dead bodies found behind your hotel that week, weren't there? I can't help but think that whatever you're covering up goes deeper than financial misconduct. You really don't want to get in the middle of a federal murder investigation."

Now the man's sunburned face turned a shade paler. "Nobody here had anything to do with that."

"But the victims were staying here, weren't they?"

Walthers shook his head fiercely. "No, they weren't. No way. A lot of people made that mistake because of where the bodies were found. They were booked into some honeymoon cottage half a mile north of here."

"Then what were they doing outside your hotel?"

"I have no idea. The police never said it involved me or my people, because it didn't. One of my maids found the bodies on a cigarette break. That's all."

"That would be easier to believe if you weren't working so hard to cover up what was really happening at your hotel back then," Bourne said. "Were the victims here to see some of your mystery guests?"

"I told you, I don't know. I never heard who the victims were. A Chinese couple, that's all. Beyond that, you'll have to talk to the police. I didn't know a thing about the people staying here. It was a blanket booking for the hotel, not individual reservations, and they brought in outsiders to manage the whole thing. Even if I did know something, I couldn't tell you."

"Why not?"

"I signed a nondisclosure agreement. It's airtight. If I say anything about those bookings eight years ago, I'm on the hook for the entire revenue from that week, plus a penalty of twenty-five thousand dollars."

"That's pretty onerous."

"Yeah. No shit. Believe me, I don't want that kind of trouble, even if it means stiffing the IRS. So you want information, you need to do better than saying pretty please."

Bourne nodded. "Am I likely to get the same story from the other hotel owners around here?"

"That's my guess. My joint wasn't the only one."

"Sounds like a big event."

"No comment," Walthers said again.

Bourne thought about it.

If multiple hotels were involved, that drove up the scale of attendees. Not just a couple dozen people—probably one hundred or more. It took a lot of work and a lot of money to erase all evidence of who they were and what they'd been doing. Travel always left traces, clues, breadcrumbs. Those people had to get here from around the country, maybe from around the world. They had to drive, eat, and fill up their gas tanks. They had to fly. Multiple planes coming in from multiple places. Even the best spies couldn't cover all the tracks.

Someone had seen something.

Someone would talk.

But *who?*

Every event had last-minute emergencies. Plans changed. Accidents happened. Someone missed a flight. Someone *always* missed a flight.

"How about you answer a question that has nothing to do with your hotel," Bourne said. "Your NDA wouldn't cover that, would it?"

"Maybe," Walthers replied, his brow furrowing with curiosity. "What you got?"

"Let's say I was in a jam eight years ago, and I needed to charter a plane to go get a VIP to bring him to the peninsula. Is there a pilot around here who could do that for me?"

The man's sly smile returned. "In fact, I know just the guy."

ROGER DUPREE FLEW A TWIN-ENGINE BEECHCRAFT BARON G58 OUT OF the airport in Sturgeon Bay. Bourne found him in his private hangar on the airport grounds, tinkering with one of the engines with tools from an old metal box. He was in his seventies, tall, thin, and slightly stooped, with a fringe of snow-white hair and a white beard making a halo around his face. His forehead was high, his skin freckled. He wore black glasses and a blue short-sleeve shirt over black slacks and dress shoes. An electric space heater on a long extension cord warmed the area near the plane as he worked.

"Eight years," he murmured after Bourne explained what he wanted. "Sure, I remember three or four charters that weekend. Last-minute jobs."

"You remember them because . . . ?"

"Because they paid me a shitload of money to keep my mouth shut."

Bourne nodded. "Did that include an NDA?"

"Yup. Sure did."

"What did that cover?"

"Pretty much everything. Where I went, who I picked up, how much they paid me. It wouldn't have mattered anyway, because I didn't know who any of them were. Eight years later, I don't even remember what they looked like. Old age is a bitch."

"Were any of the other pilots around here picking up the same kind of charters?" Bourne asked.

"Like, would they have looser lips than me?"

"Yeah. Pretty much."

Dupree shrugged. "Sorry. I think I was the only guy. None of the other pilots mentioned special jobs, and with what they were paying, somebody would have boasted about it. I've got the most experience anyway. If people need long-range charters, usually I'm the one they talk to first."

"You've been flying a long time?"

"Fifty years. I started in ATC, then got my pilot's license. A commuter airline in Chicago hired me, and I spent fifteen years with them. When they went under, I shifted to an executive charter service. Did that until I retired. Most of the time, I just fly myself now. I'm happier in the air than on the ground. But if I can make a few extra bucks on a job now and then, I don't mind doing that."

"Is there anything at all you can tell me about those flights back then?" Bourne asked.

Dupree put a power drill back in his toolbox and then wiped the grease off his hands with a dirty towel. "You ask odd questions for a tax man."

"Do I?"

"Damn straight." The pilot scratched his chin, studying Bourne. "Tell you what, you want a crappy cup of coffee?"

"Sure."

Dupree led him across the hangar, their footsteps sounding hollow under the high metal ceiling. At the back of the building, where several model airplanes dangled on wires over their heads, he grabbed a dented metal thermos that looked as if it had been through a war and back. He poured two cups of coffee into foam cups.

Bourne took a sip. "Thanks. And you're right. This is really bad."

Dupree chuckled. "Yeah, sorry about that. I do a fair number of things pretty well. Making coffee is not one of them. But I'm not paying five bucks for coffee at one of the froufrou shops around here. *Salut.*"

He raised his cup in the air, then took a sip, grimaced, and wiped his mouth. "So do you want to tell me who you really are and what this is really about? Because you sure as hell aren't some IRS agent named Sands. Believe me, I've crossed paths with enough spooks over the years to know the look. And I doubt that Glock you're carrying inside your jacket is standard IRS issue."

"You're smart," Bourne said. "And observant."

"Yeah, I don't miss much. Most good pilots don't. Details are what keep us alive. Fact is, I also heard stories about a couple anonymous bodies found shot to death north of town last night. Not exactly what you expect in Door County. And a day later, you show up asking me weird questions about high-buck charters from eight years ago? That doesn't sound like a coincidence."

"It's not. But I can't tell you much. All I can say is, the people you flew into the area eight years ago were on their way to some kind of special gathering. I need to figure out what was happening and who was running the show."

"What are you thinking? Drugs? White supremacists?"

"You tell me."

"I'd say neither, actually." Dupree drank more coffee, which was steaming hot even if it tasted like battery acid. "I assume you can keep my name out of this? Because if people are still getting killed over this years later, it makes me wonder if I'm safe talking to you."

"I was never here," Bourne said.

"All right. Fuck my NDA. The whole thing bugged me. I did four flights over three days. Pickups in Duluth, Fort Wayne, Grand Rapids, Davenport. I landed, picked up my passengers, and flew them back here."

"How many?"

"One per flight. That was it. Three men, one woman. I'm serious that I don't remember what they looked like, and I didn't get any names. Well, I did, but everyone was 'Mr. Smith' or 'Mr. Jones' or 'Ms. Johnson.' Real clever. None of them said a word to me during the flight, and my instructions were *not* to engage them in any conversation. So I didn't."

"You didn't recognize any of them?" Bourne asked.

"No. But I don't remember thinking I was acting as a mule for Nazis or cartel members. They must have looked pretty ordinary."

"Then what?"

"I landed my Baron right here. A car met the plane. Same car each time. Tesla Model S. Black. Honey of an engine, thing runs like a flame. Me, I remember machines, not people. Nobody got out, and I couldn't see the driver. Smoked windows. Each of my passengers would get out, climb in the back seat, and off they went."

"How did they pay you?"

"Cash. Crisp hundreds. And yes, I declared all of it, just in case you really do work for the IRS." Dupree winked.

"Who hired you? Who set it all up?"

"It was done by phone. A woman called me with the details. I don't know who she was, never saw her. She said the cash would be waiting for me at the airport desk, and it was. I didn't bother asking who dropped it off."

Bourne shook his head.

So far, the planners on the other side of this arrangement hadn't missed anything. They'd covered their tracks well.

"Is there anything else you can tell me, Roger? Any detail that might give me a clue about who your passengers were or what they were doing here?"

"My passengers? No. I don't know a thing about them." Dupree gave a little smile as he forced down more coffee. He had more to say.

"But?"

"But here's the thing. I live on the north end of the peninsula, up in Ellison Bay. A couple days later, same week, I was heading home on Highway 42 after dark, and some guy passed my Corvette. Not sure if you know many pilots, but we aren't exactly grandmas when it comes to speed. In fact, I'm not sure anyone has *ever* passed me before. But this guy blazed by me like I was standing still. Had to be doing a hundred, maybe a hundred and ten. At night. It was the Tesla Model S."

Bourne found himself liking Roger Dupree. "I don't suppose you happened to see where it went."

"In fact, I did see where it went. I was pretty curious, so I sped up to keep it in sight. The Tesla turned toward the water on Porcupine Bay Road. That pretty much told me everything I needed to know."

"Oh? Why is that?"

"Well, there's really only one house tucked along there. It's almost invisible in the woods, but from the upper floors, it must have a view of the bay to die for. Honestly, I'd call it a castle more than a house. I've driven over there a few times to goggle at the place, but a guard always shows up to shoo me away. It's the most expensive house in Door County. Might be the most expensive house in Wisconsin."

"Who owns it?" Bourne asked.

"Alvin Bakk."

"Bakk? The billionaire? He's the one with the Tesla?"

"That's right," Dupree told him. "One of the five richest men in the world."

10

NIGHT FELL.

Bourne drove in darkness through the hissing snow. The temperature outside had fallen to ten degrees, and the cold seeped through the windows of the Taurus despite the car's heater. He squinted through the high-beam headlights, trying to see where he was going. The illuminated route map on his phone told him a turn was approaching, but he didn't even see a crossroad ahead.

"I think I'm lost," he told Laney.

Her voice crackled through the phone's speaker. "You can only get so lost around here. If you hit water, you've gone too far."

"Funny. Hang on, I see something." Bourne slowed, trying to make out the highway sign through the snow that had crusted over it. "Looks like a turn for County Road E. Does that sound right?"

"Yeah, make a left. You're only about ten minutes away. Stay on E through another turn, and eventually you'll cross over Kangaroo Lake."

"Okay."

"You didn't have to come out here, you know. I could have driven to White Gull. I'm used to winter driving."

"No, I want to check your house."

"For what?"

Bourne hesitated. "Surveillance."

"What, you mean like bugs? You think people are listening to me?"

"Maybe watching you, too. Given your history, they've probably been keeping an eye on you for a while."

"Well, that makes me rethink a lot of the things I've done in my house. Jesus."

"Can you go outside? You should be able to talk safely there."

"Jason, do you know how cold it is?"

"Sorry."

Laney sighed. "Yeah, yeah, let me throw my coat on and get some boots on my feet. This can't wait ten more minutes until you're here?"

"It can, but clearing the house will take a while."

"Fine. Whatever. Okay, I'm out on the deck. This is a night where I wish I hadn't given up smoking. What's going on?"

"Alvin Bakk," Bourne said.

"Mr. Big Stuff. What about him?"

"He lives here?"

"Yeah, he built a fucking palace near Ellison Bay. Huge, like the biggest house in the state. Although most of the time he's in DC now because of his government contracts. Everybody around here knows him."

"What's his connection to the area?"

"He grew up here. His father worked for the park service up

on Washington Island. Bakk was your classic loner nerd. Homeschooled. It didn't take his folks long to figure out they had a prodigy on their hands. He started his first company at sixteen, never bothered with college. Now it's worth like, what, a trillion dollars or something? Since then, he's branched out into rockets, AI, fusion, lots of science fiction shit."

"Do you remember anything special going on with his companies eight years ago?"

"I don't remember much of anything from back then, Jason."

"Right. Sorry. The thing is, Bakk seems to be involved in whatever was happening. The people coming to town back then, they were coming to see him. I think he got all the records erased, kept the whole thing anonymous."

"Okay, well, I guess I'm not surprised. Bakk has the leverage to make just about anything happen, and he has a fetish for privacy. He's in and out of Door County all the time, but we never know when he's here. And nobody ever gets past the gates of his estate. I don't know what the hell goes on in there. I've tried to interview him a few times, and nothing. The security around his operations is amazing. But I suppose it has to be, given all the government work he does."

Work that the Chinese would kill for, Bourne thought.

"Listen, I want you to talk to my friend Mo," he said.

"What does he do?"

"He's a therapist."

"Isn't it a little early for couples counseling?"

Bourne smiled in the car. "I want him to try to regress you remotely. I think you saw something back then—we both did—and I'm guessing it relates to Bakk and his companies. Maybe Mo can peel back some of what's in your head. Even a fragment of memory would tell us something."

"I guess I'm up for anything. Why not?"

"Okay, sit tight. I'll be there in five."

She didn't answer.

"Laney?"

The silence dragged out, but the call hadn't dropped. He could hear the wind, as loud as a train.

"*Laney?*"

Then he finally heard her voice again, a panicked whisper on the phone. "Jason, someone's here."

THE FOREST GAVE WAY TO DARK WATER AS BOURNE PASSED OVER THE narrow inlet of Kangaroo Lake. He saw fresh tire tracks in the snow ahead of him, not yet blown clean by gales whipping across the bridge.

Someone had passed this same way only minutes before.

He followed the tracks to the other side of the lake, where they turned right at a small dead-end road. Bourne switched off his headlights, driving slowly. The birch trees and evergreens made thick walls on his left and right, interrupted only by an occasional driveway leading toward unseen homes by the water. His phone map told him he was close to the lakeshore, where Laney lived, so he eased the Taurus to a stop and shut it down.

He got out into the teeth of the winter storm. Snow poured over his head, turning him into a white statue in the few seconds he stood there. He drew his Glock, but the cold made his fingers stiff and numb. Above him, dark clouds and treetops blocked out any glimmers of light. With his free hand, he switched on a penlight and shined it on the ground. The tire tracks in the snow continued, showing him the way forward. He jogged in the darkness for twenty or thirty yards, then almost collided with a black Denali parked where the tire tracks ended.

The hood of the truck felt warm to the touch. He listened, hearing no noises except the howl of the wind. In front of him, a faint pale cast to the trees showed him that the lake was close by. Briefly, he used his penlight again. He saw three sets of footprints marching side by side down the snowy path that led toward Laney's house.

Three men. One to stay outside and watch their backs, two to close in on the house from opposite sides.

Bourne moved slowly, staying at the fringe of the trees. The first man, the guard, wouldn't wait in the open. The man would stake out a place in the trees to ambush anyone who came up the path. Step by step, Bourne inched forward. Snow pricked his face like needles and forced him to squint. Ice balls began to form on his lashes, little frozen pellets he had to rub away. The cold burned his nose and throat with each breath. His eyes adjusted to the blackness, enough to see the dark outline of the house where the path ended. The first killer was close. He felt it.

Listen to your senses.

Treadstone.

He peered through waves of snow, but saw no one in hiding. Silently, he holstered his Glock and replaced it with a tanto switchblade that unfolded with a quiet click. He stayed on the rightmost edge of the woods, trying to isolate the silhouette of a killer from the rest of the night. He watched, listened, and smelled the air. Nothing.

Maybe he was wrong. Maybe all three men had gone after Laney.

Then, like a screech owl, a scream rose above the wind, drifting from near the lake.

Bourne kicked into a run, then skidded to a stop. The dark shape of a man rose from the ground where he'd been squatting near the trees. The guard had heard the scream, too; he was focused on the direction of the house. Bourne could make out the shape of a rifle in his hands and night vision goggles poking out from his eyes.

If he turned, he'd see Bourne like a ghost in the night.

Jason charged through the snow. The man didn't hear him coming. Only at the last second did his instincts alert him, and he began to turn, swinging the gun around. Bourne led with the knife, plunging the hook of the blade into the man's windpipe and wrenching the man's hand away from the rifle trigger at the same time. The blade kept cutting, opening the man's throat, spraying blood against the white snow. Still alive, still fighting, the man swung his loose fist at Bourne's head, connecting and dizzying him. But that was all the man had. He staggered backward, giving up the rifle, fingers clutching his throat. He slipped to his knees, then pitched face-forward.

Bourne snatched up the rifle and slung it over his shoulder. He ripped off the man's goggles and positioned them on his own head, watching the black night immediately turn emerald green. He could see again. The house. The trees. The path leading through the snow toward the lake. He saw no one else around him, and the distant scream had come from behind the house, so he ran that way. As he crossed the corner of the house's rear wall, an elevated wooden deck rose beside him, with steps leading down from the second floor to the ground. He saw footprints in the snow heading away from the steps.

Laney's footprints, sprinting for the lake. Bourne ran again.

Then a bullet splintered wood off a beam of the deck near his head.

He lunged under the cover of the deck, but the bullets continued, blasting through the wood flooring, burying themselves in the soft ground. He didn't fire back; he had nowhere to aim. He threw himself into the wall of the house, dodging wild fire that rained down all around him. As he hit the wall, he braced himself, aiming the barrel upward, but still he didn't fire. A shot would give his location away. He waited until the barrage ceased, as the killer over his head assessed whether one of his bullets had found its target. Carefully, the man took a step on the deck, and the wood groaned. Bourne tried to pinpoint the sound, but it disappeared into the wind.

Now the man ran. Heavy boots thumped over Bourne's head. He followed the track with the barrel of the rifle. The noise of the boots crossed to the opposite side of the deck, and another second later, Bourne saw a man leap from the second floor to the ground. The man landed, taking the impact with his knees, then spun around, firing. The first few shots flew wide, but behind his goggles, the killer could see Bourne as well as Bourne could see him. It was a question of who delivered the kill shot first.

Jason fired.

The other man fired.

The two rifles spat flame and metal at each other, one round after another, kicking up snow, wood dust, and flakes of concrete. A bullet missed Bourne's neck by an inch, close enough that he could feel the heat. He ignored it and kept firing, and an instant later, the other rifle went quiet as the killer took a round through his face and out the back of his skull. He dropped instantly.

Bourne didn't wait. He charged from cover. Ahead of him, on the other side of thirty feet of deep snow covering the sloping grass, was the frozen surface of the lake. He could see the glow of two people close to shore. Laney, running. And the third killer running after her, narrowing the distance between them. Soon the man would be near enough to take her down with his rifle, or she would crack through a patch of thin ice into the frigid water.

Snow blew straight into Bourne's face. He ran into the wind, plunging awkwardly through high drifts. He crossed from the land to the water, hearing the belch of the lake bumping up below the ice. The gales had blown the snow into strange sculptures, creating mountains and pyramids and then stretches where the gray ice was ribbed and rocky but completely clear. He was still too far away for any kind of shot, and a missed bullet was just as likely to hit Laney as the man behind her. But the killer was getting close to her.

Bourne needed a distraction. He fired in the air, once, twice, three times. Even in the whirlwind of the lake, the third man heard it and froze in place. When he spun, he fired back, but none of the bullets landed near Bourne. The man reversed course, running straight for Bourne, firing as he came. Sharp bangs snapped in the air like fireworks. The bullets came closer now, kicking up puffs of snow near him. Bourne dodged sideways, taking cover among the jagged four- and five-foot peaks.

The firing stopped. The man was near him, only a few feet

away, but *where?* Bourne could see, the whole world glowing green, but he couldn't hear anything except the wail of the storm. He kept the rifle level, ready to shoot. Keeping low, he kicked from one drift to the next, expecting a blast of fire to trail him. None did. The killer was smart; he was waiting, not giving up his position.

The chilled wind felt like a tornado, spinning and changing direction. The longer Bourne stayed in one place, the more his body stiffened in the cold. Ice and water coated the lenses of his goggles, blurring his vision. His senses felt stripped. He turned his head slowly, watching the lake and the snow from every direction, looking for any glimpse of the hot bright glow of the man he was stalking.

There!

Fifty feet away, behind a pile of snow blown into sharp points like dragon's teeth, he saw the fringe of something warm and white against the cold green background. It appeared for a moment, then disappeared.

Someone moved. Someone was hiding there.

The killer?

Or was it Laney? Had she backtracked on the lake, knowing he was here? Was she hiding, waiting for him?

It *had* to be the third man. Bourne braced the rifle on his stiff shoulder, aiming for the drift. The bullets would pierce the snow. Multiple bullets, fired one after another, no delay for the killer to escape. He wiped the goggles again, clearing his sight. His finger slowly applied pressure to the trigger.

Then something huge and bright loomed above him. He turned in time to see the killer, as surprised as he was, edging from the other side of the drift where Bourne was hiding. They saw each other in the same instant. The man swung his barrel down to fire, and Bourne only had time to jerk his body sideways as a bullet grazed his calf and shot through snow and ice into the lake. Bourne's foot lashed out, kicking the man's ankle, and the killer lost his balance as he fired again, slipping on the slick ground. He fell backward, and Bourne leaped on him, the two men face-to-face.

They rolled and fought, dislodging their goggles, leaving them in total darkness. A fist came out of the night, hammering Bourne's throat, making him gag. Bourne's return blow caught the man under the chin, slamming his head against rock-hard ice. The man let go of his rifle, then grabbed a knife from a pocket and slashed toward Bourne's midsection. Bourne caught the man's wrist, shoving it down just as the point of the blade began to jab toward his kidney. He hammered the wrist until the knife came free.

With his other hand, Bourne found the butt of his Glock.

In one motion, he yanked out the gun, shoved the barrel below the man's ear, and pulled the trigger.

Even in the shrieking storm, the blast was loud. The killer died instantly, bone and brain spraying over the high drift. Bourne pushed himself onto his back, his chest heaving. Then he clawed at the snow and staggered to his feet. His balance returned slowly as he swayed in the wind. He kept the Glock in his hand and walked unsteadily toward the crown of snow where he'd seen someone hiding a minute earlier.

He came around the far side, gun pointed down. The person below him screamed, seeing a figure standing over her in the darkness. Then, as he knelt in front of her, she recognized him and threw her arms around his neck.

It was Laney.

He'd been a fraction of a second away from killing her.

11

AMONG HER GIG JOBS, LANEY WATCHED THE HOUSES OF SEVERAL DOOR County snowbirds who were in Florida for the winter. Bourne drove to one of the empty seasonal homes, a sprawling farmhouse on several acres outside the town of Valmy. Laney said little along the way, her voice robotic as she gave Bourne directions. When they got there, she let them in with her key, and Bourne told her to keep the lights off. It was cold inside, the thermostat set to fifty-five degrees, but the water was on, which meant they could both take hot showers.

Laney went first. She stayed in the shower for a long time. When she came out, she was wrapped in a bath sheet, her curly brown hair still damp. She slid down to the thick chocolate-brown carpet in front of the king-size bed. Her face, mostly lost in shadow, was far away. She still didn't speak to him.

Bourne showered next. The hot water eased some of the soreness in his muscles, but it stung where it found the abrasions on his skin. He toweled off in the cold, dark bathroom, then found a terry-cloth robe on a hook and shrugged it on. He slid down to the floor next to Laney and wrapped an arm around her shoulders. At first, he felt her coolness, but then her body finally relaxed, and she melted against him.

"They came after *me*," she murmured.

"Yeah. I'm sorry."

"Not just you. *Me.* Why would they do that?"

"Because we're together. Because with your help, we may be able to figure out what they wanted us to forget."

"You know what this is all about, don't you?" Laney asked. "You know what we're trying to find."

Bourne waited a moment before answering, but he chose not to lie this time. He'd almost killed her; she'd almost died. And before he and Mo went looking for the secrets inside her head, she needed to know the truth. "There was a foreign intelligence operation going on eight years ago. That's what this is all about."

"Here? In Door County?"

"Yes. I think I saw whoever was behind it, and that person has become very important. That means I know who he is, and that scares them. Except I *don't* know, because I don't remember any of it."

"You think it's Alvin Bakk?"

"I think Bakk is part of this, but I don't know how he fits in. I'm hoping you saw something eight years ago and that your memories aren't as walled-off as mine. Obviously, that prospect worries them enough that they want to eliminate you. They definitely don't want you and me working as a team."

"Who are *they*?" Laney asked.

"The Chinese. Their spy wing here in the U.S."

"Hence the honeymoon couple with Chinese passports."

"Yes. That man was an assassin. The woman, too. I don't know for sure, but my suspicion is—"

"You killed them," Laney said.

"Yes."

She shook her head. "Jesus. I need a drink."

Laney slipped the towel off her shoulders and stood up. He could barely make out her naked body, the deep trough of her spine and the creaminess of her bare skin. She disappeared for a few minutes, then returned with an open bottle of wine dangling from one hand. The shadows fell across the front of her body now, but she made no effort to hide from his eyes or cover herself as she returned to the floor next to him.

"Wayne and Alicia have great wine," she said. "This one's an Italian something or other. Red. You want some?"

"Sure."

He took the bottle and tilted it to his mouth, taking a brief swallow. The wine was excellent; her snowbird friends had good taste. He passed it back to her, and Laney took a much longer swig. She spilled a little, which she wiped from her lips. Then she put the bottle on the floor within easy reach.

"So is that what you do?" she asked. "Kill people?"

"Sometimes."

"It seems like you're pretty good at it."

Bourne let that go without a reply.

"I'm not saying I have a problem with it," Laney went on, as if debating the morality with herself. "Not really. Some women might. But there's no point in being naive about how the world works. I figure you're one of the good guys. You are one of the good guys, aren't you? Because otherwise I'll feel stupid."

"At a certain level, good and bad lose their meaning," Bourne replied.

"Well, that's an interesting answer. It sounds pretty wise, but also sad." She reached for the bottle and drank more. "But you work for us? I mean, the U.S.?"

"Yes."

"Feds?"

"Yes."

"FBI? CIA?"

"It's an agency you wouldn't know."

"Ah. One of those. Can you tell me anything about who you really are? Is Jason your real name?"

"My real identity got lost long ago."

"I guess I can relate to that. You said you weren't married. Was that a lie? Part of your cover story? Because I can't help but notice that I'm naked here, and you haven't tried anything."

"I'm not married," Bourne said.

"Girlfriend?"

"It's complicated."

She smirked. "Complicated sounds like yes, but you'd rather it was no. Particularly with me sitting here with no clothes on."

He didn't explain about Shadow. They drank more wine. Her, then him. They drained the bottle quickly, and his head grew light as the alcohol affected him and his adrenaline bled away.

"Does your girlfriend have a problem with you killing people?" Laney asked.

"She kills people, too," Bourne said.

"Oh. Super. Good to know. Guess I should think twice about making her jealous. Is it serious?"

"I don't know what it is."

"Are you in love?"

"Not with her, but there have been others," he told her, not sure why he was sharing things with Laney that were better left unsaid. Maybe it was the wine. Maybe he just needed to talk to someone. "Johanna. She was another agent. She was killed last year. I loved her."

"I'm sorry."

"I'm over it now," he said blandly, not trying to hide that he was lying. "Before that, there was a woman named Abbey. She was an outsider. We tried to make it work, but in the end, she did have a problem with what I do. She couldn't live with it. Honestly, I didn't want her to try. Those are the kind of compromises that corrode your soul. Now it's better if I stick with women who play the same game as me."

"Or women who don't expect anything from you," Laney said. "Was I clear about that? I don't expect anything from you. I just want tonight."

"That's not a good idea."

"Not-good ideas are sort of my specialty."

"You don't really know me."

"I know enough. And what I know, I like."

"We should call Mo," he said, trying to change the subject.

"Is that what we should do?"

"Yeah."

"I disagree."

He found himself with nothing to say, no more objections to make. The silence between them drew out, becoming electric, and the cold room got hotter. He wanted her enough to take his breath away, and she knew it. Her seduction moved inexorably from words to action, like water slowly penetrating stone. Her fingers located his thigh, gently tracing ripples of muscle and scars, and then moving upward to zero in on what she wanted. Her brown eyes were close enough, even in the darkness, to draw him in.

"You don't need to respect me in the morning," she went on, fingernails on his skin. "All you need to do is not kill me."

"I almost did."

"Yeah, but that's kind of meet-cute, right? 'I hooked up with this assassin, and he almost blew my head off, but then we made love, and it was all good.'"

"Not funny."

"It's a little funny. Hell, if it were Christmas, we'd have the makings of a Hallmark movie. You don't want to spoil that, do you?"

Bourne finally smiled.

"See, I think Mo can wait," Laney purred.

Her mouth found his neck, her lips kissing his shoulders. He smelled floral shampoo in her hair. The warmth of her hand traveled up his leg again, and this time she found what she was looking for and curled her fingers around it. He returned the favor, finding the source of all that heat between her legs, and her breath caught with a little rumble of pleasure. They didn't stop; they couldn't stop. They were way beyond that. He pushed her onto her back on the carpet, and her scrawny legs wrapped tightly around his hips with a strength that surprised him, and he forgot about Abbey, Johanna, and Shadow for a while.

MO KNEW. HE READ THEIR FACES AND THE CHEMISTRY BETWEEN THEM, but he was discreet enough to say nothing, although he gave Jason a sharp, unhappy look.

He'd blurred the background on his Zoom screen, wanting all of Laney's focus on his face and the sound of his voice with no distractions. That was his way. When Bourne introduced them, the power of Mo's personality had its effect on her. She couldn't seem to take her eyes off him. Bourne knew Mo so well that he sometimes forgot how good he was at what he did. That was why the CIA and Treadstone had turned to him for years in their worst psychological trauma cases.

"What do I have to do?" Laney asked, her voice calmer and more submissive than Jason had heard it before. With him, she'd been the aggressor, going after what she wanted. Now she seemed like a child awaiting instructions.

"This should be easy for you, Laney," Mo replied. "It's like going into a dreamless, restful sleep. Your mind will do the work, but you won't even be aware of it."

"I've never been hypnotized. I don't know whether I can be."

Mo had expressed his own doubts to Bourne about this, but he showed no doubts now. "Everyone can be hypnotized. We can all separate our brains from our senses without being conscious of what's going on around us. Have you ever fallen asleep watching television? We all have. But the television keeps playing, even if we're not aware of it, and then we wake up and realize everything we've missed. This is much the same, Laney."

"Okay. Whatever you say."

"Just close your eyes. Listen to my voice. I'm going to read you something. All right? Think of it like a bedtime story. It's from *A Tale of Two Cities.* I'll read, you'll listen, and very soon you'll be asleep. But you won't really be asleep. You'll keep hearing my voice, and we'll go exploring your past together."

"Yes, all right."

"Close your eyes, Laney."

"Yes."

"Focus on my voice. On the story. Just listen. *It was the best of times, it was the worst of times, it was the age of wisdom, it was the age of foolishness . . .*"

Mo kept reading, his voice following the up-and-down prose like calm ocean waves landing on the beach. He hadn't made it through more than a page of the book when Bourne noticed that Laney's breathing had gone steady, her mouth slightly open, her whole body very still. She was awake, but she was not awake.

"Laney?" Mo said quietly. "Are you still with me?"

"Yes."

"How do you feel?"

"Happy. Peaceful."

"Okay. That's good. I'm glad. I want you to keep that feeling of satisfaction. Whatever else you see now, whatever you remember, you're still happy and peaceful. No harm can come to you."

"Yes, all right."

"I'm going to have you open your eyes, but when you do, you won't see the room around you. You won't see the darkness or me or Jason. You're going to travel back eight years, and you're going to take us on a trip."

"What should I think about?"

"Don't worry about that. Let your brain do the work. Your mind will carry you there, and you'll see what you're supposed to see."

"Okay."

"Are you ready?"

"Yes."

"You can open your eyes now, Laney."

She did. Her lashes blinked several times. Her dark eyes had an empty, glassy look, and her forehead deepened into lines, as if she were searching for something. Her breathing stayed calm, her chest swelling under the blanket that was pulled around her.

"Where are you, Laney?"

"I'm in a car. I'm on the road. I know the area. It looks like I'm between Ephraim and Fish Creek. The trees are beautiful, full of reds and golds. Leaves are blowing with the wind. It's sunset. Shadows everywhere."

"Are you alone in the car?"

"Yes."

"Where are you going?"

"I don't know."

"What are you doing on the road?"

"I'm following a black SUV. I'm nervous. I shouldn't be doing this. But something doesn't feel right to me. These people don't belong here."

"These people? Who is in the SUV?"

"At first, it was just two of them. A man and a woman. Both Chinese. Twentysomethings. He's driving. I don't like the look of either of them. You can see it in the eyes. People with cruel eyes, you always know. I have a friend who runs a little rental cottage north of Ephraim. She told me about them. She said they were acting weird. So I've been sort of spying on them for the past day. Tonight I watched them leave the cottage and get into their SUV. Both of them dressed in black, both of them looking around, checking everything out. I was afraid they spotted me, but I don't think they did. I just knew they were up to something."

"What did they do?"

"They drove south, then turned inland to a different rental house. They picked up three Chinese men. Older. Wearing suits, like CEOs or bankers or whatever. Then they came back to the main road. They're heading into Fish Creek."

"Keep us with you, Laney. Describe the scene."

"It's almost dark. There are still a lot of people around. Tourists. We're going down the hill through town. I don't know, maybe I'm nuts and this is nothing. They could be going to dinner somewhere, like a family thing. Chinese dad and uncles taking the married kids out. I'm thinking I should turn around and forget all this. But I don't know, it still feels weird to me."

"Where is the SUV now?"

"It's heading along Main Street. It's going straight ahead toward the water, past the intersection where the highway turns left. Oh, man, what the hell?"

"What is it, Laney?"

"I can see ahead of me. The road is closed."

"Closed?"

"Yeah, it's blocked off on the way to White Gull. A couple of cops are monitoring the traffic, deciding who gets through. Hang on, no, they're not cops. They're beefy-looking guys in reflective jackets, but they're private. I don't know them."

"And the SUV?"

"One of the guys is checking a list. They're letting them through. The truck is continuing down the street to the hotel. I can't see them now. It's too dark. I'm parking outside the roadblock a few blocks away. I don't know what to do now. I'm calling a friend of mine at the hotel to see what's going on."

"Do you reach him?"

"Yeah. Yeah, he's answering his phone. But he's not at the hotel tonight. He has the weekend off with pay. No idea why, but he's not complaining. The people who are there now, they're not hotel staff. I should have heard something about this. How can they be keeping this so quiet? Jeez, somebody's got juice."

"What are you doing now, Laney?"

"Heck with it. I'm going to figure out what's going on. I'm going to get closer on foot. I'm cutting through the Founder's Square mall to the woods. I'll come up on the hotel from the back. If someone catches me, so what, I'm just out for a walk. I'm pushing through the trees now. Leaves are falling in my face. It's almost night. Wait, that's weird."

"What is?" Mo asked.

"Suddenly it's hard to see. It's like a fog has come down through the trees."

"Fog?"

"Yeah. Everything is white. I'm walking through a cloud."

Bourne watched Mo frown. The therapist mouthed to him: *Memory loss.*

"Go through the fog, Laney. It's not real. It can't stop you."

"It's cold. It's wet. I can hardly see."

"Keep going."

"I'm coming up behind one of the cottages. God, I'm so cold!"

Bourne reached out to put an arm around Laney's shoulders, but Mo shook his head sternly and waved him off with a finger.

"What do you see?"

"A window," she murmured. "There's a rear window on one of the cottages. I'm going right up to it, I'm looking inside. I hear voices. People talking. But the fog is so thick. I've never seen fog like this. It's *inside* the cottage. How can it be inside the cottage?"

"Try to see through the fog, Laney. Who's in the cottage?"

"The three old Chinese men. They're talking to someone."

"Who?"

Bourne watched Laney blink uncomfortably. Her face became a mask of worry and fear. Mo saw it, too. "Remember, Laney, you're happy and peaceful. Keep that warm feeling inside you, like you're floating. Just look in the window and tell me what you see."

"There's someone in the fog, but I can't see him."

"Him?"

"Or her. I don't know. All I see is a cloud, a blur, it keeps changing shape. It could be a man, it could be a woman. Oh, my God!"

"What is it, Laney?"

"The man! The young Chinese man! He's here. He found me! The man and the woman saw me spying, they're dragging me away from the cottage. They're pulling me into the woods. The woman has something around my mouth. I can't shout, I can't call for help. Oh shit, oh shit, the man has a gun! He has a gun! He's pointing it at me! He's going to kill me! I see him, he's going to kill me!"

Laney's mouth clamped shut. She breathed through her nose. Bourne didn't think she'd last much longer under hypnosis.

"We're waiting for you, Laney," Mo said calmly. "What's happening now?"

She didn't answer for a long time, and when she did, her voice became a monotone, stripped of emotion. "They're dead."

"What?"

"They're dead. Someone shot them. First the man, then the woman. A man killed them both. He saved my life."

"Who is this man?" Mo asked.

Laney screamed suddenly and broke out of the trance with a violent start. Now she was awake in the cold house, and tears began to pour down her face. She slapped the phone screen to end the call with Mo and then threw the phone against the wall.

She turned to Bourne.

"You," she said. "It was you. Your name is David."

12

"THE FOG WAS THE STRANGEST THING," LANEY TOLD HIM. "IT WAS LIKE I was staring at my memories, but parts of them had been rubbed out with an eraser. Or painted over in white. And yet at the moment I was there, the fog felt real. Looking back, it seems as crazy and fake as a dream, but I was *there*. I've never gotten so close to anything in my past before. Has that ever happened to you? Have you experienced anything like that?"

"Not quite like it, but similar," Bourne said. "Although I've never *visualized* my memory loss the way you did."

"It was creepy."

They lay in bed next to each other, her head on his chest, her arm around his waist, her bare leg thrown across his. The house had finally begun to warm as the furnace fought back the winter cold. It was still the middle of the night, still pitch-black outside. He'd checked the windows. No one had found them. The Taurus was well hidden, out of sight from anyone passing on the highway.

"David," she said. "David what? Can you tell me your last name?"

He hesitated, but the man he was had died long ago. There was no point in hiding it from her. "David Webb."

"I like that. David Webb. Okay, so now you know what I remember, David. I'm sorry, it's not much. Except for my hero coming to my rescue. What about you, do you remember any of it? Did what I say trigger anything more for you? Do you remember what happened that night?"

"No, I don't." Then a moment later, he went on. "I do remember following the Chinese assassin. He was called Fang. I chased him from Florida to Wisconsin, along with the others. The woman, Rose. The older Chinese men. But for me, that's where the trail ends. I don't remember anything after that."

"The person in the fog. The one in the cottage that I couldn't see. Whoever he or she is, is that the person you're looking for?"

"I think so."

"So you were there. You must have seen him, too."

"Yes, but for me, it's all gone."

"What do you think happened next?" Laney asked.

"We must have been caught," Bourne concluded. "You said there was other security in place near the hotel, so they must have grabbed us after I shot Fang and the woman. They took care of the bodies, and then they dealt with us. Everything I remember was manipulated. Same with you—the whole car crash staged."

"Why not just kill us?"

He frowned. "Whoever was in charge probably thought that killing us would raise too many questions. My agency would investigate when I went missing. So would the local police if you disappeared. All the efforts they made to keep this operation secret could have blown up in their faces. But if neither one of us remembered anything, we wouldn't be in a position to give away whatever was happening here."

Laney propped herself on one elbow. "So what happens now?"

"Now I try to figure out how Alvin Bakk fits into all this," Bourne said.

"You think he was the person in the fog?"

"Could be."

"But I didn't actually see him."

"No, but Bakk was part of whatever was going on eight years ago. My bet is, he and his allies are the ones who made all the arrangements and kept it quiet. He was already one of the superrich back then. That kind of money buys a lot of silence when you want it. So I need to confront him."

"I suppose I can't tag along for that," Laney said.

"No."

She chewed her lower lip. "And after that, you go?"

"Yeah. Then I go."

"What happens to me?" she asked. "I mean, I wasn't giving you bullshit when I came on to you. I was only looking for someone to be with me tonight, and you gave me that. No strings, no expectations. But people tried to kill me, too. Will they keep coming after me when you're gone?"

"Can you leave town for a while?" Bourne asked. "Buy some time?"

Laney shook her head. "Not with my mom in a facility. I have to stay near her. But I can keep a low profile for a few days. Stay in the seasonal homes I watch, rather than going back to my place.

Nobody will see me if I don't want them to see me. That will work for a while, but then what?"

"I think once I'm out of the area, you'll be safe," Bourne said. "If you're not with me, they'll consider you low risk again. At that point, going after you isn't worth the questions it would raise around here."

"Lucky me. What about the three dead bodies at my house?"

"My people will take care of that," Bourne said. "When you eventually go home, it will be like nothing happened."

"Jesus. I can see why the other girl—Abbey?—couldn't deal with it."

"Yeah. She was smart to let me go. So are you."

Laney glanced across the bedroom toward the windows that looked out onto the darkness. She climbed on top of him, her knees on either side of his hips. "But you can stay until morning, can't you? I'm not ready to be alone quite yet."

Bourne reached for her face and pulled her close. "I can stay."

"MO GAVE ME A REPORT," SHADOW TOLD HIM TWO HOURS LATER ON A video call, her words clipped and concise. "It sounds like the regression with this woman, Laney Reese, didn't give us any breakthroughs about eight years ago. It simply confirmed much of what we already suspected about your role in this."

"That's true," Bourne replied. "I was hoping for more, but Mo did his best. Whatever they did to her, they were thorough, like they were with me."

"So that relationship proved to be a waste of time."

He heard ice in her voice, and he saw it in her face, too. Her burgundy lips were pushed together, as tight as a flat line on a heart monitor. Her steel-blue eyes barely seemed to blink, and her nostrils flared with each breath. Every bone in her face seemed to show sharp edges, and her normally lush blond hair appeared flat and unwashed. Shadow always had a way of running hot and cold to keep him off balance, but he wondered how detailed Mo's report had been and whether the therapist had shared his suspicions about the sexual affair between Bourne and Laney.

It was early, still dark in Door County and not even dawn yet on the East Coast. Shadow was already in her DC office. Behind her desk, in the low light of a Tiffany lamp, he could see the Mexican painting that covered her private safe—the safe where she kept the laptop that contained the Files. All he could see of her clothes was a black turtleneck that made her look like a cat burglar.

"It wasn't entirely a waste," Bourne said. "The regression gives us an insight into the psychological experiments the Chinese have been conducting and how advanced they've become. I don't know if they're using drugs or hypnosis to do the work—maybe both. But it appears to be very effective. This was eight years ago, and they were already able to erase memories for me and Laney. I'm sure they've gone even further since then. That's a dangerous new weapon they can use in espionage operations."

"Agreed," Shadow replied. "But right now, the question is Alvin Bakk and how deeply he's involved in the Chinese spying. Do you suspect Bakk is Bai Ze?"

Bourne thought about it. "He certainly fits the profile. Brilliant, possibly autistic, limitless resources, huge ego and ambition. His range of businesses gives him connections throughout the government and corporate worlds. He's experienced in leading large, complex organizations, so he could certainly manage the Chinese domestic strategy. Bakk would also be in a position to assess key pressure points throughout the country and develop schemes to exploit them."

"Unfortunately, his connections also make him largely untouchable. Everyone's scared of him. But if he really is Bai Ze, I'm more curious about why Bakk would bother getting in bed with the Chinese. He's not a communist, and I can't see him giving up control to anyone, let alone a foreign government."

"So maybe he isn't in bed with them. Maybe they're spying on *him*. On the other hand, Bakk has plenty of business interests in China, so for now, their interests may align."

Shadow eased back in her leather chair. She folded her slim, elegant hands together under her chin. The rest of her arms were practically invisible, encased in the black fabric of her turtleneck. "Do you know anything about Bakk's wife? Or rather, his ex-wife? They divorced a couple of years ago."

"I don't."

"Her name is Mei Sun. She's Taiwanese. Thanks to the divorce settlement with Bakk, she now runs one of the most well-financed, most influential NGOs in the world. She's passionately anti-China, too. That's not surprising given that she grew up in the shadow of all the CCP threats."

"Why did the marriage fall apart?"

"If you believe the tabloids, it was the usual reason. Bakk couldn't keep it in his pants. He had dozens of affairs, fathered several kids with mistresses. God knows random fucking is a common enough problem with powerful men. Not that I care one way or another what anyone does between the sheets."

Bourne said nothing, but he didn't miss the subtext.

"But you think their split was more than that?" he asked.

"Well, maybe Sun began to suspect that she and Bakk didn't see eye to eye on China. She would have found that intolerable, particularly given her background."

"You mean her childhood?"

"Not just that. Sun was CIA before she married Bakk. She was active in the Taiwan arena, some serious black ops stuff. She was one of Holly Schultz's top agents."

"So was Chess," Bourne reminded her. "The hit man who tried to take me out when I got to Door County. Holly's name keeps popping up in this operation."

"Yes, the question is which side she's on, or whether she's playing both sides against each other. With Holly, I never know."

"I'm sure she feels the same way about you," Bourne said.

"No doubt."

"How did Mei Sun meet Bakk?"

"She was sent in by the CIA to do a full-scale background check on him when his government contract work began to ramp up. Apparently they hit it off. Everyone says Bakk can be charming in person, and money is always an aphrodisiac."

"Or Holly wanted an agent on the inside and sent her after him."

"Yes. I thought about that, too. Sun might have been on a mission to seduce him. That's sort of like shooting fish in a barrel, though, right? With most men, it doesn't take much more than the woman saying, 'How about it?'"

Bourne sighed. Again her meaning was crystal clear. He sat in the darkness of the Taurus, parked near Sunset Beach, and wondered how much of his face she could see. "Is there something you want to say to me, Marlen?"

He only used her real name, her birth name, when they talked as man and woman, not as Treadstone spies. Not as agent and handler.

"No. Why would there be?"

"I assume Mo told you that I had sex with Laney Reese."

"Yes, he did."

"Your face tells me that's a problem."

"Then you're reading my face wrong, Jason. I don't care who you fuck on a mission. We both know it's necessary from time to time. I'm the one who said sex didn't have to be anything but chemical. There's nothing romantic between us. There never can be, we both know that. You and I are sleeping together, which is fine. But don't fool yourself into thinking of me as a jealous lover. I'm not."

"Understood," Bourne said, but he didn't believe her.

"Good. Next subject."

"All right. What else can you tell me about Bakk? I need to get inside his head, and I only know what I read in the papers."

Shadow shook her head. "His intelligence file is about six inches thick. I've been through it, but that still doesn't give me a lot of insights into who he is. Bakk is simultaneously one of the most public billionaires and also one of the most private. He's on social media constantly. He's a scientist, a genius, virtually never sleeps, a futurist full of wild ideas. And yet he's been able to make a surprising number of them work. He builds a team of giants at every company he starts, and that takes social skills. On the other hand, he's also as reclusive as Howard Hughes. He's hardly ever seen at public events. He seems to run all of his companies remotely, never goes to board meetings. His employees come to him, not vice versa."

"Parents?"

"Dead."

"Any serious relationships after Mei Sun?"

"It doesn't seem that way. Just flings."

"So what motivates him?"

"As far as I can tell, he wants to be the most important person in the history of the human race. Honestly, he's made a fair start of it."

Bourne frowned. "Is any of that consistent with him being a Chinese spy?"

"That depends on the game he's playing. I'm smart, but I don't pretend to be on his level."

"All right, let's narrow it down. For now, we need to look at the small picture and not the big picture. Did you find any evidence to suggest what he was doing eight years ago? What supersecret event was happening here?"

"There's no record of it," Shadow told him. "If Bakk's intention was to keep it off the books, he succeeded. Flight manifests, credit card statements, restaurant receipts—nothing shows up. It's a black hole."

"What about the Files?" Bourne asked. "The AI engine figured out *I* was here. It must be able to give us something we can use."

"That's where things get unusual."

"What do you mean?"

"I ran that week eight years ago through the Files again—this time adding in Alvin Bakk as a variable. I got back a list of almost one hundred names, all scientists with a wide range of specialties and backgrounds. Some university, some corporate, some government. All with top secret clearances."

"You think they're the ones who came to Door County?"

"I do, but I have no way of proving it. Every one of those names is on record as being *somewhere else* during that week."

"Like me."

"Like you. I find travel receipts to back that up, plus plenty of photographs on social media. Vacations. Conferences. Elective surgery. All those scientists took a trip during that week, but the one place *none* of them went was Wisconsin."

"And yet they were here," Bourne said.

"That's my guess. Plus, there's something else. Something you need to know."

"What is it?"

"Ten of the names are people who were working for DARPA."

"DARPA? The crazy-ass government scientists?"

"That's them. They've dabbled in everything from ESP to insect drones over the years. Some of it's way out on the fringe, but they've had plenty of successes, too. And Jason? DARPA has been doing memory experiments for decades."

13

BOURNE PUSHED HIS WAY THROUGH A TANGLE OF WINTER-BARE TREES.

Inside the woods, it was still mostly dark in the few minutes after dawn. He moved slowly, his boots crunching on snow. He knew he was close to Alvin Bakk's estate, but he couldn't see it yet. With each step, he used a flashlight to watch for surveillance and security, lasers and cameras hidden in the branches, traps and trip wires strung between the birches. Even in the middle of nowhere, he assumed Bakk would be alert for strangers and would take measures to discourage them from coming closer.

At first, all he found was a rusted *No Trespassing* sign. Not far after that, the next sign warned: *Private Property—Do Not Approach.* Then he finally reached the fence surrounding the property, which was black like wrought iron but was probably made of titanium. The fence was eight feet high with spikes like arrowheads running along the top. A ten-foot border had been cleared in the woods leading up to the fence, to prevent anyone from climbing the tall trees and jumping to the other side. He assumed there were also motion sensors, not sensitive enough for false alarms with every bird or squirrel but plenty sensitive enough to alert security that a person had breached the perimeter.

The sign on the fence read simply *Beware of Dog.*

He decided to test the interior triggers. At the fringe of the woods, he chose the heaviest broken branch he could find and hoisted it like a javelin over the property fence. It landed among the dense trees on the other side, as if it had simply fallen in the wind. Bourne took cover in the forest and stretched out in the snow, watching and waiting. He didn't have to wait long. He heard a strange metallic clicking in the trees, and then he saw something bright green coming toward the fence at high speed.

It was a dog, all right. A *robotic* dog, glowing in the dim light like a futuristic hound of the Baskervilles. It was all body and metal legs, with a video camera for a head attached to the rest of the device by a long, jointed metal neck. The thing galloped up to the fence, and its elongated neck extended, the camera swiveling to do a 360-degree review of the area. Bourne wondered whether the camera was heat-sensitive and whether it could detect him hiding in the woods. But it didn't seem aware of his presence. The dog's neck came forward, its head poking between the titanium rails. Then a recorded message played in a mechanical voice.

"*Private property. Do not try to enter. All trespassers will be caught and prosecuted to the full extent of the law.*"

Bourne wondered whether that was true or whether trespassers would simply be shot. He waited, and after another couple of minutes by the fence, the robot finally withdrew and disappeared through the trees on the other side.

Bakk was definitely serious about his privacy.

The day began to lighten around him, despite a gray blanket of low overhead clouds. Bourne emerged from the forest and went up to the fence again, and he could see the roof of the estate now, looming above the treetops. The house looked as wide as a football field; the interior square footage had to be enormous. But for now, his primary obstacle was the fence and the arrival of Rover if he made it to the other side.

What he needed was another human being.

Bourne followed the fence southward. At some point, he expected to find an access gate, and he did. It was secured by a digital keypad, and beyond it, a plowed trail led toward the unseen estate. He used a universal key card that the tech experts at Treadstone had devised, and it unlocked the code in a matter of seconds. He let himself through the gate, expecting the robot dog to return when it received a sensor notification of someone inside the property line. But he didn't want the dog; he wanted whoever was in charge of the dog. Bourne ran to the nearest evergreen tree and threw his Glock to the ground. Then he kicked away snow to avoid footprints and squeezed himself upward inside the branches of the tree. He climbed until he was ten feet high and basically invisible unless someone looked directly at him. From where he was, he could see the gun in plain sight, a suppressor threaded onto the barrel.

Rover arrived quickly. He heard the frantic clicking of the robot legs running through the woods toward the gate. When the dog showed up, it surveyed the area, and the camera at the end of its jointed neck latched onto the Glock almost immediately. Seeing it, the robot froze where it was, obviously broadcasting an alert. Bourne waited, his backup gun within reach. About five minutes passed, and then he heard human footprints coming at a run down the trail that led from the gate toward the house.

Two men.

They appeared below him. Both wore yellow down vests and black jeans, and both were armed with Ruger LC9s. Alvin Bakk wasn't messing around. The first of the men was the bigger physical threat; he was at least six foot four and built to fight. The man with him was older and smaller, with bowl-cut blond hair, but he seemed to be the one in charge. The smaller man squatted and picked up Bourne's Glock from the ground. His face darkened into a severe frown, and Bourne could read his mind. A Glock inside the fence was bad enough, but a suppressor meant real trouble. Anyone carrying equipment like that didn't simply drop it during a random break-in.

There was an intruder, and he had to be close.

Bourne watched the man's eyes. They looked left. They looked right. And then, as if driven by gut instinct, the man tilted his chin upward and stared into the evergreen tree next to the trail. He saw Bourne, but before the man could shout a warning, Bourne leaped. His body crashed down, not on the smaller man, but on the larger man with him. Bourne landed on his upper back, and his weight took the big man heavily to the ground. The Ruger came loose from the man's wrist, and Bourne scooped it up and swung it hard into the man's temple. The guard's eyes rolled back, and his body went limp.

Bourne sensed motion near him before he saw it. The surprise wore off in an instant, and the smaller man began to back away, raising his Ruger to aim at Bourne's chest. The Glock was still in his other hand. Bourne expected a shot, but none came. Instead, the man barked a command.

"Loki, *disable!*"

The robotic dog reared back on its metal legs. Bourne rolled away just as Loki fired the cables of a Taser that landed harmlessly. He kept rolling another few feet, colliding with the smaller man, who lost his balance and stumbled backward. Bourne pushed himself onto his knees and shot upward, his hands grabbing for the man's wrists, spreading his arms away as he squeezed the trigger of both guns. Bullets went wild into the trees, left and right. Bourne's forehead punched into the man's gut, and he heard a gasp of air, but the man stayed standing, struggling for control of the pistols.

The man shouted again, repeating his command. "Loki, *disable!*"

Bourne spun, holding the man, then letting go and throwing himself clear. Loki shot a second Taser, and this time the electric probes ripped through the smaller man's vest and into his skin. The man screamed and twitched, his knees buckling as he fell to the ground. Bourne's Glock came loose, and Jason snatched it up, then took aim at the electronic panel at the base of the robotic dog's neck. He fired, tiny spits from the suppressor, his rounds shattering glass and sparking circuits with little tongues of flame before ricocheting into the air.

Loki went dark, green lights turning black. Its metal body stiffened.

The smaller man on the ground moaned, his body moving like rubber. The bigger man was still unconscious and would be for a while. Bourne grabbed the two Rugers and shoved them into his backpack, then knelt before the twitching man, whose eyes seemed to go in circles. Bourne brought the Glock up, then down, cracking his skull and drawing blood.

Like his partner, the man went limp.

Bourne got to his feet and ran down the trail.

ALVIN BAKK'S HOUSE APPEARED TO BE DESERTED.

It was a two-story grand estate, sided with gray shake and flagstones, and chambered windows stretching from one end to the other on both floors. The structure was shaped like a boomerang, the outer curve looking down through the trees with an expansive view of the waters of Green Bay.

Bourne figured he had, at most, fifteen minutes before the alarm was raised. In that amount of time, he'd barely scratch the surface of searching a home this large. But all he could do was play the hand he'd been dealt.

The middle doors on the sweeping veranda overlooking the lake were unlocked. He slipped inside and found himself in a huge sitting room, with a stone fireplace in which a warm fire was lit. Someone was home. The hardwood floor was covered with a Chinese rug, and Chinese art and tapestries hung on the walls. He wondered if that was Bakk's tastes, or whether the decor was left over from his marriage to Mei Sun.

He walked from room to room, overwhelmed by the sheer size of the place and the elaborate decorations. Glistening gold chandeliers. Wood-and-iron staircases. A library larger than Jason's Paris apartment, with thirty-foot windows and thousands of hardcovers stocked on mahogany shelves. Antique furniture, polished and shining; Civil War guns and photographs; a moon rock under a glass dome.

Every room also gave evidence that the house was occupied. He found incense candles burning, a half-drunk mimosa on an end table, an open book of Hemingway on a sofa cushion. But he saw no one. It was as if they'd all been called away and were in hiding. He also felt watched. He saw no cameras, but he was sure they were there. He thought about shouting out a greeting, because he had the uncomfortable suspicion that the owner of the house had been expecting him.

He climbed to the second floor.

There, with the best panoramic view of the lake in the house, he found Alvin Bakk's office, its walls covered over in blue leather and brass rivets, its light provided by a dozen LED bulbs encased in square crystal fixtures. The furniture was sleek and modern, unlike the rest of the house. The centerpiece of the room, positioned in front of the windows, was a thirty-foot desk with seven computers and at least a dozen 4K monitors. All of the displays were powered on, tracking everything from the Nasdaq to the price of Japanese steel to video feeds from Bakk's manufacturing facilities all around the world.

There was also a video feed showing the trail near the property gate, where the two unconscious guards were beginning to stir.

Bakk had been tracking him.

Bourne turned to escape, but he was too late.

Two more guards appeared silently in the wide doorway behind him, both armed with CZ Bren 2 automatic rifles. They took up positions on either side of the door, barrels focused on Bourne's chest. Two others followed, similarly armed. Bourne glanced at the veranda beyond the wide desk and saw half a dozen men taking up position there, in case he tried to make it outside and jump for freedom.

He was trapped with nowhere to go.

"Weapons," one of the men snapped.

Bourne held out his hands, fingers wide. Carefully, he withdrew his Glock, then the two Rugers, then his spare gun, and set everything on the marble floor in front of him.

"Back up."

Bourne did.

The man came and collected the weapons from the floor, then backed out of reach. Another man came forward and searched Bourne thoroughly, locating the knives he'd kept hidden and stripping them away. When the search was done, he was unarmed. At that point, he was surprised to see the guards leave. One by one, they backed out of the doorway and disappeared from the veranda, until Bourne was alone in the office.

A minute passed. Then two. He wondered if he was being given a chance to leave.

Then a panel in the leather wall opened. A secret door. He kicked himself for not spotting it before. A man appeared from an adjacent room, and the door closed behind him with a gentle click. He was around forty years old, not tall but in athletic shape, with a mop of messy black hair and strawberry-colored round sunglasses. He wore a tight-fitting black T-shirt that bared a couple inches of his midriff; the shirt advertised a German industrial rock band called Rammstein. His trim black pants ended in slip-on Skechers, and he wore no socks. He held a fluted champagne glass with a bubbly orange drink in one hand. On his other wrist, he wore a Hublot Big Bang watch that probably cost seven figures.

It was Alvin Bakk.

"Mimosa?" he asked Bourne. His voice was nasal, and he had a way of talking fast. "It's my favorite drink. People think the key is the champagne, but really, it's the orange juice. I fly in oranges three times a week from my favorite grove in Florida. Well, actually, I own the grove. Bought it a few years ago. If you don't want things to change, you have to control them yourself. Not just oranges, of course. That's true of just about anything in life. Own your future. Otherwise, someone else will."

"What about things you can't own?" Bourne asked.

Bakk winked. "I'll let you know when I find something like that, but so far, it's a short list. Excuse me for a moment, will you? The markets just opened."

The billionaire wandered past Bourne to the far end of the desk, where he sat in an ergonomic chair on wheels. His knees bounced, as if he were dancing to music only he could hear. He manipulated the mouse on one of the computers and tapped in instructions on the keyboard one-handed. Then he whizzed the chair along the desk at high speed, whistling like a train, and repeated the process at another of the multiple computers. With his back to Bourne, he waved at the veranda overlooking the lake.

"You want to go outside? Go take a look. The view is amazing. I spend hours just staring at it. That's my meditation."

"It's a great view," Bourne agreed. "But I'm fine where I am."

"Suit yourself."

Bakk typed at an astonishing speed for several more minutes, then pushed a button under the desk that shut down all of the computers simultaneously. He pushed another button and piano music by Grieg filled the room. He spun around in the chair, his fingers steepled together under his chin.

"*Cain*," he said. "Welcome. I'm Alvin Bakk."

"Yes, I know."

"By the way, do you prefer Jason? Jason Bourne? Or Charlie Briggs—that was the name you used at the White Gull, right? My goodness, you have so many identities for one man. I have surveillance all over the peninsula, so I've been watching you since you arrived. I've kept an eye on your adventures. Including your dalliance with Ms. Reese. You have good taste—she's lovely. Anyway, I figured you'd show up here sooner or later."

"Are you the one who's been trying to kill me?" Bourne asked.

"Me? Hardly. Forgive my arrogance, but if I wanted you dead, you'd be dead. But obviously, there are threats afoot. I've admired how you dealt with them. You have impressive skills. That's why I've been looking forward to meeting you. I do appreciate your not killing *my* men on the trail, by the way. That was a calculated risk—it could have gone terribly wrong—but I needed to know the kind of man you are. I'm pleased to see that I was right, that you have discretion about when to use violence and when to show mercy. Few intelligence agents have that subtlety." He took another sip of his mimosa. "Of course, you did shoot my dog. Not cool."

"It was a robot."

"Oh, Jason, Jason, really? That's what you think? In a few short years, when humans are dating robots and having sex with robots and marrying robots, a sentiment like that will seem brutish and Victorian. Loki's the best dog I've had since a golden retriever when I was nine. But I suppose you couldn't know that, could you? Hopefully, I'll be able to fix him up, but I'm worried that his memory will be fried and he won't remember who I am. You of all people should know how devastating that can be."

Bourne shook his head, his patience wearing thin. "What am I doing here, Mr. Bakk?"

"We both know exactly what you're doing here," the billionaire replied. "You're trying to figure out if I'm the spy known as Bai Ze who is running Chinese espionage operations in the U.S. The American behind Volt Typhoon."

"Are you?" Bourne asked.

Bakk whipped off his strawberry sunglasses and gave him a sharp, wicked stare. "I'm not, although I can understand why you might think so, given what you've discovered. In fact, I think the Chinese have been dropping breadcrumbs to lead you to me. They're hoping you'll do their dirty work for them."

"By doing what?"

"Killing me," Bakk said.

"Well, either way, they'll be disappointed. I don't want to kill Bai Ze."

"Of course. You want to squeeze him."

"That's right."

"Then we're on the same page, Jason. We're looking for the same thing. That's why I'm glad you're here. You see, I want to find Bai Ze every bit as much as you do. And I think I know who he is."

PART TWO

14

ALVIN BAKK GAVE BOURNE A GUIDED TOUR THROUGH THE THIRTY-FIVE thousand square feet of his sprawling estate. He walked so quickly that Jason sometimes felt as if he had to run to keep up with him. The man never stopped, never stopped walking, never stopped talking, never stopped twitching, never stopped pulling out his fourteen-inch tablet and flipping from video to video to show off feeds from cameras he kept all over the world.

"Just how much surveillance do you do?" Bourne asked, shaking his head at the things he was seeing.

Bakk swiped his thumb, making the images on the screen change at a crazy pace. "Oh, I have thousands of webcams. Some legal, but most not. Some are for business, some just because I'm a horrible voyeur."

"Aren't you afraid I'll tell the FBI?"

Bakk waved his hand in a dismissive way. "I'm not. Not at all. For one thing, there isn't a bureaucrat in the DOJ who doesn't have skeletons in their closet. They don't want to take me on. But really,

I want a partnership *with* you, Jason. That's why I'm being honest about who I am and what I'm willing to do. As you get to know me, you'll realize that I'm endlessly curious about everything. People fascinate me, from ordinary people to kings. I want to know their secrets. Secrets are what make the world go round. Hence my network of surveillance."

"I like my secrets," Bourne said.

"Yes, I can tell, but that doesn't mean you can hide them, Jason. Not from me. When you showed up in Door County, naturally I made it my new hobby to find out everything about you. I did rather well, don't you think?"

"What do you mean?"

Bakk withdrew a remote control from his pocket. They were in a humid solarium filled with plants, with natural light pouring in from a wall of glass windows facing the lake and multiple skylights overhead. An interior wall of the room featured dozens of paintings of flowers, kept behind glass, original works by O'Keefe, Van Gogh, Cassatt, Hiroshige, and Van Oosterwijck. With a few buttons on the remote, Bakk darkened the windows to black, and the glass of the art frames dissolved into a series of high-resolution screens.

The screens all showed Bourne.

Bourne watched pictures and video clips of himself shuffle through the frames, one after another. Some were from the past couple of days in Door County with Laney, but most were from years earlier, in places where he'd had no idea he was being observed. He saw himself hand in hand with Abbey Laurent near the Eiffel Tower. He saw himself and Johanna taking a boat called the *Stormy Weather* out of a port in Greece. He saw himself with a

Treadstone agent called Teeling, waiting in the rainy doorway of a church in Sofia, Bulgaria.

And then the last one. The worst one.

He saw himself on a shallow hillside in Maryland, with the barrel of a sniper's rifle aimed at the estate of the former U.S. secretary of state.

The screens turned clear again, revealing the paintings of flowers. The windows of the solarium let in the morning light. Bourne saw Bakk staring at him, his expression full of sly confidence. "See what I mean? You can understand why I'm not concerned about you turning me in."

"How the hell did you get all that?"

"Your boss, Shadow, has the Files for the answers she wants. Good for her. I tried very hard to get them, too, but you beat me to it. But that's okay. I already have years of surveillance records on a scale the government would envy, plus the facial recognition software to find anyone, anywhere, any time. Wherever someone goes, chances are, I'm watching. You can run, Jason, but you can't hide."

Bourne said nothing, but he understood the lesson in raw power that Bakk had just delivered. Any time this man wanted to destroy a life, he had the ability to do so with just the push of a button. That included Bourne's life. Bakk knew things about him that were otherwise nothing but redacted black lines in a government file.

"If you have all this power, why do you care about Bai Ze?" Bourne asked.

"Because Bai Ze wants what *I* have. What I've built. My companies. My technology. My surveillance. If the Chinese can get control of my operations, their influence would be limitless. You can imagine the destructive effects."

"Surely with all of those secret cameras, you can find Bai Ze faster than me."

"You'd think. But he knows I'm watching. As a result, he's very, very careful." Bakk pointed at the open door of the solarium. "Come on, let's continue the tour. We have a lot more to see. I have so much to show you."

They went from room to room, each one showing off the fruits of the man's billions of dollars.

A gourmet chef's kitchen designed by Geoffrey Zakarian.

A shooting range with a wall full of advanced pistols and rifles—some that Bourne hadn't seen before.

A rooftop helipad, complete with a Bell 525 Relentless helicopter ready for takeoff.

A SCIF for secure communications.

A virtual reality room, filling 360 degrees of space, including the floor. With yet another push of the button on his master remote control, Bakk took Bourne to the streets of Paris, in such vivid detail that he felt transported back home. It wasn't like a movie. He felt as if he were *there.* Somehow, even the aromas had been recreated, the sweetness of a patisserie battling with the *chocolat* left on the street by the dogs.

All the while, Bakk kept talking, an endless stream of consciousness.

"You have no memory," he said as they passed through a fitness facility that could have accommodated a football team. "No recollection of your past, your childhood, your parents, the things that made you who you are. That must be incredibly frustrating. Like you're constantly looking for something you can't find."

"It is."

"That makes you vulnerable, doesn't it? You never know what threat is around the next corner. You might not even see it when it's in front of you. You were shot in the Med, yes? A drunk English surgeon took the bullet out on a French island called Port Noir. That's when it happened. Your past disappeared."

"You're well-informed," Bourne said.

"Of course I am. I never deal with anyone without knowing everything about them. But now you're wondering if something happened earlier, aren't you? Eight years ago, you lost several days of your life here in Door County. Bai Ze and the Chinese did something to you."

"Yes," Bourne said, then added, "Or you did."

"Now you're learning. Trust no one."

"I never do."

The billionaire led him into a humid room with an Olympic-size swimming pool in the middle of a marble floor, surrounded by rare, kitschy collectibles from the U.S. and Britain in the 1960s. Bakk obviously had a fetish for the Beatles, because Bourne saw guitars, letters, photographs, and clothes in display cases, all with connections to John, Paul, George, and Ringo. The floor of the huge swimming pool was made entirely of small colored tiles, which re-created a photograph of a blond woman in a blue bikini top. Behind her, amid hundreds of red roses, was George Harrison, looking away from the camera.

"That's Pattie Boyd," Bakk explained. "You know, the sixties it girl. She married George, then left him for Clapton. What a time that was, what a revolution. Some days I wish I'd been born in that era, although I would have missed the modern technology. My scientists tell me that time travel is a bridge too far, that none of the theories of relativity make it possible. But who knows? I haven't ruled it out. If I could make it work, I'd go back there and hang out with all of the bands. What about you, Jason? Is there an era you'd like to experience if you had the chance?"

"I play the cards I'm dealt," Bourne said.

"I suppose in your shoes, I'd feel the same way." Bakk began undressing, peeling off his clothes layer by layer. "Do you feel like a swim?"

"No."

"I always do twenty laps at this time of day. It won't take long."

Bakk continued until he was stark naked, his ass ivory white against tan skin. He executed a knifelike dive into the swimming pool and began a series of laps. He had good form, as if he'd done freestyle racing in his past. It made Bourne wonder if Bakk had connections with David Abbott of Treadstone, who'd been an Olympic swimmer himself decades earlier.

When he'd completed his workout regimen, Bakk pulled himself up on the edge of the pool. An attendant appeared seemingly from nowhere, bringing a towel and a robe. Bakk dried himself, then led Bourne through another doorway to an outside porch that overlooked the lake. The cold didn't seem to bother him. A large wooden table had been set with breakfast, including pastries, scrambled eggs, sausage, and two fresh mimosas. The two men sat down, and Bakk devoured his meal with his usual frenetic energy.

"Why not eat something, Jason?" he asked.

"Why not tell me what's going on?" Bourne replied. "Talk to me about Bai Ze. And about eight years ago."

Bakk said nothing for a while as he speared his eggs with a fork. When he was done, the attendant returned almost immediately to clear the table. Bakk waited, sipping his mimosa and staring at the azure blue of the lake. The ribbed dark clouds moved quickly across the sky from west to east.

"Eight years ago, I launched a hiring fair for my businesses," Bakk said finally. "I was diversifying. I'd already started and sold several companies. GPS, payment processing, internet nuts and bolts, that kind of thing. So I had several billion dollars to play with. But that was just the down payment to make my real dreams possible. I think big, Jason. I always have. My vision is to lay the groundwork for the next millennium of human experience. That involves revolutionary thinking in a wide variety of intersecting fields—space, medicine, communications, transportation, energy, the building blocks for where we go next as a species. I had vast start-up capital to launch these projects, but I needed the *human* capital, too. The right people. Do you believe in the Great Man theory of history? Because I do. Individuals make a difference. History doesn't always move forward or upward; it moves in sync with the quality of its leaders. You've heard it said that I try to build a team of giants at my companies, right? Well, I do. And eight years ago, I was on a mission to find those giants for the next wave of my vision. Not just smart people. Leaders. Achievers. Doers."

"Why keep it all so secret?" Bourne asked.

"As you said, I *like* my secrets," Bakk replied. "The reality is, I have to work hard to keep them. When you do what I do, you deal with spies all the time. Not just government spies like you—although

I encounter plenty of those. But corporate spies, foreign spies, everyone trying to see where I'm going and make money off my ideas or get there ahead of me. Plus, I needed to preserve the anonymity of my candidates. Many had top secret clearances, many others were from overseas. Some could have been jailed simply for talking to me about their research. I confess, I wasn't just looking for employees. I also needed a fleet of my own spies—well-paid insiders at other organizations prepared to deliver advance notice of useful intelligence and scientific breakthroughs that would provide a kind of synergy with my operations."

"In other words, stealing *their* secrets," Bourne said.

"If you like. That's how the game is played. People try to steal from me, I try to steal from them. But in my case, it's not simply to beat them to the patent office. More often than not, I'm looking for advance word on companies I should buy to enhance my existing businesses. Unethical? Perhaps. But no one ever lost money dealing with me. When I buy a company, I always pay a premium to keep the founders happy. Anyway, my point is, that was the event taking place in Door County eight years ago. I brought in dozens of superstars to vet for their roles in my empire."

"And Bai Ze found out."

"So it seems," Bakk said. "It appears that Bai Ze and the CCP infiltrated the operation from the beginning. They knew who I was talking to, what I wanted, who I hired. More than that, I'm convinced that they either tricked me into hiring people who have proved to be moles—Chinese double agents—or they've begun to use their influence to turn key members of my teams against me. In the long run, they want me *out.* They want to be in a position to take over my businesses and then use them to achieve their own nationalist goals."

"Didn't you have security for the event back then?" Bourne asked.

"Of course. Very competent security. But in Bai Ze, we're dealing with a brilliant adversary with advanced techniques of his own. As I'm sure you now realize."

"Memory manipulation."

"Among other things, yes."

"Did you consult with American intelligence? Did the U.S. government know what you were doing?"

Bakk scoffed. "I don't trust government intelligence. The NSA, FBI, CIA, and, of course, your own Treadstone. Sorry, you're all compromised, all riddled with spies, leakers, fools, and bureaucrats. My ex-wife was CIA. Did you know that?"

"I did."

"Mei Sun. I'm pretty sure our entire marriage was nothing but a spy operation concocted by Holly Schultz. A costly mistake on my part, but Sun is beautiful, and the sex was amazing. So I can't complain too much. Thanks to her, I learned that lesson about trusting no one, not even someone who shares your bed. Maybe especially not them. It was less than a year after the hiring fair that we divorced."

"Did your wife know what you were doing back then? About the operation in Door County?"

"Of course."

"Do you think she leaked it back to Holly?"

"Possibly. I was already having her followed—I did that as

soon as we got married—but Sun is one of the few people I've met who is as smart as me. She revealed nothing. My surveillance never showed me anything to prove my suspicions. But that doesn't mean I was wrong about her."

Bourne gave in and took a sip of the mimosa in front of him. Bakk was right. The orange juice made all the difference. "You said you're convinced that Bai Ze has infiltrated your operations. Why are you so sure?"

"Because things have been going wrong," Bakk snapped. "In the last two years, we've been having setbacks—all of them designed to tarnish my public image, diminish the value of my companies, leave me vulnerable to outside pressures. A crewed rocket launch exploded. A catastrophic failure disrupted our fusion research. A series of unexpected side effects in clinical trials set back our breakthrough diabetes treatments."

"Those could be coincidences."

"No, no, that's just the tip of the iceberg, the high-profile incidents that make headlines. There have been many others. This has all the earmarks of a coordinated operation—someone attacking me on multiple fronts. The Chinese and Bai Ze are targeting me the same way they're targeting U.S. infrastructure, politicians, media, utilities, the cohesion of our culture, everything they need to destabilize our society. I'm a line item on Bai Ze's list."

Bourne eased back in the chair. He felt a gust of the cold wind off the lake. Bakk, in his robe, didn't shiver. "You said you think you know who Bai Ze is."

"That's right."

"Who? And why do you suspect him?"

Bakk pushed another button on his omniscient remote. The

wooden beams in the middle of the table where they were sitting separated, and another computer monitor rose into place. On the screen was a photograph of a man about Bakk's age, with untamed brown hair and black glasses. His eyes stared at the camera, but blankly, as if they didn't even see it. His skin was pale, his nose bumpy and long. Across his neck, Bourne saw a small green tattoo that looked like a human brain.

"Meet Simon Harris," Bakk said. "Doesn't look like much of a spy, does he? But looks are deceiving. Simon is brilliant. He's a behavioral psychiatrist. Once upon a time, he was also my best friend. My only friend, really. We grew up together on Washington Island. I took the entrepreneurial road, Simon did the university thing. He has three doctorates, plus his MD. Eight years ago, he was working for DARPA."

Bourne frowned. "Specializing in memory?"

"Among other things. Simon's like me. We feel a compulsion to be good at everything. Which would make him perfect for the Chinese."

"How did he know about your hiring fair?" Bourne asked.

"Because he was an integral part of it. I invited him. I trusted him—again, one of those mistakes that leave you feeling foolish. But given our history, our friendship, I felt safe making him a part of my evaluation team. He led the most important part of the process—personality assessments. You see, success is about much more than pure knowledge or experience. It's about values, ego, self-assurance, empathy, a hundred different traits in just the right combination. I brought in Simon to assess all of my candidates. He had access to everything, their records, their backgrounds. He interviewed them, tested them. Unfortunately, it put him in a unique position to steer certain candidates our way or veto others. In other words, he could open a path for people who could be compromised. I believe that's what he did. As a result, I'm convinced I have saboteurs working throughout my companies. Simon betrayed me."

"You think he's Bai Ze?"

"Either he is, or he's one of the top people in the network, which means he can blow the whistle on the others."

"Have you talked to him?" Bourne asked. "Confronted him?"

Bakk shook his head. "That's the problem. That's why I'm so sure Simon is our man. He disappeared four years ago, right around the time things began to go wrong. The first crisis—the rocket explosion that killed the four astronauts. He knew I'd suspect him, so he vanished and went off the grid."

"Or the Chinese killed him," Bourne suggested. "Eliminate any trail."

"No. Simon's alive. Six months ago, my facial recognition algorithm caught this image on one of my webcams." Bakk pushed a button, pairing the photograph of Simon Harris with a blurry photograph on the screen of a bald man wearing a red leather jacket, its collar turned up. He was on a city street, getting out of a cab, his face in profile.

"I wouldn't pick him out as the same man," Bourne said.

"Neither would I, but my computer says it's Simon. I may not trust people, but I trust my software. It's him. After this came up, I sent a team in to find him. They blanketed the area, but came up empty. No clues, no evidence of what he was doing there or what identity he might be using. But I think you're likely to succeed in finding him where my team failed. You've got the killer instinct. Plus, we both want Bai Ze. Simon is the way in."

Bourne stared at the two photographs. He listened to his mind, hunting for any instinct that he knew this man, that he'd seen him before. Eight years ago, had he stared through a window at a Door County inn and seen Simon Harris talking strategy with a group of Chinese spies? Is that what had been stripped away from his memory before he wound up back at the Mandarin Oriental in Miami?

But nothing came. The more he tried to push his brain to reveal its secrets, the more he felt the knife behind his eyes, burning him with red-hot heat. He squeezed his fists together, fighting through the pain until it finally subsided.

If Simon Harris was part of his memories, he was well hidden. Even so, this was a clue he didn't have before. He had to follow it.

Bourne shifted his stare to Bakk. "All right. If Simon's alive, I'll find him. Where was this picture taken?"

Bakk smiled. He was used to winning. "Kansas City."

15

THE SNOW IN WISCONSIN BECAME RAIN IN MISSOURI.

On the rental car shuttle, a heavy downpour sheeted across the windows, making it impossible to see the green Kansas City landscape outside. Bourne sat in the last row, where he could keep an eye on the airport passengers crowding the bus. His gut told him he was already being followed. Maybe that was paranoia after meeting with Alvin Bakk and learning about the breadth of his surveillance network, but he didn't think so.

Someone was on his tail. They'd picked him up when he changed planes in Chicago, and they'd been with him ever since.

Who?

Was it Bakk's men? Bourne would have been surprised if Bakk didn't feel the need to keep a close watch on his newest asset. Or maybe it was Treadstone. Shadow was equally possessive and liked to keep Bourne in her sights.

Or maybe it was Bai Ze.

Bourne examined the faces around him. The business travelers looking bored. The couples coming back from vacation, tired and hung over, leaning on each other's shoulders. The parents trying to keep their strung-out Disney kids in check for another few minutes before they got home. Normally spies were obvious to him in a crowd. Alone, always alone. No eye contact, no matter how long Bourne stared at them. Ordinary people felt it and looked back. Spies felt it and pretended they didn't.

But no one on the shuttle fit the pattern.

Paranoia!

He was beginning to doubt himself. Question his senses. Second-guess his instincts. A strange sense of dislocation filled his mind, and stress tightened his chest. His heartbeat thumped with the pounding of the rain. The last few days had dealt a blow to everything he thought he knew about himself, and that wasn't much to begin with. His memory had been tampered with *before* that violent night on the sea. Even the parts of his past he thought he could rely on now seemed suspect. And the people who'd given him any kind of grounding were dead or out of his life.

Geoffrey Washburn. Nash Rollins. Nova. Johanna. Murdered and gone.

Abbey Laurent. Back in her own world, where she belonged.

Even Shadow, who'd somehow become his lifeline as he put his mind back together, had turned cold.

Bourne shook himself. He needed to focus. *Watch, observe, analyze.* Someone on this bus was a traitor. *Who?*

Then he saw her.

A young woman was seated near the rear door, mid-twenties, cow ring through her nose, earbuds, lavender hair. She was dressed like a Ragstock refugee to draw attention to herself, which was a way of *not* drawing attention from Bourne. As he watched her, she noticed him and stared back, not hiding from his gaze. She scratched her cheek with her middle finger, sending him a crystal clear message. *Fuck off.*

A spy wouldn't do that, wouldn't break cover. But a spy pretending *not* to be a spy would. So which was it? Jesus! The layers within layers of deception suddenly weighed on him, until he no longer knew what was real and what was not.

When the bus reached the underground access to the rental car center, Bourne waited as the passengers unloaded. He grabbed his backpack after the shuttle was empty and headed for the nearest rental car counter. Amid the crowd, he noticed that the woman had vanished. He didn't see her anywhere. Somehow he'd allowed her to slip away, and again he felt frustrated with himself.

Uneasy. Out of sync.

Trust no one.

Treadstone. But also Alvin Bakk.

A few minutes later, he drove a black Toyota RAV4 into the Kansas City rain. His windshield wipers beat fast against the storm. The suburban area north of the metro looked remote, nothing but a few hotels and corporate buildings set among green fields. He took I-29 on the east side of the airport and drove south for a long time before he caught up with the urban development. His eyes kept watch on the mirrors, but it was early evening, already dark, and all the gauzy headlights behind him looked alike through the rain-streaked window.

As he crossed the towering suspension bridge above the Missouri River, Bourne cut across three lanes of traffic and took the exit onto Front Street. He watched for another car veering to follow, but none did. He stayed on the parkway along the river, passing through an industrial area, until the skyscraper lights of downtown came into view. In the maze of city streets, he made multiple turns, left, right, left. Several times, he pulled to the curb and stopped, letting other traffic pass by him. Twice he made illegal U-turns.

After half an hour of evasive maneuvers, he was convinced he wasn't being followed. Or if anyone had picked him up near the airport, he'd lost them.

Bourne changed direction and left downtown for his real destination.

The photograph of Simon Harris—if it really was Simon Harris, looking nothing like he had years earlier—had been captured in the background of an Instagram post taken in a downscale section of the city, outside a beauty supply store on Troost Avenue. That was where Alvin Bakk's video search engine had matched his face. But Bakk had sent half a dozen men to scour the area, showing Harris's photo up and down the street. No one knew him; no one remembered him. They'd tracked down the woman with the Instagram account, who'd taken a selfie in her new wig from the beauty store, but she hadn't even noticed the man in the red leather jacket on the street behind her.

Whatever Harris was doing there, he'd come and gone without leaving a trace.

Bourne parked the RAV on a deserted side street opposite the beauty store. He got out into the cold rain that sleeted across his face. Streetlights lit up the darkness, but no one else was around. With his phone, he compared the Instagram photo to the real-life neighborhood, noting Harris's position. Based on the angle in the picture, the man seemed to be heading south on Troost on foot.

Going where?

Bourne followed the street. He wiped rain from his eyes, passing auto repair shops, plumbing stores, gas stations, an African market, and a Chinese take-out restaurant. He assumed Bakk's men had checked out all of those places, but interviews were a crapshoot when you were looking for someone. If someone actually saw Simon Harris—and remembered him, one man in a red leather jacket on the street—they were a needle in a haystack.

Instead, he tried to put himself inside Harris's mind, to think like his target thought. Harris knew Alvin Bakk was looking for him. He knew the reach of Bakk's technology, so he'd be very careful. Obviously he *was* careful, staying clear of online photos and webcams for years. He was also brilliant, formerly of DARPA, the kind of man who was more than capable of building an entirely new life for himself on the run. New name, new documents, new past, new face.

But what would he be doing *here?*

What drew him out of hiding?

If he was Bai Ze, or connected to Bai Ze, what would a top Chinese spy want in this neighborhood?

His phone rang. It was Shadow. He left the street and found shelter under an overhang at a nearby strip mall and grabbed his phone from his pocket. He heard her voice, sharp and demanding. This was Shadow, not Marlen, not the woman he'd slept with. But regardless, something about her voice always had a physical effect on him.

"Are you in Kansas City?" she asked.

"Yes, I'm in the area where Harris was spotted. Assuming it really was him."

"Do you see anything?"

"Not so far. But I'm pretty sure I was followed at the airport. Was that you? Did you send someone to watch me?"

"You work best alone, Jason. You've been very clear about that."

"Well, if Bakk is right, if Harris is part of the Chinese network and he operates out of Kansas City, then he might have people watching the airport."

"Maybe so, but you can't trust anything Bakk says. He's playing his own game."

"I know that, but for now, we want the same thing. What did you find out about Harris?"

"I tried running him through the Files," Shadow said. "I used both of the photos, plus the location in Kansas City. I got nothing, which is unusual. But the Chinese developed the software for the Files, so Harris might know exactly how it works. He could structure his life to make sure he stays off its radar."

"What about Harris's personal life? What did he walk away from?"

"Divorced several years ago. No kids. Parents died when he was in his early twenties. He didn't have much to leave behind."

"Any siblings?"

"One brother. Eight years younger. Josh."

Bourne did the math in his head. "If their parents died when Simon was in his early twenties, Josh would have been a teenager. What happened to him?"

He heard Shadow's fingers tapping on the keys of her computer.

"Josh lived with Simon for several years in an apartment in Virginia. Simon was just out of school and already working for

DARPA. He looked after his little brother. Josh went into the Marines right out of high school. He did a tour in Afghanistan, got seriously messed up. When he came back, he was hooked on drugs. Looks like he was in and out of VA hospitals for several years. He was living in Denver at that point."

"Where is he now?"

"There's no current record on him. I don't think Simon knew where he was, either. He sent letters to the VA trying to find him. His brother's mail started coming back undeliverable. Phone number out of service. It reads to me like Josh dropped out of the world about six years ago."

"So Josh fell off the grid before Simon did his own disappearing act," Bourne said.

"Right."

"Are there any ties between Josh Harris and Kansas City?"

"Not that I can see in his records."

Bourne frowned. "Listen, send me a picture of Josh, okay?"

"I will."

He hung up the phone. Seconds later, he heard the ding of an incoming text and saw a picture of a teenage Josh Harris, in uniform, dark hair buzz cut. His young face had a Marine's toughness, square jaw, grim expression, ready to take on the world. Except Josh didn't have a clue what the world had in store for him.

Rain poured off the strip mall roof like a waterfall. Bourne stared through the empty parking lot at the Kansas City street, taking his mind backward. Simon Harris had been walking along that street six months earlier, coming out of seclusion for the first time in years. That was a big risk. Why put himself in jeopardy like that? What kind of emergency would lure him into the open?

But Bourne knew the answer in his gut. Simon had found his missing baby brother.

He returned to the street, walking southward through the rain, following in Simon's footsteps. There were no sidewalks here, so he used the gravel shoulder. He was soaked and cold, but he felt a surge of adrenaline, a sense that he was finally on the right track. One more block passed. Then two. Ahead of him, he saw an overgrown field, surrounding the ruins of what had once been an apartment complex. All that remained was the long concrete frame that marked the building's parking structure, its gray stone painted over with graffiti. A high fence surrounded the ruins, but the fence had been pushed over, its mesh cut away in multiple places, leaving easy access.

It was the kind of place where the addicted and the homeless would gather. Where drugs would be sold and used. Where lives would wither away.

Where a vet in the grip of mental illness might take refuge.

Bourne found a gap in the fence and pushed into the weeds. With his penlight, he lit up the dirt, seeing trash, syringes, and empty pill bottles. He listened, and above the rain, he heard music from the ruins. People were inside. As he neared one of the square gaps in the wall where cars used to come and go, he smelled the pungent sweetness of marijuana. He went inside, escaping the rain, moving his Glock from his holster to his jacket pocket. From his wallet, he grabbed cash.

In the darkness, he heard dozens of low voices. Down the long stone wall, a couple of fires burned. In addition to the marijuana, he now smelled bacon, burnt toast, urine, and feces. His flashlight revealed a city of tents, shopping carts, blankets, dogs, broken glass, and broken men. Their eyes squinted into the light as Bourne passed them. Most had a glazed look, beyond communication, but when he found an old man who seemed conscious and sober, Bourne stopped. He approached slowly, hands up to show no threat. The man had a sleeping black Lab beside him and a shotgun within easy reach.

"What do you want?" the man demanded, his voice burned to a raspy whisper. "You another one from the church?"

"No. Not me."

"Yeah, I figured. Most of the church types think they're gonna save my soul. You don't look like the type who cares about souls."

Bourne knelt in front of him, putting a twenty-dollar bill on the ground. "I'm looking for somebody. Maybe you've seen him."

The old man snatched up the cash. "Yeah? Who you looking for?"

Bourne took out his phone and opened up the blurry photograph of Simon Harris. "You remember this man coming around here? He might wear a red leather jacket."

"Nope. Haven't seen him."

"How about this guy?" Bourne switched to the young Marine photo of Josh Harris. "He'd be older now, in his thirties, probably heading downhill. Name's Josh."

The man's eyes narrowed. "Hard to say. Maybe. People in here don't look like themselves, know what I mean?"

Bourne nodded. "Any other vets in here?"

"A few."

"Marines?"

"Yeah, some. You think the jarheads stick together?"

"That's what I'm thinking."

The old man gestured toward the far end of the building. "Try a guy called Nickel. His pitch is that way. When he's sober, he works, makes a little money, gives most of it away. The brothers around here look up to him. If anybody knows your Marine, it'll be Nickel."

"Thanks."

Bourne petted the man's dog, which woke up long enough to wag its tail. He gave the man another twenty, then continued down the long, dark corridor of the stone building. His boots crunched on glass and jagged pieces of mortar. He swung his penlight left and right, lighting up the homeless on both sides. Open doors and empty window frames let in the rain, which shone on the floor in dark puddles.

Behind him, near where he'd entered the building, he heard the scrape of footsteps coming from outside. Instantly, he spun, shooting a cone of light in that direction, but the beam didn't go far enough to illuminate anyone near him. He switched it off, not wanting to make himself a target. He shifted sideways, then stopped where he was, listening, but he heard nothing more. His eyes adjusted. He thought he could see a couple of shadows standing like faraway statues in the corridor, but when he blinked, they seemed to disappear.

He kept walking.

Every now and then, he stopped to ask about Nickel's location, and everyone pointed him onward, all the way to the building's west wall. There, in the corner, safe from the rain, he saw a lean-to built of blond wood, painted in wild colors like a tie-dyed T-shirt. Blankets were piled into a kind of wall from one side of the pitch to the other. Several feet of debris—marbles, bells, fragments of bubble wrap—protected the lean-to like a moat, alerting the owner if anyone came close.

Bourne kept his flashlight off. He couldn't see inside the deep pitch, but he smelled cigarette smoke. Nickel was awake. The next noise Bourne heard was the slow, unmistakable racking of a slide, loading a cartridge into a semiautomatic pistol.

Then a voice rumbled from the darkness. "You want something, man?"

"Are you Nickel?"

There was no answer.

"I'm looking for a Marine," Bourne went on.

"Your Marine got a name?"

"Josh. Josh Harris."

Nickel was silent again, and a cloud of smoke wafted from the lean-to. "What do you want with Josh?"

"Actually, I'm looking for his brother."

"To kill him?"

Bourne squatted and stared into the pitch, but he still saw nothing. The only signs of life were the voice and the smoke—and the gun, which he was sure was pointed outward at the middle of his chest. "Why would you think that?"

"Because that's what the last guys were here to do. A month ago. Three bad mothers. They grabbed Josh in the field and kept asking him, *Where's Simon?* But Josh is a Marine. He didn't talk. He didn't give them fuck all. So they slit his throat."

16

BOURNE MADE HIS WAY INTO NICKEL'S LEAN-TO, WHICH SMELLED OF whiskey and cigarettes. He heard the snap of a glow stick, which lit up the pitch with a dim green light. Nickel's face was painted with camouflage, and he held a Ruger an inch from Bourne's forehead. The Marine's finger was on the trigger.

"I'm not looking for trouble," Bourne said.

"You look like a dude who finds trouble whether you're looking for it or not."

Bourne shrugged. "I can't argue with that."

"So tell me what you want with Simon Harris. And why my best friend got killed because of him."

Bourne eased himself to the ground and leaned against the far wall of the lean-to on a floor covered with multicolored Mexican blankets. Nickel did the same on the opposite wall. In the green glow, Bourne could see that Nickel was in his thirties, still with the fitness of a soldier. He wore a dirty baseball cap with the number *1887* stitched in blue on the canvas. His bangs were chocolate brown and greasy below the brim of the cap, his smeared face ready for jungle warfare. Every few seconds, one of his eyes twitched, as if someone had poked him with an electric shock. He had a half-full bottle of Jack on the floor, and he took a swallow, with the Ruger still rock-solid at the end of his other arm.

"Talk," Nickel said.

"You don't need the gun."

"I'll decide that. See, I've been expecting someone like you to show up. They came for Josh, so I figure sooner or later they'd come for me, too. I've tried to stay off the booze as much as I can. Keeping my head clear so I was ready. And sure enough, here you are. Now, why are you trying to find Simon Harris?"

Bourne glanced out of the lean-to into the darkness of the ruins. He still had the sense that someone was close by. Watching. Listening. "Honestly, I thought Simon might be a dangerous man, but now I don't know. If people are trying to kill him—if they were willing to kill Josh to get to him—then maybe he's something else. Either way, I think he's got information that will help me."

"What kind of information?"

"I'm not going to tell you that."

Nickel chuckled. "All right. TS/SCI. That's fair."

"Do you know where Simon is?"

"No."

"Did Josh?"

"I don't think so. I don't think Simon ever told him where he was hanging. He probably thought that was for Josh's protection, but it didn't work out that way. Josh told the guys who were torturing him that he hadn't seen Simon in years, but they knew he was lying. Didn't matter. That was his story, and he stuck to it."

"But Simon was here, right?" Bourne said. "I have a picture of him on the street six months ago."

"Yeah. He came to visit his brother a few times."

"Does he know Josh is dead?"

"He knows. He came back the last time, and I told him. He asked if I could arrange for a proper burial, but the bastards who killed Josh took his body, too. Dumped it in their truck and drove off. They probably wanted to see if Josh had anything on him that would point to his brother. I imagine he's at the bottom of the river now."

Bourne shook his head. "Tell me the story, okay? Josh. Simon. I need whatever you know about them, how you found them, how they got together. Even if you don't know where Simon is, you may know *something* to help me find him. And believe me, if the people who killed Josh get to him first, he'll be dead."

Nickel finally let the Ruger go limp in his hand. He laid it on the ground next to him. "Josh and I served together in Asscrackistan. Good kid. Tough. Loyal. But he made some bad choices over there, went down the rabbit hole and never climbed out. Believe me, I know the drill. I go down that hole sometimes, too, but once it gets bad enough, I dry out for a while. Last time I did, I stayed at the VCP. They're good people."

"VCP?"

"It's a community project for veterans. Not far away. Little houses for vets who need help, everything paid for. It's a way to get back on your feet, you know? Helps you transition into real life again. Let me tell you, we need places like that in every fucking city, brother. I swore off the booze, got a tiny house there, was hoping I'd fixed myself for good. Once I was thinking clearly, I got to remembering some of the buddies who went off the rails. Like Josh. Especially Josh. We were tight. I wanted to see if I could help him out."

"What did you do?" Bourne asked.

"Some of the VCP guys helped me dig into the VA records. I heard Josh might be in Denver. So I went out there, started looking for him. I was there for days, going to shelters, going to shitholes like this, trying to find him. Weird thing is, I wasn't the first. Everywhere I went, I heard his brother had been doing the same thing. No luck. I crossed paths with him one time. Simon was nothing like his brother, more like a genius nerd, you know? Didn't tell me anything, didn't tell me where he lived. But dude loved his brother, I'll give him that. He gave me a PO box in Billings, said someone went and checked it for him every week. He said if I ever found Josh, I should write to him. He'd make sure Josh got help."

"And you found Josh?"

Nickel nodded. "A few months later, yeah. I heard from a buddy in Philly. We all served together. He said Josh showed up at his door, almost dead from drugs. Wouldn't go to a hospital, kept ranting that people were looking for him, trying to kill him. Sounded nuts. Of course, turns out he wasn't just seeing monsters in the closet, you know? My buddy let him crash there for a couple of days, but his wife said Josh had to go. Can't blame her, an addict in the house with two little kids. So I went out to Philly and brought him back. He stayed with me in the VCP for a while, but that wasn't a good scene. He was still using. Bad for me, bad for the others. I tried to get him help, but Josh ran away. He ended up here. It didn't take me long to find him, and when I did, I wrote to Simon."

"When was this?" Bourne asked.

"Eight, nine months ago."

"Simon showed up?"

"Eventually. I got the impression he'd been watching us for a while. I get it now. He was making sure it wasn't a trap. And he was right to be suspicious. Not long after Simon showed up, a bunch of guys started asking around about him, showing his picture. Fortunately, nobody but me knew him, and they didn't know anything about Josh. Next time Simon showed up, I warned him. After that, he didn't come back to this place, but I'd meet him sometimes, get money for Josh. But Josh was pretty much beyond help by then. There wasn't anything anybody could do."

Bourne held up his hand, stopping Nickel's story. They both listened in the silence, although the ruins were never completely quiet. The sounds of life were always close by. Bourne shined the penlight out of the pitch, but he didn't see anyone watching them. Even so, he removed his Glock from his pocket and kept it in his hand.

"What happened a month ago?" he asked.

"I told you. Three bad mothers came looking for Josh. I wasn't here, but someone called me, and I came as fast as I could. Too late. Josh was already gone. Some of the other boys told me what happened."

"How did the killers find him?"

"Ah, shit, I don't know. Somebody talked to the wrong person, I guess. It happens. Hell, for all I know it was me. I was trying to help Josh, but maybe I opened my mouth too many times and word got spread. Anyway, I've been hiding out since then, staying away from the VCP, hanging out here. Bad place for me. The temptation's always here, and sometimes I figure, what the hell, have a drink. But I don't want to put any of the other vets in danger if the shitholes come back."

"Did anyone recognize them? Were these the same ones asking around about Simon a few months ago?"

Nickel shook his head. "No. These dudes were Asian."

Asian.

Bourne knew who'd sent them. *Bai Ze.*

Which meant that Simon Harris *wasn't* Bai Ze. But regardless, Harris knew something that put the Chinese spy at risk.

"Does Simon live close by?" Bourne asked. "Is he in Kansas City?"

"I assume so. Or he was. He may not be here anymore after what happened to Josh. If I were him, I'd clear out of the city, get lost somewhere else. But I don't know where he is. He never told me, and I didn't want to know."

"Nickel, I need to find him. Fast. Is there anything else you remember? Anything he said? Did you see what he was driving when you met him, or where he came from? I need some kind of clue to figure out where he's living, or what identity he's using."

Nickel took off the grimy baseball cap he was wearing and tossed it to Bourne. "That's all I got."

"The hat? Was it Simon's?"

"Sort of. One of the last times I met Simon, he brought a box of clothes for Josh. Goodwill stuff, nothing fancy. This hat was at the bottom of the box. I'm betting Simon didn't realize it, because the next time he came, Josh was wearing the hat and Simon freaked. Ripped it off his head and took it away. I didn't think much about it, except the next day, one of the other dudes around here was wearing the hat. Said he found it in a trash can a few blocks away.

I took it, figured I'd give it back to Simon. But I forgot about it after Josh was killed. Found it in a drawer at the VCP a few days ago when I went back to take a shower. I didn't think anybody would care about it now, and I was sure Simon was never coming back here."

Bourne studied the number stitched on the front of the cap. "It says *1887*. What does that mean?"

"No idea, man. History ain't my thing. But like I said, Simon didn't want Josh to have it. Maybe that means something."

"All right. Thanks, Nickel. Get yourself back to—"

Bourne stopped.

This time, he heard an unmistakable noise outside the lean-to. A marble, rolling, kicked by a shoe in the darkness. Nickel heard it, too. He shoved the glow stick under a blanket, restoring blackness to the pitch just as a series of low spits filled the space, bullets rapping against wood and stone. Bourne threw himself forward, arms extended, Glock in his hands. Nickel did the same, but his reactions were slow, and Bourne heard the man exhale with a grimace. He'd been hit.

The shots continued, bouncing crazily around the lean-to. Two directions, not one. Two shooters. Bourne targeted the tiny orange flash from one of the barrels and squeezed off a tight circle of shots with the Glock. He heard a cry of pain, a woman's voice, involuntary, high-pitched. Outside the lean-to, a gun clattered to the ground. Then something heavier followed. A body.

After that, he heard footsteps. The second shooter was running. Escaping.

Bourne bolted from Nickel's pitch. He slipped on the debris of the moat, his boots colliding with the body at his feet and knocking him to his knees. He heard the footsteps getting farther away down the corridor, and he couldn't risk any more shots. Whoever it was, was already gone. Shouts of panic and fear filled the ruins, and others fled, too, disappearing into the night. It was chaos.

Nickel appeared beside him. Bourne turned his penlight on the man and saw him clenching his sleeve, a bullet wound in his arm.

"How bad is it?" Bourne asked.

"Mosquito bite. I'll live. I've seen a lot worse than this. But you better go. The cops mostly ignore us, but gunfire's different. They'll check this one out. I gotta disappear, too. Don't worry, no one will rat me out around here."

Bourne dug in his pocket for a wad of cash and shoved it all into Nickel's hand. "Get yourself back to the VCP. Get your life together."

"That's the plan. Thanks, brother."

Before he left, Bourne turned the flashlight down to the body at his feet. He saw a woman in her twenties, her dead eyes open and angry. She had purple hair and a cow ring through her pierced septum.

It was the woman from the rental car shuttle.

17

1887.

Half an hour of searches on his laptop brought Bourne no closer to figuring out the significance of the year stitched onto the baseball cap. And yet it had meant enough to Simon Harris that he didn't want anyone finding it. Someone—probably Simon—had also ripped out the tags, so there was no clue where it had been made or sold.

At one in the morning, Bourne finally gave up for the night. He located a cheap motel near the Speedway and slept hard.

The next morning, he found an alehouse for an early lunch. He ordered a beer and a burger, then opened his laptop and searched again. He had no more luck than the night before. None of the newsworthy events in Kansas City in 1887—construction of the 8th Street Tunnel, the opening of the New England Building downtown, the first of twenty-five Priests of Pallas parades—seemed to have any relevance to a DARPA scientist almost a century and a half later. So what did it mean?

He knew he could turn to Shadow for help—she could run it through the Files—or to Alvin Bakk, who had a team of tech geniuses around him to paw through the web. Either one could probably determine the provenance of the hat in a few minutes. But at least for now, Bourne didn't want to involve them. If Bai Ze had infiltrated Treadstone, and if he'd done the same with Bakk's various companies, then the wrong word to the wrong person might expose Simon's location.

Plus, the second killer at the homeless camp was still out there.

Then, as he drank his beer, Bourne got lucky.

The waiter brought his burger and put down the plate next to Bourne's laptop. The thirtysomething man's eyes drifted to the baseball cap lying on the counter, and he said pleasantly, "Great whiskey, huh?"

Bourne's head cocked in confusion. "What?"

"The hat. That's a Rieger's hat, right?"

"Rieger's? What's that?"

"It's a distillery down near the river. My roommate had his bachelor party there. Cool drinks, smooth whiskey, kind of a speakeasy vibe."

"And this is their hat?" Bourne asked.

"Yeah, I think so. I remember it, because one of the groomsmen bought the same hat there. I think the 1887 thing is when the distillery was founded, but for him, it also happened to be his birthday. You know, January 8, 1987."

"Good to know," Bourne said.

"Sure. You should check the place out while you're in town. Anyway, enjoy the burger. You need anything, just flag me down."

"Thanks."

Bourne took a bite of his burger, then went back to the laptop.

He quickly found the website for J. Rieger & Co., a Kansas City distillery originally founded in 1887 and then reopened in 2014 by a descendant of the original founder. The website included an online shop for distillery merchandise, and the first item he found was the same cap he was holding in his hand.

1887.

That was the connection Simon Harris had been desperate to hide. The hat tied Simon to the distillery. Hopefully, that meant someone at the distillery would know who Simon was and where he was hiding.

THAT EVENING, BOURNE PARKED HIS RAV IN THE LOT ACROSS FROM THE three-story redbrick building that housed the distillery. It was night again, and he wanted the darkness. He got out of the SUV and examined the industrial area around him. Railroad tracks ran adjacent to the lot, running parallel with the Missouri River a few blocks away. An elevated trafficway crossed over the tracks and loomed immediately behind the building. It was cold and damp, the air still. He followed the train tracks toward the rear of the distillery, his boots crunching on stone. Near the overpass, he found a low fence that bordered an outdoor patio that was closed for the season. Behind the patio, bright lights glowed on the second floor of the brick building. But he saw no one outside.

He retraced his steps and used the main entrance. Inside, the building came to life with music and noise. It was a large, wide-open factory space with high glass windows, blond-brick walls, and fat pipes crossing the ceiling overhead. Small groups of people, mostly in their thirties and forties, hung out in leather chairs placed strategically around the room. A counter shop sold bottles of whiskey and gin, and behind it, he could see the huge copper tanks and gleaming aluminum of the distillery itself. The yeasty smell in the air was a reminder of the fermentation taking place.

Near him, someone screamed happily. He saw a young woman in a pink dress spill off a metal slide that wound from the floor above him. She giggled as she tried to stand and then fell into Bourne with an apology. He held her up by the elbow. A few seconds later, one of her friends whooped as she exited the slide, too, and the two women laughed as they staggered back to the steps that led upstairs.

Bourne followed.

On the second floor, he found himself in a lounge with a long bar that overlooked the distillery equipment through tall windows. Most of the high-top tables were full, and the hardwood floor shined under the overhead lights. He took an empty chair near the end of the bar and waited for the bartender to get free. She was small, in her twenties, with shoulder-length reddish hair hugging her face and a spray-on tan that made her skin unnaturally dark. She wore an untucked men's dress shirt with a loose paisley tie, over a knee-length black skirt. Her name tag read *Jazzi*.

"What can I get you?"

"What do you suggest?" Bourne asked.

"You look like a whiskey man. Are you a whiskey man?"

"Sometimes. I hear yours is great."

"It is," Jazzi told him. "Try the Monogram. That's my favorite.

We age it in sherry barrels, so you get a little bit of sherry taste on the tongue."

"Sold."

She brought out a shot glass and poured from the bottle, and he downed it in one swallow. Her face crinkled into a smile as she watched his face.

"Was I right?" she asked.

"Definitely. Smoky and sweet. I like it."

"Want another?"

"In a little bit. First I'd like your help."

"What do you need?"

"I'm trying to find someone. Either he works here, or he comes in here a lot." He put his phone on the bar, with the Instagram photo enlarged to show the blurry face of Simon Harris. "This is him. Does he look familiar?"

Jazzi tried to keep a poker face, but she failed. He watched her brown eyes get bigger and her neck jerk with a tiny double take. She knew him, and she was trying to cover her reaction. "No, sorry, I've never seen him before. Why are you trying to find him?"

"Friend of a friend," Bourne replied. "You sure you don't know him?"

"Nope, I don't."

"Okay, thanks. I'll keep asking around. Maybe someone else here knows him."

"Yeah, sure, go ahead, but I don't think you'll have much luck. If I don't know him, nobody else around here does."

"You're probably right. Look, how about you pour me another shot?"

"You got it."

She filled his glass again and gave him a broken smile. He put a hundred-dollar bill in her palm, and he noticed that she didn't even look at it before she shoved it in her pocket. Her face grew strained; her hands were trembling. She was scared. She retreated to the far end of the long bar, but she kept looking back at him, and he made a point of not meeting her eyes. A few seconds later, he saw her call over one of the other servers to take the bar, and then she disappeared down a corridor toward the other side of the building.

Bourne finished his drink with another swallow and set off after her. The corridor overlooked the production floor, and he saw Jazzi rushing that way down a winding metal staircase. When she was downstairs and out of view, he used the door that led to the staircase and wound his way to the main floor of the distillery. The sweet smell of the fermentation was intense here, and he heard the hum of machinery, but no voices. The bartender had already disappeared.

His hands in his jacket pockets, right hand around the barrel of the Glock, he walked slowly beside the giant stills and fermentation tanks. Ahead of him, beyond the equipment, he saw a warehouse with thousands of whiskey barrels stacked almost to the high ceiling. He slipped into the next room, where it was cool and dark. Row after row of barrels loomed over his head. He walked slowly, making no sound, but he heard the excitable voice of the bartender somewhere on the other side of the barrels.

"He's looking for you! He has a *picture* of you! I'll stall him if I can, but you've got to get out of here! Now!"

Jazzi's high heels tapped sharply on the concrete floor. Bourne heard her getting closer, and he pressed himself into the shadows among the whiskey barrels. She passed him at the end of one of the rows without looking his way. When she was gone, Bourne heard more footsteps. A man's footsteps. He drew his Glock and emerged from among the barrels. He found himself standing outside the windows of a private dining room built into the middle of the warehouse. A man stood in the doorway, and Bourne could see a laptop on an elegant, inlaid wood table behind him.

The man's face had changed from his earlier photograph. It was older, thinner, the wild brown hair now cut short near his scalp. His long, bumpy nose had been smoothed out with plastic surgery, and he no longer wore glasses. But it was Simon Harris. The man looked up, his eyes distracted.

Then he focused on Bourne and the gun.

Harris ran. His panic made him fly. Bourne ran, too, but Harris knew the corridors of the warehouse like the back of his hand. He widened the gap with a few sharp turns, then disappeared out a door near a loading dock. Bourne crashed through the door seconds later and leaped down a short flight of concrete steps. In the darkness, Harris was sprinting for the overpass that ran beside the distillery. Bourne went after him, narrowing the gap quickly. Harris was no more than twenty or thirty feet ahead, looking back over his shoulder, eyes wild with fear.

But he had nowhere to go. The ground thundered and vibrated under their feet as a long train pulling dozens of crude-oil cars slouched along the railroad tracks, rattling below the overpass and blocking Harris's escape. The man looked both ways, realizing he was trapped, backing up as Bourne came closer. The train cars banged and shook immediately behind him. Bourne holstered his Glock and put up his hands.

"Simon, I'm not here to hurt you. I want to *help* you. Alvin Bakk sent me."

Uncertainty crossed the man's face. He took a step toward Bourne, then changed his mind and suddenly leaped for the moving train. He jumped unsteadily onto one of the cylindrical oil cars, nearly slipping under the train wheels, then squeezed his way to the other side of the platform. Bourne swore and followed, pulling himself up on the next car. The train was picking up speed. Not far away, Harris threw himself off the train onto the tracks, but he landed badly on a parallel set of rails, his ankle twisting below him. He got up, tried to run, and fell. Bourne timed his own leap, then rolled as he hit the ground. When he was on his feet again, he caught up to the man, who was frantically crawling away.

"I'm not lying, Simon," Bourne said, standing over him with a boot on the man's shoulder. The boom of the train made him raise his voice. "I just want to talk to you. Bakk thinks you're Bai Ze. A Chinese spy. He thinks you betrayed him during that hiring fair in Door County eight years ago. He thinks you manipulated the tests and planted spies inside his companies."

"I didn't do that!" the man begged from the ground. "For God's sake, it wasn't me! Alvin's wrong!"

"You ran, Simon. You disappeared. Why run if you were innocent?"

"Because I *knew* something had gone wrong. I knew we were compromised. I was being watched. *Stalked!*"

"You met every candidate. You interviewed them. You ran

them through a gauntlet of psychological tests and gave the go/no-go on each one. Now Bakk is convinced his operations have been compromised. Infiltrated. If it wasn't you, then who was it? Who else had that kind of access?"

Harris pushed himself up until he was sitting and winced as he massaged his ankle. "They killed my brother. They murdered Josh."

"I know. I'm sorry."

"After he was gone, I knew I should get out of town, but I'm tired of running. It was just a matter of time until they found me."

"Who's behind it, Simon?"

The man on the ground closed his eyes. "I was having an affair. It was her. It had to be her."

"Who?"

Harris kept talking, the words tumbling over each other. "I betrayed my best friend; I betrayed Alvin. I know it was my fault, but I was weak. She seduced me, pushed all of my buttons. I didn't see that she was doing it to manipulate me. Play me! I told her everything. We talked about the candidates, the strategies, the pros and cons. I didn't see the harm. She was part of the whole operation. I mean—she was Alvin's wife."

"Mei Sun," Bourne said.

"Yes."

"Did you know she was ex-CIA?"

"Of course. That's one of the reasons I trusted her. She had a top secret clearance like me. I never dreamed that she—"

"Why do you suspect her?" Bourne interrupted. He knelt in front of Harris, the pounding of the train still loud in his ears. "Why do you think she's the one who leaked information to the Chinese?"

"I told you, things began to go wrong all over Alvin's companies. There was too much for it to be random. I started poking around, connecting the dots, and I began to realize it was the people *I'd* vouched for. I'd been set up! There was only one other person who knew enough to do that. Mei Sun."

"Did you talk to her about it?"

"No. We broke up years earlier. I was no longer of any use to her, so that was the end of it. And how could I talk to Alvin? How could I tell him *why* I suspected his wife? But I never had a chance to confront Sun anyway. After I began to look into the leaks, I realized I was being followed. My security camera showed someone tampering with my car. They were trying to *kill* me. So I went underground. I've been running ever since."

Bourne extended a hand to help the man to his feet. "Can you walk?"

Harris tested his ankle, gingerly taking a step. "Slowly. Where are we going?"

"To talk to Bakk. You need to tell him your story."

"He'll hate me."

"He already thinks you betrayed him. Better a cheater than a spy, Simon. And he and Mei Sun are long divorced."

Harris nodded. "Yes, all right. I suppose I should have done it years ago."

They limped toward the tracks, Harris leaning against Bourne. Ahead of them, in the darkness, Bourne saw the last car in the long oil train shouldering by, finally clearing the way. As it passed, the distillery building came into view.

So did a figure in black, barely visible on the other side of the tracks.

When the figure moved, Bourne saw the outline of a rifle take shape against the lights of the building. The barrel was aimed at them.

"*Get down!*" he shouted at Harris.

But the scientist panicked and ran, limping, then falling. Smoothly, patiently, with a handful of shots, the killer zeroed in on him and eviscerated his body with multiple rounds. It took less than five seconds. In the next instant, as Bourne grabbed his Glock and returned fire, the shooter ducked, delivering a barrage that forced Bourne to the ground. With a few moments of freedom, the shooter sprinted after the train and jumped aboard the caboose before its speed carried it away. Bourne was out of range to make any kind of shot, and he couldn't risk hitting a train car loaded with crude oil. He pushed himself up and dashed along the tracks, but the killer sprayed the area with more fire to drive him down again.

By the time it was over, the train was too far away, moving too quickly, for Bourne to catch it. All he saw was a faraway glimpse of the assassin's face as the train passed under the lights of the bridge.

But not a face. A mask.

A Chinese opera mask, garishly painted in yellow, black, and red.

The killer had come from Bai Ze.

18

THE FOLLOWING EVENING, BOURNE WAS BACK IN WASHINGTON, DC.

He sat on a stone bench outside St. Thomas's Parish Episcopal church near Dupont Circle. Diagonally across Eighteenth Street was a clay-colored Queen Anne row home that housed the Yellow Kite Foundation, an NGO focused on combating prostitution and child trafficking throughout Asia. Mei Sun had joined the organization's board a few years earlier, and after bringing several million dollars of Alvin Bakk's divorce settlement to the table, she now chaired the board.

It was a worthy cause doing worthy things, no doubt about that. But Bourne couldn't help but notice that the organization was also located steps away from the Hong Kong trade office, which likely provided cover for many of China's DC-based spies.

He checked his watch. It was after eight o'clock. Over the past two hours, most of the organization's workers had left for the day. However, he'd watched Sun arrive at the office during the afternoon, and he hadn't seen her leave yet. Only one light was still illuminated on the building's third floor, and every few minutes, he spotted a silhouette moving behind the curtains. Sun was working late.

While he waited, he did more research on Alvin Bakk's ex-wife. He knew about Sun's CIA background as a deep-cover agent for Holly Schultz, but none of those secret details appeared in the public records about her. Instead, magazine and newspaper articles written during and after her marriage to Bakk called her a former State Department policy analyst. That was vague enough to cover a wide range of sins. The media also mentioned her childhood in Taiwan, but left out any reference to the years she'd spent in her twenties doing wet work behind the Chinese border.

But she'd seemingly left her spy life behind her—or so she wanted the world to believe. Today, she was best known for her work at the YKF, testifying before Congress and the UN, flying all over the world, shaping the foundation in her own image. Even the new name of the organization bore her stamp. It had previously been known by a bland moniker invoking child welfare, but Sun changed it when she was chosen to lead the board. The name Yellow Kite Foundation originated with her childhood in Taipei, when she used to fly a yellow kite as a little girl with her father in Daan Park. The kite, she said, represented the innocence of childhood that the foundation sought to preserve and protect.

Plus, it was a better name for fund-raising.

Mei Sun. Bourne didn't know what to believe about her.

It was almost ten o'clock when he finally saw her leave the office. She came out the front door and paused in the glow of the streetlight, almost as if she were modeling for a camera. Her eyes flitted both ways, watching for surveillance the way a careful agent would.

Sun crossed the street to the ultra-modern building of St. Thomas's Parish. She was attractive and athletic, with an unusually tall, lean frame. Her black hair hung simply at her shoulders, no special curl or style. Her skin was golden, with a pointed chin and sharply arched eyebrows. Her dark eyes moved constantly, missing nothing. They were spy's eyes. She wore a white knit top under a gray suit jacket, with a black skirt and stiletto heels. Her attitude was smart and confident, but other than the two-thousand-dollar Prada purse dangling from a gold chain at her shoulder, no one would have taken her for one of the richest women in the world.

Their eyes met briefly as she passed near him. Bourne on the bench. Sun on the corner. She showed no reaction, and he kept his own reaction off his face. But inside, turmoil swarmed his brain at the sight of her. He felt an instinct of lost memory. He *knew* her; he'd *seen* her before. An image of Sun from the past flitted across his mind, this same woman years younger, striding on a dirt path toward a cottage tucked into the trees.

It was night.

It was Door County.

It was eight years ago.

Sun disappeared down Church Street. He pushed a fist against his forehead, trying to wrest more details from his psyche before the pain took over, but no more memories came. All he remembered was that one image, a snapshot from his forgotten past.

He got off the bench. At the corner, he turned to follow her, passing beside Victorian homes and under the skeletal branches of oak trees. Sun was already a full block ahead of him. Even at that distance, in the quiet, he could hear the fast, sharp click of her heels. Before she reached the next intersection at Seventeenth

Street, he saw her leave the sidewalk, and then he heard the metal rattle of a gate being opened. She was out of view, and Bourne ran, closing the distance in a few seconds.

Sun had gone into a narrow walkway between two buildings, protected by a high wrought-iron fence with spikes along the top. She was already out of sight. He jogged past the next building to the intersection at Seventeenth, then turned right and found a gap where the walkway from Church Street opened into an alley. Cars were parked on both sides, leaving barely enough space for one-way traffic. He waited and watched, not seeing Sun, not hearing any more footsteps from her heels.

Bourne took a few steps into the alley. He moved slowly and quietly, his hands in his pockets, the Glock in easy reach. There were no lights around him, and the buildings and cars along the alley were lost in the blackness.

Then he felt the barrel of a gun pressing into the back of his head.

"Hands in the air," Mei Sun told him, her voice cool and calm. "Gently now. Don't make me pull the trigger. Leave the gun in your pocket. I'm sure that's where it is, so don't play dumb with me. Plus you've got another gun at your ankle, switchblade in the small of your back. Right? How am I doing?"

"As well as I'd expect for a CIA agent."

"Thank you. Now take two steps forward and turn around. Keep those hands wide, please."

Bourne did, obeying her instructions. Sun lowered her Ruger and slipped it back into the pouch of her Prada purse, but he could tell by the way she held herself that she would be a formidable fighter, gun or no gun.

"*Cain*," she said, a little smirk on her lips. "Do you think I wouldn't know who you are? I may not be active agency, but Holly and I stay in close touch. I still have enemies, so she keeps me in the loop on people I need to know about. You've come up in our conversations many times."

"No doubt."

"It's strange to see you in person after hearing so much about you. I have to ask, is it true that Sugar likes you? I didn't think that dog liked anybody other than Holly. Every time I see her, she growls at me like she'd like to rip open my throat."

"Holly?"

Sun smiled. "Sugar."

"Well, Sugar and I have history. She's a good dog."

"If you say so. I prefer cats myself. Holly told me about Adam Hill, by the way. Good job forcing him out. A Chinese mole that close to the Oval Office. I wish it were more shocking to me, but at least he's dead and gone. One thing you can say about our friends in Beijing, they know how to take out the trash."

"Assuming it was the Chinese who killed him."

"Oh, it was them. Count on it. I also heard about you and Johanna. Word spreads fast about that kind of thing. I'm sorry. Love is hard enough to find in the normal world, let alone the one we live in."

Bourne said nothing, but the sound of Johanna's name sent him right back to a cemetery in Salzburg, where he'd held her dead body in his arms for hours until dawn. He felt a surge of anger again, and the same word stormed back into his mind.

Revenge.

"So I guess the question is what you want with *me*," Sun said.

"You know about Bai Ze?" Bourne asked.

"Of course. American. He leads the Chinese spy operations in the U.S. known as Volt Typhoon. Believe me, I keep a close watch on what the CCP is up to, even if I'm out. I assume Treadstone has you looking for him."

"That's right."

"And are you close to grabbing him? Do you know who he is?"

"I thought I did. So did your ex-husband."

Sun's pretty face furrowed in the darkness. "Alvin? You've talked to him?"

"Yes. He's convinced that Bai Ze and the Chinese have infiltrated his companies. Planted spies and moles. Bribed or blackmailed others into doing their dirty work. They've begun to target his operations, open up cracks so they can push him out and take over his empire."

She frowned. "The failure of the rocket launch? He thinks that was Bai Ze?"

"Among other setbacks in his businesses, yes. Bakk thinks it began eight years ago in Door County."

"The hiring fair," Sun said.

"Right. He's convinced Bai Ze penetrated the entire operation. He was also sure he knew who betrayed him."

"Who?"

"Simon Harris."

Sun flinched. "*Simon?* Good God. I don't believe it."

"Well, as it happens, I think Bakk was wrong. Harris convinced me."

"You mean you found Simon? You talked to him? I wasn't even sure he was still alive. When he went off the grid, I thought he'd gone into the woods somewhere and blown his head off."

"Why would he do that?" Bourne asked.

"Simon was a genius. Like Alvin. Sometimes the weight of being a genius is too much to bear. Those DARPA guys are highly strung."

"Well, he didn't kill himself. But he's dead now. He was living in Kansas City. That's where I found him. But the Chinese were able to track me when I went after him. They gunned him down."

"That's terrible. Poor Simon. I'm truly sorry to hear it."

"Are you?"

"Of course."

"I was able to talk to him—briefly—before he was killed. He didn't say much, but he had enough time to point his finger at the person he thought had leaked all of the information to the Chinese."

"Who?"

"You."

"*Me?* That's crazy. Simon thought *I* was Bai Ze?"

"He said you were the only one other than him who knew all the details of the candidates eight years ago. He told you everything. You discussed all of them, the pros, the cons, the results of the personality tests. You had the information you needed to pick people who would become moles inside your husband's companies."

Sun's dark eyes flashed with anger, and she hissed at him like a snake.

"If you knew my background, Cain, you'd know better than to accuse me of something like that. You have no idea what I've been through. The things that were done to me. You're lucky I don't break your neck just for saying that. I am the *last* person in the world who would help the Chinese."

"But you were having an affair with Simon Harris."

She sighed. "Yes, I was. That's true."

"He thought you seduced him to get information out of him."

"Of course I did. I was a honey trap, absolutely. But not to help the Chinese. To help *Holly*."

"You were working for the CIA," Bourne said.

"I still do, from time to time. In my current role, information occasionally comes my way that's useful to Holly. So yes, eight years ago, Simon was a *mission* for me, that's all. Alvin's operations were expanding. His power was expanding. He had incredible leverage throughout the government. On top of that, he had contacts in Beijing right up to the level of Xi. We were concerned about who he might bring into his team of giants. Simon gave me names, told me who he was recommending and who he wasn't, told me their strengths and weaknesses. I passed it along when I was back in Washington. But not to Bai Ze. To Holly and *only* to Holly. Neither one of us trusted the rest of the intel community. If the information went beyond the two of us, we assumed it would be leaked."

Bourne shook his head. "Holly Schultz was in Adam Hill's pocket. She's the one who ordered Johanna's murder."

"Holly's ruthless, Cain. We both know that. But she's not corrupt. No way. I know her too well, and so do you. She was trying to keep the Adam Hill situation *controlled*. It wasn't about her working for the Chinese."

"Well, somebody leaked the information eight years ago. If it wasn't Simon, and it wasn't you or Holly, then who?"

"Isn't it obvious?"

"Tell me."

Sun leaned closer to him. Her voice went lower. "Why do you think I was married to Alvin Bakk? Why do you think I was gathering information from the inside about him and his companies? We didn't trust him then, and we *don't* trust him now. Neither should you. You want Bai Ze? You want to know who made the final call about putting Chinese spies inside his companies? Talk to Alvin."

"Why would he sabotage his own operation?" Bourne asked.

She shrugged. "Alvin plays 4D chess, Cain. He thinks eighteen steps ahead. You don't understand his ambition, his megalomania, his paranoia. Did he show you his surveillance? How he spies on people illegally all over the world?"

"He did."

"That's the kind of person you're dealing with. Alvin truly believes he's the most important human being to ever walk the face of the planet. Do you know what kind of ego it takes to think that? He doesn't care about governments, the U.S., China, any of them. To him, governments are obsolete bureaucracies whose time has come and gone. Capitalist, communist, doesn't matter, they're all useless to him. He's planning a post-government world. The *Bakk* world. He'll manipulate political figures, spies, investors, scientists to get whatever he wants, and then he'll jettison them as soon as he doesn't need them anymore."

Bourne felt like a baseball player caught in a hotbox, with the ball going back and forth, forcing him to keep changing directions. "Bakk sent me to find Simon Harris. Why would he do that if Simon wasn't involved? That could only be a risk to himself. Simon suspected *you* were the leak, but he could easily have suspected Bakk and pointed me to him."

"And now Simon is dead," Sun snapped. "Don't you see? You did exactly what Alvin wanted. He'd been looking for Simon for years and hadn't been able to find him. So he used you instead. You led the Chinese right to him, and they *killed* him. You're just lucky they didn't get you at the same time. You're being manipulated, Cain, don't you realize that? They're playing mind games with you."

Mind games.

Memory games.

Everything Mei Sun said made sense. Everything she said about Alvin Bakk tracked with the kind of man he was.

And yet.

"The thing is, I remember *you*," Bourne said.

"What are you talking about?"

"I remember seeing you in Door County outside the White Gull Inn. Eight years ago. You were *there*. So were the Chinese."

"No way. You're wrong."

Bourne felt fireworks behind his eyes. "I can see it in my head."

"Then what's in your head is a lie. I was never at White Gull during the hiring fair. It never happened. I was at Alvin's estate the entire week. That's where Simon was based, that's where the interviews were done. I seduced Simon to spill all of his secrets, you bet I did. When Alvin wasn't around, I fucked Simon until he would have done anything for me. But I did not go to White Gull. I didn't leak any information to the Chinese. I'm *not* Bai Ze."

Bourne's voice rose. He felt sweat gathering on the back of his neck. "I saw you. *I remember!*"

Sun took a step forward in her high heels and put a hand on his shoulder. "Cain. I know your story. I know your background. I know what happened to you, and I can't imagine the pain and dislocation that goes with that. But you have to ask yourself, can you trust *anything* you remember?"

BAI ZE NODDED TO THE NINE ELDERS, WHO SAT LIKE A ROW OF DRAGONS behind the long table in Beijing, their faces obscured by the terrifying opera masks. Tonight they were silent, and their silence was always intimidating.

"I have news," he told them, his gaze moving from one man to the next on the video screen that took up the entire wall. "Simon Harris is dead. One of my agents killed him in Kansas City, where he had been hiding. This is thanks to Jason Bourne. As I suggested to you during our last conversation, Bourne can indeed be a valuable asset to us while he is alive. He was able to locate Harris when our own efforts had failed."

"*Your* efforts," hissed the man in the middle, wearing the angry black-and-white Li Gang mask. "*Your* failures."

"Yes, of course. I regret that we searched for Harris for so long without success. But the end result is what matters. Harris could have exposed many of our most valuable allies. Now he has been removed."

"And Bourne himself?" another of the Chinese men asked sharply.

Bai Ze hesitated. "He is still alive."

More hissing rose from the table.

"Do we know what Harris told Bourne *before* he was killed?" the man in the middle interjected again.

"We do not. But there was very little time—"

"Then Bourne is as much a risk as ever!"

A long silence followed the outburst. Bai Ze took a deep breath.

"Gentlemen, your concerns are justified. I share them. If my agent had eliminated Bourne, I would have celebrated with you. As soon as the next opportunity presents itself, I will make sure he is no longer a threat. But until then, I urge your patience with me. I have been developing a plan for Bourne."

"What kind of plan?" another of the masks asked.

"Bourne's mind is increasingly fragile. The stress of this mission is opening up cracks along the fault lines of his brain. The pain is getting worse. The illusions we placed in his head are mixing with reality, almost to the point of madness. As a result, he is uniquely vulnerable to us at this moment. I believe we should exploit that."

"Exploit it how?" the leader in the middle demanded, but now his raspy voice was tinged with curiosity.

"You are aware that there is one thing we want more than anything else," Bai Ze reminded them. "We have been pursuing it for two years without success. Once we claim it, our plans will be complete. Our power will be limitless, and whenever the conflict with the U.S. begins, we will be able to cripple them without firing a shot. Gentlemen, I believe Jason Bourne is the one man who can deliver what we seek. He will give it to us to save himself. And then we will destroy him."

19

BOURNE GOT UNDRESSED IN HIS ROOM AT THE HYATT REGENCY NEAR the Capitol. He took a long shower, and when he was done, he put on a pair of boxers and dragged a straight-backed chair to the hotel window. He kept the lights off, the room mostly dark. He put his Glock and binoculars on the window ledge and a bottle of Teeling whiskey on the carpet between his legs.

Eight stories below him, New Jersey Avenue was quiet at one in the morning. He used the binoculars to examine each of the parked cars, and then he studied the rooms in the hotel directly across the street. Habit. Protocol. For now, he saw no surveillance, no one looking for him. That was different from the last time he'd been here. Two years earlier, he'd stayed in this same room at the Hyatt with Abbey Laurent. His former partner and lover, Nova, had kept watch on them from the opposite hotel.

Jesus, the past. Some things were better forgotten, left to slip into the white cloud along with everything else that had been taken from him.

It had been a mistake to come back to this hotel.

Never sleep in the same bed twice.

Treadstone.

That was a rule with more than one meaning. It was about not establishing routines of where you went and where you stayed that could be used to find you and burn you. It was also about not making commitments. Every relationship that meant anything at all made you weak. Made you vulnerable. Put you at risk.

Bourne drank a slug of Teeling straight from the bottle. The elixir warmed his chest, but it failed to drive away the headache behind his eyes. Usually the headaches only came when he tried to push his brain toward places it didn't want to go, but for days now, it had never gone away, like someone pinching his optic nerve with sharp fingernails. He closed his eyes and rubbed his chin, which was rough with a day's stubble. He needed to focus, to think about next steps, but his mind kept going backward, not forward.

To the past.

What a strange, crazy road he'd traveled these last few years.

He'd started alone, and now he was alone again. But his situation today felt different, more permanent, as if he had no way to escape. Johanna had been his last chance to be someone other than who he was. She was *like* him, a kindred spirit struggling with who Treadstone had made them. Alone, they were damaged, but together, they became more than the sum of their parts. Those last few months with her, drifting on a boat in the Mediterranenan, he'd been *happy*. He'd allowed himself to believe that he could stay that way. But that was one more lie.

Instead, Johanna was in the cold ground, and he was back on

the Treadstone carousel, going round and round, faster and faster, until the spinning forces threatened to throw him out into space.

The real world intruded again. Bourne heard a soft rapping on the hotel room door.

Instantly, he shook off the fog he was in and snatched up his Glock. No one knew he was here. He'd told no one. He pushed the chair back as he stood up, then ducked under the level of the window, making sure he wasn't a target even in the darkness. With his back to the wall, he made his way to the door, which he threw open recklessly. He already had his finger around the trigger; he was ready to kill. Or be killed.

"Hello, David."

Bourne blinked. "Shadow."

She didn't flinch at the barrel of the gun, held no more than an inch from her bloodred lips. Calmly, she waited for his adrenaline to crest and wane. When it did, he finally lowered the Glock and let it go loose in his hand. He stared at her, and she stared back at him. Shadow looked cool and amused, as if wondering whether he would invite her inside. She was dressed with the sexy elegance of a night at the opera, her blond hair loose and long. She wore a sleeveless yellow crochet dress, with Dolce & Gabbana buttons down the front. The open weave teased her bare skin, leaving no mystery about what she was not wearing underneath.

Finally, he stepped aside, opening the door wider. She brushed past him, her shoulder caressing his chest. He closed the door and turned around, and she was right there, no more than a foot between them. Only the faint glow of the city through the window gave any light to the room.

"How did you know I was here?" Bourne asked.

"I make it a point to know exactly where you are. I keep my blue eyes on you so you don't run away. But you're getting predictable. The Hyatt again? That's dangerous. People know you've been here."

"I like it. It's one of the few places I remember."

"I understand, but you need to let that go. You're obsessed with the past. Don't be. The past is overrated."

"Why are you here?" Bourne asked impatiently. "Do you want a report about Mei Sun? I would have called you in the morning. I saw her tonight, but it wasn't helpful. We're being led in circles. Alvin Bakk points the finger at Simon Harris. Harris points the finger at Mei Sun. Sun points it back at Bakk."

"*And the end to all our exploring will be to arrive where we started, and know the place for the first time*," she murmured, quoting T. S. Eliot. "Thank you for the update, but I don't care about that."

"Then what do you want, Shadow?"

"I'm not Shadow. Not tonight. I'm Marlen."

Her manicured fingers moved to the first of the Dolce & Gabbana buttons, which yielded to her pressure and came loose. She repeated the process slowly, carefully, one by one, until every button had given way and the dress hung open at the front. Her fingernails—burgundy, like her lips—dragged up the corridor of bare skin from between her legs to her taut stomach and through the valley of her full breasts until they were in the hollow of her neck. She nudged both straps of the dress sideways, and they slipped down her arms, taking the dress with her and making a yellow pool around her ankles. She was naked in the darkness.

"I lied to you," she said.

"About what?"

"I told you that Laney Reese didn't matter to me. I didn't care about her. I'm not a jealous lover when it comes to you. But that's not true. Maybe she doesn't matter to Shadow, but she matters to Marlen. I hate the idea of you fucking her. It makes me crazy. It drives me *insane*. I only want you fucking *me*. And I know that Shadow can't give you that order. She has to tell you to do whatever the mission requires. Don't pretend that where you stick your cock is any concern of mine. That's Shadow, but Shadow is full of shit."

She took a step—one small step was all she needed—and she slid down his boxers, and he stepped out of them, and they were both naked. Her arms slid around his back and pulled tightly on his shoulder blades, trapping his erect shaft between their bodies. Something was different about her; *everything* was different about her. Her lips drew close enough to kiss him, but instead she whispered fiercely, "Got it? Are we clear about this? Now you know what Marlen wants. Now you know what I need. Don't pay attention to what Shadow tells you. *Only. Fuck. Me.*"

AN HOUR LATER, THEY LAY IN BED, BODIES INTERTWINED. MARLEN HAD drifted to sleep, her blond hair covering her face, while Bourne stayed awake, staring at the ceiling in the darkness. He thought about the first time they'd made love—the first time he *remembered* being with her—in a bed in Greece the previous year. She'd been unreachable then, strangely detached from what was going on between them, as if he were making love to a statue sculpted out of marble. But not this time. This time she was wild, open, unrestrained. She'd let him see her new identity, someone he barely recognized.

His eyes closed.

He slept, and he began to dream. And yet it didn't feel like a dream. Was it something else? Was this *real?* His mind went back eight years, to a time when he was David Webb, hiding in the darkness of the autumn trees, with dead leaves raining down around him as the wind blew. Behind him, the waters of Green Bay glistened under the moonlight and surged like thunder against the beach. David focused on a car parked on the dead-end road half a block away. He could see two figures inside. A man and a woman. Chinese assassins.

Fang. Rose.

Click.

The doors of the car opened. Both of them got out, readying weapons, checking their surroundings. No one else was around at midnight. The two killers headed away from him, toward a small cottage in the woods lit up by bright lights behind its windows. In the stillness, the man hissed a quiet order to his companion. The two separated as they left the road, taking trails twenty feet apart.

David Webb emerged from the trees and went in pursuit. He walked quickly, Glock in hand, his footsteps silent on the wet bed of fallen leaves. He couldn't follow both of them, so he chose the route of the young man. *Fang.* Fang was his target. Fang had been his target since he spotted him in Miami.

But what was the assassin doing *here?*

What operation had David wandered into?

Fang walked deliberately, and David stayed hidden behind

him, matching footsteps in the shadows. He didn't have to go far. The cottage was located in a small grove, among dense clusters of white birch trees that dangled their branches over the roof. There were other cottages not far away, plus the hotel's main building, but they were all dark, almost invisible. It was late, and most of the guests were asleep.

The assassin stayed along the cottage's east wall, approaching the rear. Not far away, Rose followed the west wall, the two of them conducing a pincer sting. David stayed back, watching the maneuver unfold. At the corners of the cottage, the two killers timed their assault, and then both struck at the same time, disappearing behind the back wall. David heard the beginnings of a scream, quickly choked off.

Someone was there.

Someone had been taken.

He ran, hoping the two killers didn't hear him coming in the tumult of the ambush. He sidestepped along the east wall and stopped to listen as he reached the back corner of the cottage. Not far away, someone fought, struggled, kicked at the dirt and leaves, grunted moans and cries through a gag. The noise got louder, closer. David aimed his Glock at the end of his arms and waited. In the shadows, he saw Rose emerge first, dragging a prisoner who squirmed and tried to escape as Rose carried her backward toward the trees. Fang followed, a Chinese QSZ-92 pistol in his right hand, a suppressor threaded onto the barrel.

The prisoner was a woman. David could see that. And the woman knew she was about to die. They wanted to talk to her, find out who she was, why she was there, what she knew, what she'd seen. But she was making too much noise. Someone would hear; someone would come to investigate. Better to end it now.

David heard Fang bark an order. Rose stopped, the prisoner still wriggling in her arms, growing more frantic as Fang came closer. David had no more time to wait. If he didn't move, if he didn't act right now, the woman was dead in seconds. He watched Fang's gun arm rise, locked and stiff. In the same motion, David took two steps into the open from the wall of the cottage, his own suppressed Glock already aimed at the assassin's head. He gave him a chance to surrender, knowing he wouldn't take it.

"*Fang.* Drop the gun."

The man was quick. He fired as he spun, fast enough to get off a bullet that came within an inch of David's neck. David fired back at the same time, a single headshot that dropped the Chinese killer where he stood. His partner howled, then silenced herself and placed a hand on either side of her prisoner's head. The woman—she was maybe thirty years old, with stringy brown hair—stared back at him, her eyes wide and terrified. David aimed his Glock at the Chinese killer. Just one eye. Half a face. That was all he could see with the prisoner's body blocking her. It was a long, tough shot in the darkness.

If he fired, he might hit the prisoner. Or he might miss altogether. And if he did, Rose would break the woman's neck before he could fire again. Or he could let them go, and then the young woman died anyway.

An evil smile crept across the Chinese woman's face. Rose understood his dilemma. *What are you going to do?*

David fired. One squeeze of the trigger, one low spit barely audible above the wind. The bullet drilled into that dark eye. Her hands dropped from the prisoner's head, and her body thudded down onto the soft dirt.

Now free, the young woman took a fragile step toward David, toward her *rescuer*—but then she screamed and pointed, extending a finger. David turned around, Glock still in his hand. Four men, dressed in black, had melted out of the darkness, their guns focused on the two of them.

Behind the men, arms across his chest, a smile on his face, was Alvin Bakk.

Bourne bolted awake. *You are dreaming. Wake up!*

Except he didn't.

He shook himself, but the dream refused to let go of his mind. He couldn't make it stop. He was still there in the woods, still trapped eight years ago, still David Webb with a sharp pain burning behind his eyes. He tried to focus, tried to keep the details in his head of the man he was seeing. But Alvin Bakk disappeared into a milky cloud. When a wind whipped through the trees, the fog separated, and he saw someone else. Someone new. He saw Mei Sun. Then she was gone, too, and the fog lifted, and a new face appeared. *Faces.* Multiple faces. They clicked through his brain, smiling at him, laughing at him because he didn't know what was real. What was a dream, and what was a memory?

Abbey.

Nova.

Nash.

Vandal.

Johanna.

Bourne shouted as he woke up. His mind took several seconds

to orient itself. He lay in bed at the Hyatt, his skin bathed in clammy sweat. It was still the middle of the night, the city lights glowing beyond the window.

He was alone.

Shadow was gone. *Marlen* was gone. Her yellow dress was no longer on the floor, and Bourne's boxers were draped over the back of a chair, not near the door, where he'd left them. The pillows on the other side of the bed looked neat, unused. He lowered his face to the sheets and caught no essence of the perfume Shadow always wore. Wind Flowers.

Had he noticed the aroma on her body when they first embraced? Or was she not wearing it this time? Was that why she'd seemed different to him? Was that why he'd felt like he was making love to a stranger?

Or had she never been here at all?

Bourne staggered from the bed, his knees buckling. He went to the window, holding himself up by gripping the frame on both sides. The streets of Washington stretched below him, dirty and deserted. He noticed the bottle of Teeling on the floor and wondered how much he'd drunk tonight. It was half-empty, and yet he only remembered a swallow or two before Shadow arrived.

If she'd really been here. If his brain hadn't made it all up.

Something was wrong with him.

His dreams had begun to creep into his real life, and his real life had taken on the forced, unreliable quality of a dream. And his headache. Jesus, his headache refused to go away. It kept getting worse and worse.

Bourne could only think of one explanation.

I'm going crazy!

20

MO PANOV MET HIM AFTER DAWN, WHEN THE CITY WAS STILL QUIET AND cold. They sat on the steps near the Grant Memorial, with the dome of the Capitol looming on the other side of the winter-brown lawn. Mo wore a trench coat and black leather gloves, and his breath steamed in the frosty air. A fedora covered his bald head. He sipped his Starbucks coffee and said nothing at all, his head turning casually as if to admire the view around them.

Bourne knew Mo was waiting for him to talk. But he didn't know where to begin or what to say.

"I appreciate you meeting me so early."

Mo shrugged. "I said to call me if you were having problems, and you did. That's good."

"Can we keep this between us? Nothing in your records? I don't want Shadow to get a report about this."

"I'm sorry, David," Mo replied after a brief pause. "I'd like to say yes, but you know it doesn't work like that. I can't have typical patient relationships the way an ordinary psychiatrist would. The whole reason that Treadstone and the CIA send me their agents in crisis is so I can assess their fitness for the field. Lives are at stake. If I send someone back who's not ready, that creates risks in ways I can't anticipate. So you can talk to me, or not talk to me, that's your choice. But at the end of the day, if you tell me things that make me believe you're not mentally capable of doing your job, that's what I'll tell Shadow."

"Yes, I get it," Bourne replied.

"So what will it be?"

Bourne thought about the night and about his dreams. His instinct was to say nothing, to deal with it himself. But instead, he told Mo everything. Somehow, letting it all out, admitting what was going on inside his mind, took away some of the sharpness from his headache.

"Was it just this past night?" Mo asked. "Was this a single instance?"

"No, it's been getting worse since I took this mission," Bourne admitted. "It's like having to dive back into what happened eight years ago is screwing me up. They did something to me back then. I know it. And the ripple effects haven't stopped."

Mo frowned and drank more coffee. "Well, let's start with reality. It should be easy enough to determine whether Shadow was really in your room last night and whether the two of you had sex."

"You think I'm going to call her and ask?"

"No. I wasn't suggesting that, but I'm sure she left evidence behind."

"If she was there, she was thorough in keeping it hidden," Bourne said. "I didn't find anything to prove we were together. I think that was intentional. This wasn't Shadow visiting me. It was her alter ego, the woman she once was, the woman she can't afford to be anymore while she's the head of Treadstone. Marlen. Like I told you, she didn't even wear her usual perfume."

"You sound pretty convinced it did happen."

"I guess I am."

"Then go with that. From what you say, Shadow had plenty of reasons to pretend this affair has nothing to do with your relationship as handler and agent. To keep it separate from your real lives to the point that you might wonder if you imagined the whole thing. But you didn't. So hold on to that. Then you can deal with the rest."

"You mean the dream."

"Yes, for me, that's the more concerning part of this. Then again, it's hardly a surprise that you would dream about what you saw eight years ago, given that you've spent the last several days immersed in that part of your past."

"It felt like a *memory*," Bourne said. "Not a dream. It was clear. Vivid. Real. Chronological. Right up until the end, when the faces of everyone close to me began to cycle through my head like a deck of playing cards. Plus, the events I saw aligned with what Laney remembered during your session with her. She was at the cottage. Fang and the woman surprised her. I killed them. And then, apparently, Bai Ze and his team captured the two of us. It's just like the Files suggested. I *saw* him. But I don't remember who it was."

"This vision happened while you were sleeping?" Mo asked.

"I think I was asleep. I don't know. I'm not sure of much of anything anymore."

"And the headaches? They've gotten worse?"

"Way worse." Bourne shook his head. "This all feels new. Fresh, recent, not eight years old. Like something has been done to me that's fucking with my head, and it *just happened.* I mean, could this really still be a by-product of what they did to me in Door County?"

"Have you suffered any time loss recently? Blackouts? Stretches where you were unaware of what was happening around you?"

"I don't think so."

"Then it seems unlikely that Bai Ze could be manipulating you *now.* But your mind has suffered plenty of shocks since that first event. You lost your entire memory more than once. Whatever Bai Ze did to you eight years ago, that was probably the start of it, the first disconnection between your brain and your past. With anyone else—an ordinary civilian like Laney—that might have been the end of it, and your mind could have begun to heal itself over time. But, of course, your life is anything but ordinary, David."

"You're saying I have a screw loose."

Mo smiled. "Sort of. Once the threads are stripped, the screw never really tightens again, does it? The Chinese messed with your memory when they captured you. It certainly seems that you're correct about that. Sometime later, you were shot in the head, and you nearly died. A few years after that, you were caught in an explosion. Same thing. Each time your brain came more undone. You lost more of the past, more of who you are. That's bad enough, but it probably also makes you susceptible to further dislocations."

"Great."

"I won't sugarcoat any of this, David. Even before the explosion last year when you had your latest memory loss, Shadow warned you that none of us were entirely sure about the long-term effects of what had happened to you. She told you that because *I* gave her that warning. Obviously, it proved prescient. And that was before we had any kind of hint that something had happened to you earlier—that in fact, Bai Ze had already put your brain through an initial trauma. That makes it worse. It tells me that your mental condition will always be fragile. Up to now, the effects have only been memory-related, but here you are telling me that you've begun to question your daily life, too. Last night, you temporarily lost the ability to distinguish what was real and what was not. That's a red flag. Maybe it will be a one-time thing, maybe not. I can't answer that now, but it's possible the day will come when you'll lose your sanity altogether. If that happens, you may be unable to get it back."

Bourne closed his eyes. "Jesus."

"Understand, I'm not saying it *will* happen. Just that it's possible."

"That's some bedside manner you've got, Mo."

"Look, you don't come to me for lollipops. You come to me for the truth. I'm giving you my best assessment of your condition. But none of this is exact science. I don't mean to be arrogant about it, but this is my specialty, David. There are very few people in the world with more experience in this field than me, and even I can't give you hard-and-fast answers. The fact is, it's easier to do the damage than to fix it. Despite all the money, all the research, we're still in the infancy of brain work. In fact, we're probably at the most dangerous stage, when we don't know nearly as much as we think we do. Scientists suffer hubris like anyone else, and that's when we make mistakes."

Bourne stood up. He stared at the Capitol and thought about the way his life had been turned upside down by the people who worked inside that building. "Do you have any good news for me?"

Mo stood up, too. "I wish I did, but honestly? No. If anything, I have more bad news you need to be aware of."

"What's that?"

"There could be other time bombs in your head. Things that were planted there. Misleads, misdirections. Like sleeper moles waiting to be awakened."

"From eight years ago?"

"Yes."

Bourne slipped sunglasses over his bloodshot eyes. Around them, Washington had begun to wake up. "I don't know, Mo. I still feel like I'm missing something important. Whatever's going on with me didn't just happen eight years ago. It's happening now, too. So what do you suggest I do?"

"I assume you're not going to stop," Mo said. "You won't give up the mission."

"No. I'm going to find Bai Ze, and he's going to tell me exactly what he did to me. I'm going to get answers."

"I could tell Shadow to pull you," Mo pointed out.

"Are you going to do that?"

"I should. But no. Despite everything, it's obvious to me that you're still capable of doing your job. In fact, physical and mental obstacles only seem to make you stronger. More intense, more determined. I'd be a fool to stand in the way of that. This mission is no longer just about Treadstone. It's personal."

"Very personal," Bourne agreed.

"All I can say is, be careful, David. Your worst enemy may not be Bai Ze. It may be yourself. You're obsessed with the idea of revenge, but that kind of obsession can get turned against you."

"I appreciate the warning." Bourne took a couple of steps down from the monument, then stopped and turned back. "Tell me something, Mo. What's the endgame here?"

"What do you mean?"

"You said I might go nuts, but not necessarily. If somehow I hold on to my marbles, what then? Do I stay in this fog forever? Like a nowhere man?"

"Possibly," Mo admitted. "That depends on a few things."

"Like what?"

Mo exhaled more steam into the winter air. "The life you lead."

"You mean Treadstone."

"Yes, Treadstone. I'm sure you figured out long ago that you're not a human being to Treadstone. You're an asset, that's all. To David Abbott. Even to Shadow, no matter what other relationship the two of you have. They don't care what happens to you, what these missions do to you. They care about the ends, not the means. I'm not saying you should walk away, find a different life. That's up to you. Believe me, trying to live a life without a daily dose of adrenaline carries its own challenges. But I can tell you that if you stay in Treadstone, you will never recover who you really are."

21

SIX BLOCKS AWAY, AS BOURNE WALKED TOWARD UNION STATION, A black stretch limousine pulled up next to him on D Street. The rear door clicked open, letting a blast of German punk rock music into the air. Alvin Bakk leaned outside, his black bangs falling across his forehead. He hoisted a champagne glass in Bourne's direction.

"*Cain!* Why walk when you can ride?"

Bourne glanced up and down the street, then climbed into the back of the limo. Bakk slid across the smooth leather to the opposite side, giving him room. The billionaire wore jeans with ragged cuffs, his feet bare, plus a white T-shirt with a photograph of Jack Webb next to the tagline *Just the facts, ma'am* in red letters. On the limousine's large television screen, with the sound muted and English subtitles, Bourne saw what appeared to be a South Korean game show featuring a zombie apocalypse.

Bakk tapped a button on his limousine remote control, and the deafening rock music ended. Then he switched off the television.

He settled back into the leather seats, and his sharp eyes studied Bourne.

"I haven't heard from you," he said. "I was concerned. I need an update."

"I don't work for you," Bourne reminded him.

Bakk waved a hand in the air. "Oh, let's not dot the i's, Jason. The day will come sooner or later—probably sooner—when everyone works for me. So let's speed things up. Did you find Simon Harris?"

When Bourne said nothing, Bakk unleashed an exaggerated sigh.

"Fine, fine, fine, let's trade, shall we? We can do this the old-fashioned way with the barter system. I have something you want. You have something I want."

"What do you have that I want?" Bourne asked.

"Proof that you're not nuts."

Bourne's eyes narrowed. "Excuse me?"

"Really, Jason, did you learn nothing from our first meeting? I have surveillance all over the world, but I sure as shit have surveillance everywhere near the Capitol. Believe me, if a senator has a burrito on the Mall, my cameras catch every fart on his way back to the office. Naturally, I've had my facial recognition software keeping an eye out for you—and there you were first thing this morning, having a little chat with Dr. Panov."

"You know Mo?"

"Of course I know Mo. I know everyone in DC. And they know me. But that doesn't matter. I pushed a few buttons and zeroed in on your conversation. Very illuminating, my friend. It told me a lot about you. You're concerned that you're cracking up? Sorry to hear it. Then again, it's your vulnerability that makes you so interesting, isn't it? Not many spies can ride the moral gray line without becoming addicts or alcoholics. But it seems to be your specialty."

Bourne was quiet for a long time. "You're lucky I don't kill you."

"Yes, I get that a lot. Anyway, first comes the quid, then we'll get to the quo." Bakk pushed a button on the remote control, and Bourne saw a brief video begin to play on the television screen. It took him a moment to place the location, and then he realized it was the lobby of the Hyatt Regency. This was his hotel, obviously in the middle of the night. He waited, and a few seconds later, he saw a woman in a yellow crocheted dress cross from the elevator banks to the escalator that led up to the street.

Shadow.

"See? She really was there last night. You didn't imagine it. So—you're welcome. Although, you have to ask yourself, why would she want you to believe she *wasn't* there? That's a conundrum, isn't it? Unusual woman, Shadow, but I see the attraction."

"Did you have cameras inside the room, too? Did you get off watching us have sex?"

"If I did, I wouldn't tell you," Bakk replied. "I have a pretty good idea how far a man like you can be pushed. Anyway, you have what you want, so let's get back to what *I* want. Tell me about Simon Harris."

"All right," Bourne said. "I found him. He was in Kansas City, just like you said."

"Was?"

"He's dead."

The billionaire's face darkened. "Shame. Simon was my best friend in days gone by. Was it you? Did you kill him?"

"No."

"The Chinese?"

"Probably. Or maybe it was you, Alvin. Or maybe there's no difference."

Bakk clucked his tongue in mock disdain. "Still on about that? Still thinking I'm Bai Ze? I thought we were past that and becoming good friends now. Why the suspicion again? What did Simon tell you? Or did he get killed before you could interrogate him?"

"We talked."

"And?"

"You failed to mention that Simon was having an affair with your wife," Bourne said.

"What difference does that make?"

"Did you know about it? I assume you did, because you know everything."

"Of course I knew," Bakk replied. "Remember what I told you? Trust no one. I didn't trust Sun, and I didn't trust Simon. I keep an eye on everyone close to me, on the assumption that sooner or later they'll betray me. I'm rarely disappointed. Although the affair did come as a surprise. Not that I blamed Simon. I'm sure Sun was the aggressor, and I know from experience that very few men say no to Sun. Frankly, very few women, either, based on my observations. I didn't particularly care. Simon's use to me was his brain. What he did with everything else was up to him. But the fact that Sun seduced him convinced me of what I'd already begun to suspect—that Sun's interest in me was nothing but a cover. She was reporting on everything I did to Holly Schultz."

"Or to someone else," Bourne said.

Bakk put down his champagne glass and slowly folded his arms across his chest. His eyes took on a speculative look. "Meaning what?"

"Simon thought your wife was Bai Ze. Or she was one of Bai Ze's top agents. Either way, she was feeding the Chinese everything about the people you were recruiting into your companies. He said she was the only one who had the depth of knowledge about the operation in Door County to do it."

"Sun? Work for the Chinese?" Bakk shook his head firmly. "That would be like Zelensky inviting Putin to play golf and share some onion rings afterward. She hates them. They hate her. No way Sun gets in bed with them."

"Yes, she told me pretty much the same thing."

"You talked to her?"

Bourne frowned. "Don't play me for a fool, Alvin. If you have cameras in DC, then I'm sure you have them focused on your wife's NGO."

The billionaire smirked. "I do, yes, but it's a bit of a tit-for-tat game between her and me. Unacknowledged, of course. She has the area screened constantly for cameras. She uses jammers, filters, really good tech to block me out. I get devices placed, she disables them, I place more. It's almost better than sex. Almost. As it happens, she's had me on blackout for a couple of days."

"Well, I did talk to her. She said exactly what you said. There's no way she would work for the Chinese. On the other hand, what better cover for Bai Ze than hiding in plain sight as an anti-Beijing activist?"

"Do you really think that's possible?"

"Possible, yes, but there's one other option."

"Namely?"

"According to Sun, I should be looking at *you*. She thinks you're the most likely candidate to be Bai Ze."

"Ah. So that's why the change of heart."

"It's not a change of heart," Bourne said. "I don't trust either of you. You two were the only people who had intimate knowledge of the hiring operation eight years ago. Simon Harris provided his intel on candidates to both of you—to you in the office, to her in bed. Harris ran because he was afraid of Mei Sun, but he didn't get killed until you sent me after him. As far as I'm concerned, you're both suspects."

Bakk shook his head slowly. "You think I'd work against my own interests? I'd sabotage my own rocket? Why would I do that?"

"Sun says you're like a chess player. A grand master. While everyone else is thinking three or four moves down the line, you're about twenty or thirty moves ahead. She says you have plans for a post-governmental world where you run the whole show. Normally I'd think it's impossible for any man to have that much ego, but in your case, I believe it. So you tell me, Alvin. What's your plan? Use China to weaken the U.S., disrupt our infrastructure, lose a big war, destroy our credibility? And then what? I'm sure you have plans for China, too. But watch out. They may conclude you're expendable before you ever reach that part of the game."

Bakk finished his mimosa and mixed another. He didn't look at all upset by the accusation. "Sun really does know me. It's a shame she was a spy. Like I said, the sex was great. It's almost worth it to see if she'd like to try again."

"Is she right about you?" Bourne asked.

"What, that I'm a billionaire with an ego? Guilty as charged. Do I think I could run the world better than the idiots we keep electing? Um, yeah, my robot dog could run the world better than anyone we've got now. Am I trying to use the U.S. *and* the Chinese to get what I want and then lay the groundwork for a civilization where government isn't needed at all? Absolutely. You bet, that's my dream, that's my vision. But that's more likely to happen on Mars in about a hundred years than it is on Earth right now. So do I want the Chinese to defeat the U.S. in the next war? No, I don't. I'm not a communist. The fact that the Chinese want to tear me down and take over my business should tell you everything you need to know. In other words, am I Bai Ze? No, I'm not."

Bourne had to give the man credit. He was as smooth as a carnival barker.

"Okay. Then who else knew what Simon Harris had developed about the people you were recruiting? Who saw the test results? The interviews? The background checks?"

"Nobody. That's the problem."

"Lawyers? HR people? Outside recruiters?"

"They only saw bits and pieces. A name here, a résumé there. Simon and I saw the big picture, but nobody else. Remember? Trust no one."

Bourne leaned across the limousine seat. "*And yet the Chinese found out.* They had people in Door County eight years ago. They infiltrated the entire operation, and they've been undermining you ever since. How do you think that happened, Alvin? Somebody talked. Somebody leaked the information. Simon Harris has been on the run for years, so it wasn't him. Now you're telling me it wasn't you. That leaves Mei Sun."

"If it were Sun, I would know."

"Are you sure?"

"Of course I am. Not because I'm naive. That's the last thing I am. I was *watching* her, Bourne. I had eyes on her everywhere she went while we were married. I'm *still* watching her today. If she were running a Chinese espionage operation, don't you think I'd have caught on to it by now? The idea is ludicrous. If she was meeting with Chinese operatives in Door County eight years ago, I would have seen it. *I'd know.* Was she cheating on me? Sure, she was. So what—I was cheating on her, too. But passing secrets to Bai Ze? No. Somewhere along the line, there would have been a red flag."

"You don't think an experienced CIA agent could outsmart your surveillance? Figure out a way to evade anyone who was tailing her?"

"Everywhere she went, I was there, too," Bakk insisted. "My cameras watching her. My people following her. I know where my wife was that entire week."

Bourne's eyes narrowed. "You've got surveillance videos from Door County eight years ago? You haven't deleted it?"

"I never delete anything."

"Then show me," Bourne said. "Let's see what we can find."

THEY SAT SIDE BY SIDE IN BAKK'S DC OFFICE, WHICH WAS IN A TEN-story building on the north shore of the Potomac, not far from the Watergate. There was no signage outside to identify the building, and they accessed the facility via a tunnel under a parking garage two blocks away. Bakk's electronic pass and retinal scan allowed him to avoid the other people who worked there and take an elevator directly to his private suite on the top floor. From there, he had a sweeping view of the city and the monuments.

Bakk typed fast. He sifted through his cloud-based surveillance records, and dozens of camera feeds spilled across the huge 4K screen. When he was done, Bourne estimated that Bakk had opened up more than two hundred video archives just from inside his Wisconsin estate and the small towns of Door County.

He tapped one of them and froze the video, which revealed an intimate moment between his wife and Simon Harris.

"This is my favorite," Bakk said with no jealousy in his voice. "I still can't figure out how she got her body into that position. Like I said, Sun's good in bed. Porn star good. Do they teach that at the CIA, or what? Poor Simon. He didn't stand a chance."

"This was during the hiring operation?" Bourne asked. "That same week?"

"Yes. The feeds captured them going at it like bunnies throughout the house."

"Only in the estate?"

"Only in the estate. Sun never bothered with hotels or secret rendezvous spots. I guess she figured I was too busy to pay attention with everything else going on. Or maybe she didn't care if I knew. It's not like I was hiding my own affairs."

"Did you know about the two of them at the time? Or did you only discover it later?"

"I knew. These were my unwinding videos at the end of the day. Pour a mimosa and watch my wife do her best Cherie DeVille impression." He clicked on several of the boxes and made them disappear from the screen.

"Did Simon discuss the hiring operation with her?" Bourne asked.

"Not that I saw. When they were together, it was just about sex. It would have worried me if he was discussing individual candidates with her. The intel that Simon was developing for me was proprietary. Deep personality shit, the kind of data I needed to make the final calls. Nobody else had that info."

"And yet Simon claims he told her everything. If that's true, then Sun figured out a way to avoid the cameras for those discussions. If she did that, then maybe she figured out how to get off the grounds, too."

Bakk frowned. "Interesting, but that doesn't prove she told the Chinese."

"Well, the meeting I remember—the one where the Chinese were involved—took place at a cottage in the woods near the White Gull Inn. Late, after midnight. Sun told me flat-out she was never at the hotel that week. That should be easy enough to check, right?"

"You remember the meeting?" Bakk asked. "Or are you simply saying what they put in your head?"

"I don't know. It could be either. But regardless, if Sun was lying about being there, that tells us a lot. Did your cameras catch her anywhere outside the estate that week? She told me she barely left the grounds."

Bakk began typing again. "I have no idea. It was eight years ago. My memory that long ago isn't much better than yours. Back then, of course, I didn't have any kind of AI interface to analyze my surveillance. The software was still too primitive for that. I did it the slow way, flipping through feeds until I found her. But I had security teams following her whenever she left the estate."

"Assuming you knew about it," Bourne said.

"Yes, that's true. I guess I wouldn't put it past her that she was able to leave the estate without my spies catching her."

"Do you have an AI interface now?" Bourne asked.

"Naturally. It's nowhere near as sophisticated as the Files, but that's because I don't have access to the underlying data hacks. But now I can run AI queries on all my surveillance feeds, current and historical. That's a lot of data, though. A thorough analysis of all the archives in Door County from eight years ago would take several hours."

"You never ran it before?"

"I had no reason to. I didn't—I *don't*—believe Sun was working with Bai Ze."

Bourne thought about it. "You don't have to run the entire analysis to get what we need. Just the area around White Gull. Did you have surveillance there?"

"Sure. I booked the entire hotel, and I had multiple candidates staying there. Obviously, I wanted to keep track of their movements. Trust no one, Jason. So, of course, I had cameras on the hotel entrance and the dead-end access road that entire week. I didn't spend much time reviewing it myself. Mostly, I had my security team watching the live feeds for anything suspicious. But I didn't use night vision technology. If anything was happening late at night, I'm not sure my team would have spotted it in the dark."

"Maybe AI would," Bourne said.

"Yes, maybe."

Bakk's fingers made another furious assault on the keyboard, fast enough that Bourne couldn't keep up with the code that the billionaire appeared to be writing on the fly. But soon after, he watched multiple surveillance feeds unfolding across the computer screen at a pace beyond what any human could follow. Periodically, the images froze, as if the software were taking a break to study something that looked suspicious.

"I'm including feeds in and out of town, as well as at the hotel," Bakk told him. "If you're right that Sun was there that week, she had to get there somehow. There are only a couple of roads that lead into Fish Creek. Any of the cars at my estate would trigger a flag in the software. I set it up that way."

Bourne and Bakk waited.

Fifteen minutes passed.

Then half an hour.

Then an hour.

Finally, the computer beeped. On the screen, a fragment of video appeared, labeled as no more than thirty seconds in length. Bakk played it raw, and Bourne recognized the nighttime surroundings near the Fish Creek hotel. It matched the images he'd seen in his dream—or his memory, whichever it was. This was the area near the cottage where he'd killed Fang and his Chinese partner, Rose.

But the thirty seconds of video footage didn't show anyone at all.

"I don't see her," Bourne said.

Bakk's mouth pushed into a thin, unhappy line. "Nor do I."

He tapped a few more keys, and the video replayed. This time, fourteen seconds into the feed, the screen froze and an orange box appeared around a faint silhouette among the forest's dense trees. It didn't look like a human outline, but when Bakk restarted the video, Bourne saw the silhouette appear and disappear in a couple of seconds, as if someone had walked past the camera, trying not to be seen.

Words appeared around the orange box.

Mei Sun. 20% probability.

"It seems that's as good as we get," Bakk said. "I wouldn't take that to the bank. With a twenty percent likelihood, the software may simply be giving us something because we asked for it. AI has a personality that aims to please. It doesn't really look like Sun to me. Hell, it could be a deer."

Bourne leaned forward, squinting. "Can you enhance the image?"

"I can try."

Cracking his knuckles, Bakk opened up an editing software and began tackling the profiles of light and color in the video. As he did, the visuals sharpened, becoming crisper, more distinct, both the individual trees and the strange shape that appeared momentarily between them. When he was done, the shape looked distinctly human now, but to Bourne's eyes, it still wasn't recognizable.

However, when Bakk reprocessed the enhanced video through his software, the percentage of a likely match increased.

Mei Sun. 47% probability.

"That's getting better," Bakk said. "The software sees what the human eye doesn't. Odds are, it's trying to do a match on a body outline in some other video that it knows to be Mei Sun. Now it's telling us the image here is almost as likely to be her as it isn't. But is that enough to confront her? In her shoes, I'd simply say the software made a mistake."

"The question is, if it *is* her, who was she meeting? The assassins were outside the cottage. Someone else was inside. You said you had the entire hotel booked, but the local records have all been erased. Do you still have records on your own system of who was staying where?"

"I do, but people came and went throughout the week." Bakk checked the date-time stamp on the video. "This was recorded shortly after the hiring fair began. The first weekend, Saturday night."

Bourne nodded. "That's the period when I was there. I arrived from Miami late Friday, and I was back in my Miami hotel the following Tuesday—with no memory of what went on in between. So the timing fits."

Bakk reran the video, and then he froze it with a blurry view of one of the hotel cottages in the background. "I can't tell from this clip exactly which cottage that is, but let's see who was there that weekend."

He opened up a new window and called up a list on his screen, including names, dates, and hotel room numbers. Bourne didn't recognize any of the names. They looked generic. Peter Smith. George Marshall. Deborah Jones. The kind of names that didn't look obviously false, but would include hundreds of matches around the country if anyone tried to search for them.

Bakk noticed his confusion. "Yes, the names aren't real. I used pseudonyms for everyone who attended. Another layer of security and anonymity. If anyone happened to get hold of the hotel records, the names still wouldn't tell them who was there."

"Do you have the key to who was whom?"

Bakk tapped his head. "Up here, I do. That's how my brain works. On that Saturday night, we had seventeen guests at White Gull. Several from Harvard, a few NSA, a few from overseas. I only hired three from that cohort, and they're not in positions that would have allowed them to undermine my operations. On the other hand . . ."

Bourne waited. "On the other hand?"

Bakk tapped one of the names on the screen. "Judith Parker. She's a problem."

"Why is that?"

"She was a no-show. Judith—real name Nicola Felton—was an MIT astrophysicist. She died the day before she was due to arrive. Hit-and-run in Waltham. The police never found whoever ran her down, but they concluded it was an accident. She was in the wrong place at the wrong time."

"Didn't that make you suspicious?" Bourne asked.

"I had no reason to suspect foul play at the time."

"Who took her place?"

"No one. The candidates I brought in were all unique. It's not like I had a B candidate waiting to stand in for an A candidate. I only hire A candidates. Plus, there was no time for replacements. The operation was already under way."

"In other words, the cottage where Nicola Felton was staying *should* have been empty that Saturday night."

"Correct."

"I'm betting it wasn't," Bourne said.

"Maybe not, but we have no way to prove it."

Bourne eased back in the chair next to Bakk. "Can you find the original surveillance feed that matches this clip? Your software plucked out an excerpt because it thinks the shadow there is Mei Sun. I want to see the video before and after that moment. It might tell us something more."

"All right."

It didn't take Bakk long. A few seconds later, a new video feed filled the screen. Bourne asked him to back it up by half an hour before the appearance of Mei Sun, and then they watched the scene together in real time. At first, he saw no one else in the woods, nothing he could distinguish as human. Fifteen minutes passed before Bourne saw another silhouette flit in and out of the camera range.

"Freeze it."

Bakk did. The shadow on the screen was clearer this time, and Bourne had no trouble recognizing the person in the frame.

"That's me," he said. "I was there. This is the night everything happened."

22

MEI SUN LIVED IN THE ELITE KALORAMA NEIGHBORHOOD OF DC, NO more than half an hour's walk—or a six-minute limousine ride—from the offices of her Yellow Kite Foundation. Bourne parked his motorbike outside the high-security area, off the Potomac Parkway near a bridge over Rock Creek. Then he headed south on foot through the woods toward the lineup of billionaire estates.

A freezing sleet filtered through the trees, ice-cold where it trickled down his back. But the noise of the rain covered his footsteps. He moved quickly up the slope from the river, using no light, and then he stopped where a thick stand of bamboo blocked the narrow street ahead of him. It was late and completely dark. He listened to the woods, trying to pick out any unnatural sounds amid the precipitation. He heard nothing, but his instincts overrode his senses.

Someone else was close by. He felt their presence.

Nighttime security for the neighborhood?

Or guards for Bai Ze looking for *him?*

Bourne waited, frozen where he was. A few minutes passed as he tried to outlast the patience of anyone near him. He slid his Glock into his hand, ready for an assault. Silently, with his other hand, he lifted night vision binoculars to his eyes, trying to see through the impenetrable brush. But no green glow betrayed anyone nearby.

Time to move.

He pushed deeper into the nest of bamboo. When he was close enough to see through the woody branches, he spotted Mei Sun's three-story brick mansion across the street from him. Before he could slip onto the road, he spotted the glow of headlights to his left and he ducked quickly out of view. Slowly, a black Escalade rolled down the street, casting searchlights in both directions, toward the old brick houses and into the woods, where Bourne was hiding. He lay flat on the ground, hoping he was out of sight. A bright light passed over his body, but he heard no squeal of brakes, no doors opening. The SUV continued its slow traverse, disappearing around the next curve.

Bourne broke from the trees and ran to the brick steps that led up to the front of the house. He saw no lights in any of the windows. Hopefully, that meant Sun was asleep. From his backpack, he removed an RF jammer, activated it, and put the device on the ground near the wall of the house. If Sun had a security system—he was sure she did—the jammer would disable the entry sensors and let him get inside without triggering the alarm.

Crack.

Bourne stopped, crouching in the brush near the house. Noise came from the grove of bamboo across the street. Again he used the night vision binoculars; again he saw nothing. But he didn't want to stay in the open any longer than necessary. He made his way to the back of the house, where he climbed an iron fence into the sprawling yard. At the nearest window, he used a glass cutter to make a small parabolic cut near the interior lock. It was loud, but lasted only a couple of seconds. With a small suction cup, he detached the segment of glass, then unlocked the window and pushed it open. No alarm sounded. No dog barked. He put his backpack inside, then slithered through the opening and dropped to the carpeted floor. He closed the window behind him.

The house was warm, dark, and quiet. He used a penlight to illuminate his surroundings. He'd entered into a large fitness room, stocked with weight-lifting and cardio equipment, plus an aerial kit mounted from the ceiling. Sun was serious about her workouts. On the wall, she kept a collection of swords and knives that would have been at home in a Tarantino film. He switched off his light and slipped through the door into a dark-wood hallway with rooms on both sides. His eyes took a few seconds to adjust. He continued down the hall, passing a sunroom, a cardroom, and a conservatory behind glass doors. He saw no sign on the ground floor of Sun's home office, which was what he wanted to find.

If she was involved with the Chinese, then somewhere in the house would be evidence of espionage.

Evidence of a connection to Bai Ze.

The hallway ended in a large chef's kitchen. He smelled sesame oil in the air. He took two steps into the room, but immediately knew he'd made a mistake. He sensed a presence behind him, and as he began to turn, a foot lashed out, pounding a deep blow into his kidney. Pain shot through his side, making him double over. Before he could recover, another kick hit him in the side with such force that he felt a rib fracture, and his body went airborne over the kitchen island.

He landed on his back and heard her coming after him, like a cat following gracefully across the smooth marble island and landing on all four paws. He grabbed his Glock from his holster, but a hand swatted it away, nearly breaking his wrist. Then she pounced. She was on top of him, in red pajamas, black hair tied behind her head. Mei Sun. A chop hit his throat, making him gag. Fingers snaked between his legs and squeezed his testicles in a vise, and his eyes rolled back with a sharp wave of agony. He freed one hand, slamming her skull against the wall of the island. Her grip loosened, and he hit her again, square in the chest. As her muscles temporarily went limp, he threw her off, then scrambled to his feet. His ribs stabbed him with a shot of electricity with each breath.

Sun jumped to her feet, too. She kicked; he blocked her leg. She jabbed with her fist; he ducked out of reach. Smoothly, in one motion, she dodged sideways and unsheathed a butcher knife from a wooden block, then slashed it across his chest, stinging him and drawing blood. As the blade swung past him again, he grabbed her wrist and shoved it down hard into the island, the knife coming free. Then she spun around, delivering a backhanded roundhouse across his head that dizzied him.

He staggered away. So did she. He dove for the backup gun at his ankle, and in the darkness, he saw her reaching for a holster in the small of her back. They aimed their guns simultaneously, two barrels of two Glocks pointed across a short distance where neither of them could miss. Both of them had their fingers curled around the triggers, but neither one fired. The only sound in the room was their panting as heavy, exhausted breaths came and went from their chests. Her face was screwed up with pain, and he assumed his face looked much the same.

"Are you here to kill me, Cain?" Sun asked.

"No."

"Well, that's good, because I'll kill you first."

"Don't be so sure."

"Let's not find out. Okay? Do we call this a draw, or do we keep fighting?"

"Draw," Bourne said.

"Holster on three. One . . . two . . . three."

Simultaneously, they both secured their guns. Sun switched on the kitchen lights, dazzling their eyes. She moved with awkward steps, going to a kitchen cabinet and locating a plastic bottle of alcohol and a tight wheel of gauze. With a wave of her hand, she told Bourne to lift his black shirt, and he did. She used a towel to drag alcohol across the cut made by her knife, then wound gauze around his chest.

Bourne eased himself onto a high-top chair next to the island. Sun nodded at a liquor cabinet on the other side of the kitchen. "We both look like we could use some tequila. What do you say?"

"Just don't smash the bottle over my head."

"Twenty-year-old Garcia? Are you kidding?"

She retrieved the bottle and two shot glasses, then joined him on a stool at the island. They slammed them down together, and she poured again. "What are you doing here, Cain? Why the cloak-and-dagger?"

"I think you know why."

Sun reached behind her head and undid the tight bob, letting her shoulder-length black hair hang free. Her red pajamas were the only color in an otherwise-white kitchen. "I thought we dealt with that. I'm not Bai Ze."

"Maybe not," Bourne said, "but you lied to me."

"What are you talking about?"

"You told me you weren't at White Gull during the hiring operation eight years ago. But I have you there on video."

"No way. That's not true."

Bourne retrieved a phone from his pocket and played the enhanced video clip from outside the hotel. Sun watched it once, twice, and then three times, a frown on her face. "Forty-seven percent probability? Come on, Cain. Even Alvin's AI wizard gives it less than fifty-fifty odds that this is me. Mostly because it's *not* me. I wasn't there."

"There's more," Bourne said. "After we found this clip, we did a search on the other cameras on Bakk's property. We couldn't find you anywhere during that time period. Not in your bedroom. Not on the estate grounds. If you weren't at White Gull, where were you?"

"It was eight years ago, Cain. I have no idea. Maybe I was with Simon."

"No, we found him. He was alone in his room."

"It's *not* me."

He switched to another video clip on his phone. "Two hours earlier, the exterior cameras caught you leaving the house, taking a trail into the woods. See? You pass close enough to the light that it's obvious it's you."

"So what? I like walking at night."

"You didn't come back for four hours," Bourne told her. "That's a long walk."

Hesitation crossed Sun's face. "*What?* Are you sure?"

He showed her another clip, this time showing her returning from the woods and mounting the steps that led inside Alvin Bakk's estate. The time stamp showed that the video had been captured at two in the morning.

Sun's brow furrowed in confusion. "I don't understand. This can't be right."

"Really? It seems pretty obvious to me. You knew where Bakk kept his cameras throughout the grounds. The only ones you couldn't avoid were the ones that monitored the immediate exterior of the house itself. So there you are, leaving and coming back. But once you were in the woods, you could make it to the rear wall unseen, and from there you could get to the road. Did you have a car waiting for you? My guess is somebody picked you up and took you to Fish Creek. You came in through the trees near the hotel to make sure there was no surveillance to catch you. You almost made it, too. There's just that one blurry shot that even AI software isn't sure is you. But we both know the truth, Sun. It's you."

She shook her head. "These videos are manipulated. Deepfakes. That's the only explanation. Alvin doctored the videos. He's the one with business interests across China and contacts throughout the CCP. Do you think he can afford to lose those? Do you think he's not in bed with them? He's trying to steer you off the track, so he wants you to believe I'm involved."

"You *are* involved."

Her fist pounded on the marble of the island. "I would sooner slit my throat than help Beijing! You have no idea, Cain. No idea at all."

Bourne showed her his phone again. He played more videos.

"We checked the camera feeds for the rest of the week. Two nights later, you left again. Gone for hours. Two nights after that, same thing. That's three times during the week that you left the estate. You were passing along intel, leaking details about the people Bakk was hiring."

"I didn't do that!"

"Simon says he told you everything. You found a place in the woods where there were no cameras, and you talked about the personality tests. Right? You got it all out of him. Every candidate, every vulnerability. You had everything you needed to infiltrate and undermine Bakk's operations."

"Yes, sure, Simon loved to talk. And yes, I seduced it out of him. But I told you, it wasn't for the Chinese. It was for Holly."

"Then what were you doing at the hotel?" Bourne asked.

"*I. Wasn't. There.*"

"The cameras say otherwise."

Her fingers pulled at her hair with angry frustration. "These videos are not real."

"Everything else about them *is* real. Everything else fits. You. Me. We were both there that first night, the right place at the right time. What were you doing at the hotel? Who did you meet?"

"This is crazy! It didn't happen! I don't remember any of it!"

Bourne took another shot of tequila.

He examined the stricken, changing expressions on Sun's face, and he saw no evidence of deception. She was CIA, which meant by definition she was a good liar, but he didn't think she was lying. Not about this. The revelations of the videos—of seeing *herself* outside the estate that night—seemed to be genuinely shocking to her.

She'd also used the most important word of all.

Remember.

She didn't remember what she'd done that week.

Was it possible?

"Think back," Bourne said. "Try to piece together that week eight years ago. Is there anything strange about it in your head?"

"Strange? What do you mean?"

"You said you don't remember leaving the estate. Going to the hotel. Coming back. What *do* you remember?"

She closed her eyes and was silent for a while. "Almost nothing. It's like part of me is missing, empty, gone. I feel like I'm staring into a fog, just this white cloud. When I think about that week, all I remember is, God, I slept well. That's the only thing in my head. I'm usually a terrible sleeper, but I remember how well I slept that whole time. It's odd. It makes no sense, Cain. If I were gone for hours—if I left the estate multiple times—I would *know* about it. I'd know why, and where I was going, and what I was doing. But I don't. How could I forget something like that?"

"Because I think they manipulated you like they manipulated me," he said.

"Manipulated me how?"

"Erased your memory."

"*Impossible!*"

"Tell me what happens if you try to remember," Bourne said. "If you force your brain to look back. What do you feel?"

Sun winced, her fingers massaging her forehead. "It hurts. There's a stabbing pain, like a knife behind my eyes."

"It's the same for me. When you try to get past the wall in your head, your mind rebels. That's what they did to us. They blocked out what really happened. I *saw* Bai Ze that night. I think you saw him, too. You know who he is. But like me, you don't remember."

Sun got up from the stool and paced in the kitchen, her fists opening and closing. "There's no way I would work with the Chinese."

"You didn't know you were."

"But how could I not know?"

"How could my past vanish? How could I lose my whole life? But I did. It's gone. I'm still in the dark."

She shook her head. "If you're right, you have no idea what a betrayal this is. A *violation!* Fuck, how those bastards must have been laughing at me. Listening to me condemn them in public while I did their bidding in private—not even aware that I was doing it. My body wasn't enough for them. They took my mind, too."

"Your body?"

Sun stiffened, but told him nothing. Then she went on. "*How* did they do it? That's what I don't understand."

"The mechanics? I don't know. I assume they use drugs, hypnosis, or some combination of both. Memory is fragile."

"It still makes no sense. When did they take me? When was I vulnerable? The one time they blew my mission, I remember every second of it. Believe me, I'll never forget those days. So how did they—" She stopped, and her hands covered her mouth as a look of horror and revelation spread across her face. "Oh, *Jesus.* Oh, shit."

"What is it?"

"We need to go. We need to go now."

"Go where?"

"To see Holly," Sun said.

"You think she's involved?"

"Holly's involved in everything, you know that. But no, I don't think she's dirty, not about the Chinese anyway. Or God, I hope not. The thing is, she knows both of us. She knows our history, our weaknesses, our secrets. This isn't just about you or me separately, Cain. If we were both targeted, there has to be a common denominator."

"You sound like you know what it is."

"Maybe I do, but I hope I'm wrong. That's why we need to talk to Holly."

Bourne frowned. "All right. Let's go."

"Give me five minutes. I'll drive. We'll take the Lamborghini."

Sun padded out of the kitchen in her bare feet with quick steps. He heard the thump of her footsteps as she ran up the stairs to her bedroom.

He switched off the lights in the kitchen, preferring the darkness. Light was a threat; light exposed him and made him a target. He went to the rear kitchen door that looked out on the yard. Streaks of rain came down the glass. When he tried to open the door, air pressure pushed back on his hand with an odd strength. He fought his way through it, then went out onto the deck in the cold night.

Sleet kept falling, leaving a thin layer of ice under his feet. He gripped the wooden railing, listening to the patter of precipitation around him. He didn't care about getting wet. As he stood there, seeing nothing, he thought about Holly Schultz, and a new wave of anger washed over him.

Holly.

Holly had given the order that killed Johanna. She was the one who had destroyed his life. He didn't know if he could see her without putting his hands around her throat.

Bourne forced his mind out of the past and back to the present. His eyes tried to penetrate the darkness, and he pricked his ears for any sound above the machine-gun fire of the rain. No one was here, and yet uneasiness settled in his stomach. His instincts screamed with foreboding.

Something was wrong.

What was it?

Bourne looked back at the kitchen door. He felt the pressure of the wind again, shoving hard against him, but out here in the yard, the breeze was calm, just that icy, drizzling spatter falling straight down from the sky. Suddenly, he knew. He understood the shift in air pressure and what it meant.

A window was wide open somewhere else in the house.

Someone was inside.

Bourne skidded awkwardly across the ice and charged back into the kitchen. In the darkness, he found the main hallway and crashed up the stairs. On the next level, wind blasted through double doors that led into a huge master bedroom suite. The Glock in his hand, he paused briefly at the doorway, then spun inside. Light from the street gave the room a faint glow. His eyes swept the scene, and he saw that he was right. A large window on the far wall, looking toward the river, was open, the heavy white curtains whipping like ghosts.

Then his gaze turned downward.

In front of him was a body.

Sun lay facedown at his feet in the middle of the floor, her arms and legs spread wide. Blood pooled in her black hair; a bullet had violated the back of her skull. He hadn't heard anything. No shot.

That meant a suppressor. A pro.

The bedroom looked empty. And yet it was *not* empty. He could feel the killer's presence, hidden somewhere nearby. Bourne had reacted too quickly; the killer hadn't had time to escape. He studied the large suite, looking for places of concealment, swinging his Glock as his shoulders turned.

The closet—door closed. The bathroom—door open, mirrors exposing what was inside. The king-size bed—near the window, near the curtains that flapped and spun.

The *bed.*

He re-created the scene in his head. The killer comes from behind the door as Mei Sun enters, and he shoots. Then he kneels over Mei Sun to confirm the kill, but only a few seconds later, he hears Bourne's footsteps running upstairs. There's no time to get back to the window, no time for the closet or bathroom. He throws himself across the bed. Bourne could see the off-kilter wrinkles of the comforter where the assassin had slid down to the other side.

He was hiding there.

Bourne leveled his Glock.

But the assassin fired first. Bullets tore through the foam mattress, kicking up a kind of snow in the darkness. Bourne leaped sideways, landing on the floor near Sun's body. In the tumult, he heard running footsteps. He twisted onto his back, seeing a lithe figure jump for the open window. Quickly, he got off a shot, but it went wild and missed. The assassin shot back without looking, two shots that forced Bourne to roll away to cover.

As he brought up his Glock again, in the instant before the

killer jumped, their eyes met. But Bourne saw no eyes, no face. The killer wore the mask that Bourne had seen in Kansas City as he watched an assassin escape on the back of a train after the murder of Simon Harris. It was a Chinese mask, painted in many colors, its mouth frozen in a permanent, violent scowl.

The mask of death.

Then, with a swish of the curtains, the assassin was gone, and Bourne's next bullet disappeared into the air.

He scrambled to his feet and ran to the bedroom window. Below him, an athletic shadow used the branches of the nearest tree like a trapeze artist to swing to the ground. From there, the killer sprinted through the darkness below him, a phantom crossing the street and disappearing toward the woods and the river.

He shook his head and closed the window.

He went to Mei Sun, where her body lay on the floor. Her skin was still warm, but she was gone. The search had led him to another dead end.

Then Bourne heard a low ping behind him like the strum of a chord.

He brought up his Glock again, but he was alone in the bedroom. Except he wasn't entirely alone. A small green light had appeared on the wall-mounted television. At first he thought the screen itself was black, but when he looked closely, he realized that he was wrong. The television revealed a room somewhere in almost complete darkness. The longer Bourne stared at it, the more he could make out objects.

Bookshelves.

Paintings.

Computers.

A desk.

A man—was it a man?—sat behind the desk. His body melted into the darkness; no clue where the shadows ended and he began. His breathing was unnaturally loud, as if the microphone were positioned near his throat. They stared at each other. Bourne was sure the man could see *him*, too.

A computer-generated voice came from the speakers. It was metallic and fake, stripped of any features that would reveal who was behind it.

No gender. No ethnicity. No identity.

"Hello, Cain. I believe you've been looking for me. I am Bai Ze."

23

"YOU AND I HAVE MET BEFORE," BOURNE SAID TO THE UNKNOWN MAN IN the shadows of the television screen. "Eight years ago, we were both in the woods in Door County. I stumbled onto your espionage operation. I killed two of your assassins."

"Yes, I remember," Bai Ze replied. The metallic voice somehow managed to convey a smile as he went on. "Do you?"

"No."

"No, of course you don't. We took care of that. It gets worse when you try to recall the details, doesn't it? The pain comes. But even so, you never stop. That's who you are. You push into the cave no matter how many monsters wait in the darkness. Be careful, Cain. Caves are tricky things. Turn enough corners, and you lose your ability to find your way out."

"What do you want?" Bourne asked, his words clipped, his anger rising. He tried to hold on to himself, tried to *think*. He needed information, he needed clues, he needed anything that would help him identify this man and expose where he was.

But Bai Ze gave nothing away that would help him. He'd been two steps ahead of Bourne since this mission began.

"We'll get to what I want soon enough," the Chinese spy continued. "First, let's discuss what *you* want."

"What I want is simple. Revenge."

Bai Ze was quiet for a while. When he leaned forward, the camera made his eyes shine like diamonds against the shadows of his face. "Yes, of course. Revenge for the death of Johanna. You blame me for that. You blame *us*."

"I *loved* her. You had her murdered, and you're going to pay. You and all of the traitors you've buried inside the country. I'm going to root them out, take them down one after another. I'm going to dismantle Volt Typhoon piece by piece."

"Hmm. We'll see. Honestly, I don't think it will play out that way. But strange as it sounds, I do admire you, Cain. The trauma of what's gone on inside your head would have broken weaker men. But you've kept going. You've drawn strength from it. That's impressive. Of course, you're still just one man, with an army arrayed against you. You're going to lose, but I respect the vanquished when they fail honorably. As for Johanna, my saying so may mean nothing, but I'm sorry it unfolded the way it did. We had no role in her death. That was Adam Hill, as you know. He used Holly Schultz as his tool. I knew nothing about it until after it happened."

"Hill was *your* spy."

"Yes, you're right, he was, so I understand why your search for me is personal. With Hill gone, you still feel the need to lash out. You're grieving. You need to punish someone for your loss. If it had happened to me, I would feel the same way. But you're making a mistake, Cain. Revenge isn't what you really want."

"No? Then what is?"

Bai Ze's words shot like an arrow out of the shadows. "You want your life back. I can give it to you."

"What do you know about my life?"

"I know *everything*. You can't defeat an enemy if you don't understand him, if you don't know how he thinks, what he values. I've followed you since you were first in Treadstone. Somehow I had a sense that our roads would intersect at some point. But having you show up in Wisconsin—well, I admit, that was a surprise. You could have ruined everything. You were in a position to destroy me, destroy what we were building when it had barely begun. So I had to take quick action."

Bourne sat down heavily on the bed, the pain stabbing his eyes again. He holstered his Glock and stared down at the body of Mei Sun at his feet. One more death in an endless line. He couldn't even feel angry about it anymore. He just felt empty.

"How did you do it?" Bourne asked.

"Do what?"

"Erase my memory. Like you did to Laney. Like you did to Mei Sun. How? It's not like you could flip a switch."

"No, it's complicated, crude, risky. We've been experimenting with numerous techniques for more than half a century. We keep refining our process, making it better, making it more targeted. As does the U.S., by the way. I don't mean simply the scientists at DARPA, oh no. Do you think there aren't black box corporate and university research projects on memory going on around the country? Please don't think you've got some kind of moral superiority when it comes to ethics. As for the specifics, well, there are certain drugs that interfere with the brain's ability to consolidate events into long-term memories, assuming you act quickly enough. There are also ways to target specific neurons in the hippocampus using proteins, in order to produce memory modification. It's a field called optogenetics. I won't say the science is exact, not yet, but the results are either extraordinary or terrifying, depending on your perspective. You wound up on the extreme end of memory loss, Cain, but the problem wasn't what *we* did to you. Not really. It was the bullet in your head a couple of years later. Until that happened, be honest, you were barely aware that your memory had been erased. You woke up in Miami and thought you'd had some kind of blackout."

Bourne shook his head. "Why not just kill me?"

"And alert Treadstone that we were penetrating Alvin Bakk's empire? No, no, that wasn't a plan. My Chinese colleagues wanted you dead, but I argued forcefully that we should try an alternative. It was an opportunity in a real-world setting to see how effective our techniques had become. Besides, what was the downside if the procedure failed? You'd be a vegetable, or your memory would still be intact. Either way, we'd simply kill you anyway."

"*Jesus.*"

"Don't pretend to be shocked. We live and work in morally ambiguous worlds, Cain. Both of us. You know that. I'm only telling you this, I'm only revealing what we did to you, because I want you to understand how far our capabilities have grown. The science is *real.* I need you to appreciate the power I have, the things we're able to do."

"Why does that matter?"

"Because I want to make a deal," Bai Ze told him.

Bourne stared at the screen, alert and suspicious. *Trust no one.* "What kind of deal?"

"I told you, a deal that gives you what you want. A deal that gives you your life back. This is me talking, no one else. It's a bargain between the two of us. Believe me, my superiors still want you dead, Cain. Nothing has changed. If they had their way, we would have killed you when you first came after me. As you know, we tried more than once. But the more you managed to stay alive, the more I realized it would be a waste to kill you. You could be much more valuable working *for* us."

"That's not going to happen," Bourne said.

"No? We'll see. Human beings respond to incentives. You're no different."

"There's nothing you can offer me."

"I disagree. I can give you the one thing you want more than anything else."

"And that is?"

"I can give you your memory back."

Bourne felt the breath leave his chest. He tried to hide his reaction, to keep the impact of those words off his face. The hunger. The longing. Bai Ze did know him—knew him only too well. For years, Bourne had lived with a black hole that sucked him down with its inexorable gravity. He kept going up to the edge, kept staring into the deep well, in the hope that one day it would reveal its secrets. But it never did. He didn't know who he was, what kind of man he was. He didn't know where he came from. He had no idea what dangers lurked around every corner, or whether he would even recognize a threat when it stood in front of him.

His whole world had been stolen.

Jesus, to erase that emptiness? To finally *remember?*

He would do almost anything to fill that void.

"You're lying," Bourne said, his voice even. "You have no way to do that."

"I'm not lying. Science taketh away, and science giveth back, Cain. You know your memories are still there. If they weren't, you wouldn't feel the pain when you pushed your brain to remember. You'd feel nothing at all. How many times have you relied on your instincts? Places you've been, people you've met, the details of missions, the numbers in a code, they all come back, it's all there when you really need it. You *know* things even when you can't remember them. You can *feel* your memories inside you, Cain. They're not gone, they're hiding from you, waiting for you, trapped behind a wall. I can tear down that wall for you."

"How?"

"The same way we built it."

"I don't believe you. My past is gone. It's never coming back."

"You're wrong on both counts. Your past still exists, and I can get it back. Let me prove it to you."

"Prove it?"

"That's right. Naturally, I expected you to have doubts. You wouldn't take my promises on faith. So I've arranged a demonstration."

"What do you mean by that?"

"There's a street that runs through the arboretum. Eagle Nest Road. Go there. See for yourself."

"Why the arboretum? What will I find?"

"I told you. Proof. You'll realize that I'm not lying."

Bourne felt off balance, much as he always did with Shadow. He didn't have a chance to steady himself. The blows to his mind kept coming, one after another. "Why would you want to help me?

If I get my memory back, I'll remember what happened eight years ago. I'll know who you are. I'll be able to destroy you."

"True, but I'll take that risk."

"*Why?*"

"Because to make this deal, to give me what I want, you'll need to destroy yourself first. Burn all your bridges. When it's done, you won't be with Treadstone anymore. You'll be on the run from your own people. Permanently hunted. But you'll do it with your memories intact. In the end, I think you'll decide that's a reasonable trade. You won't be Jason Bourne. Bourne will be gone. You'll be who you were in the beginning. David Webb."

Bourne felt his fists clenching; he felt the pounding in his head.

"*What do you want?*"

"Something was stolen from us," Bai Ze replied. "*You* stole it, and now I want you to steal it back. You're the only one who can."

Bourne closed his eyes. He knew. It all made sense now. "The Files."

"That's right. Shadow has the Files. We built them, they belong to us. Bring them to me. That's the price for your life, Bourne."

PART THREE

24

EARLY SUNLIGHT BROKE ACROSS THE OPEN FIELDS OF THE NATIONAL Arboretum. The grass was brown, the trees bare. Dead leaves from the previous fall still filled the woods. Bourne arrived on his motorbike just as the gates opened for the day, with nothing but a few joggers and bicyclists joining him in the cold. He found the paved trail called Eagle Nest Road, but he didn't know what he was looking for.

Proof. You'll realize that I'm not lying.

That made no sense. What was he supposed to find in the park? Did Bai Ze expect him to *remember* something about this place? But there was nothing here that had any connection to his life or his past. Maybe he'd come here as a child, but if he had, that memory was long gone. When he listened to his instincts, he felt no familiarity being here.

So maybe it was nothing but a ruse, a game, a threat.

Bourne drove slowly, the engine of the motorcycle popping and throbbing with an urge to go faster. He passed benches and walking trails, and he tried to stay alert—but for *what?* On his right, a gentle slope climbed into the trees; on his left, empty fields rose and fell as far as he could see. Eagle Nest Road wasn't a long trail. He was through it in no time. He drove as far as the T intersection, where it ended, and a new crossroad, Azalea, took over. In both directions, he saw nothing but parkland.

Proof.

But there was no proof here.

He stopped at the crossroad, switching off the bike and parking it. Serene silence took over when the engine was quiet, just the noise of the city in the distance. He got off the bike and shoved his hands in the pockets of his jacket. Staring around the park, he frowned, trying to understand what he was missing.

But he found it difficult to concentrate.

His mind kept going back to the offer Bai Ze had made. The deal was so simple, so obvious that he should have expected it. The Chinese had built the Files, and they wanted them back. With the Files in their hands again, they could tackle any obstacle to their espionage operation. The Files gave them a rich source of blackmail, leverage, knowledge, dirty tricks, virtually limitless data, and the software to find any secret hiding there. They'd already built a machine of spies and hacks throughout the U.S. infrastructure. The Files were the engine that would allow them to put that machine into motion across the country.

Yes, of course, they were desperate to get the AI software back and to get it out of Shadow's hands. *The Files belong to us. Bring them to me.*

In return, Bourne's past would emerge from the mist.

Could Bai Ze really make that happen? Could he give Bourne

his life back? The proof was supposed to be here somewhere in the arboretum, but he had no clue what he was supposed to find.

Bourne retraced his steps along Eagle Nest Road on foot, feeling the chill as the cold breeze overwhelmed the weak morning sun. He'd missed something. Something was here, something he would recognize. Bai Ze wouldn't send him on a wild-goose chase, not with the Files at stake.

Up the slope, he noticed a redbrick wall surrounding the Morrison Garden, where a collection of azaleas grew. But it was too early in the season for flowers. He climbed through the bed of wet dead leaves to look inside the walls, but again he found nothing. When he skidded down the hill again, he left the road and walked out into the grass, which crunched with frost under his feet. He focused on each tree, each bench, expecting to find something that had been left for him. A message. A note.

But the park gave up no secrets.

He walked farther into the open land. Clouds swarmed overhead, coming and going over the weak sun. By habit, he studied the high ground, wondering if he was being watched, if a sniper had a target trained on his chest. But he felt nothing. It seemed strange that Bai Ze wouldn't follow him, wouldn't make sure he took the bait, but he detected no surveillance around him. The handful of other people braving the early-morning cold of the park weren't threats.

The trade kept echoing in his head.

Your life, your past, your memory for the Files.

Jesus!

If that was real, could he actually betray Treadstone? Could he betray Shadow? Could he make a devil's choice? But there was no point in thinking about it, no point in obsessing about it, because it wasn't real. His past was gone.

So *why* was he here?

Bourne listened to the crunch of his boots and the in and out of his cold breath. He was in the middle of the grassy meadow now. To his left, he saw Eagle Nest Road, empty and quiet. On the other side of the park, at the summit of a low hill, he saw a collection of almost two dozen Corinthian columns, standing in formation like concrete soldiers. They held up nothing, no walls, no roof. The columns stood on their own. From where he was, he could see an empty reflecting pool at the base of the platform and steps that led to the columns, which guarded the hill like a kind of American Stonehenge.

No one was there. And yet he found himself walking that way, drawn by instinct. Squinting, he saw something, but he was far enough away that he couldn't detect what it was. Something lay on the ground among the columns, and whatever it was looked out of place. Without knowing, he *knew*. This was what he was here to find; this was what Bai Ze had left for him. He walked faster; then he ran. His boots punched through the frosty grass. At the steps, he ran up the slope. The columns stood high above him, casting long shadows, dark against the morning sky. The floor of the platform was a checkerboard of white stones.

Something was sprawled across the stone in front of the middlemost column. Not something—*someone*. A body.

It lay on the cold ground, covered by a wool blanket. Bourne drew his Glock, but whoever it was didn't move. As he got closer, he saw a woman's arm stretched across the platform. When he knelt, he touched the skin of her hand and found it cool. The woman lay facedown, her features covered by a mess of stringy brown hair. He lowered the blanket by a few inches and put a finger to her neck.

He found a pulse. She was still alive.

Slowly, carefully, he turned her over. The motion awakened her, and she began to stir, a whimper in her throat. He pushed the strands of hair from her face, watching her eyes blink in confusion and squint against the weak light. She moved, then winced with a jab of pain, her cheeks contorted. She tried to get up too fast and sank back with dizziness. He put a hand behind her head and eased her back to the ground.

Finally, her mind seemed to focus. She stared up at him, struggled for a moment to place him, and then gave a weak smile as her face bloomed with recognition. "*Jason.*"

It was Laney Reese.

OVER THE NEXT HOUR, THE TWO OF THEM SAT ON THE STEPS BELOW THE Corinthian columns, looking down on the empty basin of the reflecting pool. Laney leaned into his shoulder, wearing his leather jacket to stay warm, the blanket still nestled around her body. She said nothing, and he asked her nothing about what had happened to her. Not yet. Even out here, in the middle of nowhere, he worried about spies listening to their conversation.

When she'd recovered enough to walk again, he led her slowly across the open field to his motorbike. He kicked it into action, and she clung to him as he rode, her arms wrapped tightly around his waist. He didn't bother going back to the Hyatt. For now, the Hyatt was burned, a place where either side could find him and watch him. He wanted privacy.

Instead, he drove to a bland little UK safe house on Morse Street across from a neighborhood park. When he parked outside, he waved at the cameras, knowing that his arrival would trigger an alert on a computer somewhere in London. Minutes later, he got a call from one of his contacts at MI5, a man named Tony Audley, who was only too pleased to discover that Bourne was in the U.S. and not England. Audley had cleaned up violence on Bourne's UK missions too many times in the past. He gave Bourne the digital code for the lock at the safe house and promised him a head start of twenty-four hours before he alerted his American counterparts of Bourne's location.

Bourne took Laney inside and settled her on the sofa in the living room. Then he went into the kitchen to see if there was anything to eat. He didn't find much. "Nothing but Twiglets and Marmite," he told her when he returned. "I can go out and get us something more."

She spoke for the first time, her voice weak. "I'm not really hungry."

"Do you need to lie down for a while?"

"No. Actually, it feels good to be awake for now, although I've got a splitting headache. Where the hell am I?"

"DC."

"I'm in *Washington?* Are you kidding? How did that happen?"

"You tell me."

He sat down next to her, his arm around her shoulders. Laney wore a checked flannel shirt over jeans and black sneakers. Her skin was pale, sunken dark moons below her eyes. Her hair hung limp and flat. She reached around to the back pocket of her jeans and found her phone, but when she went to turn it on, she found that the battery had died.

"What day is it?" she asked.

Bourne told her.

"*Jesus!*" she exclaimed. "I've lost three days. I don't remember anything."

"What happened? What's the last thing in your head?"

Her eyes squeezed shut. "I remember you leaving. We made love again in the early morning, and then you left. I spent most of the day in the house. I didn't know whether it was safe to go out, to go home, to do anything. But it's not like I could stay there forever. So I went and saw my mom—God, my mom! I need to know if she's okay."

"You can call her later," Bourne said.

Anxiety stayed like a shadow on her face. "Anyway, then I went home. Your people had been there, just like you said. No bodies, no blood. It was weird, like everything that happened didn't really happen, you know? Like I'd dreamed the whole thing. That night, I barricaded all the doors and didn't sleep. But nobody tried to break in. No one tried to kill me. The next day, I figured what the hell, and went back to my life. With you gone, I thought I was safe."

"And then?"

"Three days ago, I—or was it four? I don't even know now. The sales manager of the Door County website asked me to do an article about a gift shop on Washington Island. I guess they agreed to advertise on our site. So I was driving along the road to the ferry, and I had to stop because a van was blocking the road. I couldn't get around him. The driver was outside, squatting by one of his tires. I got out to see what was going on. I thought life was back to normal, you know? I really didn't think that—"

"It might be a trap," Bourne said.

"Right."

"What happened?"

"I don't know. I remember getting out of my car and walking toward the guy. That's it. Then nothing."

"What about the last few days?"

She shook her head. "For all I know, the van in the road could have been ten minutes ago. Everything else is black. I got out of my car, and then the next thing I knew, I opened my eyes and there *you* were. It doesn't make any sense."

"So you weren't awake at all in between?"

"Not that I remember. Jason, what's going on? Why did they kidnap me, only to let me go? How did you find me?"

"Bai Ze told me where to look," Bourne said. "But he didn't tell me what I'd find. I didn't know anything about you."

"*Bai Ze?* You know who he is?"

"For now, he's just an electronic voice on a television screen. But he made contact. He offered me a deal."

"What kind of deal?"

Bourne said nothing. He got up from the sofa and went to the window of the safe house. The street looked clear. His motorcycle was hidden inside the garage. Tony Audley had kept his word, not giving up Bourne's location yet. He turned around and saw Laney watching him with a curious expression on her face.

"Jason?" she asked. "What's going on?"

"You said you had a headache."

"Yeah."

"The usual kind? Behind your eyes?"

"No, this is different. It's just— I don't know what it is."

He nodded. "I'm going to ask you some questions. They may sound odd, but just answer them as fast as you can. First thing that comes into your head."

"I don't understand."

"I get it, but humor me, okay? Nothing but answers as fast as you can." He snapped his fingers. "Who was your best friend in high school?"

"Lynn Kessler."

"How did you meet her?"

"We had English class together freshman year. She spilled Coke over my desk."

"Did you have any pets growing up?"

"My parents always had cats. Jason, what—"

"What were their names? The cats, what were their names?"

"Um, Martini, Tequila, Rummy. My dad liked his booze."

"When did you lose your virginity?"

"Hey!"

"Quickly, when, with whom."

"Sophomore year of college, Bobby Moran. We'd been dating for a couple of months, and then it was one and done. Asshole." Suddenly, Laney bolted to her feet, both of her hands slapping across her face. Her brown eyes went wide. She ran to Jason and threw her arms around his waist. "Holy shit! *I remember.*"

"Yeah."

"It's there! It's back, my memory's back! How? What happened to me?"

"I don't know, but Bai Ze said he'd give me proof. Proof that he could do what he said—restore memories that had been taken away. You're the proof. And given that he abducted you several days ago, he's been planning this little game for a while."

"My headache. Is it related?"

"I assume that's because of whatever they did to you. Did you know any of that information before? Did you remember any of what I asked you about?"

"Some, but only because I read about it, or people told me about it. Bobby Moran was new. I never told anyone about that. It's always been weird, not knowing anything about my sex life or where I first did it. But now I remember him. And I'm still friends with Lynn. She jokes about spilling the can of Coke over my homework, but I can see it happening now, can see us both giggling about it. The memory's there."

"How much?" Bourne asked. "How much is back?"

"I don't— I don't really know. I don't even know what to think about. Ask me something else."

"What was the first concert you went to?"

"Britney Spears."

"Seriously?"

She punched him in the arm. "Don't judge me."

"Where was it?"

"Chicago. Lynn and I drove down there."

"First memory as a child."

"I was on the beach with my dad. Lake Michigan. He brought a grill and made hamburgers. Oh my God, Jason, it's all back. I can remember everything. I'm not a stranger to myself anymore. For the first time in years, I feel . . . *normal.* Like I know who I am, like I can draw a line between who I was in the past and who I am now."

"I'm happy for you," Bourne said.

And he was.

He also realized that Bai Ze was smart and knew exactly what he was doing. He'd gift wrapped his proof in a way that Bourne would find irresistible. Listening to Laney answer his questions, he understood what she was feeling, the emotional power of what she'd regained. What he felt inside himself was an overwhelming desire for the same thing. He wanted to be able to look into his mind and find answers for the most basic of questions. He wanted what had been taken from him.

Just like the Chinese wanted the Files back.

It truly was the perfect trade.

But Bai Ze was also right about the cost. If Bourne crossed that line with Shadow, there was no going back.

"What about eight years ago?" he asked.

"What?"

"Eight years ago. What do you remember about that night in the woods?"

For the first time, Laney hesitated. She stepped away from him, her eyes confused. Her brow wrinkled. "I don't know."

"You were on the highway following the young Chinese couple. The assassins. You followed them to the White Gull Inn that night."

Her voice was tentative. "Yes."

"Do you remember that?"

"I'm not sure. I still remember what I saw when your friend regressed me. But I don't know if that's real. I mean, I can't tell if it's an actual *memory* now, if it's any different from what I saw before."

"What about the cottage?" Bourne asked. "You went up to the

rear window at one of the cottages and you looked inside. But you weren't able to see *who* was there. A fog blocked your mind. You said it was like a literal fog, a cloud inside the cottage. Is it still there? Or can you see through it now?"

She grimaced as she tried to put the pieces together. "I don't see anything. I don't remember being behind the cottage. I don't remember the Chinese couple taking me away. Or you. I don't remember you being there at all. There's nothing."

"So you don't remember Bai Ze," Bourne said.

"I'm sorry, Jason. I wish I could tell you who he is, or what I saw, but I can't. I can tell you what Bobby Moran and I had on the pizza we ate before we had sex that first time. I can tell you the first song I danced to at my high school prom. But the night that changed my life? The night I met you? That's still gone."

25

BOURNE COULD SEE IN LANEY'S FACE THAT SHE WAS EXHAUSTED FROM everything that had happened to her. He led her to one of the bedrooms in the safe house and helped her undress. He checked her naked body for any injuries she may have suffered during her abduction, but there were no physical signs of what she'd been through. She made a half-hearted attempt to coax him into sex, but she looked relieved when he smiled and told her to get her strength back. He tucked her into bed and then waited with her until he knew she was asleep.

He checked his watch. It was midmorning. They would need to be out of the house by nightfall. In the meantime, he had a lot to do.

He opened up a contact entry on his phone for someone named Lucien Argaud, a plumber located at an address in Paris. Argaud really was a French plumber, and the business address associated with his contact info was correct. But the mobile phone number for the entry was fictitious. Instead, in his head, Bourne added one digit to the first number, two to the second, three to the third, until he had an entirely new phone number.

That number belonged to the private and personal cell phone of Holly Schultz of the CIA.

She'd given it to him to be used in an emergency, and he'd never had an occasion to use it before. But he texted her now. *Need to meet. Cain.*

He didn't know how long it would take her to reply, or whether she would choose to reply at all. The last time he'd seen her, shortly after the death of Johanna, he'd broken into Holly's apartment and come very close to killing her. He was sure Holly would be wary of meeting him again, but apparently that didn't matter. Her return text arrived on his phone in less than ninety seconds.

One hour. The Chain Bridge.

Bourne left a note for Laney, then took off on his motorcycle across the city. It took him forty minutes at high speed, weaving in and out of traffic, to reach the Chain Bridge over the Potomac, which connected DC with the northern Virginia suburbs. The bridge was a few minutes away from the CIA headquarters complex, where Holly worked. He parked on the Washington side of the bridge, then took the sidewalk over the water, alert for any kind of ambush. But he saw no agency vehicles guarding the scene.

Ahead of him, in the middle of the bridge, Holly waited with her yellow Lab, Sugar, at her side. As he got closer, Sugar gave one bark, announcing him. Holly snapped her fingers twice, giving the dog permission to greet Bourne and allow him to make a fuss over her. Jason and the dog had been friends for several years. Then, when Holly snapped her fingers again, Sugar came back to rigid attention.

Bourne leaned on the bridge railing, watching the slow-moving water below them. He remained alert for threats on the low bluff hugging the riverbank—a glint of sunlight on a rifle barrel—but he saw nothing. Next to him, Holly clung to Sugar's leash and tilted her chin to enjoy the cold morning breeze.

Holly was small, in her early fifties, with a thin, birdlike physique. Her dark hair, streaked with a few strands of gray, was cut in a short, functional bob. She had the quiet look of a piano teacher who was afraid to open her mouth, but Bourne knew she was actually brilliant, tough, and absolutely ruthless. She lived in a world where the ends justified any means, and that meant she'd lied to him and betrayed him more than once.

Including ordering Johanna's death to protect the secret of Adam Hill.

Bourne felt his rage well up again. Without seeing him, Holly somehow sensed his emotions.

"The present doesn't change the past," she murmured. "We talked through all of this last year, Cain, but I realize that you'll always hate me for what I had to do. Is that why you're here? Do you still want revenge?"

"I do, but not necessarily against you."

"Well, Adam Hill is already dead."

"But his employer lives on."

Holly was quiet for a while. She was the kind of intelligence agent who thought for a long time before she spoke. "So this is about Bai Ze."

"That's right."

"Interesting. I heard a rumor that Shadow had a lead on finding Bai Ze. From the Files, presumably. I should have guessed that you'd be involved. Have you located him? Do you know who he is?"

"Not yet."

A ghost of a smile crossed her lips. "I assume you and Shadow gave some thought to the idea that *I* might be Bai Ze. Given my relationship with Hill."

"You're right, we considered that possibility. Actually, I'd be pleased if you *were* Bai Ze, because it would give me a new excuse to kill you. But I don't think that's true. You're too public. Too many people know who you are and *where* you are at any given moment. Bai Ze works in the shadows."

"Then why the urgent meeting?" Holly asked.

"First, to warn you. The agency is compromised. Bai Ze has infiltrated it. You probably have double agents close to you."

"How can you be sure?"

Bourne thought about his first night in Door County. "You had an agent working for you under the code name Chess."

"Yes. He has a star on the wall."

"Chess wasn't killed on that mission in China years ago. He was killed in Wisconsin last week. By me. He was freelancing as an assassin for Bai Ze. If there was one, there are others. Not just outside the agency, but inside, too."

Holly's face turned his way. She waited as a truck with a loud engine passed them on the bridge. "Are you sure about Chess?"

"Shadow ran the photo. The ID was confirmed."

"That's disturbing."

"There's more. Bai Ze's team was *waiting* for me in Wisconsin.

They knew I was coming. What it suggests is that Volt Typhoon goes even deeper than we feared. Bai Ze must have high-level sources in Treadstone. If that's true, then the CIA is vulnerable, too."

"So Shadow has you operating on your own," Holly concluded. "Keep the information compartmentalized, rather than risk leaks."

"That's right."

"Well, can you tell me what you've learned? I know it's asking a lot to trust me, Cain. I've given you precious little reason to do that and every reason to hate me. But you're here, which means you want something from me. I can't help if I don't know what's going on."

Bourne knew that. He'd expected it.

"Eight years ago, Alvin Bakk conducted a supersecret hiring operation near his home in Door County. He brought in top people from around the world for potential recruitment."

"His team of giants," Holly said.

"Right. Not just employees at his own businesses, but spies who would stay in place and supply him with intelligence. But Bai Ze was there from the beginning. He penetrated the whole operation. The information he gathered put him in a position to influence or turn key people throughout Bakk's empire. Multiply that across numerous other sectors, and you can imagine the time bombs that are ready to go off whenever the Chinese pull the trigger."

"I assume the operation in Wisconsin is also your one clue to finding Bai Ze," Holly said.

"Yes. Shadow used the Files and discovered that *I* was there eight years ago, too. I was chasing a Chinese assassin, and I saw

Bai Ze. But apparently I was taken, and my memory was changed. Erased. I didn't remember where I'd been, what I'd seen. As far as I knew, I'd had a blackout. I lost several days of my life."

Holly frowned. "No doubt that also left your brain vulnerable when you were shot. That's why you lost everything."

"Exactly."

"Jesus. I knew they were working on memory manipulation, but I didn't realize their research had gone so far."

Bourne thought: *And what they did, they can undo. They can reverse it. They can give me my memory back.*

If I give them the Files.

If I betray who I am.

"So why am I here, Cain?" Holly went on. "What do you want from me?"

"You knew about Bakk's operation, too. Didn't you? You had a mole."

Knowledge spread across Holly's face. "Ah. You found out about Mei Sun. Yes, okay, I recruited her to spy on Bakk and get close to him. He's a genius, but also a security risk. A billionaire with that kind of government influence and access? With that kind of power? I needed to know what he was planning. Mei Sun was my way in. She was perfect for the mission. One thing we knew about Bakk is that he had a weakness for sex, and Sun, well, she's very good at what she does. Ultimately, it worked out very well for her, too. She became one of the richest women in the world."

"She's dead," Bourne told her.

"*What?*"

"Last night. Someone will find the body today. Word will get out."

Darkness filled Holly's expression. "Was it you? Did you kill her?"

"No, but I was there. I confronted her. Actually, Sun and I were about to come see *you*, but one of Bai Ze's assassins got to her first. He was tying up another loose end. Which makes me think *you* could be at risk, too. You need to be careful, Holly. Tighten up your security. Make sure you trust everyone on your detail."

"I don't understand. Why would I be a target? If you think I'm in bed with Bai Ze, you're wrong."

"I don't think that, but Sun thought you could help us find him."

"How? I'm no closer to finding Bai Ze than you are."

"Yes, but there's something you don't know. Eight years ago, Sun wasn't just feeding intel about Bakk's hiring operation to you. She was supplying it to Bai Ze, too."

Holly gasped in shock. "Sun a double agent for the Chinese? That's crazy."

"She said the same thing. So did Bakk. But we found her on video going into the hotel where Bai Ze was hiding. That whole week in Door County, Sun was meeting with the Chinese, passing along information about Bakk's team of giants. I suspect whatever data she gave *you* was faked. She was misleading you, sending you down the wrong road."

"I don't believe it. Sun was one of my top agents. You have to be wrong about this."

"I'm not wrong. She was working directly with Bai Ze, feeding him everything. She knew who he was. But like me, she didn't remember any of it. When I showed her the video, she was genuinely shocked. Horrified."

"So you think her memory was manipulated."

"Yes. Like mine."

Holly's lips pushed into a flat line. "Well, I had suspicions that something was wrong, but it seemed impossible. Mostly because I knew Sun so well. But none of the intel from that week panned out. Sun gave me names of people Bakk brought inside, but I found no evidence that anyone was compromised. When things began to go wrong at Bakk's companies, I couldn't tie the problems back to any of the names. Obviously, I was played."

"And in the meantime, the real spies spread like a virus throughout Bakk's companies," Bourne said.

"Okay. I feel like a fool for not seeing it, but I believe you. But I don't see how this gets us any closer to finding Bai Ze."

"I'm not sure, either, but Sun thought you'd be able to figure it out. You knew her better than anyone. You were her handler. The thing is, the Chinese already had Sun in their pocket when the operation began in Door County. That's different from what happened with me. I showed up by accident. They had no idea I would be there, chasing Fang. They caught me, they manipulated me. But they'd already made Sun their spy before that week, and she didn't even realize it. *How?*"

Holly turned around and faced the river. She couldn't see it, but she seemed to absorb its presence through her other senses. The cold flushed her cheeks. Sugar turned around, too, and nestled against her leg.

"There was a mission on the mainland years ago," she told him. "Before Sun was with Bakk, when she was a field agent out of Taiwan. You have to understand, our biggest intelligence gap is *inside* China. We struggle to recruit double agents, moles. That's where they have a huge advantage over us. They have people throughout our universities, tech, government, whatever. Hell, we invite them in, we give them visas! There are so many of them, with such good background covers, that they can slip spies right under our noses. Plus, for years they were able to flood agents over the southern border. But Americans in China? It's not the same thing. It's much more difficult, much more dangerous. So we launched a program a decade ago to find and recruit more Chinese double agents. People inside the country who wanted to undermine the CCP. Sun led the effort. She could blend in; she had friends and relatives. She began to build a network in China much like Bai Ze has been able to build here. Or so we allowed ourselves to believe."

"The Chinese knew," Bourne said.

"If they didn't know from the beginning, they found out early on. They turned double agents into triple agents and played them back against us. When we began to suspect a problem, they took action. Sun got lured across the border on what she thought was a significant recruitment opportunity. A senior party official. She brought a couple of agents with her as backup. Including—"

"Chess."

She nodded. "That's right. It was a sting. They were all captured. Chess and the other agent were killed immediately. Or that's what I believed. Apparently that was a ruse so they could be turned and sent back here under new identities. As for Sun, I tried to do a prisoner swap, but the Chinese denied even having her. They didn't want to give her up. In the meantime, they tortured her. The things they did to her—when I eventually read about it in Sun's report, it turned my stomach. It takes a lot to do that, Cain."

"How did she get free?"

"She escaped from the prison where they were holding her about six months later. A guard helped her, someone who still had a semblance of conscience. She was able to get out of the country and back to Taiwan."

"Or the whole thing was arranged," Bourne said.

Holly's fingers gripped the bridge railing tightly. "Yes, now I wonder if you're right. They spent those six months destroying her mind as well as her body."

"What happened after she got back?"

"She was useless for the field at that point," Holly replied with a sigh. "Mentally, physically, she never made it back to her old self. Months of counseling didn't work. Some agents can get past the trauma, some can't. You did, but Sun was finished as far as missions overseas. So I looked for other ways that she could be useful."

"Bakk," Bourne said.

"That's right."

"Was that your idea or hers?"

"Hers. In retrospect, I guess I should have wondered about that. But it was a nonviolent op, so it seemed like there was no danger. I didn't think twice about sending her out. Once again, I played into Bai Ze's hands."

"He's good. He's had us chasing our tails for years."

"Well, Sun's history explains how they were able to get inside her head," Holly said. "I take responsibility for that, and for not doing a better job of vetting her when she got back. But I still don't see how that gets us any closer to Bai Ze."

Bourne was silent.

He was sure Holly was wrong. The truth felt close now, almost within reach.

He stared off the bridge at the Potomac, his gaze lost in the muddy water. In his mind, he replayed everything she had just told him. Step by step. From the beginning. He realized it was like standing too close to a painting and then stepping back and watching the picture take shape in front of you.

He thought about what Mei Sun had told him, too, when she was trying to fit the puzzle pieces together.

The one time they blew my mission, I remember every second of it. Believe me, I'll never forget those days.

And then:

This isn't just about you or me separately, Cain. If we were both targeted, there has to be a common denominator.

And then his own voice: *You sound like you know what it is.*

Maybe I do, but I hope I'm wrong.

No, Sun had not been wrong.

There was only one answer, one way to look at the picture in front of him. Bourne knew. He knew everything now. And he knew what he had to do. A wave of regret rolled over him, a mix of fury and loss that he could never seem to escape. It happened over and over, again and again, a song played endlessly on repeat.

To be alive was to be betrayed.

"Actually, I think you've given me everything I need," Bourne said.

26

WHEN BOURNE GOT BACK TO THE SAFE HOUSE, HE KNEW IT HAD BEEN breached. He drove by on the motorbike and saw that his old-school security alert—a small piece of paper wedged into the doorframe—had been triggered. The paper was gone. It was possible that Laney had awakened and opened the front door, but he didn't think so. He kept on driving, and when he was out of sight, he parked the bike on the street and approached the house from the rear. He let himself in through the back door, but the electronic lock announced his arrival with a soft beep.

Whoever was waiting for him in the house knew he was here.

Bourne tensed, Glock in hand, waiting for an ambush, but he didn't get one. He headed for the hallway and checked the bedroom where he'd left Laney. When he cracked the door open, he saw her still asleep in bed, undisturbed.

What was going on?

Then, when he reached the living room, he understood. Alvin Bakk sat on a sofa near the front window.

The billionaire said nothing at Bourne's arrival. He was dipping Twiglets in the jar of Marmite, and he had an open bottle of Tanqueray on the table in front of him. He wore a Brewers baseball cap low on his forehead and a black T-shirt emblazoned with the motto *Rich people suck.*

Bourne holstered his Glock and sat in an old worn recliner near the sofa. "No limo?"

"I didn't think you'd want me to be so obvious," Bakk replied, crunching on another Twiglet and washing it down with gin. The man hadn't shaved, and his normally buoyant expression was hangdog.

"You heard about Mei Sun," Bourne guessed, his voice soft.

Bakk nodded, not saying anything more.

"I'm sorry."

Bakk leaned back in the sofa, his arms now limp at his sides. "I still loved her. She really was my soulmate. Getting divorced didn't change that. I knew she was playing me the whole time, I knew she was a spy, but despite that, I loved her. I had this idea in my head that we'd get back together someday and rule the world. You talked to her. Do you think it was mutual? Do you think deep down she loved me, too?"

It would have been hurtful to tell him the truth.

"I have no idea."

Bakk laughed sourly. He knew the answer anyway.

"So did you kill her?" he asked, which was the second time today Bourne had faced that question. "Was it you?"

"No. I tried to stop it, but I was too late. Bai Ze sent an assassin."

"But you were right? She was working for him, giving him

intel about my companies?" Bakk shook his head. "Sun a Chinese spy. That undermines everything I thought I knew about people in this world."

"Well, it wasn't by choice," Bourne told him. "She was manipulated. Like me."

"I guess that's something." Bakk pursed his lips, then dipped another Twiglet. "These things are pretty good when you dunk them. God Save the King."

"How did you find me?" Bourne asked.

The billionaire shrugged, as if the question were irrelevant. "Do we have to go over that again? I have eyes everywhere in DC. And I know Tony Audley. I told you, I know everyone. When the police called me about Sun, I needed to talk to you, to hear what really happened. I was surprised that you didn't call me."

"You're right, I should have done that," Bourne said.

"But you wondered if I already knew, is that it? If I was Bai Ze and I'd sent a killer after my ex-wife?"

"I know you're not Bai Ze."

Bakk worked his tongue into his cheek to loosen a piece of Twiglet stuck between his teeth. "When I got here, I looked in the bedroom. I was expecting to find you, but instead, there was Laney Reese, asleep. What's the deal with you two? Are you an item?"

"No."

"But you slept with her in Door County."

"That's true."

"Are you going to sleep with her again?"

"Why do you care?"

"I don't. I'm just a voyeur. I like to know what goes on behind closed doors."

"No, we're not going to sleep together," Bourne said.

"Then why is she here?"

"Bai Ze abducted her. He told me how to find her."

"You *talked* to Bai Ze?"

"He talked to me. After Sun's murder. He did a video call on her television. I couldn't see him."

"What did he want?"

Bourne waited a beat before answering. "To brag, I guess. To prove that he's still one step ahead of us."

Bakk tapped a finger on his lips, his stare fixed on Bourne. Then he shook his head. "I would expect you to be an accomplished liar, Jason. But that was not a good lie. Not good at all."

"Well, that's all I can tell you."

"Then let's go back to the question of Laney. Why is she here? Why did Bai Ze abduct her, only to give her back to you? My guess is, he wanted something from you. He needed you to do something for him. See, I still think you killed Sun. Was that the deal? You murder her, you bow your knee to the throne, and Bai Ze lets you rescue Laney Reese like a knight in shining armor."

"That's not what happened," Bourne replied.

"Then again, I'm asking you, why is she here?"

Without looking toward the hallway, Bourne saw movement out of the corner of his eye, a shift in the shadows that led to the bedrooms. He heard the faintest noise of a footstep. "She won't be here for long. I'm sending her back home. End of story."

"Do you think I'm stupid, Jason? I'm a very smart man."

"I know."

"Then why treat me like a fool? Obviously, Laney is an important piece in whatever game Bai Ze is playing."

"Leave Laney out of this."

Bakk sighed. "All right, have it your way. Enough about her. Let's go back to Bai Ze. He's inside my companies, and I want him taken down. What happens now, Jason? What's your next step?"

"That's my concern, not yours. You'll have to trust me."

"You know how I feel about that," Bakk replied. "*Trust no one.*"

"Then don't. But I already told you, I don't work for you."

"You're still a company man, is that it? Does Treadstone know your next step? Have you told Shadow what you're planning? I wonder how she'd react if I called her up and told her that Laney Reese was naked in your bed right now. That Bai Ze told you how to rescue her, but you won't say why. I think she'd have questions for you. She'd probably also wonder why you asked Tony Audley not to give away your location."

"It's not complicated. I work best alone."

Bakk's eyes narrowed. "Another lie hidden in the truth. Interesting. You know, there's something different about you, Bourne. Something darker. Somehow I get the feeling that your loyalties have changed."

"Nothing's changed."

"Okay. Fine. I see I'm not getting any blood from the stone." Bakk stood up from the sofa and wiped Twiglet crumbs from his T-shirt. "I should go. But I hope you know what you're doing. Whatever Bai Ze wants from you, you're playing with fire."

Bourne said nothing.

Through the front window, he saw Bakk's limousine pull to the curb, as if summoned by magic. The billionaire went to the door, took a last look at Bourne, and then left the safe house without another word. Outside, the back door of the limousine opened automatically for him, and Bourne watched from the window as Bakk's car drove away.

"You didn't tell him," said a voice from the hallway.

Bourne turned around. Laney stood there, a sheet wrapped around her body, her shoulders bare.

"So tell me," she went on. "Answer the question. Why am I here?"

LANEY LEANED INTO HIM, HER LEGS STRETCHED OUT ALONG THE SOFA, her head on his shoulder. The sheet slipped down the shallow hills of her breasts. Her long hair spilled across his neck, and her skin smelled sweet and clean. They both drank gin, but they left the bag of Twiglets and the jar of Marmite untouched.

"Proof," he said. "Remember? That's what Bai Ze promised me. Proof that the Chinese have the ability to restore lost memory. That's why he took you, why they did whatever they did to you. He needed to show me it was possible."

Laney was quiet, thinking about it. "He offered to do the same thing for you, didn't he?"

"That's right."

"Give you your life back. All your memories."

"Yes."

She pushed herself up on the sofa, her face very close to his. "*Jesus.* And now you're thinking about it?"

"I'm thinking about it."

"The price must be pretty high," she said.

"The price is incredibly high."

"Can you tell me what it is?"

Bourne took a long, slow breath. "Bai Ze wants me to get something for him. I can do it. I know how to do it. But if I do, I'm betraying the people I work for. One person in particular. Then again, she's betrayed me many times."

"Is this the other woman?" Laney asked. "The girlfriend who kills people?"

"Yes."

"Do you think she'll kill you if you do this?"

"I don't know. Maybe. Maybe I'll have to kill her to get what Bai Ze wants. We've both known the road we're on might lead us that way sooner or later. But she's like two different people, that's what makes it such a difficult choice."

"What do you mean?"

"She has two identities when she's with me. One is called Shadow. One is called Marlen. Shadow is ruthless, cruel. She lies to me without giving it a thought. She'd sell my soul if it got her what she wanted. Marlen is someone else entirely, a real human being that Shadow has to keep locked away. That other woman is someone I'm half in love with, even when I don't want to be. If I betray Shadow, I can live with that. But I don't want to walk away from Marlen."

"Marlen is why you don't want to sleep with me again," Laney said. "Right? I heard what you told Bakk."

"That's right."

"Did it cause problems when we slept together in Door County?"

He thought about that night at the Hyatt. He heard the angry, hungry whisper in his ear.

I told you that Laney Reese didn't matter to me. I didn't care about her.

I'm not a jealous lover when it comes to you. But that's not true. Maybe she doesn't matter to Shadow, but she matters to Marlen. I hate the idea of you fucking her. It makes me crazy. It drives me insane. *I only want you fucking* me.

"Yes, it did."

"Sorry."

"It was my choice."

Laney let the sheet slip farther down her body. "I'm not going to lie or pretend. I don't know Marlen, and I don't care about her. I'm attracted to you. I haven't felt this way about a man in a long time. I'm not trying to screw up your life, but I want you. And I'm pretty sure you want me, too."

She was right. Bourne couldn't deny the physical attraction. He wanted her, too. But he wanted a lot of things that he was never going to have.

"I can't let that happen."

She put a little distance between them. "Okay. What now?"

"Right now, you're going to get dressed, and I'm going to take you to the airport, and you're going to get on a flight back to Wisconsin. Go home. Live the life you remember. I'm not part of that."

"Are you sure?"

"I'm sure."

"What are you going to do?"

Bourne reached out and caressed her cheek with the back of his hand. "I'm going to betray Shadow."

"And Marlen?"

"It's a package deal."

Laney kissed him on the lips. Just once, soft and quick. She climbed off the sofa, leaving the sheet behind, as if to taunt him with what he was giving up. She crossed the living room in her bare feet, but stopped halfway and turned back, her hands on her hips, her body on display. "Will I see you again?"

"After I do this, I'll need to disappear," Bourne told her. "Run. Treadstone will never stop. They'll hunt me forever."

"I'd run with you, but I can't."

"I wouldn't ask you to do it anyway," Bourne said.

"But will I see you again?"

Bourne forced himself to get off the sofa, forced himself to cross the room and wrap up her body in his arms. She clung to him; her fingers scratched him. He kissed her back, and there was nothing quick about it, nothing soft. The kiss told her that he meant every word he was saying. The kiss was as far as he could allow himself to go. And then when it was over, he looked into her brown eyes and made sure she believed him.

"You'll see me again."

27

SHADOW ARRIVED HOME AT ELEVEN O'CLOCK IN THE EVENING. SHE RODE in an armored Escalade with a Treadstone agent as the driver. His code name was Zero. He was ruthless and obedient, the kind of man who would fight to defend her until all the blood had drained from his body. Those were the men she wanted around her.

She lived half an hour from the Bloomingdale brownstone where Treadstone was headquartered. Her home—much larger than she needed as a single person—was a two-story redbrick Georgian colonial on the fringe of Rock Creek Park. She'd bought it two years earlier when she took over Treadstone, and she'd spent that time carefully choosing artwork and furniture that matched her antique tastes. It was beautiful now, upscale, tasteful, everything in order, like a museum.

Even so, there were days when she missed the rustic British cottage where she'd lived for years. It had been a cold island getaway whenever she was between her fieldwork, a place with very few people. She was one of those women who wasn't lonely when she was alone. Or so she told herself.

"Any instructions?" Zero asked from the front seat.

"Not tonight. Thank you."

"Let me clear the area, ma'am. Then you'll be good to go."

Zero got out of the Escalade. First, he checked with the agent in a Tesla Cybertruck parked in the driveway. There was always an agent waiting for her overnight, in case Shadow needed to make an emergency departure, which happened often enough. When he got the all clear from the driver, he made a transit around the house to review security. Upon his return, he got back behind the wheel of the Escalade.

"Clear, ma'am."

"Thank you. I'll see you in the morning, Zero."

"Five o'clock as usual?"

"Yes, please."

Shadow got out of the back seat, her briefcase in one hand, her other hand curled around the Domina pistol in the pocket of her long wool coat. Despite the green light from Zero, Shadow took no chances with security. She gave a wave to the woman inside the Tesla, then continued up the steps to her front door. She let herself inside, deactivated the alarm and reset it immediately to armed stay, and hung her coat in the closet. She let the Domina swing from her middle finger as she went to the library, where she locked her briefcase in a wall safe identical to the one she kept at Treadstone headquarters. Then she poured herself a glass of Macallan, removed a hardcover copy of *The Great Gatsby* from a bookshelf, and settled into a wingback leather chair that dated to the early

1900s. Her Echo device shuffled instrumental music by Ludovico Einaudi.

For the next hour, she read. This was the one peaceful hour she allowed herself every night, that lone hour from the time she got home to the time she went to bed. Her therapist had said it would relax her and help her sleep. She was half right. This hour had become the most precious part of Shadow's day—the Marlen hour of her day—but by the time she went upstairs to her bedroom, her relaxation always bled away. The real world crept back into her thoughts, and she struggled to sleep.

She didn't even notice the time passing, but soon enough, the Howard Miller grandfather clock in the library chimed midnight. The hour was done. Time for bed. She returned the Fitzgerald book to the open space on the shelf. She finished the last of her Macallan, rinsed and dried the crystal glass, and then took the marble staircase to the upper level. The Domina was still loosely cradled in her hand. She noted that the heavy curtains in her bedroom suite were closed, as they were supposed to be. She turned on the Tiffany lamp near her bed with a voice command, then checked the various spaces where anyone might hide. That was her typical routine.

When she knew she was alone, she placed the Domina under her pillow for easy access overnight. She entered her walk-in closet and removed her clothes down to her black panties. After that, she went into the bathroom and got ready, removing her makeup, brushing her teeth. When she was done, she returned to the closet and took a nightgown from a hanger and slipped it over her body. Her fingers sifted through her blond hair, separating the strands.

She went back to the bedroom, humming one of the tracks by Einaudi.

She wasn't alone anymore. Jason sat in a wooden chair in the corner.

Shadow controlled her reaction, showing no surprise at his arrival. Her gaze shot to the pillow, noticing that the Domina was gone. He was dressed all in black, and he looked annoyingly handsome, as he always did.

"My guards?" she asked calmly. "Are they alive?"

"They're fine."

"You got past the alarm."

"I know your code."

"Why take my gun?"

"You won't need it."

"Who are you here to see?"

"*Marlen.*"

Her breath caught and her voice fell to a whisper. "I was hoping."

She didn't hesitate. Between her legs, her arousal was already building. She pushed one strap of the nightgown off her shoulder, then the other. With a tug, she slid the black lace past her breasts and hips and let the nightgown pool at her feet. Her thumbs tugged on her panties and peeled them down inch by inch, leaving her naked. After she let him enjoy the sight of her, she turned off the lights.

The room went dark, and they were invisible.

She crossed the room to him. He was already standing up, waiting for her. The coolness they both hid behind vanished. They embraced wildly, passionately, their mouths fighting to kiss each other. She loved the feel of his rough hands all over her body; she loved being naked while he was still fully dressed. She let him scoop her off the ground and carry her to her bed in the darkness, and then she pulled him down with her, pawing at him, grasping for him, wanting his weight on top of her, needing it *now* with no foreplay. Her fingers released him; her legs spread wide. A moan escaped from her mouth like a sigh as he pushed deep inside.

It was crazy, breathless, wanton, two lovers coming together with all the pent-up need of a first time. Maybe that was because, in the back of her mind, she knew it was the last time. But she didn't let herself think about that.

BAI ZE SAT BEHIND HIS DESK, WAITING FOR THE MIDNIGHT CALL. WHEN he checked his watch, he saw that he had ten minutes before the screen in his office came alive. The men from Beijing were always on time.

For now, the screen was black, like the rest of the space, with no lights. He could barely make out his own shadowy reflection in the glass. He was always amused that his superiors had insisted on a screen that took up an entire wall, as if they were players in an IMAX movie. That was their power move, making them appear larger than life, making him feel small in their presence.

As if he didn't know exactly what they were doing.

Head games.

There were days when he wondered if it was worth the risk to engage in treason. Yes, it was partly about ego, to see whether he could pull it off. Tom Cruise didn't need to do his own stunts, but that was part of the challenge. Yes, the Chinese paid him a not-so-small fortune to betray his country. When he retired someday, he would live in splendor, probably in a condo on Hainan Island, with views over the South China Sea. Of course, that was assuming they didn't kill him first. He was no fool. When a spy's usefulness ran out, so did his lifespan. So he'd taken steps to protect himself, and hopefully that would be enough.

No, it was about more than ego, more than money.

It was about revenge.

Almost no one knew the truth of who he was. Only his mother knew, and she was long dead, taking the secret to her grave. If anyone looked at his background, they would see his father listed as a professor at Columbia. In fact—his mother had told him when he turned eighteen—his father had been a handsome neighbor boy on her New York street, the love of her life, who had been sent to die in the jungles of Vietnam. But he *didn't* actually die. He went missing. MIA. Left to rot and suffer torture in a foreign hellhole.

The government forgot about him. The people forgot about him. His sacrifice became an asterisk to a war from which America wanted to move on as quickly as possible. But his unacknowledged son never forgot. His unacknowledged son burned with rage at the country's betrayal.

If you begin a war, you honor the soldiers.

If you begin a war, you wage it to win.

Well, soon America would learn that lesson when the war came to their own shores. A cyberwar. A drone war.

He checked his watch again. Five minutes remained until the opera gang would appear on his screen. He used the time to make a phone call, and his agent answered on the first ring. Efficient as always. His killer. His *assassin*. Simon Harris, Mei Sun, plus many more over the years they'd been together. When hard work needed to be done, you always sent your best.

"Where is Bourne?" Bai Ze asked.

"He's with Shadow."

"Is our surveillance working?"

"It is. I hear them perfectly."

"What has he told her?"

"Not a thing. For now, they're fucking."

"Keep listening."

"My pleasure," the agent replied.

"I need to know everything he says. I need to know if he suspects a trap."

"Understood. I'll be in touch."

Bai Ze hung up the phone. He stroked his chin, thinking about Bourne and Shadow in bed, like two angry tigers mating. Did Bourne suspect a trap? Of course he did. He was a man who lived his life without trust, a man who knew nothing but lies. But that didn't mean he would fail to deliver. If a trap was constructed well enough, the mouse has nowhere to go but forward.

The wall across from him came to life. It was exactly midnight.

He saw them lined up in a solemn row, the CCP men hiding behind their garish opera masks, concealing their identities. The man in the middle, the one in the fierce Li Gang mask to whom the others deferred, spoke first, as usual. Bai Ze half wondered if it was Xi himself.

"You said you had news."

"I do," Bai Ze replied. "The Bourne operation has been a great success so far. To begin with, Mei Sun is finally dead. She gave away nothing before we removed her. Bourne himself is behaving like a marionette, dancing as we pull the strings, acting precisely as I anticipated he would. Our surveillance indicates that he has begun to keep secrets about his true intentions, hiding his plans from his superior. I expect him to make a move against Treadstone very soon."

"What kind of move?"

"To infiltrate headquarters. To steal the Files. Soon the AI engine will be back in our hands, where it belongs."

Mumbles of satisfaction came from the opera masks.

"And after we have confirmed that the Files are real?" the man in the middle demanded. "After we know we have what we want? Then will Bourne be killed?"

Bai Ze shook his head. "No."

Quickly, the satisfaction turned to stirrings of anger. Bai Ze held up his hands to quiet them.

"Gentlemen, gentlemen, let me go on, please. Death is too good for Bourne. It is too quick, too easy. No, we have dangled the promise of getting his life back in front of him. We have let him see what it means to *remember*, to get a taste of what he has missed all these years. I want him to believe we are delivering on our promise. I want him to close his eyes and imagine the fog lifting on everything he grew up with, everyone he loved."

"What then?" the Li Gang mask asked.

"Then we will strip it all away," Bai Ze snapped, his voice ice-cold. "We will erase his entire mind this time. We will leave him with nothing, no name, no identity, no past, no way of getting it back. He will be a stranger to himself, nothing but a homeless drifter on the streets. Jason Bourne will cease to exist."

SHADOW AWOKE TO AN ALARM ON HER PHONE. WHICH WAS STRANGE. She hadn't set an alarm.

The bedroom was dark; she saw nothing at all. No light came through the blackout curtains, but she didn't think it was anywhere close to morning. Her long fingers reached for the phone on her nightstand to turn off the blaring alert, and she saw that it was almost two thirty. She'd been asleep for barely two hours.

When she reached the other way across the bed, she found it empty, the sheet still warm where he'd slept next to her. Jason was gone, but he'd left recently. Had he set the alarm? *Why?* She slipped a hand under her pillow and realized that he'd replaced her Domina pistol before he went. Softly, using Marlen's voice, she called his name, wondering if he was still in the room, watching her.

But no. She was alone.

The glow of sex lingered on her body and in her mind. Every muscle ached in a good way, and she could still feel the highs he'd given her. When they were together like this, she loved him. When he left her, she felt the emptiness. God, she was *so good* with him. If this was another time or place, if things were different . . .

But things were not different.

Nothing could change who he was and who *she* was. She was not Marlen. She was Shadow.

There was no way she could sleep again. Her mind was too

full. With a command to her Echo, she turned on the soft light of the Tiffany lamp. She threw back the sheet, still naked, her body still tingling from his touch. Part of her wanted to shower, but she also didn't want to lose the sensation of him all over her skin. If she washed it away, she had the feeling it would never come back.

She showered anyway.

The hot water revived her, awakened her, and made their interlude in the darkness feel not real. The longer she stood under the spray, the more she found herself growing cold. Not temperature cold. Cold in her mind. Cold like a spy. She thought about the agent she knew as Jason Bourne, the man who had once been David Webb, and she realized that this entire night was not like him at all. He was behaving strangely. He did not break into her house, a ghost in the darkness looking for sex.

So what was really going on?

He'd set the alarm. He wanted her awake.

She dried off and went back into the bedroom. She didn't bother getting dressed. She went to the curtains and pulled them aside by a couple of inches, looking out on the front of her house and the wilds of Rock Creek Park across the street. The Tesla was still in the driveway, as it always was.

She went and got her phone, and she texted the Treadstone agent behind the wheel of the car. Her code name was Sweet, which she wasn't. She was lethal. *Everything okay, Sweet? Any problems?*

The agent responded immediately. *All clear, boss. Is something wrong?*

Shadow didn't answer right away. Yes, something was wrong. But what?

She retrieved her Domina from under the pillow. The weight

told her it was still loaded. She found a silk robe and slipped it on, and then she crept downstairs, still in her bare feet, the gun in her hand. The house felt cool; she always let the thermostat go down overnight to help her sleep.

"Jason?" she murmured again, hoping to hear his voice.

But he was gone.

She went into the library and turned on the lights. He'd been here; she could feel his presence. The first thing she noticed with a gasp was that the door to her wall safe was ajar. She ran and checked, relieved to find that her briefcase was still there, still locked. He'd taken nothing. And yet he was telling her something.

The code to the safe here was the same as it was in her office.

Bourne knew them both.

Sweat settled across her skin. Shadow blinked, trying to understand, trying to make sense of it. *Jason, what are you doing? What's going on?*

She knew only one thing. She had to get to the office. Now. Immediately.

Shadow pulled her briefcase out of the safe. In doing so, she dislodged something that shouldn't have been there. A tri-folded piece of paper fell out and floated lazily to the carpet. She picked it up, recognizing Jason's handwriting, and she began to read the long note he'd written to her.

As she did, her heartbeat accelerated until it felt as if it would beat out of her chest. "*Jesus.*"

28

BOURNE WONDERED IF YOU COULD HAVE DÉJÀ VU FOR SOMETHING THAT had never happened.

Years earlier, David Abbott—and Shadow—had both been convinced that David Webb had turned traitor. He'd come to New York and broken into the brownstone headquarters of Treadstone on Seventy-First Street, where he'd stolen its secrets and killed all of the agency's senior leaders. The whole thing was a lie, of course. The assassination had been carried out by an impostor, while the real David Webb was thousands of miles away, in Paris, struggling with no memory of who he was.

But today he was really here, getting ready to break in. It was three in the morning, and Bourne was one hundred yards away from the Washington brownstone that housed the new headquarters of Treadstone. He crouched among the graves on the slope of Glenwood Cemetery, examining the small gap on Capitol Street that led to the alley behind the three-story building. A streetlight gave a dim, flickering glow. Every couple of minutes, headlights marked a car taking an early run south into the heart of the government district. Otherwise, this was a residential area, quiet in the middle of the night, the windows all dark.

Very few people knew about the supersecret agency hiding in their midst. There was plenty of security, but that drew no special notice. This was Washington. Someone who needed extra security always lived close by. Bourne knew there were always six agents on street duty, three in front, three in back, to guard the exterior twenty-four hours a day, plus two more inside on the second floor. They would be in contact by radio every few minutes, so once the operation began, he had to move quickly.

He slipped invisibly down the hillside of the cemetery. Across the street, he spotted a black Mercedes, its windows smoked. A Treadstone agent was behind the wheel, eyes on the alley, radio in his ear. Bourne crept along the wrought-iron fence guarding the cemetery grounds until he was well behind the Mercedes, in a place where the overhead streetlights didn't reach. Carefully, he pulled himself up between the spiked rails of the fence. Swinging up a leg and bracing himself with one foot, he shifted his weight to the other side, then dropped heavily to the sidewalk.

An elevated frontage road ran next to the cemetery. A low stone wall separated the higher road from the divided lanes of Capitol Street. The Mercedes was fifty yards away. Bourne saw no traffic in either direction, so he ran to the wall, keeping low, and dropped to the street below. He was conscious of the car's mirrors, so he didn't cross to the far sidewalk. Instead, he stayed in the traffic lane in the shadows. Bent over, he ran quickly until the Mercedes was directly across from him.

The street was empty. So was the alley. No black SUVs

screamed around the corner to target him. He'd made it this far undetected. He couldn't see the man or woman behind the Mercedes windows, so he didn't know whether it was someone he knew. But he hoped that anyone in Treadstone would recognize *him*. He was counting on the few seconds of cover his identity would give him.

Bourne took out his signal jammer and activated it. That was a risk. If the agents noticed their communications were down, they'd immediately suspect a trap and switch into active-threat mode. But he couldn't allow the agent in the Mercedes to alert the others. He crossed the street, still avoiding the mirrors. Crouching low, he came up on the driver's door. His gun wasn't in his hand. The streetlight was nearby, and he'd be visible as soon as he stood up. He reached the car door and didn't bother trying to open it; he was sure it was locked. He rapped his knuckles sharply on the window, then took a couple of steps backward onto the sidewalk, holding up both hands.

The door flew open. A swarthy, bald-headed agent behind the wheel already had his Ruger in his hand, pointed directly at Bourne's chest. His finger was around the trigger, and in another split second, he would fire.

But then the man's eyes widened.

Bourne knew him. They'd worked together in Istanbul. The agent was a heavyset Turk whose code name was Lava.

"*Cain*," the man hissed. "What the fuck? What are you doing here?"

"We've got problems, Lava. Has Shadow been in touch? Is she here?"

"No, we haven't heard a thing. What's going on?"

Bourne didn't explain. Senior agents didn't justify their missions. "Come on, follow me, we need to get inside."

Lava scrambled out of the Mercedes as ordered. His finger slid off the trigger, and he holstered his Ruger. Mistake. *Remember the first rule,* Bourne thought. *Trust no one.* He watched the man's hand drift toward the radio in his ear to check in with the rest of the team—which he should have done before lowering his weapon.

An instant later, Lava realized the radio was dead, and suspicion darkened his face. But he was too late.

Bourne's palm shot out like a piston, catching Lava under the jaw and making him lurch off balance. Immediately, Bourne struck again, taking the man's chin and pushing his head backward until his skull hit hard against the metal of the Mercedes roof. Lava was tough; his eyes rolled back, but he didn't crumple. He began to recover, his hand fishing for the Ruger under his arm. Bourne got there first, grabbing the Ruger and slamming the barrel hard against Lava's temple.

The Turk collapsed. Bourne caught the man's body, laboring to shove him inside the Mercedes. He stripped the agent's radio and put it in his own ear, then clicked the car door shut. He checked the street. No one was around; no one had seen the fight. With a flick of the device in his pocket, he switched off the signal jammer. The radio remained silent. The other agents hadn't noticed the void.

He headed toward the alley in the darkness.

The branches of an oak tree dangled low over his head, and the side wall of one of the Capitol Street brownstones loomed high on his left. On the other side, houses stretched in a row like dominoes, each sharing walls with its neighbors. Only a couple of windows showed any life. Ahead of him, he saw a wooden fence and a tuck-under carport. Electrical wires sagged between poles.

He slowed his pace, knowing a second agent had to be nearby. Cigarette smoke drifted in his direction. Another mistake. Overnight security had a way of growing lax as the hours wore on. Bourne crept to the edge of the carport, taking cover behind vines that clung to a chain-link fence. He saw the silhouette of the agent at the alley corner, where she leaned against a redbrick wall. The woman was lean and muscled, with short dark hair. Only about thirty or forty feet separated them, but the pavement in the alley was littered with gravel. One wrong step would alert her that someone was coming up from behind.

Bourne waited, watching her, timing her. He saw the woman check her six, seeing no one in the shadows. Still Bourne didn't move. Another minute or so later, she checked again. So Bourne had a window of about sixty seconds to close the gap if she kept to the same routine. He moved into the open, taking each step carefully, avoiding the noise of loose rocks under his rubber-soled black shoes. He crossed to the wooden fence in front of him, then moved sideways step-by-step, his back tight against the fence. The darkness might buy him half a second if the agent looked back again.

Then, in his ear, a low voice crackled over the radio.

"This is Steel. Front of house clear. All other stations report."

Bourne moved faster. In a few seconds, it would be obvious that there was a problem if Lava didn't check in. He kept an eye on the agent in front of him and an eye on the ground as he sidestepped toward the corner. The fence ended; the brick wall began. He was only about ten feet behind the other agent now. He had both hands free; his Glock was in his holster and Lava's Ruger shoved inside his belt.

Meanwhile, clipped voices barked through the radio.

"Pirate. Second floor clear."

"Juice. Back door clear."

The woman at the corner spoke. Bourne could hear her whispered voice through the radio and from directly in front of him. She reported to the team leader without another look behind her. "Vandal. Alley clear."

Bourne froze, momentarily disoriented. *Vandal!* The agent in front of him was *Vandal!* But Vandal was dead; he'd *killed* Vandal in Salzburg after she murdered Johanna. Like a rogue wave, anger, confusion, guilt, and regret all rolled through his mind. Then, of course, he realized that Shadow had simply reassigned the code name. This agent was a stranger.

But time was ticking.

He took two more steps.

"Lava?" the lead agent named Steel called, no worry in his voice yet that the Turk hadn't chimed in. But one more second passed, then two, then three, and the dead air grew long. "Lava? Report."

Leaping forward, Bourne wrapped a forearm around Vandal's neck, cutting off the blood to her brain and choking off her voice. At the same time, trying to imitate Lava's guttural Turkish accent, he hissed into the radio: "Sorry. Capitol clear."

From the front of the house, Steel replied, "Roger that."

Meanwhile, the agent struggled violently in Bourne's grasp. Her boot landed hard on Bourne's foot, causing a sharp wave of pain. Her hand found Bourne's hair and pulled his head sharply forward, bone cracking against bone. Still Bourne hung on. The woman went for her weapon, and he knew that even a single wild shot would bring men running. Bourne took hold of the butt of her gun, refusing to yield as the agent tried to peel his fingers away.

His arm was still tightly wrapped around her neck. As her mind swam from the loss of blood, she finally lost consciousness. The woman's grip loosened, and she became dead weight, her whole body slumped. Bourne lowered her to the ground, then bent down and delivered a sharp swing of his Glock's butt into her hairline. The skin cut; blood flowed. She'd be out for an hour or more.

By then, Bourne would either be dead or long gone.

He glanced around the corner of the brick wall at the alley that led behind the series of brownstones. Detached garage stalls and garbage bins stretched one after another all the way to the next street. Vines climbed up the power poles. The Treadstone headquarters was halfway down the alley, its attic level slightly taller than the other homes around it. The attic was where Shadow kept her office.

Where she kept the Files.

Bourne moved through the shadows, in and out of the occasional overhead lights. He kept his Glock in his hand now. Three doors from the Treadstone building, he stopped. That was as close as he dared get without the risk of being spotted by the rear security cameras. Instead, he slipped into a nearby driveway, where an Audi was parked next to a one-stall detached garage. He climbed onto the roof of the car, and from there, onto the roof of the garage. He went up and over the peaked roof, then jumped a few feet to the next adjacent garage. He repeated the maneuver once more, and his jump put him on the roof of the garage behind the Treadstone building.

As soon as he climbed over the peak, he could lower himself to the walkway that led toward the house's back door. But he would also walk right into the gunsight of the agent manning that area.

According to the radio reports, the agent's code name was Juice. Bourne needed to draw Juice to the alley.

Reaching into his pocket, he switched on the radio jammer. Once again, the men couldn't talk to each other. Juice was on his own, even if he didn't know it. Bourne took Lava's Ruger and removed the clip, then threw the gun hard toward the walkway below him. It landed with a sharp metallic clang, crystal clear in the quiet night air. He heard a low voice from the house—"Juice, I've got noise near the alley; I'm checking it out"—but the report didn't come through the radio in his ear.

He heard boots rapping sharply on stone. Juice wasted no time investigating the sound. A flashlight beam swung through the narrow space, and Bourne shrank back on the roof out of sight. The light moved across the walkway and up the sides of the garages on both sides, and then it caught the Ruger with a shine.

"*Gun!*" Juice hissed into the radio, getting no response.

The agent ran for the Ruger. As he came into view below him, Bourne slid down the roof into the air. He landed on Juice's shoulders, taking him to the ground. With a nimble jump, Bourne was immediately back on his feet, and before Juice could recover, Bourne's steel-toed boot flew through the air in a kick that hit the agent hard in the side of the head. His eyes rolled; he was out of action.

Bourne undid the radio jammer. He needed radio signals now. He ran for the back door, not worrying about the team in front of the house. At the door, he plugged in the code on the digital lock. It changed weekly, but he knew where Shadow kept it in her phone. He tapped in the numbers and heard a soft beep as the latch opened. Inside, he walked into what looked like an ordinary Washington condo. No alarm went off, but he knew that behind the steel door on the second floor, the agent code-named Pirate and whoever was working with him were in panic mode, watching the intruder on the camera feed. Bourne didn't try to hide. He waved at the camera, then holstered his Glock and pointed upward at them.

He was sure they were shouting into their radios. "*Intruder!* We've got an intruder, how did he get past our people outside? Hang on, it's *Cain!* Definitely Cain. We've got *Cain* inside the house. What the fuck?"

Bourne took the stairs to the second floor, which he'd done dozens of times in the past. He climbed to the bulletproof door and plugged in the next lock code, which let him in with another soft beep. His foot pushed the door inward; he kept his arms wide, his hands in the air. The upstairs room was brightly lit, unlike the shadows below him. He came through the door and found two men with the barrels of semiautomatic rifles pointed at his chest.

One was small, in his forties, with dark hair. Pirate. His partner was younger, lean and muscled with a red crew cut. Bourne had met him once. His code name was River. Each stood behind desks, with computer monitors behind them. Cubicles dotted the rest of the space. A red leather door on the side wall behind the desks led to the stairwell to the attic.

Shadow's office.

Bourne took a cautious step forward. "Easy, guys. You know me. Sorry for the surprise. We've got a breach. Shadow thinks someone on the detail is dirty, and we got intel about a possible assault tonight. I need to get to her office."

Confusion ran across Pirate's face. Next to him, River studied Bourne with snake eyes, a cold face, and what was obviously an itchy trigger finger. The rifle barrels didn't move. "We didn't hear jack shit about that, Cain."

"And you wouldn't, would you? We don't know who the mole is. Shadow's on her way in. I'm here for backup."

On the monitor behind Pirate, the computer chimed with an incoming text. Bourne knew without even looking at the screen that the message was from Shadow. Pirate heard it, too, and the senior agent realized that whatever update had just arrived, he needed to read it *now*.

"Watch him," he told his partner. "If he moves, shoot him."

Then he swung around to read the message. It didn't take long, and then his breath expelled in disbelief.

"Shit!"

That was all it took. Bourne saw the brash young agent next to Pirate lock the rifle against his shoulder. River was getting ready to fire.

BAI ZE GREW IMPATIENT.

He'd been awake throughout the night, expecting a report. But so far there was nothing. He didn't dare call his agent, who was in place near the Treadstone headquarters, and risk exposing their presence. All he could do was wait.

It was after three when his phone finally buzzed with an incoming call. He answered, saying nothing.

"You were right," the low voice of his assassin murmured. "Bourne is inside Treadstone."

"The surveillance is working?"

"It was jammed for a while, but now it's back on. I'm hearing everything. I was in position to watch him make the first moves. He came via the cemetery grounds and took out three people on his way in."

"Dead?"

"No, but out of the fight. He's using his identity to defuse opposition. They know him, so that buys him time to make his move."

"What is he doing now?"

"Talking his way past the second-floor team. Next stop is Shadow's office. Hang on, wait. *Fuck!*"

There was a long pause on the line, and Bai Ze drummed his fingers nervously, restraining the urge to shout out questions. Then the killer on the phone finally continued. "Gunfire."

"From Bourne?"

"No, it's rifle fire. The second-floor agents are shooting."

"What about *Bourne?*"

"I'm not sure. I can't tell his status yet. I'm hearing a voice. One of the men is on the phone now. He's calling out *man down.*"

29

THE RED LEATHER DOOR, WHICH HID IMPENETRABLE STEEL, CLICKED shut behind Bourne. The door was locked, and he knew that none of the on-site agents had the access code. Only Shadow did. For now, no one could follow him.

For a moment, Bourne caught his breath, leaning back against the wall and closing his eyes. He wiped a smear of blood from the redheaded agent off his face. River had moved fast. Too fast. It gave Bourne no choice but to take him down. He also knew the rifle fire blasting into the ceiling would have been audible on the street. Steel and his partner at the front of the house would already be charging inside.

But for now, the attic was secure. They couldn't get to him.

He ran up the tight staircase. At the top, he opened the door carefully, even though he was sure the office would be empty. Only a pale glow came from the streetlights through the bulletproof glass in the chambered windows. He flipped the nearest switch, which activated a Tiffany lamp on the heavy walnut desk and a few sconce lights on the walls, which were decorated in a gold-and-black pattern. The angled ceiling reflected the sharp gables of the roof and cast odd geometric shadows.

He analyzed the office. The huge desk was empty of any papers, impeccably neat. He saw a fully stocked wet bar, including a Canadian whiskey called Lucky Bastard. Bourne knew that was David Abbott's preferred brand, and it made him wonder if Abbott was planning on coming out of hiding. Near the window was a century-old sofa, elegant but not particularly comfortable. That was a good description of Shadow herself. He remembered sitting next to her on that sofa, telling her that he'd destroyed the Files, that no one would be able to use them. Not the Chinese, not the Russians, not the CIA, not even Shadow herself.

She took it well, because she knew all along that she'd played him. Deceived him. She'd already taken the laptop with the Files, and what Bourne had destroyed in a lake in Estonia was a fake.

The Files.

Bourne glanced at the wall adjacent to her desk. He saw a Mexican painting of a skeleton dancing with a child in the starlight through a field of corn. He ran his hand down the side of the frame, finding the switch that unlatched it, and he pulled the painting back from the wall on hidden hinges.

Behind the painting was Shadow's safe.

The safe included a biometric sensor, activated by Shadow's thumbprint. He'd acquired her print the previous year when she'd been inside his apartment in Paris, and he'd worked with one of his non-Treadstone assets to turn it into a biocompatible image on a small rectangle of acrylic. Shadow might be his lover and his handler, but he'd known a day would come when his interests and hers would take separate paths. That meant being able to access everything in her world.

He extracted the acrylic slide from his pocket and pressed it against the biometric lock on the safe. As soon as he did, the keypad lit up. Then he plugged in the digits to undo the lock and heard the metal door open with a click.

There it was. The laptop, sitting on top of a neat stack of manila case folders. The *real* laptop—not the one Bourne had destroyed—with the AI software engine that accessed hacked databases stored around the world and ferreted out secrets that no human would detect in years of surveillance. The artificial mind of the Files gave Shadow almost limitless power that she could wield for Treadstone. And for herself. That was why everyone wanted it. That was why Alvin Bakk wanted it. That was why the Chinese were desperate to get it back.

Bourne took the laptop in his hands. He brought it to the walnut desk and booted it up, and immediately a prompt appeared, asking for the twelve-character code that unlocked the software's brain.

Enter the wrong code three times, and the laptop would self-destruct.

He knew everything about Shadow, but not this code.

"Now what?" said a calm voice from the doorway.

He turned around and looked across the office. Shadow stood there, her arms outstretched, her Domina pistol in her hands. She pointed the gun at him, and she was a superb marksman. If she pulled the trigger, she wouldn't miss.

"Now what, Jason?" she asked again. "You can't unlock it. You don't have the password."

"No. But I have you."

She smiled, her head nodding slightly. "That's why you wanted me here."

"Yes, it is."

"Except I have the gun. By the time you pull your Glock, you'll have a bullet in your head. You know that. Now put the laptop back in the safe, and get on your knees."

Bourne didn't move. "You won't kill me."

"You're wrong. I'll do what I have to do."

"If you wanted me dead, Steel and the others would be with you. They'd have rifles, and I'd already be bleeding out on the floor. But you came up here alone. You locked the others out. This is between you and me."

"Don't force me to make a choice, Jason. We'll both regret it."

Bourne came out from behind her desk. He took a single step across the office floor, moving closer to her.

"*Don't*," she repeated. "Stay where you are."

"You're not going to kill me. You won't pull the trigger. Shadow might. Shadow might be okay being the one to end my life, despite what we've been through together. Despite everything in the past, despite *now*. But Marlen can't do that. Marlen won't shoot. Because Marlen's in love with me."

He kept walking toward her very slowly. He didn't pull his Glock.

"I don't listen to Marlen," Shadow snapped.

"You can tell yourself that, but it's a lie. You *are* Marlen. She's your real identity."

"Stop where you are. Stop right now. I'll fucking shoot you, Jason. I will do it. Don't put me to the test."

He held out his hand. "Give me the gun."

"*Stop!*"

"Give me the gun, Marlen. I didn't have to give it back to you. I could have taken it with me. But I wanted you to have it, because you had to trust me. I knew you wouldn't use it. I knew you *couldn't*."

He was close to her now, the gun almost within reach. A wild kind of pleading shined in her eyes, but her arms remained solid and unmoving.

"David. *Don't.* Don't make me."

"Admit it to yourself, Marlen. You've been in love with me since we met in Switzerland years ago. The *real* you, not the robot that David Abbott created. Do you remember the painting of Mont Saint-Michel you kept for years—the place where I asked you to marry me? Do you remember the things you told me about the future? Your dreams about the two of us escaping this world together, going off to some cabin in Sweden, living in some tiny village where no one can find us. That's who you really are. That woman is not going to kill me."

Tension stretched her face tight. "Fuck Marlen. Fuck David Abbott. And fuck *you*. Get on your knees."

"Give me the gun."

His fingers could nearly touch it now. One more step, and he was there. He watched her hand, which was still rock-steady, her finger ready on the trigger. A little twitch was all she needed to shoot. A part of him, somewhere in the back of his mind, wondered if she would really do it. Kill him. If she couldn't resist the opportunity to show Marlen once and for all who the boss was.

He took the last step toward her and caressed the metal of the barrel. His hand closed around the body of the gun, touching her warm fingers gently. He pulled, expecting resistance, but she gave him none. The Domina came easily out of her hand, and he secured it in his pocket. Their eyes met, and he saw tears as she watched him.

God, she was good. Flawless.

Bourne turned around.

Then, from behind him, Shadow let out a banshee cry as she leaped forward. Her body flew into his back, toppling him, sending him down to the hardwood floor. She landed on his back, pounding his skull, dizzying him. He labored to bring up his knees, and with his full weight, he arched backward, launching her into the air. He shook himself, the room spinning, and got to his feet, but she was on him again, hands around his neck with a grip like titanium, fingernails digging deep and drawing blood.

Her eyes were like a wolf's stare. She'd waited for this for a long time. The chance to let out the animal. The chance to bury her coldness and let ice turn into fire. He couldn't breathe. The world around him spun. All he could do was pummel his fist into her stomach, once, then twice, until air gasped from her lungs, and she let go and stumbled backward. He drove in on her, throwing her against the wall with all his strength, the impact loud and ugly. He hated it, hated watching her knees give way as she sank down to the floor.

Why, Marlen?

But she'd given him no choice.

She sat on the floor, back against the wall, shoulders slumped. Her blond hair fell across her face. Her skull had hit the wall, and blood made its way from behind her ear and trickled onto her neck. She looked defeated. Bourne drew his Glock and shoved it against her chin, right below that beautiful mouth and those bloodred lips. Those lips he'd kissed only hours earlier. That mouth that had driven his body crazy with pleasure.

"Give me the code," he hissed.

"No."

"The *code*, Shadow."

"Fuck you. Take the laptop if you want. It's a brick. You'll never be able to open it."

He pushed hard with the gun barrel, forcing her head against the wall. She winced involuntarily. "Don't fool yourself, Shadow. Unlike you, I *will* shoot. You see, Marlen loves me, but I don't love her. Maybe once upon a time I did, when I was young and a fool. But then Marlen became Shadow, and Shadow has betrayed me over and over and over again. You've sold me out. You've used me. Whenever we have sex, it's always *you* in bed, isn't it? There is no Marlen, only Shadow. Do you think I don't know? Do you think I can't tell that any emotion you've ever shown me is one more lie? I *will* kill you, Shadow. I've known that moment would come for a long time. You've known it, too."

She stared back at him, her eyes crazed, part fury, part love, part anguish. He realized with a hole in his soul that she hadn't expected him to say those things, that they came too easily out of his mouth for them not to be true. He didn't love her. Even when he desired her, he didn't love her.

The only real emotion he had for her was hatred.

"You bastard," she whispered, her voice cracking as if it were her heart.

His own voice stayed frozen. "Give me the code."

"No. Shoot me if that's what you want."

"I will. I will kill you and not even think twice about it. But look in my eyes, Shadow. It doesn't stop there. That's only the beginning of my revenge for what Treadstone has done to me. I'll do what Johanna wanted to do. I will take the agency apart brick by brick, dollar by dollar, agent by agent. I'll kill your father. David Abbott is next. I know where he is. He'll be dead by the end of the week. You know I'm telling you the truth. After that, I'll go around the world, city by city. I'll take them all out. I will burn everything to the ground. When I'm done, there will be nothing but ashes. Your precious Treadstone will be gone forever. *Now give me the fucking code!*"

Bourne stood up and went back to the desk. He kept the gun on Shadow, but his other hand sat poised above the keyboard.

"Twelve characters," he said. "Go."

Shadow breathed loudly. He could hear the air dragging in and out of her lungs. "You'd really do this?"

"To get my life back? Yes, I would."

"Once you sell your soul, you can't buy it back, David."

"Look who's talking."

"You won't get out of here. Not alive. Steel and the others are downstairs. They'll shoot. I'll give the order."

"It's dark," Bourne told her with a shrug. "There's a window out to the roof right there. In a few seconds, I'll disappear, and you'll never see me again. You can look for me wherever you want. You can chase me around the world. You can send your best people after me. But once I go, I'm gone. Cain is history."

His fingers hovered over the keyboard.

Shadow sniffled and wiped her nose. She stayed where she was on the floor. A look passed across her face, something stricken and lost. Then her lips moved, and she announced the code one character at a time, slowly, waiting as he typed each one into the laptop. Her voice was loud, proud, unshaken.

Capital letters. Numbers. Small letters. Exclamation points. Question marks. Twelve characters.

He entered the last one—the number *6*—and the Files came to life with a flash of light and a single chord, like something from a symphony. The home screen waited for him to enter a question. To hunt for a secret.

Bourne slapped the laptop shut and went to the window. He had what he needed.

"Goodbye, Shadow."

OUTSIDE, BOURNE DIDN'T HAVE TO WAIT LONG.

He knew the Chinese were watching him. He didn't know where their eyes were, but he felt them following him as he made his escape. Even in the darkness, they tracked him. He made his way back to the motorbike where he'd parked it six blocks away, on the other side of the cemetery, and he waited. No one from Treadstone was nearby.

But he wasn't alone.

Less than a minute later, his phone rang. He took a deep breath, steeling himself. This was it, this was the moment, this was the final act of the play. When he answered, he heard the anonymous electronic voice that he'd heard in Mei Sun's bedroom.

Bai Ze.

"Congratulations, Cain."

"I have what you want. Now give me what *I* want."

"Of course. I'll text you an address. Meet me there."

"You get nothing until I have my life back, until my memories are restored. If you don't follow through, you don't get the password code. And you already know the Files are useless without the code."

"I understand. We have a deal, Cain. The address is waiting for you in your phone right now. *I'm* waiting for you. I imagine we've both been anticipating another face-to-face meeting for a long time. Ever since you first saw me eight years ago."

30

THE ADDRESS TOOK BOURNE OUTSIDE THE CITY, TO AN INDUSTRIAL area near the port of Baltimore. He arrived with the winter dawn still two hours away. He parked his motorcycle in the tall brush near an overpass of I-895. The headlights of a few middle-of-the-night cars and trucks flashed above his head. Sagging chain-link fences lined the road on both sides, and the pavement was wet from a spitting rain. To his right, he saw construction trailers. To his left were multiple sets of railroad tracks. A few container cars, their metal frames covered in graffiti, sat abandoned on the farthest set of tracks.

Debris littered the construction area near him. Machinery. Trucks. Stacks of plywood and scrap metal. Rusted shipping containers. Bourne walked along the shoulder of the road, the rain making him wet. His Glock was in his hand, and the backpack with the laptop was slung over his shoulder. The area looked deserted in the early hours, but that was a ruse. They knew he was coming;

they were waiting for him. He spotted cameras mounted on the light poles, following him down the street.

Someone, somewhere, was watching.

He crossed a set of railroad tracks that curved along the pavement in front of him. Not far away was an overpass for one of the Baltimore streets. Beyond the concrete supports was a white windowless warehouse surrounded by a barbed-wire fence. He stayed under the overpass, hearing no traffic over his head, following the fence until he reached a vehicle gate. He saw no security waiting for him, no electronic locks, no signs or identification. But Bourne knew. This was the headquarters of Volt Typhoon, the center of the spider's web.

Bourne walked up to the gate. He stood there, alone, for almost a minute before he heard the rumble of engines. Two dirty white SUVs approached from opposite sides, and six people climbed out. Five men, one woman. The men held military M4s, and three of them formed a semicircle in front of Bourne. Two took up positions farther back, in the unlikely event that he escaped the first onslaught.

The last agent, the woman, held only a Glock that matched his. She wore a black bodysuit that emphasized her lithe figure. Her hair was secured under a tight knit cap. She came up to the gate in front of Bourne, nothing between them but the mesh of the fence. He couldn't see her face, which was covered by a Chinese mask, its features painted in yellow, black, and red. This close, the mask almost looked alive.

He'd seen that mask twice before. Once when Simon Harris died, once when Mei Sun died. It was the mask of a killer.

"We've already met," Bourne said. "Haven't we?"

The woman said nothing. She made a circular signal in the air with her finger, and the vehicle gate slid silently open, triggered by an unseen watcher. She stepped aside to let Bourne enter, and then the gate slid closed again. When she snapped her fingers, one of the men near the SUVs put aside his rifle and came forward to search Bourne for weapons. He was good. He found them all. Gun, backup gun, knives. In seconds, Bourne was unarmed.

Then the man reached for the backpack, but Bourne shook his head.

"The laptop stays with me," he told the woman.

She nodded at the other agent, who backed off and left the backpack where it was on Bourne's shoulder.

The woman crooked her finger at him. Like a kind of parade, they all walked toward the white warehouse in the rain. Rifle barrels tracked him with every step. He had no chance to fight back or escape. Not that he wanted to. He needed to go inside. They reached a loading dock, and beside it was a twelve-foot door that gave access to the warehouse. Bourne noticed that the warehouse itself was completely unmarked, but there were ruts along the ground, indicating that heavy vehicles had come and gone from the loading dock to the street. No doubt they were transporting supplies to and from container ships arriving in the nearby port. From here, matériel went out to operatives across the country. Electronics. Copper. Computers. Guns.

He heard a series of electronic beeps as the woman keyed in the lock code. The door unlatched, and she opened it and beckoned him inside. He crossed to the interior, and the woman came with him, closing the door behind her. None of the other agents joined them. It was just the two of them now, under a high ceiling with bright overhead lights illuminating a maze of crates labeled with Chinese characters.

With the barrel of her Glock, she waved him forward. The concrete floor echoed like hollow thunder under his boots. He walked toward the far side of the warehouse, seeing nothing that looked like the central command of Bai Ze. But near the opposite wall, he spotted two stacks of shipping containers that looked out of place. Next to him, the woman pushed a few buttons on her phone, and the containers slid smoothly aside on rails, revealing another high door and lock panel. Again the woman unlocked the door, revealing an unlit space. He could see none of its secrets.

"Inside," she murmured, speaking for the first time.

The voice was familiar. He knew that voice. But of course he did.

Bourne went to the doorway, then stopped where the shadows began. He stared into the darkness of the room, seeing nothing, but he was conscious of size, of airflow, of the aroma of incense. He felt someone's presence, too. The room was not empty. Someone was waiting for him.

Bai Ze.

"Inside," the woman repeated.

Bourne turned around. She had her Glock pointed at his head.

"Why don't you take off the mask?" he asked.

The woman said nothing. She took a couple of steps backward, the gun still level at the end of her arm. Her fit frame stood ready, as if she expected him to leap for her, to grab for the Glock. But he didn't.

From behind him, in the darkness of the command center, Bourne heard a man's voice. This was not the strange electronic voice that had been used before. This was human. Like the woman's voice, it was familiar to him. He knew the man behind that voice. He'd known him for years.

"Go ahead," the man said from the darkness. "It's time."

The woman removed her disguise. First came the knit cap, which she dropped to the floor, releasing a flood of chestnut hair. Then she reached under her chin and slid off the opera mask, letting it dangle on her fingers. She wasn't hiding anymore. They stared at each other across the ten feet between them. Her face held no expression or emotion, no smile, no guilt, no lust, no triumphant ego. And yet he knew she felt all of those things.

"Hello, Jason," Laney Reese said.

"Hello, Laney. I knew it was you, but I wanted to believe I was wrong."

"I hope you don't expect me to apologize."

"Not at all. It's the job. But I give you credit for selling me on your story. When I first saw you in Door County, I really thought you were who you said you were. An innocent out of her league. A local who had stumbled into something dangerous."

A little smirk folded onto her lips. "But that wasn't the first time. We met once before."

"Yes, we did."

"You saw me for a split second. Our eyes met."

"That's right."

"Do you remember it now?"

"I do. With the right trigger, a memory comes back. Now I remember what really happened eight years ago. The Files were right. They had it all pegged from the beginning. I was there that night, and I saw everything."

Bourne turned back to the unlit space, to the unseen man.

"I remember you, too," he went on. "There's no point in hiding anymore. *Bai Ze.*"

DAVID WEBB CROUCHED IN THE WOODS, WATCHING THE CHINESE ASSASSIN known as Fang.

The killer he'd first seen near the pool at the Mandarin Oriental in Miami. One of Treadstone's most wanted men.

Fang stood outside a small cottage within steps of the beach at Lake Michigan. His partner, Rose, had disappeared to guard the other side. It was late, dark, the neighborhood quiet. Only a glow from one of the cottage's windows showed him a glimpse of Fang's silhouette. The man's head moved constantly, watching, observing.

What was going on?

He'd tracked Fang from Florida all the way to the cold nowhere of the Midwest. Whatever was happening here had to be important to draw in three Chinese men who were obviously CCP, traveling with lethal protection. The men were inside the cottage now. David had seen the door open, had heard welcomes being exchanged. They were meeting someone—but who? And why?

Meanwhile, their two assassins protected the space, making sure no one came close.

But David had to get to that window.

He studied the darkness of the woods between him and the cottage. It was difficult terrain. Trees with barren winter branches made a maze, and one snap of a twig would give him away. The soft ground was littered with fallen leaves that would scrape and rustle. The air was frigid, and his fingers were already numb. He felt the lake breeze pricking his face like needles.

This would not be an easy assault, and he had respect for Fang's talents. A kill had to be silent, immediate.

David began to push forward, but then he stopped.

Not far away, Fang tapped a radio receiver in his ear and spoke a few soft words of Chinese. The assassin shifted his position, stepping away from the window into the shadows, where he was completely invisible.

Something was happening.

David heard noise from the dead-end road that led to the hotel and the beach. A car was coming. Headlights split the night. The gravel scratched under its tires, and then the engine went off as the car parked near the trees. He heard the click of the driver's door, followed by a sharp, quick tap on the asphalt of the road. High heels. A woman. From where he was, he couldn't see who it was, but he heard her getting closer, guided by the swinging beam of a flashlight. She headed straight for the cottage door.

Fang stayed unseen. The killer didn't want the woman to see him.

The woman reached the cottage. She tapped her knuckles softly on the door. Someone answered; the door opened, letting out light, giving him a fleeting glimpse of the woman's face. A Chinese woman, unusually tall, with straight black hair and an angled chin. Attractive, but a stranger. Friendly greetings were exchanged at the door. David heard the woman's voice, but he was more focused on the voice of the man letting her inside. That low voice resonated in his mind, as if he knew that man, as if he knew *who it was. Not one of the Chinese from the CCP. Someone else.*

He struggled to place it, to take that voice from a completely different context and put it down in the Wisconsin forest.

Who are you?

David was unsure now, wondering if he should stay back and let the meeting play out. Observe, not intervene. But Fang took the choice out of his hands. The assassin came flying out of the darkness like a vampire bat. Only an instantaneous reflex saved David's life. He jerked up his hand just as a garrote went around his neck. The wire bit into his skin, yanked his hand toward his throat, but he held it back fiercely as blood oozed from his palm to his wrist. Fang had both hands on the wire, but David had one hand free, and he found the ankle of the man looming behind him. He pulled hard, throwing the man off his feet, but Fang didn't let go as he fell backward. He dragged David with him, pulling tighter and harder on the wire until the garrote used the weight of David's own hand to choke off his breath. David squirmed and flailed, but the assassin's grip was like steel. Growing dizzy, blackness creeping in, David grasped for the knife secured on his calf. He unsheathed it and buried the blade in the thigh of the man below him. Fang gasped, still not letting go of the wire. David struck again, into the cartilage of the killer's knee this time, and Fang couldn't hold back a sharp howl of pain. But his hands pulled the garrote tighter and tighter. David's lungs screamed, unable to find any air, fireworks exploding behind his eyes. He yanked out the knife and swung his arm backward in a wild, desperate arc. He missed, the blade hitting the ground. Then he swung again, landing in flesh, cutting muscle in Fang's shoulder. And once more, this time into the squishy gel of the assassin's eye, and through it, deep into his brain.

Fang screamed, but the scream cut off into sudden silence as he died. The hands holding the wire went limp.

David peeled away the garrote and rolled free. He staggered to his feet, collapsing against a birch tree, sucking in breath after breath of sweet air. He didn't have time to recover, not before the second assault. Rose would be on him in an instant. He only had time to unholster his Smith & Wesson CSX before Fang's partner leaped out of the shadows, drawn by the noise of the fight. David simply raised the gun and fired, catching her in the middle of the chest, the body landing heavily against him, then crumpling to the dirt at his feet.

The blast of the gun had been low, muffled because he'd fired so close to her body. Smoke stung his nose. He waited, listening, wondering if anyone had heard, if anyone would investigate. But the woods stayed quiet, except for the horrible death rattle at his feet. A minute passed. Then two. Then five.

The woman was dead, and he heard nothing more. No one in the cottage came outside.

David pushed through the woods, approaching the glow of the window. He stayed by the corner of the frame and edged far enough to see inside. The interior looked rustic and Midwestern, a wood fire crackling on the far wall, watercolors of the lake hung against heavy gold wallpaper, leather furniture, dim light. Only one person was in the room—the tall Chinese woman who'd come from the road. She sat in a chair, her eyes closed, her expression serene.

Then a door opened in the wall on David's right. The three Chinese men emerged. They gathered around the woman in the chair, but she took no notice of them. One of them whispered; she gave no reaction. He spoke louder, but the woman remained frozen in place, unaware of anything going on around her.

"You see?" said a new voice from the bedroom doorway. "This is what I can offer you, gentlemen. Sun will tell me everything. Give me every name. Answer every question. And when it's done, she'll remember nothing. Not me. Not you. Not being here at all. You can imagine the possibilities."

That voice!

David felt a pounding in his head, a wave of horror and disbelief welling out of his gut. Yes, he knew that voice. He knew that man. He'd spent hours with him. He'd poured out his soul to him. He'd trusted him more than anyone else in his life.

Mo Panov stepped from the bedroom into the glow of the firelight.

Mo Panov, therapist, scientist.

Mo Panov, spy and traitor.

The shock lifted David out of his surroundings only for a second or two. His senses were focused inside, not outside. That was a mistake.

In the next instant, he realized someone was behind him.

He began to turn, but his eyes only had time to process a woman whipping a billy club toward the base of his skull. He had a vision of a lithe body, chestnut hair, pale skin, a pretty face. Then the impact hit him like an explosion of fire, and he was gone.

31

BOURNE WATCHED MO FROM THE DOORWAY AS LIGHT FILLED THE SPACE.

Mo Panov. Bai Ze.

Inside the command center, hanging lanterns adorned with delicate silk hung from the ceiling, giving the room a soft, almost romantic glow—a contrast to the multiple computer screens on the cherrywood desk and the huge black glass wall. Mo stood on the plush carpet in the middle of the room, which measured at least forty feet in all directions. He looked as casual and comfortable as he always did, in pleated slacks, loafers, and a rust-colored sweater with leather patches on the elbows. His face bore a sad, enigmatic smile as he watched Bourne.

Mo Panov, his therapist.

No, more than that, his *friend!*

It was one more betrayal. The worst of all.

"Not that it will mean anything, but I'm truly sorry that it's come to this, David," Mo told him. "I've always genuinely liked you, right from the beginning. The others in Treadstone? In the

CIA? I have no sympathy for them. On some level, you must feel the same way, given how they've lied to you over the years. But you've always kept a certain *morality* about you, despite everything. I guess that sounds strange, with what you've been forced to do. But I do believe you're a moral man."

"Unlike you," Bourne replied coldly.

Mo shrugged. "Fair enough. You're right. I can't argue. But I have my reasons."

"Money? Is that a reason? Is that enough to sell out your ethics and your country?"

"Oh, there's plenty of money, yes. I won't deny it. Plus unlimited research potential. That means something to a scientist and psychiatrist like me. But that's not really why I did it. That wouldn't be enough. Actually, you're one of the few people who might understand, David. The government betrayed *me*, much like they did with you. In my case, it was my father. Lost. Abandoned. Forgotten. Left to rot in the jungle. When your country is willing to do that to a patriot, you can't expect much loyalty in return."

Bourne said nothing. He'd heard excuses too many times.

Mo pulled a heavy chair from near the cherrywood desk and put it in the middle of the room, facing the black glass wall. He tapped the seat. "Come, David, sit down. Let's talk. There are people who want to meet you."

Bourne felt the barrel of a gun pushing into his neck. Laney jabbed him forward, and he didn't look back. He went into the room and sat down in the chair, which matched the cherry desk, with legs carved like fierce dragons. Laney stood in front of him, gun still aimed at his chest. She knew him well enough to keep a safe distance.

"I meant what I said," Bourne told her. "You really are a good actress."

"I'm good at a lot of things," Laney replied, taking another step backward, as if he were trying to distract her before he jumped for the gun. "As you found out."

"What about your mother?"

"She died when I was nine."

"So you don't have to rush back to her side in Door County."

"No."

Bourne shook his head. "A very good actress."

"A good actress needs a good script. Credit Mo for that."

"No doubt." Bourne kept his eyes on Laney. "So tell me the rest. Eight years ago, I killed Fang and Rose. Then you showed up behind me. You knocked me out. Of course, I didn't remember any of that once Mo was done with me. I woke up in Miami and had no idea where I'd been for four days. But I'm curious. What really happened after you got the drop on me in the woods?"

Laney gave him an icy smile. "I wanted to kill you. You'd seen Bai Ze. Fang worked for the Chinese, he was their security, but I worked for Mo. It was my job to keep him safe. To me, it felt like too much of a risk leaving you alive."

"My Chinese friends agreed with Laney," Mo added, folding his arms over his chest as he stared down at Bourne in the chair. "They would have been happier with you dead. But I convinced them that your death had more risks than benefits. I'd already showed them what I could do with Mei Sun. They knew my work with memory was becoming increasingly sophisticated. I was confident we could get you back to Miami none the wiser. You wouldn't have any idea what had happened to you. Given your personality,

I was also pretty sure you wouldn't tell anyone. You wouldn't want to look weak with Treadstone, admitting that you'd had a blackout. Fortunately, I figured that if you did confess to anyone, it would be *me*. And if that happened, we could opt for a more permanent solution."

"As usual, Mo was right," Laney said. "You remembered nothing. But when he told me you were coming back to Door County, I was curious how that would go. I knew it would be interesting dueling with you. Seeing if I could win you over."

"So who are you?" Bourne asked her. "I mean, you're not really a Door County gig worker. Are you ex-CIA, like Mei Sun? Like Chess? Is that how he found you?"

"Very good, Jason," she told him. "Yes, I was a young agent working out of the station in Vietnam a decade ago. As luck would have it, Mo was there, too, ostensibly to run psychological tests on the field operatives. But also to hunt for his father. I helped him do that, but we got nowhere. Both the Americans and the Vietnamese threw up a brick wall. But along the way, we became friends."

"And then?" Bourne asked.

Her face darkened.

"That summer, I had a run-in with two of the other agents. They'd been harassing me for weeks, but the station chief did nothing to stop them. It was a boys' club in the agency. Still is. One night they staged a fake mission, grabbed me, tried to rape me. I had sort of a—fugue, I guess you'd call it. I went wild and killed them both. I didn't know what to do, so I called Mo. He helped me cover it up. The agents simply disappeared. It happens. Me, I quit the agency. I wandered around Europe, picking up security and mercenary work. But Mo and I stayed in touch. Then eight years ago, he reached out to me with an opportunity to help him with something new. Working for the Chinese, putting together a domestic espionage network. Believe me, I had no loyalty or patriotism to hold me back, not after what I'd been through. So he and I have been together ever since."

"I assume you never lost your memory," Bourne said.

"Oh, my memory is just fine," Laney assured him.

"The man in the truck that went off the road. The men at your house, out on the ice. You let me kill your own agents."

"A necessary setup. I needed you to trust me."

"You targeted me from the beginning. That was always the plan."

"Of course."

Mo sighed with a glance at the black screen behind him. "You have to understand, David. I know you better than anyone. Even better than Shadow. You've told me things you never told another soul. Very little of that made it into my reports. I kept it to myself. To me, you were always a potential risk, but also a potential asset. When Shadow told me she was sending you after Bai Ze—well, I saw an opportunity to turn the situation to my advantage. But I know that you're harder to manipulate when you're alone. Fortunately, I've known your weakness for a long time. You can't resist a damsel in distress. You're vulnerable when an attractive woman needs your help."

"So he sent me to seduce you," Laney said. "I definitely didn't mind the assignment, Jason. I found you attractive. That wasn't a lie. But I was worried that when you saw me, you might actually remember me from eight years ago. Or you'd realize on some level that I'd been there that night, too. That's when Mo came up with his brainstorm. My cover story. Yes, I *was* there near the White Gull Inn, just like you. I saw Bai Ze, and then the Chinese grabbed us and erased *both* of our memories. Brilliant."

"I knew Laney's story would disarm you," Mo continued with an arrogant certainty in his voice. "Here's a beautiful woman who understands exactly what you've been through. She shares the pain of living with no past. You'd find that irresistible, David. With that kind of hook, Laney could break down your walls and get past your usual cynical nature. All of it was carefully designed to lead you right here."

He gestured at the backpack.

"Which reminds me, I'll take the Files now."

Bourne didn't protest. He let the pack slide off his shoulder to the floor. With Laney still guarding him with her gun, Mo carefully approached him and retrieved it. He unzipped the pouch and removed the laptop, holding it with a kind of reverence. He put it on his desk, pressed the power button, and bent over the keyboard, watching twelve squares appear on the screen, waiting for the correct password. His fists clenched with victory.

"Magnificent. At long last. Truly, David, you're exceptional at what you do. I'd encourage you to trade sides and work with us, but as I say, I know you too well. Those ethics of yours would never allow you to do that."

Bourne let the silence drag out for a while. "You can't restore my memories, can you?"

Mo straightened up, exhaling softly. "No. Maybe someday, but no, not now. It's much easier to destroy things than to build them up."

"Fortunately, you had Laney to give me 'proof.'"

"Yes, that's what made the plan perfect. Giving Laney amnesia would make the two of you a matched set, falling into each other's arms. How sweet. Then, when Laney got her memories back, you'd see what you've been missing. Again, it helps that I *know* you, David. I know the hunger you try to hide. For you, amnesia is a wound that never heals. You'd do anything, give up anything, to remember who you are. Even if it meant betraying Shadow and Treadstone and having to live the rest of your life on the run."

Mo checked his watch. At that moment, the huge glass wall behind him came to life. Mo and Laney moved aside, and Bourne found himself facing nine men seated at a long wooden table. Behind them were heavy red draperies. The room was dimly lit, each man barely visible in the shadows, except for individual spotlights illuminating nothing but their faces. But instead of faces, Bourne saw Chinese masks, each one unique, each one garish and hand-painted into angry expressions. The light gave the masks a strange lifelike quality, seeming to hover above the table, unconnected to any bodies.

"Gentlemen," Mo said, "may I introduce Jason Bourne."

The mask in the middle spoke. Bourne wondered who was behind it. Was it one of the three CCP men he'd seen in Florida?

Or was it someone even higher in the party?

"*Cain.* So you are here. Finally. Bai Ze promised that he could bring you to us. Last year, you disrupted one of our most valuable operations. That comes with a cost, and now we will see it paid."

"Adam Hill," Bourne said.

"Indeed."

Bourne shook his head. "Hill was a pig of a human being. A deviant. He was beneath you. I'm surprised you were willing to work with him."

The man behind the mask gave a dismissive shrug. "It is easier to choose your enemies than your friends, Cain. Hill's *proclivities* were disgusting, but they also made him vulnerable, and we took advantage of that. He was a valuable asset, perhaps our *most* valuable asset other than Bai Ze. We hold you responsible for his loss."

"He had Johanna killed. Do you think I'd watch that happen and do nothing?"

"Yes, that is understandable. But vengeance is a chain that comes with many links."

"So what do you plan to do with me?"

Mo glanced at the screen, then at Bourne. "As I told you, Jason, it's easier to destroy memories than to bring them back. In this case, alas, the damage will be permanent. When we're done with you, I'm afraid there won't be much left of your mind. You won't know who you are, where you came from. You'll be an *unperson*, as Orwell would say. Maybe we'll drop you off at that homeless encampment you found in Kansas City. Treadstone will never find you. Of course, even if they did, it wouldn't matter. The process is irreversible."

A little chill ran down Bourne's back. He didn't doubt that, given the opportunity, Mo would do exactly what he said. "If you do that, you'll never get the code for the Files. I have it, remember? You don't."

Mo smiled. "Oh, but you're wrong."

Laney took a step forward. He kept an eye on the Glock, still lodged firmly in her grip. "The last time we were together—the last time I was in your arms—I planted a bug on you, Jason. I've been listening to you ever since. I heard everything. The fight between you and Shadow? I heard it all. So I heard her give you the code."

Bourne stared back at her, his face impassive.

Mo went to the laptop on his desk. Its screen had gone dark, but when he pushed the trackball, the computer came to life again, still with twelve boxes blinking on the screen, waiting for the password that activated the Files.

"Laney?" Mo said. "If you please."

She needed no notes. She had it memorized, as any good spy would. Slowly, carefully, she rattled off the code character by character, exactly the way Shadow had announced it to Bourne in her office. As she did, Mo tapped the keys with equal care. When he entered the final number *6*, there was a brief, tantalizing pause, as if the laptop would fail to respond. But Bourne knew that Laney had gotten it right. A moment later, the symphony played a single chord, and the home screen awakened.

Mo's fingers flew on the keyboard for a couple of minutes, rattling off queries, checking the results. Testing the software, making sure it was the real deal.

And it was.

Bourne had delivered it into their hands.

"Gentlemen," Mo announced, turning back to the nine men in opera masks on the huge screen. "We have the Files."

32

MURMURS OF TRIUMPH RUMBLED FROM THE MEN BEHIND THE MASKS. The man in the middle, the leader of the pack, spoke again, and Bourne could hear smug satisfaction oozing from his voice.

"Life comes full circle, Cain. *We* developed the Files. It was our superior knowledge, our superior expertise that made it possible. The software belongs to us. When the AI engine was stolen, you were the one who foiled our attempts to get it back. Now you've betrayed your own people to return the Files to their rightful place. I hope you enjoy the irony."

"Yes, it's practically an Alanis Morissette song," Bourne replied.

The joke failed to land with the men in China, but Bourne noticed a momentary frown ripple across Mo's face, ripe with suspicion. The therapist bent over and typed a few more queries into the Files, but when the software behaved as expected, he straightened up again, the concern gone from his face.

"Well, David, it seems we've come to the end of the line."

"I guess so."

"It's been a long road between us. I confess, I'm a little sad that it has to end this way."

"Me too."

"You won't want to be awake for anything that comes next. When you do wake up, well, life will be very different. Not in a good way, I'm afraid. But you won't miss what you can't remember."

"Actually, I've never found that to be true," Bourne said. "I *do* miss what I can't remember. That's what keeps me going."

Again hesitation flashed on Mo's face. His eyes narrowed, and he opened his mouth as if to ask a question. Then he seemed to think better of it. "Anyway. I have a sedative to put you out. It will make transport easier."

He went to the other side of his cherrywood desk and opened a drawer. He removed a small case, from which he extracted a syringe, plus a small glass bottle. Turning the bottle upside down, he punctured the top with the needle and filled the syringe with several millimeters of clear liquid.

Mo studied Bourne with caution as he came closer. He spoke to Laney, who remained in position with the Glock.

"If he moves, shoot him, but not to kill. Inflict the most pain, but keep him alive. Knees. Hips. Places that will do the most damage. David, I know you want to be a hero, but believe me when I say you'll only be making it worse on yourself by resisting. Laney's as good a shot as you are. Perhaps better. She won't miss. Your life won't be easy where you're going, but it will be considerably harder if you're unable to walk."

"I'm sure you're right."

More hesitation.

Mo looked for answers in Bourne's face, but Bourne kept his expression as blank as the men on the screen who were wearing masks. The therapist stepped closer, then thought better of it and changed direction to come around behind Bourne, where he couldn't be seen. But Bourne could feel Mo's presence close to him.

Ten feet away, Laney took dead aim with the Glock on Bourne's knee. Mo was right. She wouldn't miss.

"I do have one favor to ask," Bourne said.

Behind him, he felt Mo stiffen. "What is it?"

"Check your phone."

"What?"

"You should check your phone," Bourne repeated.

Mo stayed where he was for a long beat. Then he walked over to the desk, where his phone sat facedown. He picked up the gold case, and his thumb swiped from the bottom to unlock the screen. But the phone didn't respond to his Face ID. Mo tried again, without success. Finally, he tapped the screen to enter the password.

Still the phone stayed locked.

Bourne watched Mo try twice more. Then the therapist slammed the phone down on the desk and his eyes shot to Bourne with a horrified confusion.

"You might want to check your computer, too," Bourne suggested.

Mo's anxiety melted into abject fear. The therapist practically leaped over the desk to get to the other side. He used the mouse to awaken his multiple monitors, and then he tapped out a long password on the keyboard. When it didn't work, he pounded the desk and tried again. Three times. Four times.

His face looked up, flushed and furious. His voice came out in a choked whisper. "*What did you do?*"

"I didn't do anything, Mo. You did."

"What are you talking about?"

"You opened the Files. That was enough." Bourne focused on the men in China, whose masks swiveled back and forth to look at each other with growing uncertainty. "Do you gentlemen know how the Files work? Or did the designers put in that feature without telling you about it? You see, it's sort of a back door if things go wrong. Shadow found it. She took the laptop to a coffee shop and watched the software hack into every device within range. Phones. Laptops. Wi-Fi. It captured passwords, photos, data, emails—pretty much everything it could find—and then sent it all to its new master. Shadow. Treadstone."

Bourne's eyes burned into Mo.

"You see, it's all been cloned now, old friend. Hacked. Stolen. Every contact, every operative, every plan, every spy, every document, every detail of Volt Typhoon. We have it. We're going to dismantle your network agent by agent, location by location. And *you*, Mo, we'll be talking to you, too. A nice long conversation. When we're done with you, maybe we'll just drop you off at that homeless camp I found in Kansas City."

Mo pounded his fists on the cherrywood desk. "You knew. You knew it was a setup. You knew it was me. *How?*"

"You can thank Mei Sun for that. You see, that was the part I struggled with. That was what didn't make sense. I stumbled onto your operation eight years ago by accident. It was a lucky break, me seeing Fang in Miami. But Sun was already in your pocket.

She'd been manipulated long before Bakk's hiring fair in Door County. If she wasn't dirty—if she wasn't a Chinese spy—how was that possible? So I talked to Holly Schultz, and she told me about the trauma Sun faced when she was captured in China. At first, I figured that was where she was turned. But that was too far away, too long ago. Plus, Sun said she remembered every second of her torture. There were no blackouts where she'd lost time, lost memory. Then it occurred to me. What does the CIA do with agents who have been through mission trauma? What does Treadstone do? They send them to see *you*, Mo. That was when I knew. You were the common denominator. You'd been manipulating Sun for years. And manipulating me, too. When you regressed me to see what was in my head eight years ago, you started messing with my mind instead. Planting lies and hallucinations. Getting me off balance. It was all you."

Bourne glanced at Laney, whose focus had been shaken. Her eyes blinked over and over; her gun hand shook.

"That was when I realized *you* had to be involved, too," he told her coldly. "Up until then, you had me fooled, I admit it. But coming back to me with your 'proof'—remembering everything in your life except the one thing that really mattered, seeing Bai Ze in the cottage. Well, that seemed a little too convenient. So I was waiting for you to plant the bug on me. When we knew you'd be listening, Shadow and I staged a little play for you in her office. It had to look real. It had to look like I'd actually betrayed Treadstone. Otherwise, Mo would be suspicious, and he might think twice before bringing me here and plugging in the code for the Files."

With a loud click, the office suddenly darkened.

The bright light of the screen that took up an entire wall went black. The Chinese in their opera masks were gone. Mo stared at the glass wall, which now reflected nothing but his face, and his mouth fell open in horror. He knew what that meant.

"Ouch. I think they just made you an unperson, Mo."

Mo wheeled on Bourne. His lip bent like a whiplash, and he bellowed at Laney.

"*Kill this son of a bitch!*"

Bourne was ready. He threw himself sideways off the chair just as Laney's Glock exploded. In the next instant, the office, which was already dim with shadow, went completely black. The power in the building turned off, shutting down every light, every screen. Laney kept firing, spraying bullets and forcing Bourne to roll wildly to steer clear of the onslaught. But she anticipated his maneuver and shifted her fire. A bullet lashed his leg; he suppressed a grimace of pain, then rolled again. He watched for the flame of the Glock, which pointed him right at her. As she fired, he crawled, making no sound. Then he flew off his knees, taking Laney to the ground and crushing her with his weight.

The gun spilled out of her hand.

But she fought back with mad determination. Her knee drove upward between his legs, and the pain in his groin burned hot, drawing an involuntary gasp from his throat. Her teeth sank into his shoulder, clamping down hard, her jaws like an alligator. He swung a fist at her head, knocking into the bone of her skull, but it took two vicious blows before she gave way. Laney kept coming. Her fingernails found his neck, raked at the skin, and drew blood. Her other hand jabbed at one of his eyes, coming so close to blinding him that he had to jerk backward and roll free, letting her go.

In the darkness, she got up. So did Bourne. Somewhere on the floor around them was the Glock, but he didn't know where it was. He listened for her movements, tried to gauge where to attack her. But she found him first. She flew from nowhere, sending him into the chair, which collapsed beneath him. He landed on his back on the carpet, and he heard a rush of air as her boot kicked into the flesh of his side. When he grabbed for her leg, she was already gone. Another kick landed, and the toe of her boot crashed into his head with a glancing blow. He gasped again, rolling away, hoping to feel the gun beneath him.

It wasn't there.

Instead, Laney found it.

She tapped the metal barrel just to taunt him, and he heard her whisper in the darkness. "Bang bang, Jason."

She fired. The gun went off once, twice, three times, missing him, but luring him toward her. He scrambled to his feet and charged the area where she'd fired, but she was already gone. Her Glock followed the noise of his body, and the next bullet seared across the top of his shoulder, cutting through muscle.

Where was the door?

He needed to escape. Get out, get away.

But he was lost inside the blackness of the large room.

Then the lights flashed on again, and Bourne squinted at the brightness. He found himself near Mo's desk. Laney stood between him and the door, which was open behind her, leading back to the open space of the warehouse. Mo was gone. So was the laptop. In the chaos, he'd disappeared with the Files.

Laney had the Glock in her hand. He had nowhere to go, nowhere to hide. Blood made a growing stain inside his shirt and down his leg onto the floor. She aimed for his chest, the gun barrel steady. Without a word, her lips bent into a little smile of victory, and her finger curled around the trigger.

In the next instant, a single shot boomed through the office, and he expected to feel the impact throughout his body.

Instead, Laney's face disintegrated in front of him, exploding outward in a cloud of bone and brain. The gun dropped to the carpet. She fell straight forward, dead, her body landing within inches of his feet. His gaze shifted to the doorway, where he saw a woman holding a Domina pistol at the end of her outstretched arms.

"I warned you about sleeping with that bitch," Shadow said.

THEY SEARCHED THE WAREHOUSE. THEY KNEW MO HAD TO BE INSIDE, hiding. Treadstone had swarmed the facility, killing the guards, covering every exit. Bourne and Shadow walked from the command center into the giant warehouse space, which was a maze of shipping containers and water-stained crates.

She handed him his Glock. "I want Mo alive. I want what's in his head."

Bourne nodded. They split up, Shadow heading left, Bourne heading right. He crossed the open floor to the stacks of crates, all printed with Chinese characters. They rose forty feet over his head. He went from the front of the warehouse to the back, checking each row, seeing no one. Then he chose the row nearest the wall of the loading dock and marched into the shadows between the high towers.

He shouted into the silence.

"Mo! There's no point in hiding. Any exit you take, you'll find Treadstone waiting for you. You're not going anywhere."

The therapist didn't answer.

Bourne kept walking. He felt the buzz of the radio receiver in his pocket, and he shoved it in his ear. He heard Shadow's voice. "Anything?"

"No."

"Should I bring in backup?"

"No, keep the doors closed. He can't run, and he's unarmed. We'll get him."

Then, suddenly, the halogen lights overhead switched off. The entire warehouse went black, and Bourne found himself blind.

"Shadow? What the hell? Did you do that?"

"No." He heard her redirect her voice to the Treadstone team outside. "Pirate, are you there? We just lost power."

The agent's voice came over the radio. "It wasn't us."

Bourne swore. Not far away, out of the darkness, he heard the clatter of an exterior door opening and closing. "Someone just came inside. Shadow, we've got people *inside* the warehouse. Pirate, do you still control the doors?"

Pirate's voice blared over the radio. "Every team, report, report."

Bourne heard the replies one by one, but the Treadstone team on the west side of the building stayed silent. That was the door. That was where the penetration had been made. But in the darkness, he had no sense of direction.

"Pirate, get those lights back on."

Then he heard boots. At least three men. Somewhere in front

of him, he heard the clatter of running footsteps, the noise bouncing off the high ceiling. He charged ahead, seeing nothing, banging into heavy crates. The boots seemed to head away from him, and when he tried to chase the sound, he got nowhere.

Gunfire erupted.

Rifle fire.

A quick burst started and stopped. *Chaos!*

"They're shooting," Bourne said. "Shadow, if they've got night vision, we're sitting ducks."

"Stay down."

"Pirate, the *lights!*"

The stomping of the boots echoed again, closer now. He ran a short distance, then had to throw himself to the concrete floor as rifle fire above his head drove him down. With the Glock, he shot wildly forward, scattering the men in front of him. He heard the hiss of a voice not far away. "Leave him! Go!"

More thunder of boots. More voices and shouts.

Somewhere in the warehouse, a door opened and closed.

Silence came back.

Bourne waited, stretched out on the floor, his Glock aimed into blackness. Finally, he murmured into the radio. "Shadow? Are you there? Are you okay?"

"I'm fine. Where are they?"

"They're gone."

Like an instant sunrise, the warehouse lights went on over his head. Bourne got to his feet, leaving smears of blood behind him. His wounds from Laney's bullets stung, and he could feel himself getting lightheaded. He stumbled forward to the next aisle among the crates, then glanced to his right and saw the shine of spent shell casings on the floor twenty yards away. He followed them to the next gap between the high stacks.

Mo Panov lay on his back, his eyes wide open, his chest riddled with bullets.

Bai Ze was dead.

Bourne saw their entire relationship flash across his mind. The sessions in this man's house and office. The drinks, the jokes, the hours the therapist had spent pawing inside his head. Manipulating him. In the end, the Treadstone rules had been proven right again.

If you think you know someone, you don't.

"They killed Mo," he told Shadow over the radio.

She didn't answer immediately, but he heard her breathing. Then she asked, "And the Files?"

Bourne looked down at the body sprawled on the concrete in a lake of blood. There was nothing else. No laptop.

"The Files are gone."

33

BOURNE SAT ON THE SOFA IN THE DIM YELLOW LIGHT OF SHADOW'S Treadstone office.

Two days had passed since the assault on the Chinese command center in Baltimore. He'd spent a day at George Washington Hospital, but then checked himself out, his wounds stitched, his pain managed by an occasional Vicodin. He'd spent the next day sitting alone in the UK safe house, thinking about Mo, thinking about Laney, before he was ready to deal with Shadow again.

The redheaded Treadstone agent code-named River, whose face was still bandaged where Bourne had thrown the man's rifle barrel against his forehead as he fired, didn't look happy to see him. But he waved him up into Shadow's office.

It was midnight now.

"So who has the Files?" Bourne asked her.

"I've spent the last two days trying to figure that out," Shadow replied. "The intercept was so damn smooth, so ruthless and efficient. But no one knew. Hell, I only had a couple of hours to put together the operation myself. I don't know who could have mounted a counterassault so quickly."

"Treadstone knew," Bourne said. "You brought in a team."

Shadow frowned. "You think one of our people leaked it."

"That would explain how they could penetrate the mission so quickly."

Her face stiffened with anger. "If we do have a mole, the question is, who's running them? Who's behind it? It could be the Chinese, the Russians, even the Israelis. They've all had their eyes on the laptop since the beginning."

"Holly Schultz knew you had the Files," Bourne pointed out.

"I thought about that, too." Shadow glanced at the Mexican painting on the wall, as if remembering that the laptop was no longer in the safe behind it. "We probably won't know who took them until we see how they're being used. But I don't like not knowing. The Files are a dangerous weapon, no matter who's opening up the software."

"You'll still be able to deconstruct most of Volt Typhoon," Bourne said.

She nodded. "Yes, the trove of intel we captured from Mo is huge. Our tech people are already digging into a flood of Chinese viruses, working with utilities and corporations to debug their systems. The FBI is starting to round up spies, but the word's out. They know we're coming for them. The rats are sneaking into the tunnels to get away. We won't catch everybody, and God knows the Chinese will start over again soon enough. At most, we've bought ourselves a couple of years."

Shadow got off the sofa and paced in the office, her movements graceful on her long legs. Bourne watched her. Her blond hair was loose and lush, her makeup in place, her body sinuous and sensual. The late hour didn't matter. She was always perfect. And yet something was different about her tonight. He felt worry, hesitation, impatience, emotions she normally kept hidden. She didn't look in control of her world.

"I'm curious about something," she said, turning back to him.

"What's that?"

"What if you'd been convinced that Mo really could give you your life back? What would you have done then?"

"I never thought he could," Bourne replied, which was a lie. For a while, he'd believed it was possible. Bai Ze had almost convinced him. Laney had almost convinced him. He'd believed it because he *wanted* to believe it.

"But what if you had?" Shadow pressed him. "Would you have betrayed me for real? Broken in and taken the Files?"

"I don't know. I don't think like that."

Another lie.

Yes, he'd thought about it. He'd felt the temptation, raw and deep, just as Mo knew he would. He didn't know how far that temptation might have carried him.

Shadow seemed to read the doubts in his face. Her hand caressed the wall where he'd held her and pressed the Glock under her chin. "You were very convincing. For a while, I thought you might really kill me."

"I wondered that about you, too. We're both good liars."

Shadow came back to the sofa. She sat down, and her blue eyes zeroed in on him with a strange, searching intensity. "Except you weren't lying, were you?"

"What do you mean?"

"Everything you said about Marlen and Shadow, that was true. You don't love Marlen. If it comes down to it, you *hate* me. Not that I blame you. I've done terrible things to you. The first time we met in Switzerland, our entire relationship was based on a lie. Since I became your handler, it's only gotten worse. I've used you for my own ends whenever it suited me. Even in bed. So no, I don't blame you for hating me."

Jason frowned. "I don't hate you."

"Why not?"

"It's more complicated than that."

"I'm not so sure it is."

He exhaled in frustration, mostly with himself. "I told you there's no Marlen, only Shadow, but I don't really believe that. The trouble is, I never know who I'm going to find when I see you. When you took over Treadstone, I thought I knew what box to put you in. You were emotionless, hard, the ice queen. Then we started sleeping together. We began coloring outside the lines. After that, I didn't know what to think. Sometimes I wondered if you loved me. Sometimes I wondered if sex was just a new way of controlling me."

"I'm not sure I know the difference myself," she admitted.

"But Marlen is real. When you take off the mask, you *are* the woman I met in Switzerland and wanted to marry. Or at least part of you is. You *are* the woman who thinks we could run away from this world and hide out in some rural Swedish village. And you know what? There are times when I think so, too."

Shadow dragged a smile onto her lips. "This is not one of those times, is it?"

"No."

"So what do we do?"

"I don't know," Bourne said, "but the way things are now doesn't work. Me being in Treadstone, me being in your bed. I can't keep living with two different people. You have to make a decision about who you are. If it's Shadow, then I go back to Paris and wait until you show up in the Tuileries to give me another mission. If you're Shadow, everything else between us is done."

She stood up again and went to the window, where she stared out into the night and at the Washington street below her. "What if I'm Marlen?"

"Are you? Could you ever really be Marlen with me and let go of the rest?"

"I don't know. I think I could."

"I'd like to believe that, but whenever I see your face in the mirror, I'm pretty sure I'll still see Shadow staring back at me. Setting me up for the next betrayal."

"Trust no one," she said.

"That's right."

"You're smart, Jason." She brushed the blond hair away from her eyes. "You were right about one thing, though. Marlen loves you. That's real. It always has been. Even in Switzerland."

"And Shadow?"

Standing at the window, she gave a short, derisive laugh. "Shadow doesn't know the meaning of the word. That's just my reality, Jason. It is what it is."

"I know," Bourne said.

"But you were also wrong about one thing."

"What's that?"

She came to the sofa, bent down, and took his face in her hands. Her lips were soft as she kissed him. "You could never kill me.

Even if you wanted to, even if I deserved it, even if I were about to kill *you*. You couldn't do it. That's not who you are."

He wondered.

Was that true?

"Let's hope we never have to find out," Bourne said.

THE FIRST-CLASS AIR FRANCE LOUNGE AT DULLES WAS CROWDED, WITH a white noise of passenger conversations around him. The overhead monitor showed that his flight to Paris had begun to board, but Bourne didn't rush to get to the gate. He sat in a high-backed chair beside the wall of windows that looked out on the airport runways. He was on his third shot of Teeling. His mind was restless, and he wanted to dull it, turn it numb. He was anxious to leave, to be home in the chaos of Paris, in the familiar surroundings of his apartment on the Left Bank. It would be a relief to go back to his routines.

But he also found himself replaying his last conversation with Shadow, wondering if leopards like the two of them could ever change their spots. This moment in time felt like a crossroads, the kind of turning point he hadn't faced since he awoke in the Mediterranean with no memory. Just like back then, he struggled with which way to turn.

Was there any kind of life out there for him, other than the one he knew?

One of the lounge attendants came over, smiled at him, and brought him more whiskey. "Your flight is boarding, sir."

"Thanks. I know."

He didn't move from the chair by the window. Not yet. He was tired. Not just his mind, but his body. It was getting harder and harder to bounce back from his missions. Each wound, each scar, each bloodletting took its toll. He didn't remember much of his past, but the things he did remember, the darkness of the recent years, enveloped him like a black cloud. Paris was just a break between storms. Another one always came.

His eyes blinked shut. He slept for a moment, then awakened with a start.

The lounge attendant approached a woman in the opposite chair and whispered in her ear. Bourne couldn't hear what she said. The woman, with a look of surprise on her face, got up and left. He noticed the attendant do the same thing to the next couple sitting by the windows. They left, too.

Strange.

Bourne focused his gaze out the window, drawn by the thunder of a departing jet. A Delta Airbus on the runway broke free of the ground, its body turning sharply skyward, its landing gear curling up underneath it. More people leaving home, going home. He needed to do the same thing.

Get on your flight and go.

As he turned back to the lounge, he watched the attendant whispering to more people. They all left.

Bourne waited for her to come to him, to explain, to ask him to leave. Was the lounge closing for some reason? Was there a threat in the airport? He felt the absence of his Glock, packed away in his luggage in the belly of a plane.

He saw that he was alone. Just him. The entire busy lounge had emptied out in a matter of minutes. Even the lounge attendants had disappeared now, too. Quickly, he surveyed the area around him, anticipating a threat, automatically looking for something that could be used as a weapon.

Then the door to the lounge opened.

Alvin Bakk walked in.

The billionaire wore blue jeans, open-toed sandals, and an untucked black T-shirt featuring the head of a jaguar from the Natuwa wildlife sanctuary in Costa Rica. His Ray-Bans covered his eyes; his black bangs hung messily on his forehead. He dangled a bottle of Teeling whiskey from one hand and held a pink mimosa in the other. His mouth broke into a grin as he flopped down in a white chair opposite Bourne.

"Cain," he said. "Cain, Cain, Bo-Bain. Leaving so soon?"

"Alvin. I should have guessed. How did you get everyone to leave?"

"It wasn't hard. A thousand dollars per person. Everyone's a whore at heart."

"What do you want?"

Bakk lifted up the whiskey bottle, and Bourne shrugged. The billionaire filled Bourne's shot glass and then sipped his own drink from the champagne flute. "Well, first of all, I want to say thank you. Mission successful. You found Bai Ze—shocker about Mo, but as you and I always say, trust no one. The FBI is helping me clean house inside my companies. I couldn't have asked for a better result. You've earned a bonus, my friend."

"I wasn't working for you," Bourne reminded him.

"Nonetheless, I always pay my debts. Shall we say a million dollars? But I'm happy to negotiate if you want more."

"Pass."

Bakk clucked his tongue. "Yes, of course, a spy of principle. I do like that, even when I find it baffling."

"I have a flight to catch," Bourne said.

"I'm aware. Heading home to Paris?"

"That's right."

"I love Paris. There's a fantastic little bistro in Montmartre called Le Troubadour. Do you know it?"

"I do. But you didn't come here to trade tourist tips, Alvin. What's going on?"

"Straight to the point, no nonsense. Excellent. *Mais certainement.* All right, I have a proposition for you."

"Namely?"

"You said you weren't working for me when you found Bai Ze. All right, let's change that. Let's make it official."

"What are you talking about?"

"I'm offering you a job."

Bourne didn't hide his surprise. "A job? Are you serious?"

"I am. Rooting out the Chinese moles in my companies is just the beginning. My worries don't end there. In my world, there's always risk. Spies, corruption, theft, a thousand crises, the media nosing into my business. I need someone to lead my global security operations. One ring to rule them all. You're the perfect candidate, Jason. I want you to join my team of giants."

Bourne readied himself to give the man a flat no. But that wasn't what came out of his mouth. "Who would I report to?"

"Me. Only me. No one else in between. You'd have a staff around the world, all handpicked by you. If there's someone on board now that you don't like, they're gone. Bring in any assets you want from the intel agencies. You'll have complete control to run the division as you see fit. I put my faith in the people I hire."

"I thought you didn't trust anyone."

"True enough. But I do trust you. Mostly because you're like me, constantly suspicious."

"I'm suspicious of you, too," Bourne said. "You more than most."

"Fine. I'd expect nothing less. Keep me under your microscope as much as you want. As for salary, you can name your price. Suffice it to say that a few years working for me would set you up very comfortably for the rest of your life. If you wanted to disappear somewhere—to a little village in Sweden, say—you'd have the resources to do so. Bring someone with you if you want." He gave Bourne a broad wink, not hiding the things he knew.

How?

How did he know about conversations between Bourne and Shadow? About their fantasies for the future?

But Bakk had shown time and again that his surveillance knew no limits.

"I'd have to leave Treadstone," Bourne said.

"Yes, you would. Is that a problem?"

"I need to think about it."

"Naturally. Take all the time you want. Actually, I'm kidding. You have ninety seconds. Get on the plane to Paris and say no, or leave the airport with me and start immediately. Your new life begins right now."

Bourne felt his mind spinning, caught in a whirlwind. The crossroad he'd imagined was right in front of him, demanding that he choose one path or another. The easy thing was to say no, to leave his life exactly as it was. Go back to Paris. Wait for Treadstone to send him into the darkness again.

But was there another way? Could he really change direction?

He wondered what it would be like to work for a man like Bakk, who had enough money and power to change the course of the world. To spy on almost everyone, know almost everything. To get whatever he wanted.

Whatever he wanted.

A dark thought sprang into Bourne's mind. "Was it you?"

Bakk's eyebrows rose, but Bourne suspected that the billionaire already knew what he meant. "What do you mean?"

"Did you steal the Files?"

Bakk said nothing. He simply drank more of his mimosa and eyed Bourne from above the rim of his glass.

"You told me before how much you wanted them," Bourne went on. "I know how effective your surveillance is. You could have hacked our plan and seen your opportunity. You have the people and resources to move fast. Did you send in your team to kill our agents, kill Mo, and grab the Files for yourself?"

"If I did, you'll only find the truth in one place," Bakk replied. "On the inside."

"Do you think I could work for someone who would do that?"

"I think you already do."

Bourne felt that truth like a bracing slap to his face. Bakk was right. There were no secrets about this man that were worse than the secrets of Treadstone.

"Investigate whatever you want," Bakk went on. "Rip open every door. Once you come to work for me, you'll have full access. If you need to take me down, take me down. But I believe when you join me, when you see what we can accomplish together, you won't care what I did. I'm building the future of the human race. Any tool that brings the future closer is a tool worth having."

Bourne shook his head at the man's unbelievable mixture of ego and arrogance. No one could have that kind of limitless power and not be tempted to abuse it. And yet there was something intoxicating about his vision, too.

As the seconds ticked away, as he struggled with the choice in front of him, he felt his phone buzzing. He took it out of his pocket and saw that Shadow had sent him a text.

Take the job.

That was it. Nothing else, no explanation. She didn't tell him why.

Maybe this was Marlen talking, wanting him with her, wanting him to take a chance on the two of them. With Bourne out of Treadstone, they could be together. It could be like it was in the beginning.

Or maybe this was Shadow's way of sending him on a new mission.

Bakk has the Files. Destroy him.

As always, her motives were inscrutable.

The overhead speaker in the empty lounge came to life. Bourne heard the scratchy announcement, repeated in English and French so no one could miss it. The Air France flight to Paris was on its final call and every ticketed passenger needed to be on board. Bourne's home was waiting for him, eight hours and four thousand miles away.

If Paris was still home.

"Time to choose, Jason," Bakk told him. "Stay or go."